AUG – – 2018

W9-BGD-978

SAY
YOU'RE
SORRY

Center Point
Large Print

**This Large Print Book carries the
Seal of Approval of N.A.V.H.**

SAY YOU'RE SORRY

MELINDA LEIGH

EAGER FREE PUBLIC LIBRARY
39 W. MAIN ST.
EVANSVILLE, WI 53536

CENTER POINT LARGE PRINT
THORNDIKE, MAINE

This Center Point Large Print edition
is published in the year 2018 by arrangement with
Amazon Publishing, www.apub.com.

Copyright © 2017 by Melinda Leigh.
All rights reserved.

Originally published in the United States
by Amazon Publishing, 2017.

This is a work of fiction.
Names, characters, organizations, places,
events, and incidents are either products of the
author's imagination or are used fictitiously.
The text of this Large Print edition is unabridged.
In other aspects, this book may vary
from the original edition.
Printed in the United States of America
on permanent paper.
Set in 16-point Times New Roman type.

ISBN: 978-1-68324-872-9

Library of Congress Cataloging-in-Publication Data

Names: Leigh, Melinda, author.
Title: Say you're sorry / Melinda Leigh.
Other titles: Say you are sorry
Description: Center Point Large Print edition. | Thorndike, Maine :
    Center Point Large Print, 2018.
Identifiers: LCCN 2018017800 | ISBN 9781683248729
    (hardcover : alk. paper)
Subjects: LCSH: Murder—Investigation—Fiction. | Women lawyers—
    Fiction. | Widows—New York (State)—Fiction. | Large type books. |
    BISAC: FICTION—Crime. | FICTION—Romance—Suspense. |
    FICTION—Thrillers—Suspense. | GSAFD: Romantic suspense
    fiction. | Mystery fiction. | LCGFT: Thrillers (Fiction) |
    Detective and mystery fiction.
Classification: LCC PS3612.E3572 S29 2018 | DDC 813/.6—dc23
LC record available at https://lccn.loc.gov/2018017800

For Roxy aka "Rocket Dog."
We rescued each other.

CHAPTER ONE

Darkness.

Tessa had been afraid of it most of her life. For as long as she could remember, she'd gone to bed dreading nightfall, looking under the bed, double-checking her nightlight.

As if a lightbulb the size of a lit match could possibly banish her nightmares.

But tonight, she prayed for the blackest of nights. For the moon to stay hidden behind the shifting clouds. For the shadows to make her invisible.

The darkness had changed sides. Head spinning, lungs screaming, she ran into its embrace. What had once been her greatest fear could now be her savior. Her miracle.

That's what it was going to take to keep her alive until the sun rose.

"Tesssssa." The voice floated over the forest. "You can't get away."

Where is he?

Evergreen boughs grabbed at her arms and scratched her face as she plunged through the forest like a panicked deer. Her heart beat with the frantic staccato of a prey animal. She

7

slowed, her body protesting the abuse of little-used muscles. She passed the scorched carcass of a burned tree. Its blackened branches pointed upward like a charred hand reaching for the sky. She ducked behind the shelter of a towering oak. Bark scraped her back as she pressed against the trunk and listened.

Where did he go?

A mosquito buzzed around her face. To her right, she could hear the sounds of the forest that surrounded Scarlet Lake. The stillness of the night sharpened her senses. Frogs croaked. Crickets chirped. An animal, small and light, scurried through the underbrush nearby. The air was thick with the scents of pine, lake water, and fear.

Not for the first time, she wished she could shrink and disappear into a rabbit hole.

Hoot! An owl landed on an overhead branch.

Tessa startled, a gasp slipping from her lips. She covered her open mouth with a hand. Liquid dripped over her fingers, and when she lowered her hand, it came away wet with tears—and blood. She touched the corner of her mouth, where his fist had split her lip. Other parts of her face and body ached from what he'd done in the clearing before she'd managed to land a kick to his groin.

Then he'd dropped her, and she'd run. Blindly.

The owl took flight, slow flaps of its wings

sending it soaring through a break in the canopy. The clouds parted, and moonlight shone through the opening. For a few seconds, the raptor was silhouetted against the inky sky. And then it was gone.

Sliding down the tree trunk, she sat on her heels and huddled.

Despite the coolness of the September night, her lungs burned as if she'd inhaled gas and swallowed a flame. She panted; the sound echoed in her ears and seemed loud enough to carry a mile through the trees.

Quiet!

He was going to hear. She was out of shape, and her mad sprint had taxed her lungs. She hadn't gotten far. He had to be close.

"Tesssssa."

The drumming of her heartbeat muffled his voice. She couldn't tell which direction it was coming from.

She pressed her lips together, but her lungs demanded more air. Red rimmed her vision as dizziness enveloped her. Opening her mouth, she kept her breaths shallow, hoping, praying her ragged gasps weren't as loud as they sounded echoing in her own ears.

Minutes passed.

Nothing happened.

Maybe he'd gone in the other direction.

Her breathing eased. Her legs began to tremble

from the cramped position. She'd partied in the clearing countless times. But everything looked the same in the dark.

She'd lost track of her location.

She glanced around the trunk. Twenty feet ahead, moonlight cast a trail in silvery shadows. Was that the path that led to the main road? Beyond the narrow break in the foliage, the trees closed in, and darkness smothered the forest.

Sweat ran down her spine and pooled at her lower back, soaking the waistband of her jeans. She squinted. What choice did she have? She couldn't stay here long.

He'd catch up with her.

He'd kill her.

But in order to run, she'd have to come out from behind the tree.

Where is he?

No matter. She had to keep moving. If he hadn't caught her yet, he soon would. There was no way he'd let her go now. Why had she trusted him? Because he'd said he loved her?

Stupid.

He wasn't capable of love. She'd known it in her head, but her heart had wanted to believe.

And now the truth would kill her.

At the beginning of the evening, she'd considered walking into the cold lake and putting an end to her misery. But now that death was breathing down her neck, terror had taken over.

Her survival instinct overrode any fears about her future.

I don't want to die.

Her last words to her grandparents had been angry. She'd lied to them. If she didn't make it out of this, that argument would be their final memory of her. They weren't perfect, but they loved her. Now there'd be no way for her to say she loved them back, that she hadn't meant what she'd said, that she'd been upset about the mess she'd made of her life and she'd lashed out at them.

She wouldn't have a chance to say she was sorry.

She had to get away. She had to live. To apologize for hurting the two people who loved her the most. She pushed to her feet. Her thigh muscles shivered, and her head swam. Instead of running all out, she picked her way to the trail. With no idea where he was, the less noise she made the better. If she didn't know where she was, maybe he didn't either.

Underbrush snatched at her bare legs as she stepped onto the path and eased into a slow jog. The packed dirt under her sneakers felt familiar. She rounded a bend and quickened her pace. A twig snapped, and she bolted like a rabbit. A cloud drifted in front of the moon, dropping a shadow across her path. Tessa's foot caught, and she fell. Pain zinged through her kneecap as it struck an exposed tree root. On hands and knees, she paused, catching her breath and swallowing the terror that clogged her throat. Tears ran down her cheeks.

Keep going!

She got one foot under her body and stood. Forcing her shaky legs to move, she stumbled up the path and drew up short as she recognized the scorched tree. She'd run in a circle. She stumbled as she realized she was headed back toward the clearing.

Toward him.

The rustle of dead leaves echoed, loud as a crack of thunder.

Please. Please, don't let him catch me.

Tears blurred her vision. Swiping a hand across her face, she cleared her eyes, then broke into a weak run.

A shadow stepped out from behind a fat tree. She skidded to a stop, the worn soles of her canvas high-tops sliding in the dirt.

Her bones trembled as she stared up at him. He wasn't panting or sweating or the slightest bit out of breath.

And she knew. The truth struck her like an open hand against her cheek.

She was going to die.

Panic wrapped around her neck and tightened its grip until breathing was as hard as sucking air through a straw.

"Did you really think you could get away?" He shook his head.

She turned and ran, blindly shoving at the branches in her way. She couldn't outrun him. She was tired, and he was fresh. Her breaths dragged in and out of her lungs in ragged gasps. Behind her, his footfalls were even and sure.

She burst from the woods. The lake glimmered in front of her. At the edge of the dark water, a thick patch of cattails waved in the breeze. The ground was soggy underfoot as she bolted into the thick stalks. One thought dominated her brain:

Hide!

The wet ground pulled at the soles of her sneakers, the squishing sound betraying her. A hand shot out and grabbed her bicep. He dragged her toward him.

"No." She pulled back, dropping her butt toward the ground.

But resisting proved as futile as it felt.

She opened her mouth and let out a wild scream.

"Shut up!" He struck out, the movement of his arm quick and sure.

The fist connected with her jaw. She blinked. The cattails around her blurred.

She'd been right all along. The dark was not her friend. It would not save her. It was an abyss from which she'd never emerge. Never again.

This was the end.

She fell to the marshy ground. Above, cattails waved against the night sky. Then a figure was silhouetted. Something metal glinted in the moonlight and pain sliced her into pieces.

The world faded into a cold and dreaded darkness.

CHAPTER TWO

He stumbled out of the cattails and stared down at his hands.

Blood, slick and dark and oily, covered his gloves and the knife. He turned toward the water and squatted at its edge. Setting the knife on the bank, he stuck the gloves into the shallow water. He rubbed his palms together and washed away as much of the blood as possible. Then he stripped off the gloves and set them aside. Specks of blood dotted his forearms. He scrubbed at them, scooping a handful of mud from the lake bottom and using it as a cleanser.

There'd been so much blood. He'd never wash it all off.

He glanced back into the reeds. What had he done?

Something that couldn't be undone.

His gaze landed on the knife at his side. His stomach turned over at the sight, and he ripped his eyes away.

How many times had he stabbed her? He couldn't remember. Rage had completely short-circuited his brain. The last twenty minutes were a blur.

A violent, frenzied blur.

He heard screaming, pleading, crying, the sounds of pain and fear. He put his hands over his ears, but the sounds were in his head.

Stop it!

The bloody knife glared at him accusingly.

You know what you did.

And he was going to have to live with it. But how?

An idea cut through his panic.

By not getting caught.

He couldn't go to prison. He'd never survive, and even if he did, his entire life would be over. It wasn't as if a life sentence for him would bring her back. Nothing could do that.

What am I going to do with the knife? Thanks to TV crime shows, everyone knew that he'd never get all the traces of her blood off it. He needed to get rid of the knife and the gloves. His clothes too. They must have blood on them. He needed to dump everything. But where? How?

He paused and breathed.

Think!

He hadn't meant to kill her. But rage had taken over. He'd been driven by an animal urge that screamed that she belonged to him.

Even as he thought it, he knew it wasn't the truth. She wasn't his. He'd simply taken what he wanted without asking.

But then, he'd always had dark thoughts. He'd

fought the darkness inside him most of his life. Hidden it away so no one would see. But she'd broken his control.

Since the first time he'd seen her, he hadn't been able to think straight.

He pictured her now, her pretty eyes that always seemed to be on him. From the first time they'd met, she'd felt the same rush of attraction for him, even if she hadn't wanted to admit it. He was sure of it. But she was gone. Her smile would never brighten another of his dark days.

I love you.

I'm sorry.

His heart ached, acutely aware that hers no longer beat. He'd watched the life fade from her eyes, felt her soul leave her body.

Bringing the knife had been his downfall, an impulse decision.

But then, impulses were his real problem, weren't they?

Self-preservation drove him to his feet. He had work to do. He collected the gloves, now dripping with lake water rather than blood. Putting them on, he picked up the knife by the very end of the handle. He had to hide it.

Somewhere.

But first he had to pay his respects. He had to see her one final time and face the reality of his actions. Only then would he be able to put this night behind him and move forward.

On his way back to the cattails, he picked up a plastic bag from the ground, trash from someone's takeout dinner. He stuffed the knife inside the bag and rolled it up. He'd figure out what to do with it later.

After he said his final good-bye.

He returned to her. Dropping to his knees, he looked at her face—only her face. He couldn't think about the extent of his brutality. It was as if for that twenty minutes, someone else had inhabited his body. He couldn't have done that to her. He loved her.

But love had its dark side, jealousy, possession. Obsession.

A tear slid down his face at the thought of never seeing her again.

I love you.

I'm sorry.

How am I going to live without you?

CHAPTER THREE

Morgan Dane toyed with her steak salad, but the weight of the decision on her mind dampened her appetite.

The waitress returned to the table. "Anyone need another drink?"

Morgan shook her head. "No, thank you."

She'd had exactly two sips from her glass of house red.

Across the table, District Attorney Bryce Walters finished his single glass. "Is something wrong with the wine?"

"No. It's fine. I'm not much of a drinker." The truth was she had no tolerance for alcohol, and the only thing worse than a kaleidoscope of butterflies flapping in her stomach were stumbling drunk ones.

"Well, that's a good thing." He smiled, his teeth even and white.

She should probably be attracted to him, but she wasn't, which was for the best. This was not a date. As long as Bryce hadn't changed his mind about offering her a job since their last meeting, he was going to be her boss, not her boyfriend.

He set aside his empty glass and ordered coffee. Morgan declined.

The man's superior genes could not be denied. Tall and lean, he had a tan that suggested manly, outdoorsy pursuits. He balanced being a gentleman and a man's man. He'd even been gifted with a deep voice that resonated well in large rooms. In the courtroom, Bryce sold guilt like the slickest marketer.

Morgan shifted in her chair, acutely aware of the way her suit nipped in at her waist. Her tailored silk blouse fell in an elegant drape to show the single strand of pearls around her neck but never revealed any hint of cleavage. While some female ADAs strove to downplay their femininity, Morgan had chosen to highlight hers, and she was often underestimated because of it.

But today her professional attire felt more like a Halloween costume. She hadn't worked in a long time, not since John's death.

The grief she'd packed away threatened to rise, and she blinked away from Bryce's sharp scrutiny to eat another bite of steak. The moment she swallowed the meat, those damned butterflies attacked it like a swarm of locusts. Giving up on the meal, she rested her fork across her plate.

Bryce's gaze softened. He didn't miss a thing. *Damn it.*

She'd thought she could get through the meeting without getting emotional.

Time to get this done.

The rural county in upstate New York only employed a handful of assistant prosecutors. If she wanted to work near her home in Scarlet Falls, this was her best chance. She intended to grab it.

The waitress returned with Bryce's coffee.

He drank it black. "Sorry my afternoon meeting ran long. Thank you for being flexible and having dinner with me."

"Thank you for dinner." It wasn't as if Morgan had wild Friday night plans he'd interrupted. If it weren't for this dinner, she'd be in her pajamas watching a Disney movie with her kids. Truthfully, Morgan hadn't been happy about pushing their meeting back, but this was her new reality. Working moms missed the occasional bedtime.

Bryce leaned his forearms on the table and interlaced his fingers. His cross-examination focus landed on Morgan like a spotlight.

"Have you made a decision?" he asked.

"I have." She shivered as the vent overhead unleashed a stream of cool air down her back. "I accept."

Bryce grinned. Satisfaction slid over his face as he shifted back in his chair. "Excellent."

A busboy cleared their dinner dishes, and the waitress approached. "Would either of you like to see a dessert menu?"

Morgan shook her head. A few grains of silver on her skirt caught the light, evidence of her youngest child's current obsession with glitter. She resisted checking her watch. She'd only been gone a couple of hours. The girls were fine.

One evening away from her kids, and she missed them. How would she cope with being at the office all day, every day? This was ridiculous. She was thirty-three years old. Until two years ago, she'd been a successful assistant district attorney. She'd juggled a household, three very small children, and a career. Most of the time, John had been deployed to Iraq. Then an IED had exploded six thousand miles away, killing her husband. Devastated, she'd chucked everything to move back home. Now it was time to get back to being an independent, professional woman. She'd been hiding behind her grief long enough.

She needed to move forward with her life.

But why did it have to be so damned hard?

Bryce lifted his coffee. "To my newest assistant district attorney."

"To new beginnings." Morgan picked up her water glass and touched it to his cup. Soon she would feel like her old self.

Right?

"You might want to rethink declining dessert," Bryce joked. "This will probably be the last decent meal we'll have together. From now on, it's all Chinese takeout at your desk."

"I like Chinese takeout." Morgan's smile felt fake. Probably because it was.

Bryce paid the check, and they left the restaurant. On the sidewalk outside, he said good-bye with a warm handshake. "I'll see you a week from Monday. Human Resources will be in touch."

"Good-bye." Morgan walked in the opposite direction and turned the corner, her grip tightening around the handle of her tote as if she was holding her composure together by her fingers.

She'd parked her minivan at the curb on a side street. Sunset cast long shadows across the sidewalk. Her heel caught and she stumbled, the shoe wrenching off her foot. Catching her balance, she backtracked a step, bent down, and picked up her shoe. The three-inch heel hung broken from the sole, the leather ripped beyond repair.

Tears welled in her eyes, and panic swirled in her chest. *What the hell?* It was just a shoe. In one heel and one bare foot, she clumped awkwardly across the street and got into her van. Thank goodness she was no longer in Bryce's view. He didn't need to discover the fragility of her professional persona. In truth, it fractured under pressure like spun sugar.

Sliding behind the wheel, she closed her eyes and breathed until the tightness in her chest eased. Meltdown averted, she removed her intact pump and tossed it on the passenger seat with its broken mate before driving home. There, she dropped her shoes in the garbage can at the head of the driveway and went inside.

In the living room, her grandfather leaned over the coffee table and stared at a chessboard. Their neighbor, Nick Zabrowski, sat on the opposite side. Nick owned a small landscaping company and lived across the street with his dad.

"Hi Nick." Morgan set her tote on the chest in the foyer. "No plans tonight?"

"No." At twenty, Nick was too young to spend his Friday nights with an elderly neighbor. Girl problems?

"Are the kids asleep?" Morgan asked.

Scratching his chin, Grandpa touched his rook then released it. "Yes."

"How did you get Sophie to bed with Nick here?" Morgan asked. Nick was one of Sophie's favorite people.

Nick blushed. "I read her a story."

Aw.

Grandpa moved his rook, sat back, and looked at her. "Where are your shoes?"

"I broke a heel." Morgan removed her suit jacket and tossed it over her tote.

Nick jumped his knight over a row of pawns. "I should go."

Grandpa nodded. "We'll finish the game tomorrow?"

"Sure." Nick headed for the door. " 'Night."

"Goodnight." Morgan closed and locked the door behind him.

Grandpa leaned over the chessboard.

"Let me get that for you." Morgan shifted the board to a shelf, out of the way of her three small girls, who would roll through the living room like bowling balls in the morning. "Who's winning?"

"Hard to say at this point."

Nick and Grandpa had been playing chess for years. A former member of his high school chess team, Nick had the advantage, but Grandpa pulled a trick from his sleeve now and then.

"How did it go?" he asked.

"Fine," she said, sniffing.

"I can tell." Grandpa snorted. He snatched a tissue from a box on the side table and handed it to her.

Morgan blotted under her eyes. "I don't know what's wrong with me. I just accepted an offer for a job I really wanted."

"You're taking a big step." Grandpa rubbed her arm. "Change is scary. You're going to be all right. You're tough."

Morgan nodded. *Enough of this emotional bullshit.* She didn't feel tough, but she would fake it. She went into the kitchen and took a container of Chunky Monkey from the freezer. "Am I doing the right thing by the girls? They'll have to make some pretty big adjustments."

Grandpa followed her in. "They'll be fine. They'll miss you, but their lives won't change that much. You're the one who will have the big adjustment."

Taking a spoon from the drawer, she ate directly from the pint.

Fetching his own spoon, he shuffled up next to her and helped himself. "No one said you had to go back to work. If you're worried about money, you don't have to be. Even after I'm gone, I have money put away—"

"Thank you." Morgan stopped him. Tonight she couldn't bear to think of losing him too. "I know you'll always look after us." She leaned her head against his shoulder. "But that's not it. I haven't even touched the money from John's life insurance." Living back home, she was able to cover her minimal expenses with her survivor benefits.

"I'm glad to see you trying to move forward. If you're happy, the girls will be too."

"Thanks. I hope so." Morgan lifted her head. "I'm going to bed."

"I'll lock up and set the alarm." Grandpa had installed a security system a few months ago.

Morgan wiped out the pint of ice cream, and then she carried her jacket back to her bedroom, frustrated and feeling the first twinge of a sugar headache.

Going back to work was supposed to alleviate her depression, not increase it.

She stopped in the girls' room. Three twin beds crowded the space. Six-year-old Ava snuggled with her teddy bear. Five-year-old Mia curled on her side with her stuffed zebra tucked under her arm. Sophie, who didn't let a simple thing like sleep keep her still, lay flat on her back, all four limbs flung out. She'd tossed her covers to the floor. At three, Sophie was a handful. Who was Morgan kidding? Sophie was going to be a handful at every age. Morgan picked up the blanket and covered her littlest daughter before continuing to her own room down the hall.

She undressed, hanging up her suit and putting on her robe. John stared at her from the photo on her nightstand. Sitting on the edge of the bed, she picked it up. She had better photos of him, formal pics taken in his dress uniform, but it was this one that spoke to her heart. Sweat glistened on his tanned brow, and his face was deployment-thin under a head of unruly dark hair. Dressed in tan BDUs, he laughed against the desert backdrop. That was John. Always looking at the bright side.

If he were here right now, he'd say, *You can do this, babe.*

"I'm trying. I miss you," she said to his photo.

Heaviness settled over her. She opened the nightstand drawer and contemplated the sealed envelope in the back. *No. Not ready for that.*

27

She closed the drawer. Setting his picture on the nightstand, she eased onto the pillow.

She'd taken the first, huge step toward getting her life back. That would have to be enough for today.

The sound of the phone ringing startled her. She lifted her head, confused. Her bedroom was brightly lit. She glanced at the clock. Just after midnight. She must have fallen asleep. It took her a few seconds to realize it wasn't her cell that was ringing but the house phone. No one called on that line except telemarketers. The caller ID read Palmer.

Morgan lifted the receiver, expecting to hear the echo of a call center in the background. "Hello?"

"Morgan?" a woman's voice asked, the rising pitch projecting anxiety.

"Yes," Morgan said.

"This is Evelyn Palmer, Tessa's grandmother."

Morgan sat up straighter. Tessa was her occasional babysitter.

"What time did Tessa leave your house?" Mrs. Palmer asked.

Still groggy, Morgan said, "Tessa wasn't here tonight."

The line went quiet.

Morgan propped herself on an elbow. "Mrs. Palmer? What happened?"

"Tessa is gone."

"What?" Morgan shifted the phone. She couldn't have heard that correctly.

"We had a big fight yesterday, and she left." Mrs. Palmer's voice cracked. "She said she was going to spend the night at her friend's house, but I called Felicity's mother. Tessa didn't go to the Webers' house."

She'd lied.

"So you haven't seen her since yesterday?" Morgan asked.

"Yes." Over the connection, Mrs. Palmer sobbed. "Since Tessa has been babysitting for you every Friday night, I hoped you'd seen her. Then at least we'd know she was all right."

"Tessa hasn't babysat for me for weeks," Morgan said.

"So she lied about that too." Mrs. Palmer went quiet.

Morgan set her pillow aside and climbed off the bed. Tossing her robe on the bed, she rooted in her dresser drawer for a pair of jeans and a T-shirt. "Have you called the police?"

"We'd thought she'd cool off and come home tonight. But it's almost midnight and she's not here." Mrs. Palmer sniffed. "I'll call the police now, but I don't know what they can do. She's eighteen."

"Have you tried to locate her cell phone?"

"I wouldn't know how to do that," Mrs. Palmer said.

"Do you need help looking for her?" As she offered, Morgan felt under her chair for her canvas sneakers.

"I don't know. I keep thinking she's going to pull into the driveway any second. My husband is driving around now. I'm not allowed to drive at night anymore."

Mr. Palmer probably shouldn't be driving at night either. Tessa's parents had died in a car accident when she was twelve, and her grandparents had been raising her for the last six years. Unlike Morgan's robust grandfather, the Palmers were plagued with medical problems.

"I'm getting dressed." Morgan found the shoes. "I'll be at your house in a few minutes."

"Oh, thank you." Relief softened Mrs. Palmer's tone. "I'm calling the police and her friends."

Morgan ended the call, set the phone back in its cradle, and pulled her T-shirt over her head. Picking up her shoes, she left her bedroom barefoot. The phone call had rattled her, and she took a minute to peek into her daughters' room. In the slant of light from the hall, she could see three dark heads nestled on pillows. The tiny shiver of relief made her feel almost guilty.

Poor Mrs. Palmer.

Morgan couldn't imagine anything more terrifying than having one of her girls missing.

She went into the kitchen. Footsteps scuffed in the hall.

Her grandfather came through the doorway, putting one hand on the frame for balance. He wore a navy-blue robe over tailored cotton pajamas. "What's wrong?"

"That was Evelyn Palmer. Tessa didn't come home tonight." Morgan filled him in on the phone call as she sat down in a chair and slipped her bare feet into her shoes. Her grandfather walked forward, his leather slippers dragging on the tile, one steadying hand sliding along the wall.

"Where's your cane?" she asked.

He scowled. "I don't need a cane."

"That's not what the doctor says."

"My slippers are older than that doctor." He leaned a shoulder on the wall and crossed his arms, signaling an end to the topic.

Morgan gave up, for the moment. As much as she hated to admit her grandfather was aging, *he* absolutely refused to act his age. "Anyway. It doesn't sound like something Tessa would do."

Her grandfather shrugged. "No. It doesn't. But the best teens can be a handful. You have to raise them with a healthy dose of suspicion."

Morgan remembered coming home from parties to his scrutiny. She could still picture him sitting in his leather chair, a book in his lap, his sharp gaze sizing her up over his reading glasses. He had had no qualms about giving her breath a not so subtle sniff. The retired homicide detective had guided three of the four Dane siblings into

31

adulthood after their father had been killed in the line of duty and their mother had moved them from the city to upstate New York when Morgan was in high school. Her mom had had a heart attack a few years later.

"Her car could have broken down somewhere out of cell range." Standing, Morgan grabbed her denim jacket from the back of the kitchen chair. "She could have hit a tree or a deer."

Her grandfather followed her down the short hall to the foyer. "Let me know what you're doing, all right?"

He was living proof that parenting—and grandparenting—was a lifelong commitment.

"I will. I'm just going to drive over to the Palmers' house and see if I can help."

"You know that one night out isn't unusual for a teenager," Grandpa said. "Almost all of them show up within twenty-four hours. Plus, she's legally an adult. She hasn't committed a crime."

"I know." But Morgan's concern wouldn't ease. Then again, Morgan had lost both her parents and her husband. She often held her loved ones closer than was entirely healthy. But grief had wrapped barbed wire around her heart. The slightest touch made it bleed.

"Do you want me to call Stella?" Grandpa asked.

Morgan's younger sister was a detective with the Scarlet Falls PD.

"Not yet. She works too much as it is. Let me see what's going on. Tessa will probably turn up soon, and Mrs. Palmer already called the police. I'm sure the responding officer can handle the call. Like you said, Tessa hasn't done anything illegal."

Just completely out of character.

"All right. Be careful. I love you," Grandpa called. "Do you have a flashlight?"

"I do." Morgan patted her tote bag and left the house.

Outside, the darkness loomed. But as she walked down the driveway, motion sensing security lights lit up the front yard like a runway. She glanced up at the camera affixed under the eaves of the house.

Grandpa had installed it with the security system almost as a joke to catch a neighbor who didn't clean up after her dog. But now Morgan was glad for the extra surveillance.

Years ago, none of them had ever dreamed they'd need a security system in Scarlet Falls, let alone in their rural development. But these days, there seemed to be no escaping crime.

CHAPTER FOUR

Lance Kruger hunkered down in the front seat of his Jeep and stared at the one-story motel across the street. In the center of the long building, the curtains of room twelve were drawn tight. The camera on his passenger seat, complete with telephoto lens, waited.

His phone vibrated, shimmying across his dashboard. The display read SHARP. His boss.

Lance answered the call, "Yeah."

"Catch them yet?" Former Scarlet Falls detective Lincoln Sharp had retired after putting in his full twenty-five and had spent the last five years as a P.I.

"Got individual photos of each of them entering the motel room. They haven't come out yet." Photos of a lusty good-bye in the parking lot would solidify Mrs. Brown's claim of adultery.

"They're still in there?" Sharp whistled. "Impressive. I wouldn't expect Brown to have that much stamina."

"He probably fell asleep."

Sharp snorted.

"If you can't sleep, you can always take over

tonight's surveillance." Lance shifted in the seat, trying to get comfortable.

"I'm too damned old and creaky to sit in a car all night long," Sharp said. "Why do you think I hired you?"

"You're fifty-three, not ninety-three, and since when do we take divorce cases?"

"Family favor."

Mrs. Brown lived next door to Sharp's cousin. Since Mr. Brown had already been reported for sexual harassment, Mrs. Brown was hoping he wouldn't want the affair with his coworker made public. Full-color glossies would provide excellent leverage when it came time to divide marital assets and settle on alimony.

But the whole business left Lance with a foul taste in his mouth. "We're bottom-feeding."

"At times." A teakettle whistled on Sharp's end of the line. "Let me know if anything goes down. I'll be up."

Sharp ended the call. Lance set down his phone, stared at the motel room door and willed it to open so he could go home. But nothing happened.

Whatever he'd expected when he left the Scarlet Falls PD three months before, this wasn't it. Through the fabric of his tactical cargo pants, Lance rubbed the thick scar tissue on his thigh where a bullet had ended his police career. His leg was almost healed. But almost wasn't good enough. As much as he wanted to be on the force, he would not be responsible for another officer getting hurt because he couldn't keep up.

After the first four weeks of unemployed boredom had nearly driven him insane, he'd latched onto Sharp's offer to join his PI firm like a K-9 on a bite sleeve. For the last two months, he'd been Skywalker to Sharp's Obi-Wan.

Lance shifted position, stretching his leg. If he was going to spend this many hours sitting in his vehicle, he was going to have to trade up to a larger model.

Headlights swept across the pavement, and a familiar Cadillac slid crookedly into a slot in front of the motel room. Lance's spine jerked straight.

Was that Mrs. Brown?

The door of the Cadillac flew open and bounced on its hinges. Mrs. Brown slid from the vehicle and stood on wobbly legs. She staggered toward the door of the motel.

Oh, shit. Alcohol had never helped anyone make better decisions.

Lance bolted from his Jeep, but he was too far away to intercept her.

Mrs. Brown stopped ten feet in front of the door. She dug a handgun out of her purse, leveled it at the door of the motel, and pulled the trigger.

Boom. The gun jerked in her hand. Wood splintered. Lights turned on in windows across the low building.

And Lance's heart did its best impression of a cardiac event. He skidded to a halt as Mrs. Brown fired again. Lance flinched, his body pouring sweat as he remembered last November's shooting.

Get it together.

Now was not the time for a flashback.

He pulled his phone from his pocket, pressed 911, then gave the operator the address. His brain told him to return to his vehicle and wait for the police to arrive, but he couldn't do it. This crappy little motel was on the edge of town. Scarlet Falls would have just a few cars out on graveyard patrol shift. Having one nearby was unlikely.

Mrs. Brown was angry and drunk, a deadly combination. God only knew who she might shoot before the police arrived.

Lance swallowed the throbbing pulse in his throat and forced himself to move forward.

"Mrs. Brown!" he called, nearly deafened by the hammering of his own heart. "Please put the gun down."

"No," she called over her shoulder. "I'm going to shoot his pecker off." She refocused her aim—and her rage—back on the door and yelled, "Leonard, git your ass out here."

As if Mr. Brown would come out after she'd announced her intention of blowing a hole in his privates. He was already probably trying to squeeze his beer gut out the bathroom window.

"Ma'am, you can't shoot him." Lance's pulse echoed in his ears as he eased forward. The gun wasn't pointed at him, but if she turned . . .

Mrs. Brown yelled, "Why not? The rat bastard is cheating on me."

"I know," Lance commiserated. "He's a bastard. That's why you're going to divorce him, right?"

He took another step.

She paused. Her face tilted as she considered her original revenge plot.

"If you shoot him, you'll be arrested." Sliding another foot forward, Lance held his hands in front of his chest in a nonthreatening posture. "Then where will you be? Jail."

The muzzle of the gun dropped a few inches.

"You want to get even, right?" He eased forward. "Wasn't that your plan? To make him pay?"

She nodded, her eyes glistening with moisture. She sniffed. "He didn't even bother to hide what he was doing. Everyone in town knows what he's been up to." Humiliation amplified the distress on her face.

Lance nodded. "He is an inconsiderate, lying scumbag. That's why you're dumping him. Everyone knows you won't take this sort of behavior from him." Lance played up her pride. "He's going to be paying for what he did to you for a long time."

Her lips flattened into a bloodless line as she imagined her revenge.

He jerked a thumb toward his Jeep. "I already have photos of both of them going into the motel. Soon you'll be able to get him out of your life for good."

"But I love him!" she wailed, her face crumpling.

For Pete's sake . . .

How could she possibly still be in love with her cheating, lying, asshat of a husband?

"Mrs. Brown, lower the gun," Lance said.

She complied, the muzzle of the gun pointing toward the blacktop.

In one swift motion, Lance took the gun from her. She burst into tears. He unloaded the weapon as she sobbed.

Once the threat was over, Lance took a deep breath. Adrenaline coursed through his veins like a hit of speed. At least as a cop he'd had backup and body armor. As a private investigator, he was on his own in a sea of crazy.

Speaking of crazy . . .

With Mrs. Brown disarmed and subdued, Lance waited for the SFPD. Ten minutes later, a sheriff's deputy arrived instead, which wasn't uncommon. With a limited number of cars on patrol, the local force relied on the county sheriff for backup.

Lance handed over Mrs. Brown's weapon, gave

a statement, and was free to go. As soon as he typed up his own report, he would be done with the Browns and their messy divorce. Love made people nuts.

His phone buzzed with a text from Sharp. STOP AT THE OFFICE.

Either Sharp had been listening to his police scanner or he'd gotten a call about the incident. He knew everybody in local law enforcement.

Lance drove to the tree-lined side street in Scarlet Falls where Sharp owned a duplex and lived in the unit above Sharp Investigations. At nearly one a.m., all was quiet in the very small business section of town. Lance parked at the curb and climbed the wooden steps. Sharp's office occupied what was originally the living room of the converted two-bedroom apartment. Lance had set up camp in the first bedroom with a card table, a single chair, and a laptop. The sole personal item was a wireless speaker. He hooked the camera to the laptop and downloaded his pictures from earlier that evening.

"You really need to buy a desk." Lance's boss stood in the doorway. In worn jeans and a plain gray T-shirt, Sharp was wiry and ridiculously fit for his age. Twenty-five years on the police force had left him with an indelible don't-fuck-with-me expression.

"The table works for now." So far, Lance had refused to commit to a permanent position at

Sharp Investigations. He wasn't ready to give up his dream of getting back on the force. "Next time one of your family members requests an adultery surveillance, you're on your own."

Sharp ignored the comment. "We need to talk."

"Yes, Mom." Lance followed his boss into the small kitchen.

Sharp filled a teapot and put it on the stove. Then he filled one bowl with dog kibble and another with water, opened the back door, and deposited the bowls on the back porch.

"Still feeding that stray?"

"She won't come in." Sharp spooned tea into a wire basket and dropped it into a ceramic pot.

"She?" Lance teased.

Sharp pretended to be a total hard-ass, but it was a lame act.

"You're a sucker for big brown eyes." Lance led the way into Sharp's office. Two chairs faced a beat-up desk. A black couch spanned the far wall.

Sharp carried a teapot in one hand and two mugs in the other. "You've had a tough night, so I'll ignore your smart-assery."

Lance eased himself into the straight chair. "You know, most men would offer a friend a glass of whiskey after a traumatic event."

Sharp poured green tea into two mugs and set one in front of Lance. "Alcohol is a depressant. That's the last thing you need right now."

41

Sigh.

"Now that I can see for myself that you're not dead, tell me what happened." Sharp took his place behind the desk.

Lance filled him in. "Just a typical Friday night."

Sharp laughed so hard, he wheezed.

"It's not funny," Lance said.

"You're right. It's not." But his boss's voice shook.

"That was the worst job ever. I don't know what bothered me more, the flying bullets or the melodrama." Lance took a few deep breaths. "Not sure where we stand on the case."

"Not much you can do when the client loses her frigging mind." Sharp's voice sobered. "Seriously, I'm glad she didn't shoot you."

"I don't know about this PI thing. I still miss being a cop," Lance said.

"I know that, and I know why," Sharp said. "Do you think I don't remember what day it is?"

Lance's throat tightened. Twenty-three years ago, his father had vanished. Sharp had been in charge of the case.

"I understand the desire to protect and serve. I did it for twenty-five years. But being a PI is better in a lot of ways. You're your own boss. You make your own decisions. No one can order you to stop investigating a case." Sharp's mouth tightened. That was exactly what had happened to him when leads on Lance's dad's case went cold. "But if that's what you really want, then keep working on your recovery."

"More crunchy-granola-woowoo crap?"

"Bash it all you want." Sharp crossed his arms. "You're better, and you know it. You were pushing too hard and not letting your body heal. Didn't your physical therapist give you the go ahead to get on the ice?"

"I'm allowed fifteen minutes of light skating." Lance had played hockey in high school, and eighteen months ago, he'd been volunteered to serve as an assistant coach to a bunch of disadvantaged kids through a police outreach program. The shooting had benched him. He missed hockey—and the kids—more than he'd expected.

His therapist had actually cleared him weeks ago, but he hadn't set foot on the ice yet. As much as he wanted to play, it wasn't worth the risk of an injury. One fall could wipe out all his progress. He'd stick with coaching from the sidelines.

Sharp rolled his eyes. "You know I'm right."

He was. *Damn it.*

Besides, he could hardly make fun of Sharp's lifestyle. The man could still run a seven-minute mile and do muscle-ups.

"All right, but I still wish this was whiskey." Lance drained his cup of green tea. Three months ago, he would have stopped at a bar on the way home for a couple of shots. Tonight, he'd go home and make an antioxidant protein shake.

"Get some sleep." Sharp got up and walked around the desk.

Lance stood. "A solid eight hours is next on my agenda."

Did he know how to party or what?

But ten months after being shot, he finally thought maybe he *could* fully recover. That his police career might not be over. That he could get back to coaching and the active lifestyle he missed.

His phone rang and he read the display.

Morgan.

If there was one person who could tempt him away from his bed—or into it—it was Morgan Dane. He was treated to a quick mental vision of her in his bed, all tousled, no trace of her usual perfection, thanks to him.

He almost rolled his eyes at the ridiculousness of his imagination. He'd known the Danes since high school. He and Morgan had dated during senior year. They'd liked each other back then with the usual awkward teenage crushes, but when they'd left for college, neither one of them had been devastated. Nothing had prepared him for the bulldozer effect she'd had on him when he'd run into her a few months before. Morgan seemed only interested in being his friend, and he was in no position to have a relationship.

So be cool.

He answered the call. "Morgan?"

"Did I wake you?" Her tone was breathless, which didn't help.

At. All.

Lance stepped into the hall. "No. I was up."

A glance at the digital clock reminded him it was nearly one a.m. Why would Morgan call him in the middle of the night? Concern brought his puppy love to heel.

"What's wrong?"

"My babysitter, Tessa, didn't come home tonight. Her grandparents are worried. I'm going to look for her in the usual teenage hangout locations. Would you be willing to ride along with me?"

"Of course. I'll be at your house in fifteen minutes." He ended the call.

You were going to be cool, remember?

"I thought you were going to get some sleep?" Sharp stood in the doorway.

"Morgan needs help." Lance stopped in his office to remove his Glock from the gun safe in the closet. After the disaster of the Brown case, he wasn't taking any chances, especially with Morgan's safety. On that note, he returned to the safe for his backup piece and ankle holster.

"You have it bad for her. Just ask the woman

out already," Sharp called as Lance walked past his office.

Lance reached for the doorknob. "Goodnight, Sharp."

If only it was that simple. But he had enough responsibility on his plate just managing his mother's mental illness. After his dad disappeared, his mom developed severe anxiety and agoraphobia. She'd been relatively stable for the past few months, but there were times when taking care of her was a full-time job. And on top of Lance's issues, Morgan had her own freighter of emotional baggage and *three* kids.

Three.

Anyone who seriously dated Morgan had to consider that a future with her included being a father to her girls. Lance didn't see how he could possibly do the job right, and he would not half-ass something as important as parenthood. Kids deserved better.

He lowered the window of his Jeep, hoping the brisk September night was enough to cool his jets. It wasn't. He turned up the radio and shaved three minutes off his drive to the Danes' house as Green Day blasted him awake.

Parking his Jeep next to her minivan, he walked up to the front door but didn't knock. No reason to wake the sleeping members of the family. He peered through the screen door and called softly, "Morgan?"

Her grandfather, Art, came out of the kitchen and waved him into the house, Morgan's French bulldog, Snoozer, at his feet.

Lance stepped inside just as Morgan hurried down the hall toward him. She was tall and slim, with big blue eyes and legs that went on forever. Her clothes were uncharacteristically tossed on, and her long black hair was down and tumbled in messy waves over her shoulders in much the same way as it had been in his earlier vision.

Sharp was right. Lance had it bad. But he was an adult, and he'd act like one.

"Thanks for helping." Art shook his hand. Then he turned and gave his granddaughter a kiss on the cheek. "Be safe. I love you."

She hugged him. "Love you back."

Lance opened the door for her, and they went outside. She stuffed her cell phone in her gigantic purse, slung the straps over her shoulder, and walked toward her mom mobile.

"We'll take my Jeep. Teenagers like to go off-road." Lance would take a bullet for Morgan, but he drew the line at riding in her minivan.

"Good thinking." Morgan nodded and changed direction.

They got into his vehicle. He started the engine, and music blasted. He turned the volume to low. "Sorry. Where to?"

Her lips pursed. "I don't know. Her grand-mother gave me her best friend's number. The girl didn't answer her phone. I left a message. I thought we could check some of the usual hang-out spots. I was hoping you would know where the kids go these days."

"I have some ideas." Lance had broken up plenty of parties in his time on the police force. "Who's handling the case?"

"Carl Ripton came to the house, but I'm not sure what he can do. Tessa is eighteen. She walked out willingly. No crime there."

Lance pulled out his phone and dialed Carl's number. His former coworker gave him the rundown on what the SFPD was doing to find the girl. Lance thanked him and ended the call. "They put out a BOLO alert for her. No sightings of her car yet, and her cell phone GPS isn't sending out a signal. Unfortunately, she's a legal adult. Carl said none of the girl's friends would give him any information."

"Teens don't want to get their friends in trouble," Morgan said.

"When was the last time you saw Tessa?" he asked.

"About a month ago. Gianna insists on being my live-in nanny now."

Because one stubborn old man and three children under the age of seven hadn't been enough responsibility for Morgan, three months ago, she'd taken in Gianna Leone, a very sick young woman with no family. Gianna had been raised by a crack-addicted prostitute. Depressed and following in her mother's footsteps, she'd overdosed. While on duty, Morgan's sister Stella had saved the girl with a dose of Narcan, but Gianna had been left with permanent kidney damage. After Stella had befriended her, Gianna had slowly been pulled into the Dane family.

The Dane house existed in a perpetual, glitter-bombed state of chaos. What was one more monkey in Morgan's circus?

"Gianna looks much healthier since she moved in with you," he said.

"Yes. She still has to go to dialysis three times a week, but she's put on some weight and she has more energy. I hope the girls aren't too much for her to handle when I start work."

Lance drove toward the grammar school. "So you got the job?"

"Yes." The painful sigh that slipped from her lips made him ache for her.

"You sound excited."

She turned to the dark window. "I have to do something. I feel like I've been stalled out, doing nothing for two years."

"Raising your girls and taking care of your grandfather and Gianna is hardly nothing." How did she juggle it all? Lance could barely handle his mother. "You do more before breakfast than most people do all day."

"I don't know about that. Anyone with little

kids is crazy busy in the morning." She laughed.

It was a small sound, but he liked hearing it. "Crazy describes your house perfectly."

"I happen to like a little insanity in my life. Keeps me on my toes." Her tone turned serious. "I love raising my girls. I can't explain why I feel so disconnected."

"Morgan, your whole life was upended in the worst way."

Yet she still managed to take care of an entire houseful of people.

She sighed, the breath long and deep and sad.

"You're going to be all right," he said. "Sophie wouldn't put up with anything else."

Morgan's two oldest kids seemed to like Lance, but her youngest looked at him with reserve and suspicion, as if the three-year-old had X-ray vision that exposed what was really in his heart.

"No kidding." She smiled at him. "Thanks. And thanks for coming out in the middle of the night."

"It's my pleasure. We've known each other a long time, but I finally think I'm seeing the real you." Lance turned onto the rural road that led out to the lake. "I haven't seen you dressed that casually since—ever."

Even back in high school, Morgan had always managed to look perfect. That cheerleading outfit . . .

She reached up to smooth her hair.

He stopped her by taking her hand. "Don't. It looks good on you, and you don't have to put up a front for me."

She froze and her face went blank.

So much for playing it cool.

"We're friends, right?" He dropped her hand. He had no right to start something he couldn't finish. If he wanted to keep her in his life, he shouldn't screw up their friendship.

Morgan's phone rang, breaking the tension between them. "It's Tessa's friend, Felicity. I hope she knows something."

3 5353 00033 0169

CHAPTER FIVE

Morgan rubbed her hand, still warm from Lance's touch. It was nice to know she wasn't dead, but the prick of interest made her uncomfortable, clearly a reaction she wasn't ready to explore.

She'd intended to look for Tessa alone, but she hadn't protested when her grandfather suggested she call Lance. The fact was that she felt much safer with him. But tonight, he was acting . . . different.

Interested?

It must be her imagination. Like he'd said. They were friends, and friends helped each other. That was all there was to it. Her discomfort had nothing to do with the way all six feet two inches of him filled out his cargos and T-shirt, the way his blue eyes always seemed to be focused on her, or the fact that she genuinely liked his personality more than his blond buffness.

But how did she reconcile her attraction to Lance while John was still in her heart?

The love ballad playing softly on the radio wasn't helping. She reached forward and turned off the radio to answer the call. "Hi, is this Felicity?"

"Yes," the girl whispered.

"This is Morgan Dane. I called about Tessa."

"Tess babysits for you," the girl said in a soft voice that sounded as if she was trying not to be heard.

"Yes. She does. I'm looking for her. I know you already told her grandmother you haven't seen her, but I'm really worried. Is there anything you can tell me that might help me find her?"

"You have to promise not to tell my parents."

"I won't tell anyone unless I absolutely have to." Morgan wouldn't lie. A teenager's trust was as fragile as a bird's egg. Once broken, it was impossible to repair.

Felicity paused, seeming to weigh Morgan's answer. "There was a party last night."

"Was Tessa there?"

"Yeah," Felicity admitted.

"Where was the party?"

"Out at the lake."

"Did you go with Tessa?" Morgan asked.

"No. She came in her own car, but she was with her boyfriend."

"I didn't know Tessa had a boyfriend."

"She was keeping it quiet," Felicity said. "She said her grandparents wouldn't like him."

"Who is this boy?"

"Nick. His last name starts with a Z. You know him. Tessa met him at your house."

"Nick Zabrowski?" Morgan asked, surprised.

Nick had never mentioned he was dating Tessa, and Morgan saw him several times a week.

"That's him."

"Why wouldn't Tessa's grandparents approve of Tessa dating Nick?" Morgan liked Nick very much. He was a hard worker. He graduated from high school two years before and had started his own landscaping company. He was kind as well as ambitious. How many young men would read a little girl a story or take time out of his evenings to play chess with an elderly neighbor?

"He didn't go to college so he's not good enough for them."

"How long was Tessa seeing Nick?"

"About a month," Felicity said.

How many times in the past month had Tessa claimed to be babysitting for Morgan when she was actually with Nick?

"Tell me about the party."

"The party sucked. Tessa and Nick had a big fight and broke up. Tessa was still there when I left. I haven't seen her since."

"Tessa wasn't at school today?" Morgan should have asked the Palmers if they'd called the high school.

"We had the day off for a teacher in-service day," Felicity whispered. "I have to go."

"Thanks. Let me know if you remember anything else."

Felicity ended the call.

"Felicity says Tessa went to a party at the lake with Nick Zabrowski last night." Morgan summed up the conversation for Lance.

"Isn't that the kid who lives across the street from you?"

"Yes. I don't understand why the Palmers wouldn't like him." Morgan put her phone back into her tote.

"Fighting with guardians and lying about a boy isn't too unusual for an eighteen-year-old." Lance turned the Jeep around. "She probably found another friend to stay with last night."

"I hope."

The lake wasn't far away. Lance drove past the gazebo and picnic areas, then turned off the main road onto a dirt and grass lane. The local teenagers liked to hang out in a spot that wasn't part of the public area. A footpath connected the park with the clearing. But it was faster to take the service road the kids used.

Morgan grabbed the handle on the top of the door as the Jeep bounced along. It was nearly two a.m. before they drove into the clearing at the edge of the lake. Their headlights swept across trees, dark water—and a white Honda Accord parked near the bank.

Morgan pointed. "There's her car. It would be wonderful if she just went home with a friend."

Lance stopped the Jeep, and they got out.

Wings flapped overhead and a high-pitched squeak almost made Morgan jump back into the SUV.

"Was that a bat?" Morgan pulled her flashlight out of her tote.

"Probably." Lance leaned back into the Jeep for a flashlight of his own and switched it on.

"Are you armed?"

"Yes."

Morgan stepped closer. She was an independent, professional woman, but bugs and bats were not on her list of favorite things. "I should have brought my gun."

Lance chuckled. "I promise to shoot any bats that attack us."

"I'm going to hold you to that."

The soil was sandy, and in the center of the clear area, generations of kids had dug out a pit for bonfires. Lance played his beam across the pit, full of ashes and scorched wood. Empty water bottles, beer cans, and fast food takeout bags littered the area.

"Doesn't matter how many times the police run the kids out of here." Lance stood next to her. "They always come back."

Morgan spotted more litter at the water's edge. "Were we this messy and inconsiderate?"

"I don't remember being interested in food when we were out here." Lance paused. "I do remember making out in the back of my car."

"I'll bet you do." Morgan shone the flashlight on his face.

His grin was too wide. "I'll bet you remember steaming up my car windows too."

"I admit nothing." But yes, she did. "Your ego doesn't need feeding." She poked his arm. "Your head will get bigger than your muscles."

He wiggled an eyebrow. "You noticed my muscles."

With an amused snort, she shifted the light back to the ground, turning her attention—and hopefully Lance's as well—back to Tessa's car. Alarm pricked along the skin on her arms. "Her tires are flat."

"All of them?" Lance shone his flashlight on the white sedan.

"Yes."

They approached the car. Lance leaned over to look more closely into the interior. "It's empty."

The woods were thick and dark. Could Tessa have decided to walk home and gotten lost? Or maybe she'd gone home with one of the other kids. Wouldn't be the first time kids covered for a friend with their parents or the police.

Lance took out his phone. "I'll call the SFPD and let them know we found the car."

"We should probably call Nick and see if he's seen her."

Lance shook his head. "Let the police handle that in case there's a problem."

"A problem?"

"Someone slashed all her tires." His eyes were flat in the darkness as he turned away.

"Nick wouldn't do that." But Morgan didn't make the call.

While Lance called the police, she circled the vehicle, scanning the car and the ground around it for clues. Something metal glinted in the dirt a dozen feet away: a set of keys. The largest was a Honda ignition key. Why would Tessa's keys be on the ground? If she dropped them while walking away . . .

Morgan walked past the keys. She played the beam of her flashlight over the ground and saw something pink on a mossy tree root closer to the lake. She walked closer. A cell phone. She stooped to pick it up. There was something dark spattered on it.

The wind shifted, and a sense of vulnerability swept over Morgan. Shivering, she glanced around at the dark woods. Branches and their shadows swayed in the dark.

She called back to the clearing. "Lance?"

The hairs on the back of her neck twitched. Had Tessa gone this way? Morgan could see her accidentally dropping either her keys or her phone, but both? She glanced back down at the dark red dots on the phone case.

Blood?

And Morgan knew.

Tessa hadn't been walking away. She'd been running.

Morgan followed an imaginary arrow that connected the two objects. Underbrush plucked at her jeans as she scanned the ground but saw nothing but dirt, moss, and dead leaves. Continuing in the same direction, a game trail led toward the lake.

"Morgan, where are you?" Lance called from the clearing. "Did you find something?"

A twig snapped as he approached. She jumped but didn't answer. Every cell in her body was screaming that something was wrong.

Very wrong.

"I'm here." She waited until she heard Lance behind her, then followed the trail toward the lake. Cattails rose from the weeds as she neared the water. The ground turned marshy and sucked at her feet. Directly ahead, her flashlight paused on some broken cattails.

Was that blue cloth?

"We should wait for the police," Lance said behind her.

"I see something." She moved two steps closer, her need to know warring with her sense of dread. Apprehension prickled at her spine as she moved closer, her feet dragging in the mud as if they knew she wasn't going to like what she saw.

Morgan took another step forward. The cloth was blue. Denim blue. The sleeve of a jacket much like the one she was wearing. The beam of her light caught a length of long, dark hair. Her stomach went cold.

Tessa?

The cattails had nearly closed over her.

"I found her!" She rushed forward. Six feet from the girl, she froze. Morgan moved the light over the girl's body. Blood on her torso had dried to a dark red. Lance's arm swept out to block her path.

"Don't go any closer," he said. "You'll contaminate the scene."

"But what if she's . . ." Even as she said it, Morgan knew Tessa wasn't alive. There was simply too much blood.

"She's not." Lance's voice softened.

The flashlight shook in Morgan's hand. She leaned forward to see Tessa's face. Tremors spread through Morgan's body, yet she couldn't take her eyes off the trembling light and what it illuminated.

She went cold from the inside out, as if her heart was pumping slush through her veins.

Lance turned to face her and planted himself between her and Tessa. "Look at me, Morgan."

But even as she stared at the center of his chest, her mind projected its own image. Tessa, dropping her keys, trying to get into her car, seeing her flat tires, running through the woods.

Something—or someone—chasing her.

Catching her near the lake.

"Morgan." Lance's hands settled on her biceps. His fingers squeezed gently. "Come on. Look. At. Me."

But her muscles had frozen. Lance gave her a gentle shake. She blinked and looked up. In the moonlight, his lean face was all sharp angles and shadows, with an underlying paleness that suggested he wasn't as calm as he wanted to be. She felt the assessing scrape of his gaze across her face.

When he spoke, his voice was hoarse with pain rather than full of conviction. "It's going to be OK."

But she knew it wouldn't, couldn't be all right.

She looked past him, her eyes pulled back to the sight of Tessa, her body slashed to fleshy ribbons and covered in dried blood. Her face was gray and her once warm brown eyes stared at the night sky.

Across her forehead, rusty red letters spelled a single word.

SORRY.

CHAPTER SIX

"Back up." Lance steered Morgan away from the body.

Part of him wanted to take a closer look. Another part wanted to run like hell. From the brief glimpse he'd gotten of the body, it was a particularly nasty scene.

Not that it mattered. He had no business getting near that body. He wasn't a cop anymore, and the SFPD was en route.

Under his hands, Morgan's body shook, and her teeth chattered. Worry for her quickly wiped out any concern for himself. This wasn't his first death scene, but as a former assistant prosecutor, Morgan's experience with homicides would be one step removed. Viewing photos was not the same as seeing the body *in situ.*

He guided her toward his Jeep. He opened the hatchback and took out a warm jacket. He helped her into it. The sleeves covered her hands, and the hem fell to her thighs.

Before he could think, he wrapped his arms around her and pulled her to his chest. She fit against him perfectly. As wrong as the scene behind him was, having Morgan in his arms was right, and he took as much comfort from the embrace as he gave.

Morgan stirred, talking to his chest. "What happened to her?"

Reluctantly, he stepped back and zipped the jacket to her chin. "It is way too early for theories. We'd be guessing. Let's wait for facts." He appealed to the lawyer in her.

"You're right." But her blue eyes were dark pools, and her face had gone paler than the moon.

Eyes drifting toward the trees, Morgan took a huge gulp of air. "Could he still be out there?"

"I doubt it." But he kept scanning the surrounding trees just in case. He'd only gotten a brief look at the corpse, but the blood smeared on her skin had appeared dark and dry. "I suspect she's been dead more than a few hours."

Fifteen minutes later, approaching strobe lights swirled in the dark. A patrol vehicle parked next to the Jeep, and Carl got out, his face grim. They didn't bother with greetings. Lance showed Carl the body.

"Shit." Carl turned back toward his cruiser.

By the time the first gray of pre-dawn brightened the scene, two more patrol cars, the medical examiner, and a forensic team had arrived. The team hung back, waiting for the ME to do his thing. Kit in hand, the ME trudged across the clearing. His white coveralls looked ghostly in the gray light. Despite the number of personnel,

63

the clearing was eerily quiet. Normally, bad jokes would bounce around a death scene. Gallows humor was a favorite coping mechanism, but not when the victim was a kid.

A dark blue unmarked police car parked at the end of the row. Two figures got out.

Detectives Brody McNamara and Stella Dane hurried down the tract.

Stella rushed to her sister. "Are you all right?"

Morgan's stiff nod wasn't convincing, but she'd pulled herself together.

While the forensic team suited up in their PPEs, Brody and Stella followed the ME into the cattails. The horizon shifted from gray to pink as Morgan and Lance waited. Ten minutes passed before Brody and Stella emerged from the reeds.

"You must be exhausted. We'll take your statements, and then you can go." Brody motioned for Morgan to follow him. He guided her ten feet away.

Stella turned to Lance. "Tell me what happened."

Lance related the events of the evening, from Morgan's phone call to finding the body. Stella took notes, then returned her notepad to her pocket. "You'll look after my sister?"

"Of course." He nodded.

But Morgan's spine was straight and her chin high as she finished giving her statement to Brody and then returned to Lance's side.

They walked back to the Jeep. He started the engine, turned on the heat, and drove back toward the Dane house. Morgan was silent on the drive to her neighborhood. She pinched her cheeks, smoothed her hair, and climbed out of the Jeep.

A grim-faced Art opened the door before they reached it. He shot Lance a questioning look.

Lance shook his head. "Not now."

With a long police career behind him, Art understood. He nodded.

They left their muddy shoes by the door. High-pitched chatter drew them to the kitchen. Lance followed Morgan into the room. The sight of the three kids eating breakfast was a welcome dose of positive energy.

Her three little girls sat at the table. Ava was digging into a syrup-soaked pancake. Mia slathered butter on a short stack. Tiny Sophie, who seemed to survive on three Cheerios a day, hadn't touched her plate. Morgan's wild child wore purple leggings, a neon green T-shirt, and socks in two different shades of blue. Her hair looked like it had been styled with a leaf blower. Instead of eating, she smeared a glue stick on a piece of paper and shook a small container of silver glitter over it. Glitter was Sophie's crack.

Gianna stood at the stove ladling batter onto a hot griddle.

As soon as Morgan entered the kitchen,

the girls ran to her in a chorus of "Mommy!"

"Good morning, my sweets." She enveloped them in a giant hug, and the smile on her face warmed to genuine. She eased into a chair. The children surrounded her, and their chatter escalated. Lance's head spun, but Morgan seemed to be able to listen to three conversations at once. Her face relaxed as the kids told her about their morning. How much could they have done already?

"Hi, Lance." Ava climbed back into her chair. Mia zoomed over to give him a quick hug before returning to her breakfast.

Sophie crossed the kitchen, stopping in front of him and staring up, her big blue eyes seeing right through him. Seriously, the kid was a walking polygraph. "Mommy looks sad."

Clearly, Sophie blamed him.

"Yes," Lance said warily.

"Will she be happy again soon?" Subtext: what are you going to do about it?

"I hope so."

"Me too." Her nod was far too solemn for a three-year-old.

"I should go," he said. The weariness in his bones came from more than one night of no sleep. It grew from the violent and senseless death of a bright young woman.

Morgan walked him to the door. "Thank you for everything last night."

"You're welcome." He stopped over the threshold. "Call me if you need anything."

"I will."

Lance drove back to his small house in town, parked in the driveway, and went into his two-bedroom ranch. After the chaos of Morgan's house, the emptiness of his own hit him hard. Who would have thought he'd miss the incessant chatter of three small kids? Not him.

He entered the bedroom, stripped, and stepped into the shower. The blast of cold water cleared his head. Five minutes later, dried and dressed, he stared at his bed. Considering the replay of this morning's crime scene, he would pass on sleep just yet. In the dining room, he sat down at his piano but couldn't muster the desire to play. Nor did he want to sit in his cold, empty space and stare at the walls.

Even though it was Saturday, he needed the distraction of work.

Grabbing his keys, he left. The office was only six blocks away. Lance's morning commute took less than three minutes.

Sharp was at his desk when Lance arrived at the office. "You look like hell."

"Thanks." Lance went into the kitchen at the back of the space. "Do you have any coffee in here?"

"Do you really want to tax your adrenal glands?" Sharp asked in a *no you don't* voice.

"Yes." A dull ache throbbed at the base of Lance's skull.

Sharp broke out the blender and leafy greens. "Seriously, tell me what happened last night."

"As if you haven't heard." Lance dropped into a chair at the small wooden table.

"I know that eighteen-year-old Tessa Palmer was found dead near the local party spot at Scarlet Lake." Sharp shoved sweet potato greens, his latest obsession, and frozen chunks of fruit into the blender. "I know you and Morgan Dane found her, and that it was a particularly nasty killing."

Lance blew out a stream of air. "That sums it up."

But he detailed the events of the night anyway. When he was finished, Sharp pulsed the blender until its contents were a revolting shade of green. He poured the concoction into a glass. "Antioxidants are good for stress."

Knowing the shake would taste better than it looked, Lance drank it. "Do we have any cases to work on?"

"Of course."

Lance followed Sharp into the office.

Setting his mug on the desk, Sharp selected a file from a stack. "Here. Sixteen-year-old Jamie Lewis has been missing for two months. The SFPD has no leads. Her mother is desperate. This isn't the first time she's run away, but it's the first time the police haven't been able to find her."

Lance took the file and opened it. An eight-by-ten, full-color glossy of a young girl stared up at him. It was a school photo, but Jamie wasn't smiling. Her mouth was twisted in an insolent scowl. But it was her eyes that startled him. They were dark with challenge and anger that belied her age.

"I've seen convicted felons with warmer expressions," Lance said.

"Definitely," Sharp continued. "Jamie has ADD and oppositional defiant disorder. She's been on a broad range of pharmaceuticals since she was eight. By the time she was twelve, she was refusing to take her medication. Instead she self-medicated with alcohol and pot. Two years ago, her psychologist added bipolar disorder to her diagnosis. Her parents are divorced and blame each other. There's plenty of friction with the stepparents. The mother is local. Jamie's dad moved to California and remarried."

"She looks like a seriously troubled kid."

"She is." Sharp sighed. "SFPD has found no signs of her in town. They're convinced she ran far away. The parents don't deny it, but they want her found anyway."

Lance flipped through the file. Sharp had interviewed her mother in person, the father over the phone. He'd also gone through Jamie's bedroom.

She wasn't a girly girl. She liked classic rock and comics. She could draw, and some of her sketches were disturbing. "If she got out of town, there isn't much the local cops can do except enter her in the database with the million other missing kids."

If she was picked up by police in another location, they would run her through the National Crime Information Center. The NCIC would list her as a runaway, and she'd be returned to her parents.

"What do you want me to do?"

"I have Jamie's social media account information. She hasn't been online since she went missing, but kids post everything online. Go back through her posts for the last few months before she took off. See if you can find anything that might give us some insight. Friends that her parents weren't aware of. Places she always wanted to go. Online connections that could be suspicious."

Lance cracked his knuckles over the keyboard. "I'm on it."

Pulling his keys from his pocket, Sharp nodded toward his own office. Through the open door, Lance could see the black leather couch against the wall. "Try to get a nap."

"I might get bored enough."

"Have you stopped to see your mom today?" Sharp asked.

"Not yet." After finding the body, Lance wasn't up to dealing with his mother yet. "Maybe after that nap."

Sharp paused. "Want me to check in on her for you?"

As if merely checking in on his mom was all that a visit entailed. Sharp was one of the few people who Lance's anxiety-ridden mom allowed into her home. If it hadn't been for Sharp, no one would have seen her or taken her to her group therapy sessions while Lance was in the hospital last fall.

"No. I'll do it, but thanks for the offer."

"Call me if you change your mind. Do me a favor, and make sure the water bowl on the back porch is full," Sharp said on his way out.

Lance went onto the back porch. He caught the quick flash of a skinny white-and-tan body as the stray disappeared under the steps. He carried the water bowl into the kitchen, filled it, and returned it to the porch. The pup looked thin and the food bowl was empty, so he added some kibble. He could see the shine of the dog's eyes as it watched him. "You could do worse than Sharp. He acts all gruff, but he'd basically be your slave if you let him."

The dog didn't believe him.

Lance returned to his office, played a classic rock station through the wireless speaker, and settled in with his laptop. He flipped through the file to the parent information—anything to keep the image of a dead teenager out of his head.

Three hours of computer research later, exhaustion hit Lance like a brick over the head. Jamie's social media accounts revealed nothing, but then, it was likely that her parents monitored her online activity, considering her psychiatric history. The kid was probably smart enough to know her accounts were being watched.

Lance considered making a coffee-and-donut run. If he fell asleep, he'd be seeing Tessa Palmer's body in his dreams. He was halfway to the door when the stiff ache in his thigh turned him around. He went back to the kitchen and drank a protein shake, then stretched out on the couch.

He couldn't let a few nightmares—or anything else—get in the way of his recovery.

But the bloody image that haunted his sleep didn't belong to Tessa. It was Morgan's. Even in his sleep he knew that she was the one who had the power to hurt him.

CHAPTER SEVEN

It was Wednesday afternoon. Lance leaned on the outside of his Jeep and waited for Jamie Lewis's best friend. Seventeen-year-old high school drop-out Tony Allessi worked at the bowling alley. Neither the police nor Jamie's parents had been able to get any information out of the kid, but Lance wasn't an authority figure. Somebody had to know where Jamie had gone. With teenagers, friends were the best possibility.

Tony was easy to spot crossing the parking lot. On top of a lanky, six-three frame, his four-inch blue-and-red Mohawk didn't exactly blend into a crowd. He looked like a parrot.

Lance pushed off the door of his Jeep. "Hey, Tony!"

The teen turned at the sound of his name. He wore ripped jeans and a vintage Ramones T-shirt.

"I hear you're good friends with Jamie Lewis." Lance looked beyond the nose ring, eyeliner, and twin ear gauges the size of dinner plates.

Under all his facial modifications, Tony's eyes were sharp and suspicious. "Yeah. So?"

"I'm looking for her."

"Why?"

Lance handed him a business card. "You heard what happened Thursday night, right?"

Tony nodded, his mouth tightening into a solemn line. "Yeah. I didn't know Tessa that well, but she didn't deserve to get killed."

"No. She didn't. The police haven't caught the guy who did it. I hate to think of Jamie out there all alone." Lance let the implication hang in the air.

Tony leaned back, hands raised. "Dude, I can't steer the police toward a friend."

He's definitely seen Jamie.

"I'm not the police," Lance pointed out. "But her parents are going crazy. Every time the news mentions the murder, they picture Jamie."

As did Lance. Tessa Palmer's dead body had haunted him since Saturday morning. He really wanted to find Jamie before something terrible happened to her. Kids on the street were vulnerable to all sorts of predators.

"Sorry, man. I can't help you," Tony insisted. "I don't know where she is anyway."

"If you see Jamie, ask her to call me." Lance handed him another card. "Just knowing she's all right would mean a lot to her parents."

"OK." Tony pocketed it and walked into the building.

"Hey, cop," a voice called.

Lance pivoted to see a red-haired teenage boy standing next to a beat-up Toyota. The kid was

74

small and scrawny with a sunburn-over-freckles complexion.

"You were asking about Jamie Lewis?"

"What's your name?" Lance asked.

"You a cop?"

"No." Lance checked to make sure his handgun behind his right hip was covered by his shirt. It was. Why did everyone think he was a cop?

"Then it's none of your fucking business."

It was one in the afternoon. Wasn't this kid supposed to be in school?

"Do you have information about Jamie?" Lance asked.

"What's it worth to you?" Red held out his hand and wiggled his fingers.

Lance dug a twenty out of his wallet.

The kid shook his head. "It's worth more than twenty bucks."

Lance exchanged the twenty for a fifty. The kid reached for it, but Lance was twice his size. He held the money just out of reach. "What do you know?"

With a disgusted sigh, Red pulled out a cell phone that probably cost more than his car. He scrolled. "There was this big party out at the lake Thursday night."

Lance straightened. "And?"

"And Jamie was there." The kid held the phone out so Lance could see the screen. A video was playing with the sound muted. Lance watched two boys shoving each other and arguing.

The kid tapped the screen. "Look in the background."

A ring of kids circled the fighting boys. They appeared to be encouraging the fight. Red hit pause. "There's Jamie."

"Do you know any of these other kids?" The focus was on the combatants, so the people in the background were fuzzy. Lance couldn't positively ID anyone. He'd have to see the video on a larger screen.

"Dude, I'm not a squealer."

Lance waved the fifty. "Can I get a copy of this?"

Red rolled his eyes. "It's on YouTube. You can do whatever you want with it."

Lance copied the URL and handed over the cash.

"Thanks." Red took the fifty and his phone.

As the kid got into his Toyota, Lance memorized his license plate information. It would take him five minutes to identify Mr. Red Noneofyourfuckingbusiness.

Lance drove to the office. Sharp was at his desk, working on his computer. Lance headed for the empty room and his laptop. He settled in the folding chair.

"Aren't you uncomfortable in that tiny chair?" Sharp called across the hall.

"I'm fine. I like minimalism." The computer

screen glowed, and Lance opened the browser and went to YouTube. He found the video in twenty seconds. "Come watch this."

Sharp crossed the hall and watched over Lance's shoulder. Lance stopped the video at the same point Red had. "Jamie Lewis?"

"I'll be damned."

"So much for the assumption that she left town."

"When was that video taken?" Sharp asked.

"Thursday night." Lance played the video from the beginning again. He didn't see Red, nor did he spot Tony's Mohawk in the crowd, but then even enlarged, the background images were a little grainy.

Sharp leaned closer. "Is that the party Tessa Palmer was last seen at?"

"It is." Lance froze the video again. "There's Tessa."

"Do the police have this video?" Sharp eased back, scratching his chin.

"I don't know. I'll call Brody."

"You should. It's good to stay in the good graces of local law enforcement. Horner's a necessary evil and makes a really bad enemy."

"You forgot 'asshole.' I hope the mayor loses the election. Then maybe Horner will get canned." Having worked for the man for ten years, Lance had tired of his politics over policing.

"It can always be worse. Better the devil you know, and all that."

"This is true," Lance admitted.

"Do you recognize the two boys fighting?" Sharp asked.

"The dark-haired kid lives across the street from Morgan. His name is Nick. He was Tessa's boyfriend. I don't know the other boy." Lance pointed to the screen. "It looks like the video was just uploaded to YouTube today."

Lance ran the clip one more time. He turned the sound up, but all he could hear was the crowd of kids chanting, "Fight, fight, fight."

Nick was the aggressor, his face red with rage as he went at the other boy with a two-handed shove.

"I'd like to know what led to the fight," Sharp said. "I wish the video started earlier."

Tessa moved into the scene, wedging herself between the two boys. Nick backed off, but the second kid went around her, knocking her to the ground in his haste to get at Nick. Tessa ran out of view. A few more boys moved in to break up the fight and the video ended with a long shot of the ground.

"At least we know Jamie was still in town as of last Thursday night." Sharp turned toward the doorway. On his way out, he called over his shoulder, "I'll call her parents. Give me a few minutes to download a copy of that video in case the cops have it taken down from YouTube."

"I'm sure Jamie's parents will be relieved to see her alive," Lance said.

After Sharp went back to his own office, Lance called Brody, but he didn't answer and his mailbox was full. He went out into the hall and leaned into Sharp's office. "I can't get Brody on the phone. I'm going to stop at the station. Did you get that video downloaded?"

Sharp looked up from his keyboard. "Got it."

Lance went outside, climbed into his Jeep, and drove to the township municipal building. The SFPD occupied the ground floor of a two-story colonial-style building. The tax collector, zoning office, and town clerk were located upstairs. He crossed the gray-tiled lobby and entered the reception area. From the outside, the building looked homey and quaint, with blue, New Englandish siding and barn-red shutters, but inside, the space had needed a facelift twenty years ago.

The desk sergeant greeted him with a smile that creased his face like a bulldog's. "Hey, Lance. How's the new PI gig?"

"It's not bad." Lance leaned on the counter.

"Sharp treating you all right?"

"He is."

"Tell him he'd better, or I'll kick his ass." The sergeant grinned.

"Is Brody around? I tried to leave him a message, but his mailbox is full."

Lowering his voice, the sergeant said, "Horner held another press conference, so Brody is tied up with citizens calling in *tips*." Ninety-nine percent of which would turn out to be a complete waste of time.

"Poor Brody," Lance said.

"We're trying to filter them the best we can, but we're shorthanded as it is."

Weren't they always?

The sergeant sighed. "And you know how it is. All the citizens want to talk to *the detective*."

"How about Stella? Is she here?" Lance asked. "I might have some information about the Palmer case."

The sergeant shook his bald head. "No. She's not working the Palmer case anyway."

"Really?"

"Really."

"Then who's working with Brody?" When Lance had worn a uniform, he'd assisted the detectives when they'd needed help.

The sergeant glanced around. The lobby was empty. "Horner."

"Wha-at?" Of all the names Lance had expected to hear, that wasn't one of them.

"I know," the sergeant agreed. "Anyway. Maybe you should talk to him."

"Good idea." Lance would rather have a root canal.

"I'll tell him you're here." The sergeant picked

up the phone and spoke with Horner's secretary for a few seconds. "Go on back."

"Thanks." Lance bypassed the counter and went through the doorway into a long open room filled with rows of metal filing cabinets and clusters of cubicles. Uniforms sat at desks typing reports. They greeted Lance as he walked through to Horner's office.

Horner's blonde secretary waved him through with a manicured hand. "Go on in."

Lance gave the door a polite knuckle rap before going in. Even at the end of the day, not a single wrinkle dared mar Horner's starched, navy-blue uniform, and his precision haircut looked just as perfect as always.

"Lance, have a seat." Horner gestured to one of the two chairs that faced his desk. "You're looking fit. How are you?"

"Very well. Thank you." Lance eased into the seat. "It was a long recovery."

In June, seven months after the shooting, Lance had briefly returned to the force, but his leg hadn't been ready. His inability to keep up had placed his fellow officers in danger. He wouldn't carry a badge again unless he was completely fit.

"Glad to hear it. I wish you'd have gone back on disability instead of quitting." Horner's hair gleamed in the light as if it were varnished, or maybe plastic. The chief *did* bear a certain resemblance to Ava's Ken doll.

"At the time, I didn't know if I was ever going to get back to a hundred percent, and staying on disability didn't appeal. I'd rather work."

"I understand and respect that." Horner nodded. "Now, what can I do for you?"

Lance pulled his phone from his pocket. "Actually, I have something for you." He opened his YouTube app and handed the phone over the desk. "If you look at the time stamp on the video, it appears this was taken at the lake Thursday night."

Horner's eyes brightened as he watched.

"It's easier to see on a bigger screen, but that's Tessa Palmer trying to break up the fight," Lance said.

Horner swiveled to face the desktop computer on the other leg of his L-shaped desk. He opened his browser and pulled up the video, freezing on a frame of Tessa between the two boys. "This looks like her boyfriend, Nick Zabrowski."

"It does."

"How did you find this?" Irritation flattened Horner's mouth.

"I ran across it while working a missing-kid case. Jamie Lewis. It was just uploaded today." There was no reason for Lance to maintain client confidentiality since Jamie was already an open case for the SFPD.

"Do you know who took this video?" Horner asked.

"No." Lance debated about giving Red's plate number to Horner. But the police could subpoena YouTube for the account details of the person who'd uploaded the video. And Lance might need more information from Mr. Noneofyourfuckingbusiness to find Jamie. The kid would be less cooperative if Lance gave him up to the police. He'd keep the kid's ID in his back pocket for now.

"Thank you for bringing this to my attention. If you run across anything else, I'd appreciate a call." Horner held out a hand.

Lance shook it. "Of course."

"I want to let you know that I've requested to add a third detective and two more uniforms to our force. The recent rise in crime supports the budget increase. We have the full support of the mayor. Of course, the council is holding back on the approval until after the election, but I feel confident that once the mayor is reelected, Scarlet Falls will be hiring."

Lance played down his interest. "Thanks for the information. Good luck with the Palmer case."

"I've little doubt the case will be closed within the week." Horner's eyes shone with a predatory gleam.

"You have a good suspect?"

Horner smiled, his teeth as Hollywood-perfect as his hair. "All I can say is that it will all be over soon. This video will help. Thanks again. I won't forget your cooperation when that position opens up, if you're still interested in becoming a detective, that is."

"I'll give it some consideration," Lance said.

He left the chief's office with a head full of questions. He called Sharp from the car and updated him on the meeting. "Why is Horner taking a personal interest in the Palmer case?"

"Because he knows the girl's grandparents and so does the mayor. They belong to the same fancypants country club. Plus, Horner's a total publicity whore."

"That explains a lot." Lance told Sharp about Horner's vague job offer.

"You're really still interested in working for him?" Sharp asked.

"Maybe." *Yes.*

"Remember, you don't get to pick your cases. Go back to work for Horner, and you'll be at his beck and call."

"As opposed to being at your beck and call?" Lance joked.

"You're comparing me to Horner? That's an insult," Sharp retorted. "You realize Horner stole this case from Stella because of the good press it will give him and the mayor."

"He suggested they're close to making an arrest."

"Yes. I heard they're waiting on a DNA test."

"Where did you hear that?"

"I have my sources." Sharp stopped by the local watering hole frequented by his former cop buddies a few times a week to pick up gossip. The Pub stocked an organic ale just for Sharp.

"Can you find out who owns this vehicle?" Lance gave him the plate number of Red's Toyota.

"Will do. I'll text it to you." The line beeped, and Sharp said, "I have another call coming in. See how many of those other kids at the party you can ID. Somebody has to know where Jamie Lewis has been hiding."

"On it." Lance ended the call and set his phone on the console. He recognized three people on the video: Tessa, Jamie, and Nick. The only one of those three he could actually speak to was Morgan's neighbor. He turned the car toward her house.

CHAPTER EIGHT

Rain tapped on the kitchen window. Morgan sipped a cup of coffee and read her emails from the DA's office and the Human Resources department. Filling out employment and insurance forms made her new job real, and the first glimmer of interest in something outside the walls of the house flickered inside her.

Next to her, Sophie ate one tiny triangle of her peanut butter and jelly sandwich and worked on a drawing. Morgan glanced at the picture. The wild arcs of color were typical Sophie.

Fresh bursts of sadness and anger shot through her.

Once Tessa had been a little girl, coloring at her kitchen table. She should have had a long, happy life.

Morgan blinked away an image of the girl's ruined body, the same picture that appeared in her nightmares over and over every time she closed her eyes.

"It's nap time," Morgan reminded her youngest.

Sophie looked up from her lopsided rainbow. As usual, tangled hair swayed around her daughter's face. "I'm too old for naps."

Morgan ignored the protest. "I'll hang your rainbow on the fridge. Let's go."

Sophie slid from her chair and headed for her bedroom, feet dragging. But a morning of pre-school had worn her out and she was asleep in minutes. Her face was flushed, and Morgan suspected a back-to-school cold was looming. She paused to watch Sophie sleep for a few minutes. Awake, the child wasn't still long enough. Her rosebud mouth was relaxed, giving her an innocence she rarely had when up and moving.

Soon, Sophie *would* be too old for naps. Like her sisters, she would outgrow rereadings of *Goodnight Moon* and the need to have her toast cut into perfectly even triangles. Morgan was going to miss these small, peaceful bits of time.

She pushed back at the creep of sadness.

Life didn't stand still. She was moving forward.

Pulling the bedroom door almost closed, Morgan went back to the living room. Grandpa was in his recliner. He set aside his iPad. "I give up. The security camera isn't working. I'll have to check it tomorrow."

Morgan pictured him climbing a ladder. "Why don't you call the alarm company? That's what we pay them for."

"You're right." Grandpa gave her his full attention. "Are you all right? You haven't been out of the house in days. It's not healthy." Grandpa was never afraid to say it like it was. "You never called Lance back, did you? He was worried about you."

Morgan hadn't returned his call. She'd also ignored messages from several neighbors, all presumably wanting to gossip about Tessa.

Grandpa frowned. "We haven't even talked about Tessa's death."

Morgan didn't want to talk about it. She didn't want to think about it. She'd relegated Tessa's murder to the dark corner of her mind reserved for grief. But it was there, hovering, waiting for a trigger, which is why she'd successfully avoided the Internet and filled the last few days with craft projects and kiddie cartoons.

"Honey, you can't just hold it all inside." Grandpa's voice was gentle. "What happened to your therapist?"

"I really wasn't getting anywhere. It seemed pointless to continue." She hadn't wanted to make progress.

Grandpa reached over and put his hand over hers. "Then you should find another one."

She smiled, but it felt empty. "I'll be fine once I get back to work. I just need to get my life in order."

Her grandfather didn't look convinced.

Morgan stood. "And on that note, I'll get back to my paperwork before Sophie wakes up."

She didn't make it to the kitchen.

"You're going to want to see this." Grandpa raised the volume on the TV. He pushed down the foot of his recliner and leaned forward.

On the screen, the police chief, the mayor, and the district attorney gathered on one side of a podium. On the other side of the flag-festooned stage, Brody stood in the background.

Police Chief Horner stepped up to the podium. "Behind me are District Attorney Bryce Walters, Mayor Rich DiGulio—" Horner shifted his focus, "—and Scarlet Falls Detective Brody McNamara."

Flashes went off as photographers snapped shots.

Morgan returned to the sofa and perched on the edge of the cushion.

Horner turned back to the throng of media. "We have an update in the murder of Tessa Palmer."

Reporters surged forward, extending their microphones and shouting questions.

Horner raised a hand to request silence. Chatter lowered to murmurs, and he continued. "In the early morning hours on Saturday, the Scarlet Falls Police Department learned of the brutal sexual assault and murder of a female victim."

Morgan flinched at the words "sexual assault." She hadn't known.

Horner continued. "The young woman was identified as Scarlet Falls resident Tessa Palmer. She was killed between the hours of ten thirty p.m. Thursday and four a.m. Friday. Her body was found near Scarlet Lake. We are thoroughly investigating this brutal crime. Detective McNamara is the lead detective on the case. I'll leave him to answer your questions."

He gestured for Brody to step up to the mic.

Brody complied, but he didn't look happy about it.

A reporter shouted, "Detective McNamara, we heard there's a suspect."

Brody shook his head. "We have a person of interest, but we aren't prepared to charge anyone at this time."

Another reporter raised his mic. "Do you think there's a serial killer running around Scarlet Falls?"

Brody answered, "It's too early in the investigation—"

"Thank you, Detective McNamara." Horner cut him off, but behind his polite nod, he looked ready to tear Brody's head off. "We have no reason to think this murder is anything other than an individual event."

"Should the women of Scarlet Falls take extra precautions?" another reporter shouted.

"We always suggest our female residents be vigilant about their surroundings, but we have no specific warning at this time." Horner took a breath, his gaze sweeping the crowd. "I'm confident that this office will bring a swift close to a case that has shocked and appalled the residents of this town."

Grandpa lowered the volume as the press conference wound down. "Chief Horner likes to get in front of the camera."

"He'll lose his job if the mayor doesn't win his reelection. A killer running around town won't help that happen."

The police chief was hired by the mayor and city council. If town leadership changed, the chief could be fired by the next administration.

"There'll be a great deal of pressure to make a quick arrest," Grandpa said. "The election is only six weeks away."

"I feel like I should do something."

"Like what?"

"I don't know, but I want Tessa's killer caught." Five minutes ago, Morgan hadn't wanted to talk about Tessa's death. Now, she suddenly felt cowardly for hiding from the news.

"You'll get to put criminals away starting next week."

"I can't wait. Why wasn't Stella at the press conference?" Morgan asked. Her sister had responded to the scene with Brody. "Horner likes to put her in front of the camera."

"I don't know. Maybe she's working the case."

"I'm going to call her." She speed-dialed her sister.

Stella answered in two rings. "Morgan?"

"Hey. I just saw the news conference. Where were you?"

"Horner pulled me from the case." Wind weakened Stella's voice.

"What?"

"Hold on. The wind is brutal out here. Let me get in my car." Over the connection, a door closed and the wind ceased. Stella continued. "He took me off the case. He said I'm too close."

"This isn't the first time you've known a victim. This is a small town. You're bound to know some victims."

"I know." Stella paused. "I got the feeling there was more to his order."

"Like?" Morgan asked.

"I've recognized half of the people brought in for questioning." Stella lowered her voice. "I wonder if he took me off the case not because I knew the victim, but because I might know the killer."

Statistically, male homicide victims were more likely to be murdered by strangers, but women were usually killed by someone they knew. Scarlet Falls was a small town. Chances were, Tessa had been killed by one of their own.

Stella said good-bye and Morgan lowered the phone. Movement through the living room window caught her attention. Three police cars pulled into the Zabrowski driveway. Two black-and-whites and one unmarked car.

"What is it?" Grandpa asked.

"Police cars across the street." Morgan watched Brody get out of the unmarked police car.

"They're going to question Nick. You said he was Tessa's boyfriend." Grandpa climbed to his feet and joined her at the window. Brody went to the front door. Bud opened it, and Brody handed him a folded paper.

"They're serving a warrant," Grandpa said.

Morgan headed for the door.

Grandpa frowned. "You can't get involved. You're going to work for the District Attorney, remember?"

"I'm just going to see what's happening."

Worry propelled Morgan across the street. The lots in the riverside neighborhood were several acres each, the houses far apart. The Zabrowski place was a one-story, two-bedroom, no-frills rectangle. It didn't have a water view, but Bud was meticulous about his landscaping. The front lawn, with its Ireland-green grass and tall oaks, looked like a park. Nick had learned his trade at a young age.

Morgan went up the brick walk. Bud had the door open before she reached the stoop.

"I was just going to call you. I don't know what to do." The manager of the Speedy Lube in town, Bud still wore his red, logoed polo and black pants.

Morgan didn't know much about the family's

background, only that Bud had raised his son alone since Nick was little. In the ten years they'd lived across the street from her grandfather, she'd never heard any mention of Nick's mother.

Bud kept the house as tidy as his lawn. The furnishings were bachelor-plain, heavy on black leather and oak. Knickknacks were limited to framed snapshots and a couple of high school chess trophies. Brody stood in the middle of the room, giving instructions to three uniformed officers as they worked. All four policemen wore gloves as they pulled up the couch cushions and upended furniture to inspect the undersides of drawers.

Bud led the way into the kitchen. Nick sat at the kitchen table, his hands clasped in front of him in a white-knuckled grip. His face was locked in disbelief, grief, and fear. A fifth policeman stood in the doorway watching Nick.

Bud handed her some papers. "This is what they gave me. We went to the police station on Saturday, and they asked him some questions, but we haven't heard anything since. I thought that was the end of it."

Morgan thought back to her discussion with Felicity. The police would track down all the kids who had been at the party Thursday night, but Nick, as Tessa's boyfriend, would be of special interest. She unfolded the papers and automatically checked to make sure the name, address, and other information were correct. There were separate warrants for Nick's and Bud's vehicles. Her gaze moved down the page. She read over the description of property to be seized: knives, clothing items, biological evidence, fibers . . .

The police thought Nick had killed Tessa. He wasn't just a suspect. He was the *lead* suspect.

The warrant included the house, the land, and the large shed in which Nick stored his landscaping equipment. The police were also seizing Nick's computer and cell phone.

Morgan's gaze shifted to Nick. She couldn't believe he would violently kill Tessa on Thursday night, and then come over and play chess with Grandpa the next day as if nothing had happened. Actually, he'd been a little distracted, and the fact that he'd been at their house on a Friday night had been unusual.

"Nick?" she took the chair next to him.

He didn't look up, but the set of his shoulders was all tension.

With a glance at the cop in the doorway, Morgan lowered her voice. "The police asked you questions on Saturday?"

He lifted his gaze to hers. She recoiled at the wounded look in his eyes.

Nodding, he said, "Two policemen came to the door and said they needed to talk to me at the police station. They wanted me to go in their car, but Dad drove me instead."

Many people would have been interviewed on Saturday and Sunday as the police sorted suspects from witnesses.

"How did it go?" she asked.

"I thought it was fine." His brows lowered. "I guess I was wrong."

"Did they advise you of your Miranda rights?" she asked.

"Yes."

Miranda rights were generally read to suspects, not witnesses. They'd zeroed in on Nick almost immediately. By itself, that wasn't alarming. But a search warrant required the police to establish probable cause, so the police must have had more than just a hunch that Nick was guilty. The probable cause affidavit wasn't attached to the search warrant. Sometimes, to expedite the search, a judge signs the warrant with the understanding that the affidavit will be attached within twenty-four hours.

But Morgan would have liked to have known the extent of the evidence right now.

"Did you understand that you could have had an attorney with you while they asked you questions?" Morgan asked.

"Yes," he said. "But I didn't think I needed one. I wanted to cooperate. I want them to find who . . ." His eyes filled with moisture, but he blinked back his tears. "I want them to find whoever did that to Tessa."

"What were the names of the officers who asked you questions?" she asked.

"Police Chief Horner asked all the questions," Nick said. "But the detective in the living room was there too."

So, Stella must have been pulled from the case because she knew the primary suspect: Nick.

"Do not say anything else without a lawyer," she said.

"I didn't do anything. How could they think . . .?" He didn't finish his sentence.

"Nick, I want you to promise me you will not answer any more questions from the police without an attorney present. It's important."

"Yeah. I get that now." He raised his eyes. "And letting them swab my mouth was probably dumb too. But I honestly didn't think I had anything to worry about. I couldn't ever have hurt Tessa." A tear slid from his eye. He wiped it away with an angry swipe of his hand.

A sick feeling settled in Morgan's belly. They'd swabbed Nick for DNA on Saturday.

How much evidence did the police have?

Guilt swamped Morgan. She'd been hiding under a metaphorical rock for the past few days. She'd known the police would bring Nick in for questioning. Why hadn't she asked him about his interview?

"Can we go outside?" Morgan asked the officer babysitting Nick. "We're probably in the way."

He nodded and stepped back so she, Bud, and Nick could pass. The cop followed them, sticking close to Nick. Out on the front lawn, the situation didn't improve. Another police car had arrived, and two officers were searching the exterior of the property.

Nick balled his hand into a fist, and his posture stiffened. He looked like he was working hard not to cry. Maybe she should have kept him inside, but watching the police search your home was bound to be upsetting.

"It's going to be OK, Nick." Bud's voice was calm.

Nick shook his head. They waited as the policemen walked the grounds, stopping periodically to squat and inspect the grass. Morgan's heart broke at his distress. Usually, he was an easy-going kid.

The officers rounded the house and disappeared from view. Bud paced, Morgan leaned on a tree, and Nick stood stock-still in the center of the lawn. Twenty minutes passed.

"Brody!" an officer came running from the side of the house.

Brody exited the house and rounded the building. A few minutes later, he walked back toward them. His eyes were grim. His gaze flickered to Morgan. Clearly, he didn't want to do whatever was next.

Brody stopped in front of Nick. "Nick

Zabrowski, you are under arrest for the murder of Tessa Palmer."

Nick's body shook. His face went white, and his mouth dropped open. "No."

A uniformed officer stepped forward, handcuffs out and ready. "Turn around. Put your hands behind your head. Interlace your fingers."

Instead of complying, Nick backed away. "No. This can't be right. I would never hurt Tessa. I didn't do anything."

"Give him a minute," Bud said.

"Turn around." The cop reached for Nick's arm.

The cop's hand touched Nick's bicep, and his body jerked, his legs tangling as he turned to flee.

The uniform tackled him, taking Nick to the ground facedown and straddling his back.

"Stop! Get off me," Nick screamed into the grass, terrified.

Despair welled in Morgan's throat as tears burned her eyes.

"Nick, try to calm down," she said. "Fighting them will only make the situation worse. If you can be quiet and cooperate, this will be easier for you."

Nick went still, but they all knew that nothing about what was going to happen to him next would be easy.

CHAPTER NINE

What the hell?

Lance parked at the curb in front of Morgan's house. Across the street, four police cars were parked in Nick's driveway. A news van had arrived. A reporter and her cameraman scurried up the grass like rats with microphones.

In the center of the front lawn, a cop knelt on a man on the ground. Another man in a red shirt was lunging at the pair on the grass. *Nick's dad?* Morgan stood in front of him, holding him back with both hands on his chest.

The reporter shook out her hair, lifted her mic, and checked her lipstick in the lens of the camera. The cop on the ground jerked the handcuffed man to his feet.

Shit. That was Nick.

The scene came together in one, horrible rush.

Nick was being arrested for Tessa's murder.

The young man stopped struggling. His body went stiff, his face completely impassive, as if he'd simply shut down.

Lance got out of the car. He was not getting involved in Tessa Palmer's case, and Morgan

100

shouldn't either. The DA wouldn't be happy to find her at the prime suspect's house.

"Nooo!" A high-pitched yell came from behind him. Lance spun. Sophie came flying off the front step, with Gianna at her heels.

"Sophie, get back here!" Gianna shouted.

The little girl's face was a mask of panic and rage. Lance darted left and intercepted her with an arm around her middle.

"No!" she howled. "They're hurting Nick. Make them stop!"

Lance swung her into his arms and hugged her close to his chest, trying to turn her face away from the scene. Not that it would help at this point. She'd obviously already seen the worst part.

Tiny fists pounded on his chest. "Dowwwn!"

"Shh." Holding tight, he rubbed her back. "It's going to be all right."

The reporter pointed at Lance, and the cameraman swung around to aim the camera at him. He shifted Sophie to shield her from the camera's view with his body.

Across the street, Morgan's face was sheer devastation as a stiff-legged Nick was dragged toward a police car and put into the back. The cameraman went back to filming Nick. Morgan released her grip on the man in red. He slumped, wiping a hand across his face, and nodding blindly at whatever she was saying to him.

Lance carried Sophie inside.

"I'm sorry." Gianna held out her arms.

"Hold tight." Lance bent to hand her over. Sophie's spindly arms and legs were surprisingly strong, but she'd stopped fighting and started sobbing. "Keep her inside. I don't want those vultures from the press putting her on the evening news."

Gianna took the child, wrapping her arms around her small body, and walked toward the rear of the house. Over Gianna's shoulder, Sophie shot Lance a mutinous stare, her face an angry, tear-streaked red. She was never going to forgive him.

He went out onto the front stoop to see what was happening. The car containing Nick had left. Cops, including Brody, swarmed over the grass. Morgan had pulled Nick's dad to the side of the property and was talking to him. The man's face was locked in pain and despair.

Morgan touched his forearm, turned, and walked toward Lance. He met her in the middle of her driveway. Her eyes, usually deep with sadness, were on fire. Over the past few months, the only times he'd seen her truly happy and animated were when she was playing with her kids. Underneath, her grief ran deep. When she was alone, she tended to brood.

"What happened?" he asked.

"They found a knife, which appeared to be

encrusted with blood, buried behind the shed." Morgan met his gaze. That wasn't all. "They also found a T-shirt with blood on it in his hamper."

"No."

The man in the red shirt hurried across the street. "Morgan?"

Turning toward him, Morgan gestured between them. "Lance Kruger, Bud Zabrowski. Bud is Nick's dad."

"This can't be right," Bud said. "Nick could never hurt anyone. For one, he can't stand the sight of blood. Pukes every time. He could never do . . ." Bud clearly couldn't vocalize the crime Nick had been accused of committing. "*That* to anyone, let alone Tessa. He really liked her."

Bud inhaled a deep and painful-sounding breath. "What am I going to do? I can't afford a defense attorney."

"The court will appoint a lawyer if you can't afford one," Morgan said.

Bud shook his head. "Will that be good enough?"

That depended on who was assigned his case. There were good public defenders and bad ones, but frankly, they were all overworked.

"I don't know." Morgan was honest.

"I can try to mortgage the house, but I doubt there's much equity. I took out a second mortgage to help Nick buy the equipment for his business.

Do you know any good attorneys?" Bud asked Morgan.

She nodded. "I can give you some names."

"Thank you. I have to try." Bud shook her hand. "I'm going to start calling mortgage companies." He hurried back to his house.

Morgan walked to the front step and sat down. She pulled her cell phone from her pocket and began to scroll. "Even if he mortgages his house, he's going to have a hard time paying the bill of a top criminal defense attorney."

"How hard will it be for him to find someone to take the case? If DNA on the knife matches Tessa's blood . . ."

"I know."

"What if he's guilty?" Lance didn't know Nick that well.

"He's not."

"How do you know that? If Brody arrested Nick, he has enough evidence to make a case, and he's only been investigating for a few days."

Morgan raised her gaze. "A few weeks ago, Grandpa sliced his hand out in the yard with a pair of pruning shears. Nick was working with him. One glance at the blood and he threw up in the driveway. It was an immediate reaction."

"That's not enough to build a defense."

Morgan rose and dusted off her slacks. "Shadow of a doubt, right? Isn't that what Nick's entitled to?"

"It's a pretty thin shadow."

"It's a start, and we don't know anything about the case. What if the DNA on the knife doesn't match Tessa's?"

"Why would Nick have a bloody knife buried in his backyard?"

Morgan's body went rigid. "If Nick killed Tessa, why would he hold on to the murder weapon? She was killed right near the lake. He could have thrown the knife into the water or left it at the scene. Only a fool would bring home the murder weapon he used to kill his girlfriend."

"Not a fool," Lance corrected. "Someone who hasn't committed a crime before. Someone who panicked. Criminals don't always do the smart thing. That's how they get caught."

"I know, but I can't believe Nick is a killer. He plays chess with my grandfather. He reads stories to my girls."

Maybe that's why Morgan was so freaked out. Nick was a member of their community. She trusted him. She'd let him into her home, given him access to her children. If he could be guilty of murder, then how could anyone ever feel safe?

"I've never even seen him lose his temper," she said.

But Nick had been very angry on that video.

Lance reached out to touch Morgan's arm. "I know you don't want to believe it, but Brody is a good cop."

"I know Brody's a good cop, but this time he has to be wrong."

Or was he? Lance wondered how well Morgan really knew Nick. And for that matter, how well did anyone really know their neighbors and what went on behind closed doors?

CHAPTER TEN

He turned off the television. Nick Zabrowski had been arrested for Tessa's murder. His plan had worked. He should be happy, but it didn't feel real.

Standing, he walked to the window, almost expecting to see a police car outside. But the scene outside was the same as always. A squirrel bounded across the grass and raced up a tree.

Could he really have gotten away with what he'd done?

He glanced down at his hands. No matter how much he washed them, he couldn't seem to get rid of the imaginary bloodstains. He curled his fingers into tight fists. His nails dug into his palms. The sharp bite of pain was grounding.

It amazed him that he could walk around in public, and no one saw through him. He knew what he was, and it wasn't normal. Other people would be horrified at the things he dreamed about. He worked hard to pretend he was like everybody else.

All that hard work had paid off after he lost it Thursday night. He had gotten his shit back together and taken care of business.

Now he needed to act like everything was fine. But it was getting tougher to pretend. How does a monster act normal?

He listened for a few seconds but heard nothing. The house was empty. No police cars were parked outside. No one was waiting to expose his secrets.

He went to his closet, turned on the light, and moved aside a few boxes. In the back corner, he lifted the carpet, then pried up a small piece of the floor. Inside the hole was a shoebox. A chilly shiver of excitement passed through him as he held the box in his hands. It felt too light considering all that it held.

His secrets.

His demons.

His guilt.

Setting it on the floor, he opened it. Photographs of Tessa stared up at him. He picked up a picture by the corner. A tear slipped from his eye and landed onto the photo. He wiped it away with an angry gesture. The pain in his heart intensified.

I loved you. Why couldn't you just love me back?

How could he live without her?

She'd been perfect. Sweet. Innocent. Beautiful.

She'd said she hadn't loved him back. She'd tried to reject him. But she'd been lying to herself. No matter how hard she'd tried to deny it, she'd wanted him as much as he wanted her. Turning on him had been her ultimate betrayal.

But now she was gone. At first he'd blamed himself for his lack of control, but she'd forced him to do what he'd done. She knew about his temper, and still she'd backed him into a corner, she'd threatened him. He'd had no choice. He'd been relieved when he'd realized that it had been her own fault.

Why did you make me hurt you?

He flipped through the stack of photos, each one a stab to his heart. But by the time he'd reached the end of the pile, he'd become conditioned to the pain. He went through the pile again and again, until he could view each image without responding. Then he put the photos away.

He fished in the bottom of the box for the lock of hair he'd taken the night he'd killed her. He ran his fingers through it but stopped when he touched something hard and crusty. He held the hair to the light.

Blood.

Another reminder that she was gone. Nothing would ever be the same again.

His grip around the hair tightened. He left the closet and went to his bathroom. Running the water in the sink, he blocked the drain and washed the hair with shampoo.

Then he returned to the closet. The hair went back into the box. The box was placed in the hole, the floorboard and carpet put back. No one would know what he'd hidden there.

Just as no one would ever guess what he'd done. If his plan worked, the police would never suspect him. Yes, he'd lost control. He'd snapped. But he'd pulled himself together and cleaned up his mess.

Now it was time to do the same with his life.

Tessa was gone, but he wasn't. As much as he missed her, he was going to have to think about her replacement. The monster inside him had to be fed.

As long as he lived, he'd have needs.

Dark needs.

Needs someone would have to meet.

CHAPTER ELEVEN

Morgan opened her eyes to a throbbing headache. She hadn't slept much since finding Tessa's body, and Nick's arrest the day before had kept her awake long into the night. When she did manage to drift off, her nightmares were filled with images of Tessa and Nick and blood. Eventually, her subconscious got around to substituting her own girls in Tessa's place.

Wasn't that part of what drove her denial? She didn't want to believe she'd let a murderer into her home. That *she'd* introduced Nick to Tessa.

She glanced at the clock on her nightstand. Seven o'clock! She hadn't slept past the crack of dawn in years. She stumbled out into the hall and glanced in the girls' bedroom. Empty. Mia and Ava had school today. Were they ready?

She ducked into the kitchen. Used cereal bowls in the sink reassured her that they'd eaten. She poured a cup of coffee, downed two ibuprofen tablets, and continued her search.

Giggles drew her out onto the deck. In the morning light, the girls chased giant bubbles in the fenced backyard. Gianna waved a huge wand through the air, sending a shimmering bubble drifting across the grass.

All three children were dressed. And, miracle of miracles, Sophie's hair had been brushed and was fastened into two ponytails on either side of her head.

Setting her mug on the outdoor table, Morgan descended the steps barefoot. Her odd mood lifted as her three little girls raced across the lawn to greet her. She hugged Ava and Mia. Little Sophie leaped from the ground. Morgan caught her, and Sophie wrapped her clinging limbs around Morgan.

She felt her daughter's head. Her temperature was normal, but Sophie's sniff and swipe of her hand under her nose verified she'd caught a cold.

"Look." Sophie pointed at her head. "Gianna gave me kitten ears."

What a brilliant way to win Sophie's cooperation.

Sophie squeezed as hard as she could for the count of three, and then dropped to the ground and raced away. Morgan's heart swelled. There were times when her love for her children was almost overwhelming, especially when they smiled and she could see John in each of them.

Gianna walked over, grinning. "I'm counting that as a victory."

"And you should. Thanks for handling the

girls this morning. I can't believe I slept so late," Morgan said.

"You needed the sleep, and we've been having fun." Gianna set another giant bubble loose.

"I don't want them to tire you out."

"I *enjoy* them." Moisture glittered in Gianna's eyes. "I've never been part of a real family before. I love living here. I keep waiting for someone to pinch me and take it all away."

"No one is taking you anywhere." Morgan touched her arm. "We love having you."

Gianna blinked and wiped her eyes.

"Have you seen my grandfather?" Morgan asked.

"He went to the store. Why don't you go get some breakfast and a shower? I'll put Mia and Ava on the bus."

"Thank you. I really appreciate that." With a backward glance at the happy children, Morgan turned toward the house.

After a hot shower, she felt almost human. She dressed, combed her hair, and brushed her teeth. Returning to the kitchen, she refilled her coffee mug. Movement pulled her gaze to the kitchen window. At the end of the driveway, the girls and Gianna waited for the school bus. Mia and Ava wore pink-and-purple backpacks. Gianna held Sophie's hand, obviously having learned the hard way the day before just how fast Sophie's tiny legs could run.

113

Morgan looked across the street. Bud and Nick's house looked dark. How had Nick fared overnight? Had he been booked and transferred to the county jail, or was he still in the holding cell at SFPD?

She was relieved when the front door opened and Sophie burst into the kitchen. There was no better distraction than a three-year-old. Gianna was right behind the child.

"Gianna says I can be a kitten today." Sophie bounced on her toes.

They spent the next few hours digging through the craft supplies and fashioning a crude kitten costume out of black felt and leftovers from last Halloween. The morning passed quietly. Grandpa came home and fell asleep in his recliner. At noon, Sophie ate three bites of her peanut butter sandwich and set it aside.

When the doorbell rang, Morgan jumped. Leaving Gianna and Sophie at the kitchen table, Morgan looked out the window. "It's Bud."

Gianna held her hand out to Sophie. "It's almost nap time. If we go into your room now, I'll have time to read two stories." Gianna plucked a tissue from the box on the table, but Sophie bolted down the hall before Gianna could wipe the child's nose.

"Thank you," Morgan said, then went to the door and opened it. "Come in."

"Are you sure?" Bud stepped into the house.

His face was gray, his eyes bleak. "I don't want to overstep."

She waved him in. "Where did you stay last night?"

"My assistant manager let me sleep on his couch." The police had spent the entire night completing their search of Bud's house.

"Are you allowed back in today?"

Bud nodded. "I haven't been inside yet. I don't even know what they took."

"They'll give you an inventory of all items removed from the property," Morgan said. "Tell me what's happening with Nick."

"He had an arraignment hearing this morning, but it wasn't anything like I expected. Nick didn't say anything. There was a lawyer there he'd never met. I haven't been able to find him a private one yet. I applied for a mortgage over the phone, but the approval is pending. I'm hoping there's enough equity in the house to at least cover a retainer. I don't have much in the way of savings." Bud followed Morgan into the kitchen. "Anyway. They didn't even ask him if he was guilty or anything. The whole thing only took a couple of minutes."

"Nick is charged with a class A felony. The initial arraignment is really just a formality. He'll have a chance to issue a plea later."

"I couldn't even hear most of what they were saying. The judge set his bail at a million dollars. The bail bondsman said I need a hundred thousand in cash to get him out. There's no way I can come up with that kind of money. Even if the mortgage is approved, I'll need every cent of that equity to pay a lawyer. How can they lock him up when he hasn't been convicted of a crime?"

"Nick is charged with a violent and particularly heinous murder." Morgan shuddered, remembering just how heinous. "He will be held in custody pending a formal indictment by the grand jury, which should happen within six days of his arrest, which will be Tuesday."

But even the grand jury was a formality. Morgan knew Bryce. The DA wouldn't have charged Nick if he didn't have enough evidence for a conviction.

"What about after that? How do I get him home?"

"I don't know. His attorney can petition for a bail reduction."

"But you don't sound like that'll happen, which means he'd have to stay in jail until the trial, right?"

"Yes."

"How long will that take?" Bud asked.

"It could be a year before the case is brought to trial."

Bud's face went gray. "And Nick will have to stay in jail that whole time?"

"It's possible." Morgan didn't add that the case could take even longer than that.

As a prosecutor, Morgan had always believed that the vast majority of people arrested were guilty. She'd never felt that she'd put an innocent man in jail. But there had been cases in New York of innocent people who'd spent years in jail waiting for their trials. Though the percentage of innocent people held unjustly was low, when someone you cared about was included in that small minority, the situation was suddenly intolerable.

"I don't know what to do. I'll never come up with enough money to pay for years of legal expenses, and if the lawyer who represented Nick today is any indication of what he'll get from the state . . ." Bud looked lost. "I already got the feeling the attorney thought Nick was guilty."

"Public defenders carry large caseloads, but many are actually very good."

Many, but not all. Large caseloads meant less time, less attention on each case. Nick could very well sit in jail for the next year. There wasn't a special, safe place to hold people awaiting trial. He'd be in with the other inmates. Innocent or guilty, young Nick was going to be locked up with real criminals. His fledgling business would fail. He could be assaulted. He would definitely be traumatized.

Nick's life could be ruined. At a minimum, he'd be changed forever.

Morgan's next words were out of her mouth before she could think. "What if I offered to represent Nick?"

What was she doing? The Dane family put criminals *in* prison. They didn't get them out. Her father would roll over in his grave. And she didn't even want to think about how Bryce would react.

Bud's head lifted. "You would do that? I don't have much money to pay you."

"We'll work something out," Morgan said. What else could she do? Nick had no one else. "There is no guarantee I can make a difference, but I can promise that I will do everything in my power to prove Nick is innocent."

"You think he's innocent?"

Morgan pictured Tessa's body, the gruesome image as clear as the night she'd found her. "I can't believe Nick would do such a thing."

After Bud left, Morgan opened the refrigerator and stared at its contents. She needed lunch, but her appetite had been dimmed by her decision. Her mind whirled as it processed what she'd done.

She'd agreed to defend Nick. Her new job—the very thing that was going to pull her out of her current hole—was history.

Her grandfather shuffled into the kitchen. "So. I eavesdropped."

Morgan closed the fridge. "Are you going to tell me I've just made the worst decision of my life?"

Grandpa dropped into a chair. "Have you thought about this?"

"Honestly, no." She faced him, crossed her arms, and leaned on the counter. "No one else is going to believe he's innocent. No one. Bud doesn't have much money. If he finds another attorney who's willing to take the case *pro bono*, it's going to be for the publicity. Nick's case is media fodder. And no media-pandering lawyer is going to put Nick's needs first. It'll be a show."

The case had all the earmarks of a publicity rampage.

"What about your job with the prosecutor's office? Bryce Walters isn't going to be happy."

Morgan closed her eyes for a second and swallowed. "I guess it wasn't meant to be."

"You're willing to give up your entire future for Nick? You don't even know what evidence they have against him," Grandpa pointed out. "Your whole career is based on putting criminals in jail, not getting them off. Most people arrested and charged with crimes are guilty."

"Do *you* believe he's guilty?" Morgan asked.

Grandpa sighed. "No. But I'm relying on emotion here, not fact. You could be throwing away your whole career."

"I know. But I don't have a choice. What if he's innocent? Do you know what prison will do to a young man like Nick?"

The kid would be part of the most vulnerable set of prisoners. Young, good-looking, and a little naive, he'd be prey among the general population.

"That doesn't mean he's innocent," Grandpa said.

"That's why I'm going to find the truth." Morgan eased into the chair facing her grandfather. "Are you disappointed in me?"

"Why would you ever think that?"

"Because I feel like I'm switching sides. Everyone else in the family devoted their lives to putting criminals away, and here I am trying to get a man off a murder charge."

"No one in our family would want an innocent man put in prison." Her grandfather put one thin, blue-veined hand over hers. "Danes fight for justice. This is no different. Nick deserves the best counsel he can get, and I know that's you. No one will fight harder for him."

"I feel like I've been a slacker for the last two years."

"A slacker? You're kidding, right?" Grandpa sounded irritated. "Your husband died and left you with three children to raise on your own. You took time off to get your kids and yourself through grief no one should have to face at your age. You and John should have had another forty years together."

"But we didn't. Life isn't fair. It's time to accept that and move on." Which sounded easier than it was. "You don't think Dad would be disappointed that I've moved to the other side of the courtroom?"

"He'd be proud of you no matter what you did. You're taking a stand here. You're making a personal sacrifice in the name of justice." Grandpa squeezed her hand. "I'm damned proud of you. Your dad would be too."

A noise from the street caught their attention. Morgan got up and went to the window. A police car sat in the street outside Bud's house. "I'm going to make sure everything is all right."

She went out onto the front porch. A crowd had gathered in the street.

Oh. No.

CHAPTER TWELVE

There was no sneaking up on the Barone family.

Two large German shepherds barked from the end of their chains as Lance stopped his Jeep in front of the house.

Red Noneofyourfuckingbusiness, aka Robby Barone, lived with his parents on a small working farm on the edge of town.

A small satellite dish topped the roof of the two-story basic-blue farmhouse. The lawn was mostly clover but freshly mowed. There were no flower-beds, no wind chimes. No furniture adorned the weathered gray porch. Instead of children's toys or a swing set, two clotheslines and a neatly planted vegetable garden filled the rear yard.

A barn and multiple outbuildings were clustered together at the rear of the property. A dozen chickens occupied a fenced run and large coop. A second pen held two pigs, and three cows grazed in a small pasture enclosed with barbed wire. A stock trailer and an old school bus were parked alongside the barn.

Everything about the place said function over frill. There was an air around the house that felt too stark, even for a farm.

The pungent scent of manure coated Lance's throat as he went up the wooden porch steps. He closed his mouth and rang the doorbell. When he didn't hear a ring inside the house, he knocked on the doorframe.

The breeze shifted, bringing the welcome smell of herbs to Lance's nose. Flower pots filled with plants had been lined up like soldiers under a double window. Curtains moved behind the glass, and he caught a brief glimpse of a human shape. The wooden door cracked, and a woman peered around the edge.

Lance smiled through the screen door. "Good morning. Are you Mrs. Barone?"

She nodded. "What do you want?"

The woman assessed Lance. Robby had gotten his red hair, small stature, and freckles from his mother. Mrs. Barone wore a white apron over a flowered cotton dress of washed-out pale blue. Her hair was bound in a thin, tight ponytail. Below the knee-length hem, her feet were bare. She was probably in her mid-thirties, but hard living and ruddy, dry skin made her look older.

Lance smiled and tried to look nonthreatening, which wasn't an easy task for a man his size. "I'd like to talk to Robby. Are you his mother?"

Robby's car wasn't in the driveway, but one of the outbuildings appeared to be a garage, and the overhead door was down.

"Yes. Is he in trouble?" Her grip on the door-knob tightened.

"No, ma'am. I was just hoping he could help me."

Her brown eyes narrowed in suspicion.

Lance continued. "I'm looking for Jamie Lewis."

He didn't mention the video. If Mrs. Barone didn't know about the party in the woods, then Lance's squealing on Robby wouldn't help gain the kid's cooperation.

"So this isn't about Tessa Palmer?" she asked.

"No, ma'am."

Why would she think it was?

Mrs. Barone squinted, lines clawing at the corners of her eyes as she focused over his shoulder and searched the dirt driveway. "Are you with the police?"

"No, ma'am." Lance slid a business card out of his pocket. "I work for Sharp Investigations. Jamie's parents have hired us to look for her. I'm interviewing all the kids who might know Jamie."

Liar.

He told his conscience to shut up. He wasn't lying. He would interview them all if he could identify them.

Lance looked over Mrs. Barone's shoulder at the interior of the house. Through the open door, he could see into the living room. The furniture leaned toward worn and weary, but in the background a news show played on an LED TV. A new-looking laptop computer sat open on the coffee table. Clearly, the Barones spent money on electronics.

Did Robby or someone else in the family have an alternative source of not-exactly-legal income?

Following his line of sight, Mrs. Barone stepped through the door, closing the heavy wooden door behind her. She stuffed her hands into the front pockets of her apron, her shoulders curling inward. "Robby's not home from school yet."

"Do you know when he'll be home?" Lance knew that school had ended fifteen minutes before, at two o'clock.

"No." She shook her head, but her eyes strayed to the driveway again. "And I don't know how he could help. No one has seen Jamie for a long time."

"Are Jamie and Robby close?" Lance asked.

"No." Her hands slid out of her pockets and gripped each other tight enough to whiten her knuckles. "You better leave before my husband gets home."

Or what?

Was that a threat or was she afraid of her husband?

Lance made a mental note to run a background check on everyone in the Barone household, especially Robby's father. "I know I'm reaching for straws, but you never know which small detail might help. Her parents are getting pretty desperate."

Mrs. Barone's eyes went suddenly moist. "I imagine they are, especially after what happened to Tessa."

"It was a shock to everyone," Lance agreed.

"Tessa was the girl next door, so sweet and shy." Mrs. Barone walked to the edge of the porch, her arms hugging her waist. "I can't wrap my mind around it."

"It was a terrible thing," Lance said. "How well did you know Tessa?"

Mrs. Barone hesitated. "She was the same age as my oldest, Rebecca. I homeschool my girls, but Tessa and Rebecca met at youth group at the church."

"After what happened over the weekend . . ." Lance let the implication hang. "I really want to find Jamie and bring her home safely."

Mrs. Barone nodded. "Poor Tessa. I can't believe she was killed by a neighbor. Just goes to show that you don't really know folks, right?"

So much for innocent until proven guilty.

Lance bit back his comment. He needed Mrs. Barone to encourage her son to cooperate with Lance's investigation. It wasn't his place to educate the woman on the finer points of criminal law.

"Will Robby be back later today?" Lance asked.

"I don't know." She pocketed the business card Lance handed her, then rubbed her arms as if she was cold. "I'm sure he'll do what he can to help you find Jamie."

Lance was equally sure Mrs. Barone's little angel would be happy to help—for another fifty bucks.

"Thank you." Lance pulled a picture from his pocket, a still he'd printed from the video of the boy who'd been fighting with Nick. Lance showed it to Mrs. Barone. "Do you know this kid?"

Mrs. Barone took the picture. "That's Jacob Emerson."

"You're sure."

"I'm sure. Everyone around here knows the Emersons. Mr. Emerson is a lawyer. He tries to keep a tight rein on Jacob, but that boy was born to be a handful."

Good to know.

A whiny engine sound announced the arrival of Robby's ancient Toyota. Robby spotted Lance through the windshield. The car hesitated, as if Robby was considering turning around, but he parked alongside Lance's Jeep. Robby got out of the car and came up the front walk, his posture cocky.

His mother nodded at Lance. "Mr. Kruger was just asking about Jamie Lewis."

127

"OK." Robby nodded, but like his mother, he seemed more concerned with watching the end of the driveway for whoever was due home next.

"I was going to ask you if you knew who this was." Lance flashed the photo of Jacob Emerson. "But your mom already helped me out."

"Then you got what you came for," Robby said. He shared a look with his mother. "You should go. Now."

Lance turned to Mrs. Barone. "Thank you, ma'am."

Back in his Jeep, he sent Sharp a message: need full background checks on everyone else who lives at this address. He typed the Barones' rural route number into his phone.

Something fishy was going on at the Barone house. Robby and his mother were way too paranoid. Their transgressions might be totally innocent, but Lance had learned the hard way not to ignore his instincts. Was Mr. Barone a criminal? Abusive? Both?

He drove away from the Barone house. On the way back to town, without consulting his brain, Lance detoured down Morgan's street. He felt like a twelve-year-old cruising past his secret crush's house on his Schwinn. He turned the corner. His foot shifted to the brake pedal. Three houses away, a small crowd of people stood in the middle of the road. All eyes watched the Zabrowski driveway.

What the hell was going on?

Broken lengths of crime scene tape hung limply across the drive and around the property. Bud stood at the head of his driveway. An elderly couple blocked his path. The old man was bent and bowlegged with age. The woman at his side stood straight, but her frame was paperclip thin. A strong wind swept dead leaves across the lawn. Lance was surprised it hadn't knocked her over.

Morgan was jogging across the road.

Lance opened his door and slid out of his vehicle. Hurrying past the crowd of gawkers, he heard the murmurs of gossip.

"His father should have known."

"I always thought that kid was strange."

"I can't believe we had a killer living here all this time."

Lance wanted to correct all their misconceptions. Nick was innocent until proven guilty, but now wasn't the time. Crowds didn't listen to facts or reason. Crowds acted on emotion, which amplified according to the size of the gathering.

Ignoring them, he followed Morgan.

A woman in a pink track suit cast a suspicious look at Morgan's back as she walked by.

Morgan stepped up beside Bud. Her face softened with empathy. "Mr. and Mrs. Palmer, I'm so sorry for your loss."

Lance threaded his way through the crowd until he was next to Morgan.

The bowlegged old man didn't respond, but his gaze flickered to Morgan for one second before refocusing on Nick's father. "Your son killed my Tessa."

Oh no. Tessa's grandparents were confronting Nick's father.

Bud shook his head. "No."

"Tessa was a good girl, and your boy murdered her." Stepping forward, Mr. Palmer pointed at Bud with a shaking hand. "How could you not know what your boy was up to?"

"I'm sorry about Tessa, but my son didn't do it," Bud said, his voice thick with emotion.

Mr. Palmer's face reddened. "The cops say he did. They don't go around arresting innocent citizens."

Someone in the crowd called out, "They found the knife behind your shed!"

Morgan stepped between Mr. Palmer and Bud. "Mr. Palmer, Tessa was a beautiful young woman. I'll always remember how sweet she was with my own girls. Please accept my condolences."

Mr. Palmer gave her a curt nod.

Morgan continued. "Please go home. Let the police handle the case. No good can come of this."

Bud surged forward, but Morgan held him back.

Mr. Palmer leaned toward Morgan. "Whose side are you on?"

"There are no sides here," Morgan said. "Nick is innocent until proven guilty."

Mr. Palmer's face darkened. "There most certainly are sides."

"The justice system takes time," Morgan said calmly. "You have to have faith in it."

"What about Tessa?" Mr. Palmer's face turned stroke-red. "What about justice for her?"

"I'm so sorry," Morgan said. "Is there someone I can call for you? A family member?"

"There's no one. Tessa was all we had." His anger crumpled. "She's gone, and there's no way you can bring her back."

Deflated, the old man slumped and turned away. The frail blonde woman at his side stepped forward, getting right in Bud's face. She raised a hand and slapped Bud hard. Bud didn't move. Though he'd seemed prepared to hold his ground with the old man, he appeared resigned to taking whatever punishment the elderly woman dished out.

"Your son is a monster." Mrs. Palmer pivoted on an orthopedic shoe, took her husband's arm, and led him away.

Murmuring, the crowd eased away. Someone spit on Bud's lawn.

After the crowd dispersed, Morgan turned to Bud. "Are you all right?"

A red handprint colored his cheek, but Bud didn't so much as acknowledge it with a touch.

"I guess I should have expected some hate. Tessa was a sweet girl, and everyone is appalled about her death. But I thought these people were our neighbors too. I'd hoped they'd stand by Nick."

He'd thought wrong.

"They're scared," Lance said. "They don't want to think this can happen in their own backyards."

The media was fueling their fear and rage with sensational headlines like LOCAL GIRL KILLED BY BOYFRIEND and GIRL NEXT DOOR MURDERED BY LOCAL MAN.

"It's easier to take their hate out on me and Nick than face it." Bud turned toward his house. Someone had spray-painted KILLER in bright red paint on the front of his garage. "I guess I'll go scrub that off."

"I'm sorry, Bud." Morgan touched his arm. "Do you want some help?"

"No." He shook his head. "You're already doing more than anyone could ask. The work will give me something to do."

Bud disappeared inside his house. Morgan and Lance walked across the street.

"What are you doing for Bud?" Lance asked. "You should stay out of this."

"No chance of that now." Morgan's long legs covered the driveway quickly.

"What do you mean?" Lance drew even with her.

She paused. "I'm defending Nick."

What?

Lance reached for her arm and spun her around. "Are you insane?"

She was throwing her career away.

"No. Naive maybe." In her flat-soled shoes, Morgan was barely a head shorter than Lance. But with her chin up and her shoulders back, she seemed taller and more imposing. Her face held a mask of determination he'd never seen before. Her blue eyes went from pretty to piercing. If this was her courtroom face, it was intimidating as hell.

"The town has already tried and convicted Nick. When the neighborhood finds out you're on his side, they're going to turn on you too."

"I don't think so. They know me. They've known my family for fifteen years. They respect my grandfather."

"Morgan, they think Nick murdered the proverbial girl next door. Mr. Palmer summed it up. Everyone will have to choose. You will be part of the opposing side. You will be the enemy."

"So I should turn my back on Nick because I might become unpopular?"

"I didn't say that."

"Then what did you say?" Morgan asked.

Lance faced her. "I'm worried about you."

She nodded. "I can understand that, but what kind of person would I be if I didn't help Nick?"

"Do you really think he's innocent?" Lance asked.

"I do. Evidence isn't everything." Morgan looked over her shoulder at the Zabrowski house. "A group of facts can have more than one logical explanation."

"You once told me you could never be a defense attorney because you couldn't live with yourself if you had to help criminals get away with crime. I understand that you think Nick is innocent. Even if you prove it, what will you do after the trial? Bryce will never hire you after this. You'll be out of a job."

"I know." Morgan sighed. "But I can't let that stop me."

But Lance wasn't sure she understood the rage she'd encounter when her choice to defend Nick became public knowledge. People were going to be very angry—and angry people were dangerous.

"You need to see this." Lance pulled out his phone and played the video of the fight at the lake.

Morgan paled. "Where did you get this?"

"From a kid who was at the lake party last Thursday night, but it's on YouTube." Lance explained about his search for Jamie Lewis. "Your *client* has a temper."

"Shit." Morgan hurried toward the house, calling over her shoulder. "Who is the boy Nick is fighting with?"

134

"His name is Jacob Emerson." Lance rushed to catch up with her. "Where are you going?"

"I need to file an injunction to have that video pulled from YouTube before it's all over social media and the news. Our entire jury pool will be tainted." She opened her front door and went into the house.

Lance thought the chances of an impartial jury pool had sailed halfway to China already. He followed Morgan into the house.

"Morgan, you'd better look at this," Art said from his recliner.

A BREAKING NEWS banner scrolled across the bottom of the screen while the video of the fight between Nick and Jacob Emerson played.

So much for preventing the contamination of the jury pool.

CHAPTER THIRTEEN

Jail, day 1

Naked, Nick shivered as he hustled into the room, a bundle of clothes under one arm.

The door behind him closed with a surreal and metallic clank, muffling the moaning and shouting of the booking area. With almost everything made of block and steel, sounds echoed with a harsh intensity that made him jump constantly for the whole first hour at the county jail.

The small room was built of cinderblock with a locked steel door on each end. There was one small, wire-reinforced window in each door. Every few seconds a guard looked in. The room smelled like bleach and piss. A puddle of urine surrounded the stainless steel toilet in the corner. Nick needed to pee but couldn't figure out how to do that without getting piss all over his feet.

But, on the bright side, this holding area was empty.

For the first time since he'd been brought to the building, Nick could almost draw a full breath. Even though he knew the camera in the ceiling corner was watching, the absence of other inmates was a sweet, albeit brief, relief. Inside his belly, nerves hummed like a swarm of bees.

Soon he'd be entering the general population. Worse yet, he'd been assigned to D-pod, where the most dangerous inmates were held, since he was accused of committing a violent crime. Nick wasn't the only not-yet-convicted killer being held behind bars here.

Innocent until proven guilty was pure fiction.

He'd spent all afternoon going through the intake process. He'd been strip-searched, deloused, and showered. The delousing powder had gotten in his eye, turned it red, and made it tear. The process had been the most humiliating and frightening experience of his entire life. His humanity had been stripped away. He'd say he felt like an animal, but zoo animals were treated with greater respect.

He hurried to the steel bench bolted to the wall, set down the orange uniform he'd been issued, and dressed. He was grateful he'd worn white boxers. All other colors were confiscated. If he'd chosen plaid this morning, he'd be going commando. Somehow he knew the lack of underwear would have made him feel even more vulnerable.

Instead of the jumpsuit he'd expected, the uniform was more like scratchy hospital scrubs. He stepped into the pants and shoved his feet into the rubber sandals he'd been issued. They were like the soccer slides he'd worn in middle school. The shirt was several sizes too big. Cold seeped through the thin fabric.

Sitting on the chilly, hard bench, he concentrated on breathing. Every thought that ran through his head terrified him. He needed to calm down. This was no place to show fear. He pictured a chess match in his head, calculated move after move—order instead of chaos.

The door behind him opened, the metallic clack sending a bolt of fear right into his bowels. A big white man walked in, carrying his own orange uniform. Everything about him was huge, from his head-size fists to his giant, tattooed chest and arms. His beard was thick and blond, as was the hair on his chest. He dressed in a calm, unhurried, and resigned manner that suggested this experience was not new to him. Nick tried not to look scared, but from the amused expression on the newcomer's face, he hadn't succeeded.

"I'm The Man." He pronounced the word like a royal title. Then he sat down on the bench across from Nick and gave him a casual glance. "Your first time?"

Nick didn't know whether to admit it or not. He was so far out of his element, he could have been on Mars or some other hostile planet. All he could think about was trying to make his hands stop shaking. He didn't need anyone to tell him that showing weakness in jail would be like bleeding in shark-infested waters.

"You don't have to answer. I know you're a fish." The Man snickered. "Quiet can be a smart play, but don't let them think you're afraid to talk. Ignore the pod boss and you'll get your ass kicked too. Same goes for not standing up for yourself."

Nick nodded as if he understood, not that he did. He only had one thing figured out. He was so far over his head, there was no way he could reach the surface before he drowned.

The Man stretched his massive legs out in front of him. "This is my third time in here. I'm going to give you some advice. Inside, we stick together. Whites hang with other whites. We're outnumbered, and there ain't no such thing as fucking political correctness in here. It's all about survival. You stick to your own kind."

Nick listened without speaking.

"You keep your head down, and your mouth shut. You don't ask questions. You don't repeat anything anyone tells you. Snitches end up with stitches." The Man turned his arm over. A series of blue tattoos covered the white underside of his forearm. "You see these?"

"Yeah." Nick wasn't sure about the meanings of the twin lightning bolts or the number 88, but it was impossible to misconstrue a swastika.

The Man was a white supremacist.

"A young fish like you needs protection in here

or you'll end up as somebody's boy." He tapped the swastika. "This is how you get it."

Shit.

Nick hadn't thought about gangs. His lack of knowledge of jail life was one more element to his fear. Joining a gang felt like a commitment, a decision that couldn't be changed once it was made.

A serious undertaking that could have permanent consequences.

"Some of the other cons have a thing against rapists. Me? Doesn't bother me one bit."

Nick's spine snapped straight, a wave of coldness sweeping over him. "You know who I am?"

"Everyone will know who you are. Ain't nothing to do in jail but talk. Word spreads fast." The Man shrugged. "Like I was saying, I ain't got nothing against you. Women need to learn their place, and some seem to need harder lessons than others. But some dudes might want to kill you just because of what you done. Then again, some dudes might want to kill you for the sheer entertainment factor. Always remember, once they're convicted, some of these guys ain't never getting out, and they know it. They've got nothing to lose."

The words slipped out of Nick's mouth. "I didn't do it."

"Sure. Everybody in here is innocent. We all

140

got a bum rap." The Man chuckled. "You got one chance to survive." He tapped the swastika.

"What are you in here for?" Nick asked. If the fact that he was being charged with rape and murder didn't faze The Man, he must be up on serious charges too.

"Manslaughter, but it goes without saying that I'm innocent too." He leaned back and crossed his arms. "If I were you, I'd play the bum-rap card for all it's worth. Every man can empathize with being railroaded by the pigs. And if that don't work . . ." The Man pointed to his tattoos. "Because the guards don't give a fuck."

The door opened and two more naked men entered. The black guy was about twenty-five and big and beefy. His entire back was covered in tattoos. The white kid was maybe nineteen, tall but skinny as a toothpick. Nick could count his vertebrae from across the room. The Man snorted as the kid put on pants three sizes too big. He looked scared enough to piss himself.

Nick wondered if he had the same scared-rabbit gleam in his eyes. He'd better not. He was silently grateful that he was too lazy to shave daily—his thick four-day stubble aged him—and for the physical labor that had muscled his body since he'd graduated high school. The skinny kid looked like a walking target.

Like prey.

The Man went silent. Eventually, the other door

opened. The guards barked some orders, and the four inmates were escorted down the hall. They were each handed a thin, folded plastic mattress and a threadbare blanket to carry into the pod.

Nick followed The Man's example and hoisted it up on one shoulder. If nothing else, it provided him with what felt like a partial screen. Only half of the pod residents could see his face. The skinny kid clutched the mattress to his chest like a shield, and as they entered the pod, he went whiter than bleached bones, his eyes shining with terror.

Nick schooled his face into what he hoped was no expression.

He had been expecting a row of locked cells, like the prisons he'd seen on TV. But D-pod in the county jail was one big concrete room. Men walked around the pod freely. Open doorways lined one side of the room. *The cells?* Nick glanced in as he walked by. Each tiny cell contained two metal bunk beds separated by three feet of concrete, clearly designed to hold four men. Inmates stood in the openings, assessing the newcomers. Nick could feel their predatory scrutiny.

The cells must have all been full because more metal bunks lined one wall of the main room. Every one of those already held a bedding kit, and more mattresses were lined up on the floor.

The center of the space held metal tables with attached benches.

Some quick math told Nick that the space was designed to house forty men, but he counted at least sixty inmates. Other inmates in the SFPD holding cell had complained about overcrowding at the county jail, but Nick hadn't considered the ramifications. So did that mean no one was locked in at night?

Instead of the possibility that three cellmates would try to kill him, Nick had to worry about the whole pod? He'd expected order, discipline, even claustrophobia, but locking sixty criminals in a room together with nothing to do was an experiment in pure chaos.

He tried not to flinch at the comments emanating from the doorways as he passed by.

"Look at that tight white ass."

"I'm gonna get me a piece of that."

"*Mm. Mm. Mm.* Fresh meat."

Were they referring to him or the skinny kid? Selfishly, Nick hoped it wasn't him.

Another hairy white guy bumped fists with The Man, and he was welcomed into a sea of beards and scary-looking tattoos, like a Viking warrior's homecoming after a successful pillage.

Someone scurried to move his mattress and blanket, and The Man was given a top bunk. Nick didn't know much about jail protocol, but The Man garnered respect—and fear.

Nick watched the black inmate get absorbed into a group of African Americans. He seemed to know his way around.

The kid was trembling like a scared kitten.

Instinctively, Nick put some space between them. The kid was fodder, and there wasn't anything Nick could do about it. He had no room for guilt. Assessing the danger and his chances of survival was eating up every bit of his attention, and he was hardly in a position to protect anyone else. This group of men had gone all *Lord of the Flies* times a hundred. Being an accused sex offender, Nick already had one strike against him.

He eyed the floor. Unlike the holding cells, the concrete appeared relatively clean. Not knowing what else to do, Nick set his mattress on the floor at the end of a row. No one gave him any shit about it, so he figured he was good.

He sat on it, keeping his back to the wall.

The kid had already been singled out as a weakling. Who knew what would become of that, but at that moment, everyone seemed to be eyeballing Nick. He'd come into this situation with a game plan of keeping his head down and blending in with the cinderblock walls. But obviously that wasn't going to work. He needed a new plan.

For the first time, the full weight of the charges hit him.

Unless there was a serial killer amongst the inmates, there probably wasn't anyone in this pod accused of more serious crimes.

How could this have happened?

He hadn't even had the chance to mourn Tessa. Her image popped into his head, and sadness pressured his sinuses. He shut that down and channeled some healthier anger. Crying would put him in the same category as the skinny kid.

Deep inside Nick's chest, rage and frustration boiled. He was stuck in here while whoever killed Tessa was running free. Who had done it? Jacob? He wouldn't put it past that arrogant prick.

A wolf whistle brought Nick's thoughts back to the present.

At this point, Nick was an accused rapist and murderer. Hopefully the serious and violent nature of those charges would give the other inmates pause. But in reality, if they wanted to beat Nick's ass, rape him, or even kill him, there wasn't much he would be able to do about it.

There were sixty of them, and he wasn't even in a cell that locked.

At that moment, every gaze was directed at Nick. He wanted to run and scream and pound on the D-pod door.

I didn't do it.

I'm innocent.

The Man's comments rang in his mind: *The guards don't give a fuck.*

His gaze strayed to the door, as if it would open and he'd be escorted out while everyone apologized for locking him up by mistake.

But that didn't happen. Shit, he didn't even have a lawyer who gave a fuck. The one they'd given him for the arraignment read the charges against him exactly three seconds before the hearing and hadn't protested when the judge had set bail at *one million dollars*. His dad didn't have that kind of money.

Nick kept his eyes on the group of men, his ears tuned to the conversations around him, and his mouth shut. In his head, he played his imaginary chess game and forced his posture to relax.

He contemplated his options.

Play badass. *Stupid idea.* He was a middle-class white kid from a nice neighborhood. He was about as far away from badass as he could get. The only tattoos he'd ever worn were temporary SpongeBob stickers. With no ideas, he settled on staying put and minding his own business. Sooner or later, the other inmates would come to him, and Nick would have to do the best he could. For now, he'd watch and wait.

But night was coming. Would he make it until morning?

CHAPTER FOURTEEN

Everyone looked guilty in an orange prison uniform.

Friday morning, Morgan sat at the table in a cell-sized interview room at the county jail. The cobalt blue of her suit was the sole spot of color in the gray-on-gray color scheme. She'd tried to see Nick the previous afternoon, but his official transfer from the SFPD and intake into the county jail hadn't yet been completed.

Nothing was more important to the law enforcement system than paperwork.

A guard escorted Nick into the room and removed his handcuffs. Rubbing his wrists, Nick slid into the chair opposite Morgan. His face was expressionless, and a bruise darkened his chin. He stared at the wall as the guard retreated.

"He hasn't said much since we booked him," the guard said.

Good. He'd listened.

"I'll be outside the door." The guard shot Nick a warning look.

"We'll be fine, but thank you." Morgan waited for the guard to withdraw to the other side of the door.

Once the door had closed, Nick's gaze shifted to her face. "Are you really going to be my lawyer?"

"Yes."

"Why?"

"Because I know you."

He leaned back. "They all think I'm guilty." He inclined his head toward the door.

"They don't know you. I do." Morgan leaned over the table and pinned Nick's gaze with her own. "I'm going to ask you one time and one time only. Did you kill Tessa?"

Most defense attorneys Morgan knew never, ever asked their clients if they were guilty. Not only did they not want to know, but an attorney could not allow a client to perjure himself and claim innocence on the stand. Defense attorneys skated around this ethical dilemma with a don't-ask-don't-tell policy.

The justice system wouldn't work without lawyers who were willing to support both sides. Intellectually, Morgan understood that every accused criminal deserved the best possible defense, but she wouldn't be able to live with herself if she helped free criminals who were released and subsequently committed more violent crimes.

Nick didn't flinch or fidget at her question. Nor did he break eye contact. His gaze held hers, steady and sure without any trace of guile. "No."

"Then I believe you."

Nick didn't seem to know what to say. "Thank you."

"Thank me later. I want you to tell me exactly what happened last Thursday night." Morgan poised her pen over her legal pad.

"I met Tessa at a party at the lake."

"What time was this?"

"About nine," Nick said. "Anyway. Right after we got there, the guy she used to date, Jacob Emerson, came over and called her a slut. I told him he should—" Nick paused, looking away, his face flushing.

"I need you to tell me everything, Nick, even if it's not pretty." Morgan leaned her forearms on the table. "I worked for the DA's office for six years. You can't shock me."

But he wouldn't meet her eyes when he said, "I told him he should go fuck himself."

"And then?"

"And he said he didn't need to because he'd already fucked Tessa and so had every other guy in town." Nick took a breath. "Tessa tried to pull me away, but I shoved Jacob. He's such a privileged, entitled asshole."

"Then what happened?" Morgan did not want to put words in Nick's mouth.

Nick shrugged. "The fight didn't last long. A few shoves back and forth. Tessa got between us, and Jacob knocked her down trying to get at me.

That pissed me off. I punched him. He punched me back. Couple of other dudes stepped in, and that was the end of it." Nick shook his head. "I ended up with a bloody nose. You know what happens when I see blood. It wasn't much blood, but I almost puked."

Morgan took detailed notes. "I saw a video of the fight yesterday. It's been played online and on the news. Did you know someone filmed it?"

Nick shook his head.

"I've filed an injunction to have it pulled from the Internet to prevent the tainting of the jury pool, but I'm afraid the damage is already done. I'll also push for a change of venue. Though we're not likely to get it, at least the request will go on record as grounds for a possible appeal if you're convicted."

Nick's face went pale. "You think I'm going to be convicted?"

"I'm going to do my best to keep that from happening, but part of my job is to lay the groundwork for possible future appeals."

"OK." Nick chewed on a cuticle. "Who took the video?"

"I don't know yet, but I will find out." The only two pieces of evidence that Morgan had seen at this point were the list of charges and the video on YouTube. She actually preferred to do her initial interview blind. Once she started reviewing evidence, it would be hard to get

Nick's story down without injecting her own preconceived opinions. "Now that I'm officially your lawyer, I'll get copies of all the evidence the police and prosecutor have gathered against you."

He nodded.

"What happened after the fight?" Morgan asked.

"Me and Tessa got in my car. She cleaned my face up for me." He shifted in his chair. His face flushed. "Then we drove to the other side of the lake and had sex in my car."

"Consensual sex?"

"Yeah." Nick jerked upright, anger surging over his fear and brightening his eyes. "Of course. I know the police said she was raped. I could never have . . ."

Morgan held up a hand to calm him. "All right. You and Tessa had consensual sex in your car. Front seat or back?"

"Back."

"Did you use a condom?"

"No. And I know it was stupid." His jaw went tight with frustration and regret. "I didn't have one."

Morgan set her pen on the notepad. "Nick. I'm not your parent. I'm your lawyer. You have to get used to telling me personal things. If this goes to trial, every detail will come out anyway."

Nick's nod was stiff and barely perceptible.

Morgan picked up her pen. "What time was this?"

"I don't know exactly. Maybe around ten."

"What happened next?" Morgan started a timeline.

"Tessa was crying. She wouldn't tell me why. I assumed it had something to do with the fight and what Jacob said. I drove us back to the clearing. Her car was still there." Nick's eyes clouded. "Then she broke up with me."

"She had sex with you, and then broke up with you afterward?" Morgan clarified.

"Yes. I tried to get her to talk to me, but she wouldn't say why she had to break up with me." Nick's eyes filled with tears. "Finally, I just left. She was in her car. I assumed she'd drive home." He sniffed. "That was the last time I saw her."

"Did other kids witness your argument with Tessa?"

He bit off a piece of his thumbnail. "Yeah. Probably. There were a couple of people still there when we drove to the clearing."

"Did anyone see you leave without her?"

"Maybe."

"I need to know who."

"OK. I think Robby Barone was there, and Felicity, and another friend of Tessa's, Jamie." Nick concentrated, his expression desperate.

"Try to think of others." Morgan wrote down the names. "Where did you go?"

"I drove around for a while. I couldn't believe she broke up with me." Sadness quivered in his voice. "If the cops hadn't shown me pictures, I wouldn't believe she was dead either."

Morgan had a quick flash of Tessa's bloody body. If the case went to trial, she and Nick would both be seeing those images over and over. Would they ever become immune? She hoped not.

No. She couldn't think like that. She was going to prove he was innocent.

"Did you get a burger?" she asked. "Stop at a convenience store? Did anyone see you driving around?"

Nick shook his head. "No. I don't even remember exactly where I went."

"Did you make any calls on your phone?" Morgan asked, hoping the GPS might have recorded Nick's location.

"I tried to text her later, but my battery was dead."

So much for the GPS on his phone.

"What time did you get home?"

"Around midnight."

"Did your dad see you come in?"

"No. He was already asleep. He had to open the shop Friday morning." So Nick had no alibi for the entire night.

"How much of this did you tell the police?"

"Everything. I didn't think I had to hide any-

153

thing, because I'm innocent. When they said I was helping them find Tessa's killer, I believed them." Anger tightened Nick's face.

Most citizens didn't know the police could lie when interviewing suspects. It was perfectly legal, and they did it all the time.

He sniffed and swiped a hand below his eyes. "I still can't believe she's dead."

"I know. Me either." Morgan looked up from her notepad. "Here's what's going to happen next. By Tuesday, there will be a grand jury hearing where the prosecutor presents evidence and the jury decides if there is enough to officially charge you. In reality, this is a formality. We don't even attend, unless you want to testify, and I don't recommend providing any sort of testimony at this stage. The DA will get the indictment."

Nick's face creased with confusion.

"The prosecutor might offer a plea bargain, but I don't anticipate it will be much of a deal." Not with the mayor, police chief, and DA all milking the case for publicity. I also need to inform you that if you are found guilty, you could be facing life in prison."

Nick's mouth opened and closed again without any words coming out.

"I need permission to discuss your case with your dad," Morgan said.

"OK. Sure. Is there any way you can get me out of here?" Nick asked.

The bleakness in his eyes destroyed her. "The judge has set bail at a million dollars. Your dad would have to come up with ten percent of that amount, or one hundred thousand dollars."

His shoulders slumped. "He doesn't have that kind of money."

"I don't want to add financial issues to your worries right now, but a solid defense will be expensive. I'll work your case *pro bono*, but I'll have to pay for expert testimony, additional testing of evidence, and an investigator, among other things. As much as I hate this situation, you're going to have to choose how to spend your limited funds. If you tie it all up with the bail bond, there won't be any left for your defense."

"So I have to stay in jail?" Panic edged Nick's voice.

Morgan put her hand over his. "I wish you didn't."

"You don't know what it's like . . ." Nick glanced around the tiny room, fear shadowing his eyes.

"I don't want you to spend the next twenty-five years of your life behind bars." Morgan squeezed his fingers. "I'm so sorry this is happening to you."

He took a shaky breath, and then sniffed hard and lifted his chin. "I'll be OK. Thanks for everything you're doing."

"In the meantime, you have to be very careful.

Do not speak about your case to anyone in here. Not your cellmates, the guards, no one. Don't even think out loud. Other inmates might try to use information you give them as leverage in their own cases." In her days as an ADA, Morgan had seen prosecutors elicit information from other prisoners. "Do not speak about the case on the phone, even if you're talking to me or your dad. The call could be monitored and recorded. Do not waive any rights. Do not talk to any investigator unless I am with you. The prosecutor does not have to honor promises made by other law enforcement officers."

"None of this seems right."

"No. It doesn't. But I'm going to do my best to get you out as quickly as possible." Morgan summoned the guard and watched as Nick was cuffed and led away.

She shook off her depression, gathered her notes, and left the room. After exiting the jail, Morgan drove to the DA's office.

It was time to talk to Bryce. No doubt he'd already heard she'd agreed to defend Nick, but she owed him the courtesy of a face-to-face meeting. The District Attorney's office was in the municipal complex down the street from the county jail. Morgan parked in the visitors' lot and got out of her van. Her pumps clicked on the pavement as she strode toward the entrance.

"Ms. Dane?"

Morgan paused and pivoted. She recognized the man jogging toward her. A reporter with a local cable channel. A dozen strides behind him, a cameraman followed. She put on her sincere face. Nick needed someone to be his spokesperson.

The reporter stopped, straightened the lapels of his suit, and waited for the cameraman to catch up. Once the lens was up and the green light illuminated, the reporter began. "Is it true that you will be representing the man accused of raping and murdering Tessa Palmer?"

"I am defending Nick Zabrowski." Words mattered, and Morgan chose hers carefully. She would always use Nick's name or refer to him as her client. The press and the prosecutor would call Nick the defendant or the accused to cast guilt on him every time they spoke. Morgan would strive to make Nick appear as a victim of a skewed justice system, a human being caught in circumstances beyond his control. It was Morgan's job to make the public see that what was happening to Nick could happen to any one of them.

"You used to be a prosecutor. How does it feel to be trying to free a suspect rather than put one away?" He thrust the microphone back.

The press had already done Nick a huge disservice with their sensational, clickbait head-lines. Unfortunately, the first station to report news won, and success had nothing to do with accuracy. But Morgan couldn't afford to ruffle any media feathers.

"I have no comment at this time other than to say that my client is innocent, and we're anxious to get busy proving it." She lifted her chin and shot the camera a sincere and confident look.

"What about Tessa Palmer?"

Morgan softened her expression. When her eyes filled, she didn't bother to hide it. "What happened to Tessa was terrible and tragic. She was a kind and intelligent young woman with a bright future ahead of her. No one should ever have to suffer as she did." Morgan wouldn't shy away from condemning the crime or sympathizing with the victim. "But the horrific nature of the crime doesn't warrant rushing into an assumption of guilt or making a premature arrest."

She turned from the reporter to the camera. "I will prove that Nick is innocent, but I also want to see Tessa's real killer caught. My client didn't commit this terrible crime. Therefore, someone else did." Morgan paused, giving the camera a dead-certain gaze. "And so long as Nick is unjustly held behind bars, the real murderer is still out there."

She left the press with that final sound bite and went inside.

Five minutes later, she faced the DA across his desk. "I felt I owed you the withdrawal of my application in person."

"Thank you for that." Bryce gestured to one of the chairs facing his wide desk. "I can't say I'm not disappointed."

"I'm sorry you feel that way." Morgan eased onto the edge of her seat.

But under Bryce's quiet facade, anger simmered. The DA wasn't taking her decision well. "I can't believe you'd throw away a great job for a hopeless case. Nick Zabrowski is guilty as sin."

Morgan didn't comment. What was the point? She hadn't even reviewed the evidence yet. Bryce wasn't going to offer much of a plea, not on a murder case this juicy. Tessa was the girl next door. She was brutalized and killed right in her own community. Tessa represented innocence spoiled. Her murder pulled at the emotions of every parent, brother, sister, and neighbor. What did people fear more than a vicious attacker raping and killing their daughters?

Nothing.

Bryce rested his forearms on the desk. The French cuffs of his white shirt poked out of his jacket sleeves. His cufflinks were sterling-and-onyx discs, classic and understated. "Let's talk about your client pleading guilty and saving the tax payers time and money."

"Talk away," Morgan said. "As I haven't received or reviewed all the evidence at this time, the discussion will have to be one-sided."

"Before she was stabbed nine times, Tessa Palmer was sexually assaulted. DNA from the semen matches your client's. Blood scraped from under the victim's thumbnail also matches your client's DNA. This is all noted on the affidavit, in case you were thinking about challenging the probable cause for the search warrant."

How had Bryce gotten DNA results that quickly?

Bryce continued. "We have a witness who saw your client arguing with the victim shortly before she was killed and a video tape of him fighting with the victim's ex an hour before that. On the video, your client is clearly the aggressor in the altercation."

Morgan didn't panic even though the evidence seemed overwhelming. The prosecutor would spin every fact into proof of Nick's guilt. It was Morgan's job to find an alternative explanation and uncover other evidence or testimony that would cast doubt on the DA's theory.

Bryce leaned back, interlacing his fingers and resting them on his blotter, confidence oozing from every pore. The man was very good. "Did you know that Tessa was pregnant?"

Shit.

Only her experience as a trial lawyer kept the shock from Morgan's expression, but she was sure he'd seen it in her eyes.

"You'll see this in the autopsy report, but in case you were wondering, your client was not the father." Bryce watched her face.

How many favors had Bryce called in to get those DNA results expedited? And why hadn't he served the Zabrowskis with a search warrant before receiving the test results? Most judges would have signed a warrant based on witness statements that Nick had argued with Tessa shortly before her death. Probable cause was often balanced with the need to collect evidence before the suspect disposed of it. But Bryce had dotted every *I* and crossed every *T*.

Morgan simply nodded while her mind worked. When she'd worked on Bryce's side of the court, she'd been threatened and harassed by criminals. She'd learned to keep her game face through just about anything.

"Still no comment?" Bryce lifted his brows.

"Not at this time."

"Here's the way I see it. Your client found out that Tessa cheated on him. She was pregnant by another guy. She broke up with him. Your client was jealous. Enraged. So he raped and stabbed her."

"That's a pretty big stretch."

Bryce's body tipped forward. "Here's the only offer your client is going to get. If he pleads guilty to first degree murder and rape, I'll recommend a twenty-five-year sentence instead of life without parole."

In the state of New York, the death penalty wasn't an option.

"I will be sure to pass your offer along to my client after I review all of the evidence."

"You do that." Bryce straightened. The only sign of his irritation was a tightly clenched fist on the desktop. "Once the grand jury convenes, the offer is off the table."

"Thank you." Morgan stood, reached across the desk, and offered Bryce her hand.

"I will give you this, counselor." Bryce took it in a brief squeeze. "You are a class act. It's a shame you've just destroyed your career."

Morgan left Bryce's office with a weighted heart. Even if Bryce was stretching with his theory, the evidence against Nick was convincing. Juries loved DNA. She hurried down the hall and into the elevator. Some of the evidentiary documents were being sent via secure email and should start hitting her inbox in a few hours. She was anxious to get started. She had some decisions to make, like how she would hire an investigator without a retainer.

She had one option: Lance.

She drove home distracted, her mind on the case, and pulled into her driveway as if on autopilot. No one was home. She checked her watch. Not even lunchtime yet. On Friday mornings, the house was typically empty. Gianna had dialysis, Sophie was in preschool, and Grandpa played chauffeur.

Grabbing her purse, Morgan climbed out of the van and went up the front walk. Her phone buzzed with an email, and she dug it out of the pocket of her bag. She was opening her email app as she approached the house.

She was nearly to the door before she saw it. Her phone slipped from her fingers and hit the brick path.

It couldn't be.

Her brain refused to believe what she was seeing. She squeezed her eyes shut for a second then opened them again. But it was still there.

Just below the monogrammed pewter knocker, a bloody heart was pinned to the door with a knife.

CHAPTER FIFTEEN

"A knife through the heart?" Anger surged through Lance as he viewed the photo Morgan handed him.

"The symbolism is clear." Morgan rubbed her biceps and perched on the second folding chair he'd brought into his makeshift office.

By agreeing to defend Nick, in the neighbors' eyes, Morgan had turned on them.

"It's a cow heart. I reported it to the police." Morgan shivered and crossed her long legs. "They took pictures and filed a report. I doubt anything will come of it. No one in the community except Bud is on Nick's side." She pressed a hand to her forehead. "Where can you get a cow heart? I called the local grocery stores and butcher shops. No luck."

"Have you called the ethnic markets? There's an Asian supermarket out near the interstate. Sharp goes there to buy sweet potato greens. I know they carry more than the usual cuts of meat. I've seen whole chickens and pig heads." Lance handed the picture back to her. "What about your grandfather's surveillance camera?"

"It's not working." She slid it into her briefcase.

"The alarm company came the other day but they couldn't repair it. They're replacing it on Monday."

As disturbing as it was, he sensed she hadn't come to discuss the cow heart someone had nailed to her front door. So why was she here?

Footsteps sounded in the hall.

"Lance?" Sharp called.

"In here," Lance answered.

Sharp appeared in the doorway, and Lance introduced them.

"I'm glad you're here," Morgan said. "I really need to speak with you both."

"In that case, let's go into my office. I have actual chairs." Sharp stepped back and gestured across the hall. "Can I offer you a cup of tea?"

"Yes. Thank you," she said.

Sharp ushered Morgan into his office. "I'll be right back." He went into the kitchen.

Lance settled in the chair next to Morgan. Back in the kitchen, water rushed and an igniter on the stove clicked.

Morgan turned to Lance. "I don't want to spring anything on you. If you'd rather we talk in private . . ."

Lance stopped her. "It's fine. You can say anything in front of Sharp." He paused, briefly considering that he wanted to share the intimate details of his past with her and what that implied. "Did I ever tell you about my father?"

"I know he wasn't in your life, but you've never elaborated. You didn't seem to want to talk about him." Morgan's head tilted. "I assumed he'd walked out."

That's what everyone had assumed. "When I was ten, my dad vanished."

Morgan straightened. "Vanished?"

"He literally went out for bread and milk one night and never came home."

"That's horrible." Morgan placed a hand to her throat.

Lance turned away from Morgan and her pity. Outside the office window, the wind stirred a pile of dead leaves on the front lawn. They swirled into the air, then tumbled across the grass, at the mercy of the wind. Much like a ten-year-old Lance had helplessly watched his life cartwheel out of control. As much as he tried to leave his youth behind, he couldn't help but wonder if his father was dead or alive. Had he met with foul play or had he truly walked away from his family?

"Did the police ever find him?" she asked.

"No." Lance swallowed. Composed, he pivoted to face her. "Sharp was the detective on the case. He worked it for about a year until the department made him put it aside, unofficially of course. Officially, cops work each case until it's resolved. But in reality, limited resources have to be channeled to current crimes."

"That must have been terrible to live through."

"It was," Lance said. "But after the case went cold, Sharp kept an eye on me and my mom over the years."

More than an eye. If it hadn't been for Sharp, Lance wondered if he'd have gone to college or become a cop or grown into a sane, productive member of society.

"My point is, there isn't much Sharp doesn't know about me. He's more than a business associate. It's fine to talk in front of him."

"I'm glad you told me." Her eyes warmed.

Why *had* he told her? Not many people besides Sharp knew about the horror that his teenage years had become. The truth had been too painful to talk about. As a kid, it had been easier to let everyone think his parents were divorced and his mom was never around because she worked overtime to pay the bills. Circumstances had limited his social life, and he certainly hadn't shared her mental breakdown with his very few friends.

He couldn't help but wonder what Morgan would think of his mom. He certainly didn't tell any of the women he dated casually that his father had disappeared. And *By the way, my mother has a serious mental illness* wasn't the best lead-in for future dates. Lance had had several quasi-serious relationships. None had survived the meeting-the-parents stage. It was just too much to expect anyone else to deal with his mother's issues. Morgan already carried more than her share of responsibility. How could he possibly ask her to shoulder any more?

And this was why they could only be friends, no matter how much Lance would like more. Cups rattled in the kitchen. A few minutes later, Sharp carried a tray to his desk. He handed a cup to Morgan.

She took it in both hands, cradling it as if to warm her fingers. "As you might know, I've agreed to defend Nick Zabrowski."

Sharp nodded. "I saw you on the news."

"I won't lie. Defending Nick won't be easy. The DA has already convinced the public that Nick is guilty, and from what I've seen of the evidence, the case is daunting."

Lance leaned forward. "Someone pinned a cow's heart to Morgan's front door with a knife today."

"Classy." Sharp exhaled, concern and respect filling his eyes. "But that won't stop you."

"No." Morgan's eyes lifted, and her blue eyes blazed with conviction. "Nick has lived across the street from my grandfather for years. He mows our lawn. He plays chess with Grandpa. My girls love him. I just can't believe Nick could harbor the level of rage necessary . . ." Letting the thought trail off, she set her tea aside. "Our neighborhood is closely knit. I also knew Tessa.

168

She babysat for my girls. As much as I want to prove Nick didn't kill her, I also want to find the person who did."

"That's a tall order."

"It is. I won't be able to do it alone. I'm going to need an investigator."

Lance coughed. She wanted to hire Sharp Investigations? Why hadn't that occurred to him? Why else would she be here? Clearly, she hadn't come just to talk to him, and didn't that fact give him an ache right under his heart?

He tried to put it aside. He had no right to feel hurt. Morgan wasn't ready for a relationship, and as long as he had his mom to handle, neither was he.

But damn.

He couldn't entirely suppress his feelings. If he and Sharp didn't agree to help her, she'd go to someone else. Jealousy poked him in the gut. He didn't want anyone else working closely with her. But taking the case would put him at odds with Chief Horner. Lance's chance of getting that upcoming detective slot would evaporate faster than steam from an overheated radiator.

All he'd ever wanted since his dad disappeared was to be a detective. Could he give that up?

"Does your client have money?" Sharp asked bluntly.

Morgan sighed. "I'll be honest. Bud is scrambling for cash. He's remortgaging his house."

169

Sharp said, "You're working *pro bono*?"

Morgan nodded. She was sacrificing her entire career for her neighbor, and she wasn't even getting paid. "Whatever money he can amass will be for the investigation and defense. Bud's a good man. He'll pay you eventually."

"You really believe this kid is innocent?" Sharp asked.

"I do." There was no doubt in her tone.

Lance rested his elbows on his knees. "What if you find out he isn't?"

"He is." Morgan's eyes went flat with determination. "Besides the fact that I know he's not capable of murder, Nick vomits at the sight of blood. I've personally witnessed this happen. It's an immediate, visceral reaction."

"So you think he's being railroaded," Lance said.

"Horner's an ass," Sharp chimed in. "But I can't see him deliberately persecuting an innocent man."

"He expedited three DNA tests in six days," Morgan added. "That took work. I'm sure he used up quite a few favors. He *wants* Nick to be guilty."

Sharp nodded. "Bryce Walters needs the public image boost after that cluster with the Jones case a few months ago."

"I feel so out of touch. What happened?" Morgan rubbed her forehead.

170

"The police chief and DA pushed a search warrant through only to have it be declared invalid at trial for lack of probable cause. With the evidence suppressed, an armed robber walked. Three weeks later, Jones killed a liquor store clerk in Whitehall. After the press broadcast the connection, both the mayor and the DA saw their public approval ratings take a swan dive."

"That also explains why they were extra cautious with the search warrant." Morgan lowered her hand, her brows furrowed in thought. "But if they want this case solved quickly, they might have made mistakes."

"Yes," Sharp agreed. "I'd not only look under every rock, I'd blow them up and examine the pieces."

Sharp's gaze landed on Lance like a Taser barb, then returned to Morgan. "We'll need to discuss the offer. Can we have a few minutes?"

"Of course," she said.

Lance followed Sharp across the hall into the storage room.

Sharp closed the door. "It's up to you. If we work her investigation, Horner is going to be pissed. As long as he's the SFPD chief, you'll never wear a badge again in this town."

"I know." Lance scrubbed his hands over his face. Moving away from Scarlet Falls wasn't an option. He couldn't leave his mom.

"Do you know this kid?"

"A little. On the surface, I would never have suspected him capable of murder, but we both know people can be very good at hiding their sins." Lance put aside the complications Morgan's offer entailed and focused on what he knew about the case.

Sharp scratched his chin. "Irrespective of his guilt or innocence, are you prepared to give up a future with the police force to work for her?"

"Yes. I want to take this case," Lance said.

"For you, for Nick, or for Morgan?"

"All of the above. I'd pretend to be all noble, but that would be bullshit."

Sharp got up and went to a filing cabinet. "In that case, I have something for you that might make you feel better about your decision. I was waiting for the right moment to give it to you." He unlocked and opened the bottom drawer, pawed through a tight row of files, and yanked a thick accordion file free. He handed it over. "Here."

"What's this?" Lance turned it sideways. His blood chilled as he read the label: VICTOR KRUGER.

His father.

The file was two inches thick and felt heavier than mere paper should. The weight of its implications no doubt.

"My personal file on your father's case." Sharp closed and locked the drawer.

"Police detectives aren't supposed to keep personal files."

"This is true, but we all do. Or at least we did back then." Sharp sighed. "I'm sure plenty has changed since I left the force."

Lance tested the file's weight. "So you clearly worked on his case even after it was officially declared cold."

"I kept plugging away at it in my personal time." It was just like Sharp to do so without saying a word.

"You never told me."

"When you were a teenager, you needed normal and you wouldn't have gotten that if you didn't let go."

As evidenced by what had happened to Lance's mother.

Lance didn't open the file. "I've been in this office nearly every day for two months. Why didn't you give me this before?"

"I wasn't sure you'd want it, and I didn't want you to get consumed by something that happened more than two decades ago. I'm also sensitive to the impact reopening the case might have on your mom. But if you're going to join the firm permanently, I feel like I shouldn't keep this from you any longer. You should be able to make this decision for yourself."

Lance touched his dad's name. Did he want this? Once he opened the file, he'd be pulled in.

The case had the potential to be his black hole. He also had to consider his mom. Dredging up the past could have serious repercussions on her life, which was already a constant and precarious balancing act.

Sharp continued. "I know that your dad's case and my influence over the years is part of what drives you. But you don't have to be on the force to be a detective. I got pulled from your dad's case because the case went cold and the budget was tight. We were shorthanded. Officially, I had to move on to solving active crimes. In the private sector, I decide when to stop working a case. Now it's up to you."

"Thank you. I think." Lance tapped the file on his leg. He was afraid to open it.

"So you're sure you want to take Nick's case? This is an important decision. Do you need time to think about it?"

As much as it pained Lance to let go of his dream, in his heart he didn't really have an option. He'd never be able to turn his back on Morgan. His fingers curled around the edge of the file. "I'm in."

"You really do have it bad for her."

"We're just friends."

"Sure you are."

"On the bright side," Lance said. "I can't stand Horner, and not only will I never have to work for him, but taking this case will be like giving him a metaphorical middle finger."

"That's the spirit. He is a dick. I don't know why you'd ever want to go back to working for him. He was one of the reasons I took retirement as soon as it became an option." Sharp slapped Lance's shoulder. "Order some damned furniture and expense it to the office. I'm tired of watching your giant self hunch over that ridiculous card table."

Oddly, Lance felt lighter, as if letting go of his police career had somehow freed him. The tightness in his thigh didn't feel so dire.

"I wouldn't be so sure of that just-friends thing," Sharp said. "She doesn't look at you like a friend. How long ago was she widowed?"

"About two years. But we both know it doesn't matter."

"Just because you've been burned by a few selfish women doesn't mean you'll never find one who can handle your baggage."

"Morgan has enough baggage of her own. Together, we'd be a disaster." The weight of their collective burdens would drag them under. "I'll let her know we're in. What about the golden rule? Nick's father won't have a retainer yet."

"I will make an exception because she is your close, personal friend." Sharp jabbed a finger in the air. "But do not tell anyone I took a case with no money up front. My reputation will be ruined."

"Can't have that." Lance opened the door.

"I can always take the expenses out of your pay," Sharp said, probably only half-kidding.

Lance paused in the doorway. "You can pretend to be a hard-ass all you want, but now I know you're a softie."

Sharp chuckled, then grew serious. "If she needs an office, tell her she can use this room. We'll clear it out for her. I have an excellent security system for this building. Her files will be safer here than at her house. I also doubt she'll want to bring autopsy photos into her home where her children might see them."

"Good point," Lance said. "I'm going to stay close to her, Sharp. People are going to be angry. Today's stunt was only the beginning. By taking this case, Morgan has made herself the public face for a whole can of hate."

"Agreed." Sharp's gaze narrowed. "If she's right and this kid is innocent, that means there's a real killer out there, and I doubt he'll be happy with Morgan prying into the murder."

Lance went back to Sharp's desk. Morgan was scrolling on her phone.

"We're in," he said.

She exhaled and closed her eyes for a long second. When she opened them, they were full of gratitude. "Thank you."

"Do you have a game plan?" he asked.

"I'm waiting for evidentiary documents from

the DA's office. I just met with Bryce an hour ago, so that's going to take a while. But I talked to Nick this morning." Morgan pulled out her notes and gave them the highlights of her interview.

When she listed the kids who were still at the lake when Nick left, Sharp interrupted. "Did you say a girl named Jamie was one of the kids Nick left behind at the lake?"

Morgan nodded. "Yes. Nick said she was a friend of Tessa's. He didn't know her last name."

"We can help you with that," Sharp said. "Her name is Jamie Lewis. One of your key witnesses is our missing teen. You and Lance should go talk to her parents."

Lance pulled his keys from his pocket. Now that he'd made his decision, his interest in the case was piqued. Plus, working with Morgan was going to be . . .

Interesting. She stood and collected her giant purse. "Maybe there's a connection. Jamie and Tessa were friends. One is hiding. The other is dead."

CHAPTER SIXTEEN

Morgan couldn't imagine having one of her girls missing for two months. Just the thought of it made her queasy.

In the tiny living room of a two-bedroom apartment, Vanessa Lewis sat on a plaid love seat and stared at the picture of her daughter. She wore no makeup, and her straight brown hair was cut in a short wash-and-wear cap. "I can't believe this was taken last Thursday night. Why would she still be in Scarlet Falls and refuse to come home?" She blinked a tear from her eye.

"We'll find her." Sitting next to her, Vanessa's fiancé, Kevin Murdoch, reached for a tissue box on the end table and handed it to her.

Morgan and Lance sat in two wingback chairs on the other side of the glass coffee table.

"Did something unusual happen before Jamie ran away?" Morgan asked.

Vanessa nodded. Her eyes and nose had reddened. "Kevin asked me to marry him. I was so happy. But when I told Jamie he'd be moving in with us, she exploded. She's always been difficult. Moody. Explosive. Oppositional. She has ADD. When she was younger, she took medication, but she didn't like the way it made her feel. Once she got too old for me to force her, that was the end of that. I always wondered why she was so difficult to handle, but when she hit puberty, she got much worse. I took her to a new psychiatrist who said she was also bipolar. While the diagnosis was hard to take, it explained her terrible mood swings and anger issues."

Kevin reached for her hand. "This isn't your fault. You couldn't predict that Jamie would react the way she did."

"I'm a night manager at the diner," Vanessa said. "At least five nights a week, I don't get home until two in the morning." She sniffed. "I thought this was going to be a good thing. Kevin is an accountant. He works from home. I know Jamie was sneaking out to parties while I was at work. I'd hoped having an adult in the house in the evenings would be the end to the drinking and pot smoking." She looked at her fiancé. "Kevin warned me that Jamie might not see the end to her freedom as a positive outcome."

"We won't stop searching until we find her." Kevin lifted their joined hands and kissed her knuckle.

At fifty, Kevin was an average-looking middle-aged guy with a receding hairline and a small paunch, but Vanessa looked at him as if he were Brad Pitt.

"I don't know what I would have done without

Kevin. He's been my rock." She gave him a weak smile. "I keep telling him he should move in. He's here all the time anyway, but he won't do it."

Kevin shook his head. "No. Not while Jamie's gone. It wouldn't be right. She'd feel like you moved on without her in just two months. We'll wait until she's home and settled."

Lance leaned forward. "How long have you been dating?"

Vanessa smiled. "Two years."

"How do you and Jamie get along, Kevin?" Morgan asked.

Kevin's gaze met hers for a split second, then flickered to the left. He scratched his nose. "Fine."

Pausing before answering a simple question, the inability to maintain eye contact, and touching one's face were all classic examples of a liar's body language. So, what was Kevin lying about?

Morgan circled around the topic of his relationship with Jamie. "Do you have any children of your own?"

He shook his head. "No."

Lance picked up on Morgan's line of questioning. "Teenagers can be difficult. Do you have any experience with kids?"

"Um. No." Sweat broke out on Kevin's forehead. He dropped his chin and shook his head.

"I do the best I can with Jamie, but I admit sometimes I don't feel up to the task."

Vanessa jumped in. "Jamie and Kevin get along as well as could be expected. They don't fight. Kevin is extraordinarily patient with her—more patient than I am sometimes. Most teenagers are difficult, but Jamie takes that to a whole new level. Anyway, she seemed fine with our relationship right up until I told her we were getting married."

"How does Jamie get along with her father?" Lance asked.

"They talk on the phone once in a while." Vanessa frowned. "He just goes through the motions. Jamie knows he isn't interested. He has a new wife and a baby on the way."

"That must be hard on her," Morgan said.

"She should be used to it." Bitterness echoed in Vanessa's voice. "He walked out on us when she was eight. He couldn't handle her. He wanted two kids, a white picket fence, and a dog. We were hardly living the American Dream. We were broke most of the time. We were paying out of pocket for a lot of Jamie's therapy. And money aside, he just couldn't deal with the volatility."

"Has Jamie run away before?" Lance asked gently.

Nodding, Vanessa blotted her eyes with a tissue. "Yes, but she was always easy to find, which made me think she didn't really want to run away. Usually it would happen after we'd had a fight about her treatment. Getting her to therapy was a nightmare every single week. Last time she ran away, the police found her in a friend's shed. The parents had no idea Jamie had been sleeping in their backyard for two days. Her friend brought her food and clothes and let her into the house when the parents were at work."

"Does Jamie have hobbies?" Morgan asked. "Does she like music, shopping, sports . . .?"

"She listens to music, but she doesn't play an instrument or anything." Vanessa focused on her crumpled tissue. Her breath caught in her throat.

"She likes comics and she draws," Kevin finished for her.

Morgan had kept one eye on Kevin throughout the interview. As long as she wasn't asking him direct questions, his nerves seemed to settle. She turned to him. "What kind of drawings?"

More sweat popped out on his head. "They look like dark comic books."

Lance's gaze swept from Kevin to Vanessa. "What does she do after school?"

"She locks herself in her room." Vanessa sighed. "I do my best, but I'm lost as to how to get through to her."

"Did she have a cell phone?" Every teen Morgan knew had a phone.

"No." Vanessa shook her head. "I had to take it away. She was using it to access chat rooms and engage with strangers. Here at home, I have software that limits her online activity to approved educational websites."

Lance and Morgan fished for more information, then looked around Jamie's bedroom. The walls were covered with classic rock posters.

"She has good taste in music." Lance nodded toward a Rolling Stones poster. He opened the closet. "All jeans and sweatshirts."

"No nail polish or makeup either. Jamie isn't a girly girl." Morgan sat at the cluttered desk. The drawers were full of the usual junk: pens, pencils, paperclips. Notebooks. Morgan opened one. "She does draw her own comics."

Lance looked over her shoulder. "She's pretty good. Sharp took her photo to the local comic book and art supply stores but didn't have any luck."

"Look at these." Morgan leaned over to see the photos stuck in the frame of the mirror over the dresser.

"These look like some of the kids from the video." He took one down. "There's Tessa."

It was a selfie of Tessa and Jamie printed on computer paper.

"It was taken right here." Morgan pointed. "There's the Rolling Stones poster."

They took the photo to the living room and showed it to Vanessa and Kevin. "Do you know this girl?"

They both nodded.

"That's Tessa." Vanessa started to cry again. "She tutored Jamie in math last year. The school arranged the match. It didn't help her grades all that much, but the friendship was good for her. Jamie really liked Tessa. I can't believe what happened to her." She sobbed.

Kevin wrapped an arm around her shoulders and pulled her close.

"When was she here last?" Lance asked.

Vanessa hiccupped and spoke between hitched breaths. "Not since before final exams last June."

They said good-bye and showed themselves out, leaving Vanessa crying on Kevin's shoulder.

Lance pulled out the keys as they walked across the parking lot. "What do you think?"

Morgan glanced over her shoulder at the depressing brick building. "I think Vanessa Lewis is in a really tough spot."

"Mental illness can destroy your life," Lance agreed, his voice rough.

"Did Sharp do background checks on all the parents?" Morgan asked.

"Yes. I don't like that Jamie left as soon as she found out her mother was marrying Kevin, but Sharp hasn't found any red flags in either Kevin's or Vanessa's backgrounds. The father in California is clean too."

"Maybe Vanessa is right and Jamie was angry that she'd have less freedom if Kevin moved in.

If Jamie is oppositional, her motivation could have been as simple as not wanting her life to change or not wanting to share her space. It's a small apartment."

"You're right, but I still don't like the timing." Lance steered her around a patch of broken glass. "And we've established a concrete connection between Tessa and Jamie."

"Could be a coincidence," Morgan said. "Scarlet Falls High isn't that big."

"True. But it's worth more investigation."

"You know who else needs more investigation?" Morgan stopped at the Jeep. "Kevin."

"You noticed all the sweating too?" Lance pulled his key fob from his pocket and unlocked the doors.

"Yes. And I would swear he was lying about something." Morgan walked toward the passenger door. "Though excessive sweating isn't evidence."

"I think you're right." Lance looked at her over the hood of the Jeep. "Kevin has something to hide."

CHAPTER SEVENTEEN

The picture of Tessa stared back at him from his computer screen. Her dark hair was pulled away from her pretty face. It seemed like she was smiling for him.

At him.

He couldn't use the Internet without seeing her. She was everywhere. And in none of the photos on the news was she covered in blood. So much blood.

I miss you.

He looked at his hands. Clean. He closed his eyes. How was he going to get over her?

He sucked in a deep breath.

On the screen, a reporter talked to Morgan Dane. He turned up the volume. In a taped sound bite from the day before, she claimed to know that the wrong person had been arrested for the murder of Tessa Palmer.

Impossible.

Only two people had been in the woods that night, and one of them was dead. She couldn't possibly know the truth.

But doubt lingered under his certainty. He'd lived in constant fear that someone would discover his game and call him out. But people saw what they wanted to see—and no one wanted to believe a killer could actually be living next door.

He wiped his hands on his thighs. Had he made a mistake? He replayed his actions that night but found no mistakes. The cops had been satisfied. Nick Zabrowski had been arrested. The whole town thought Nick was guilty.

Nick Zabrowski was going to be convicted of murder.

Because the alternative was unacceptable. If Morgan Dane proved Nick's innocence, then the police would resume their investigation. If they dug deep enough, who knew what they'd find? No matter how careful he'd been, there was always risk. He wouldn't be able to sleep at night until the trial was over and Nick Zabrowski was sent to prison.

He clicked "Play" and watched her give her short speech one more time. The fire in her eyes made him hit pause. She was determined. She actually believed Nick was innocent.

Apprehension prickled along his skin like static electricity. Morgan Dane was going to be a problem. He could feel it.

Above all, he couldn't allow her to find out the truth.

Opening a new window in his browser, he began a random search. He needed to learn everything he could about Morgan Dane. Her address. Her family. Her friends. Anyone she was close to could be used against her.

He would use information as ammunition. He would find her weaknesses. If you drilled enough holes in any foundation, it would crumble.

Morgan Dane was a threat, and she needed to be stopped.

CHAPTER EIGHTEEN

The next morning Morgan stepped into the storage room at Sharp Investigations. Lance and Sharp were in the process of clearing the room out for her use. The closet door was open and stacked with boxes. The long table in the center of the room still held a few cartons.

"How is Sophie's cold?" Lance shifted a box. He wore what she'd come to consider his private investigator uniform: cargo pants, a snug tee, and a short-sleeved shirt worn unbuttoned, likely added to conceal the weapon behind his right hip.

"Much better." Morgan set a takeout tray loaded with three coffees and a Dunkin' Donuts box on the table. "But I suspect Ava has caught it. No doubt Mia will be next."

"You brought donuts?" Lance grinned.

"Also a couple of croissants and muffins. I didn't know what you and Sharp liked." Morgan took the lid off her coffee and inhaled. She loved summer, and this morning's autumn chill had cut right through her. In her opinion, pumpkin coffee and her suede boots were the only good things about the approach of cold weather.

Sharp walked in. "You know Saturdays, and every other day, are casual here."

"When I'm on the job, it's important for me to look the part." Morgan thought her appearance had become even more important while she was working Nick's case. Without the weight of the prosecutor's office behind her—and considering public opinion was not on her side—she would have more difficulty than usual getting cooperation. "People judge lawyers' abilities by the cost of their clothes and vehicle. I drive a minivan. The suit is all I have."

And she considered it her armor.

She offered Sharp the Dunkin' box. He made a distasteful face.

"I'll take one." Lance grabbed a glazed donut. "Sharp doesn't drink coffee or eat processed foods."

"I'm sorry." Morgan selected a Boston Kreme. "I have a wicked sweet tooth."

"Sugar and caffeine are highly addictive," Sharp said in his high-and-mighty tone.

"I'm going to live on the edge this morning." Lance took a coffee from the tray.

"I'm sorry. I won't corrupt him again. I promise." Grinning, Morgan slid her laptop from her tote. "Thank you again for the loan of your office space."

Sharp moved the last two boxes to the closet. "You're welcome."

"Our security system isn't close to what you have here," Morgan said.

Lance carried a box of supplies and copies from the hallway and placed them on the table. "What's your plan for today?"

"Reviewing evidence. I started last night, but there's a lot to get through." Morgan's head was fuzzy from lack of sleep.

Sharp opened her box. "There isn't much in here."

"Most of the discovery materials came through secure email." She opened her laptop.

Sharp frowned. "I know I'm being an old fart, but I prefer printed copies." He left the room and returned with a printer, which he set up on the far end of the table. "Start when you're ready."

Morgan began to print police reports.

"I like to work with visuals." Sharp rubbed his hands together, as if anxious to get started. "I'll put together a murder board."

She glanced up at the far wall, where a huge whiteboard spanned the distance between two windows. "I'll print multiple copies. I like to keep my files a certain way too."

The printer hummed as it spat out pages. They divvied up reports and began reading.

Morgan started with the police reports. By lunchtime, she'd gotten through a large chunk of the materials, and her head spun with details. She saved the autopsy report for last, steeling herself for the horrible details. Reading about the sheer brutality of a violent crime was hard enough when she hadn't personally known the victim. But this . . .

This was the stuff of nightmares.

She scanned the text first and then moved on to the photos. The first image of Tessa's body lying in the cattails took Morgan's breath away. The close-ups of Tessa's face and wounds were worse. Morgan closed her eyes and pictured the girl the last time she'd seen her alive, sitting at the Danes' kitchen table playing a game of Chutes and Ladders with the kids. Morgan's empty stomach churned. She reached into her tote bag for a roll of antacids and chewed two.

"We should break for lunch," Lance said, his gaze too focused on her.

"I'm going to get some air." What she needed was to get away from those photos. She took a croissant onto the back porch.

A flash of white drew her attention to the space under the porch steps. A dog huddled in the shadows. Clearly a mixed breed, its body was white with tan patches and looked vaguely bull-dogish, but leaner. Someone had docked its tail, and its ribs protruded under a short, dirty coat.

"I can't eat this anyway." Morgan tossed a piece of her pastry onto the porch. The dog slunk out of its hiding space and gobbled the food with the wary rush of an animal that didn't know when or where it would get its next meal. Morgan tossed more bits of croissant, drawing the animal closer. The dog edged forward for each bite, until it was only a few feet away. "I'm out of food."

With one apprehensive wag of her tail stub, the dog darted back under the steps.

The door behind her opened. Lance walked out and stood next to her. "Are you all right?"

"Yes." Morgan leaned on a post. "I just needed a minute."

Lance put an arm around her shoulders, and she shifted her weight toward him. A tear slid down her cheek. She wiped it away. "Some of those pictures got to me. I'm sorry."

"For what? Being human?"

"Being weak." She pushed away from him. "The only thing I can do for Nick or Tessa is to solve her murder. Crying isn't going to help anyone."

"You are the strongest person I know." Lance reached out and tucked a hair behind her ear, his knuckles brushing her cheek. "But this—" He gestured toward the building. "This is hard enough to handle even when the victim is a stranger. I'm here if you need someone to lean on."

She closed her eyes and turned her face into his hand for a few seconds. But when he shifted forward, as if to embrace her, she straightened. If he held her right now, she'd break down, and she couldn't handle the emotional storm that would follow. Grief was a quagmire that would pull her under until she suffocated. She could already feel the familiar heaviness, ready to settle its crushing weight on her chest, making each breath harder to draw than the last, as if the simple act of drawing air into her lungs could crack her wide open and leave her in pieces.

She couldn't go there again, not after she'd just fought her way out from under it.

"Thank you," she said. "I appreciate the offer. I do. But what I really need is to get back to work."

Ignoring his disapproving frown, she turned toward the door and away from him.

Back in the war room, Sharp brought her a green smoothie, and she forced herself to drink it while scanning the murder board. Using magnets, he'd organized photos under headers like Crime Scene and Suspects. He'd also written bullet points and drawn connections with arrows. He'd put a photo of Tessa at the top of the board.

"The visual presentation helps you see connections," she said.

"That's the idea. What do we know so far?" Sharp picked up his marker and started a timeline on one side of the board. "Nick and Tessa attended a party at the lake. They arrived at approximately nine p.m. The police have identified eleven other teens who attended the party." Sharp listed their names. "As far as I can tell, only Jamie, Robby Barone, Felicity Weber, and Jacob Emerson were still at the lake at the end of the party."

"Jacob is the ex-boyfriend?" Lance asked.

"Not exactly. Jacob and Tessa went on a few dates last April," Morgan clarified.

Sharp stretched his arms over his head.

"Do we know who took the video?" Lance asked.

"Yes." Morgan sifted through a few papers. "A kid by the name of Brandon Nolan."

"Did Brandon say why he didn't post the video sooner?" Sharp asked.

Morgan sorted through the police interviews. "Yes. He missed his curfew Thursday night, and his dad grounded him and took his phone for a week as punishment. The police didn't have Brandon on their initial list of partygoers. He's not in Tessa's inner social circle. The police did interview him after they became aware of the video. He said he left right after the fight."

Sharp snorted. "So the second he got his phone back, he posted the video without thinking it could be related to Tessa's murder?"

"Yes, he did." Morgan sighed. She'd prosecuted enough teens that the lack of forethought didn't surprise her. "Let's finish the timeline. Nick and Jacob fought shortly after the party started. By nine thirty, Nick and Tessa went off in his car. According to Nick, they had consensual, unprotected sex in the backseat. When they returned to the party sometime around ten, they had an argument. Nick says Tessa broke up with him. This is verified by the text Tessa sent Felicity at 10:43 p.m. The party broke up between ten and ten thirty. Nick says he left Tessa there. She had her own car."

"Did anyone confirm this?" Sharp asked.

"Yes. Robby Barone and Felicity both stated that they left after Nick." Morgan continued, "Nick says he drove around until about midnight. His phone was dead, so we have no GPS data. His father was asleep when he came home."

"So Bud can't even back him up on that," Lance said.

"Right." Morgan jotted times and events on her timeline, then pulled out the autopsy report. "Tessa died between 10:30 p.m. Thursday night and 4:00 a.m. Friday morning. She was stabbed nine times, but the ME thinks she died quickly. Considering the extent of her wounds . . ." Morgan shuddered as she looked at an autopsy photo. "One of the initial wounds was a deep puncture to the heart. If she'd lived through the entire attack, there would have been more blood."

Wounds didn't bleed much after the heart stopped beating.

Morgan flipped to the next page in the autopsy report. "The autopsy also shows bruising and abrasions consistent with sexual assault. Semen recovered from Tessa's body and blood scraped from under her thumbnail matches Nick's DNA. The ME also found traces of condom lubricant. The DA theorizes that Nick tried to use a condom, which shows premeditation and the desire to not be caught, but the condom broke."

Sharp went to the table and rifled through some papers. "In your interview with Nick, he said he had a bloody nose from the fight with Jacob and that Tessa cleaned him up. Is that in his original statement to the police, or did he say that in response to the blood being found under Tessa's nail?"

Morgan found his initial police interview. "Unfortunately, he did not include that information in his original statement. But the police didn't ask him any questions that would have prompted him to reveal that. Overall, Nick's statements are consistent."

"Did they offer him a polygraph?" Lance asked.

"No, but we should consider it." Morgan made more notes, and then returned to her narrative. "The knife recovered from Nick's yard matches Tessa's wounds, but that DNA test is still pending. There were no fingerprints on the knife. There was a T-shirt with blood on it in Nick's hamper."

"From his bloody nose," Lance said.

"That would be my conclusion. That DNA test is also pending." Morgan looked up. "The

DNA on the shirt should be Nick's. I assume the blood on the knife is Tessa's. The DA refuses to expedite those tests."

"Why would he? He already has his suspect locked up," Sharp said.

"And maybe he's used up all his favors," Lance added.

Morgan nodded, frustrated. "Things the police did not find at Nick's house or at the crime scene: a broken condom, bloody pants, or bloody shoes."

Lance interrupted. "So Nick managed to dispose of the condom, his pants, and his shoes, but he tossed his bloody shirt in his hamper and buried the murder weapon behind his shed? That makes no sense."

"There is no way he stabbed that girl nine times without getting blood on his pants and shoes," Sharp agreed. "The knife had to be a plant."

"Meaning Nick was intentionally framed," Morgan said.

"Right. Make a note to check the forensic reports when they come in, to see if any semen was found under the body or in Nick's car," Sharp said. "Was she raped and killed in the same place?"

Morgan returned to her chair and shuffled through more papers. "The forensics reports aren't in, but I see notations about blood being visible under and immediately around the body.

There is a notation of the black light picking up a small amount of semen on the backseat of Nick's car."

"Which is consistent with Nick's statement." Lance studied the board. "But the DA will argue that Nick could have raped her in the car, then dragged her out to stab her."

Sharp closed his marker. Holding it in both hands behind his back, he paced back and forth in front of the whiteboard. "She could have gotten away from him and ran. Then he chased her down and stabbed her."

Morgan rubbed at an ache in the back of her neck. "By ten thirty, Tessa was alone at the lake."

Sharp halted and frowned. "So what happened next?"

Three beats of silence passed, then Lance asked, "Did Nick know she was pregnant?"

"I don't think so. He didn't mention it." Morgan wrote the question in her notes for her next interview with Nick. "I didn't know about it when I interviewed him. But the DA's theory is that she broke up with him because she was pregnant with another guy's baby. Nick became enraged. He came back to the party and attacked her."

"It's a reasonable hypothesis." Sharp pivoted to face the board. "But it isn't without holes."

Morgan scanned the autopsy. "The ME notes that a chunk of Tessa's hair was cut from her head using a blade, not scissors. It was not found at the scene."

Sharp straightened. "A trophy?"

"Or a memento," Lance said. "May I see that report?"

Morgan moved aside, giving him access to the pages she'd spread out on the table.

Lance moved to a pile of crime scene photos and selected one. "Tessa was wearing a denim skirt. When she was found, she was fully dressed and her skirt was arranged over her legs." Lance took the photo and attached it to the murder board with a magnet. "He dressed her or allowed her to dress, suggesting the murder didn't occur immediately after the rape."

"So was the killer ashamed of the rape?" Morgan asked. "Maybe that's why he wrote *sorry* on her forehead."

"Possibly, if he's the one who is sorry. It's also possible that he thinks Tessa should have been sorry for something." Sharp stepped up next to Lance and stared at the picture. "Because I see rage in the extent of Tessa's injuries." Sharp's gaze flickered back and forth between the timeline, the photos, and the inconsistencies. "Nick said he didn't use a condom."

"Correct," Morgan said.

"Were any condoms found at his house?" Lance asked.

"No." Morgan pointed at the board. "But whoever raped Tessa brought a condom and a knife with him, making his attack premeditated."

"So her killer was very angry but planned out his attack," Sharp said in a tight voice. "At least in the time immediately preceding the murder. Possible motives: jealousy, possession . . ."

"If I can't have her no one can?" Lance returned to the table. "Do we have Tessa's phone records?"

"Yes," Morgan said. "The Palmers gave the police immediate access to their account. For a teenager, she doesn't have much activity on her phone. Mostly she texted back and forth with Felicity and Nick. Reviewing her texts for the three weeks before her death, I found complaints that her grandparents are ridiculous, they don't understand her, they want her to date Jacob. She describes him as an obnoxious jerk. She doesn't mention her pregnancy. However, on the night she was murdered, right after she texted Felicity, she placed a twenty-nine-second phone call to the landline at Jacob Emerson's house."

"Who uses a landline?" Sharp asked.

"I don't even have one," Lance added.

"In Jacob's interview, he says he and Tessa only went out a couple of times. His parents and her grandparents kept pushing them together, but he says they weren't 'into each other.' " Morgan used air quotes. "Jacob isn't permitted to have his phone at night. It gets turned off and left in the kitchen. Tessa knew the rule and called on the landline. Jacob's father answered the phone and told her to call back in the morning."

Sharp rubbed the back of his neck. "What about the connection between Tessa and Jamie?" He put a photo of Jamie on the board and drew a line connecting it with Tessa's picture.

Lance hung a picture of Kevin Murdoch on the board. "I want more background information on Jamie's soon-to-be stepfather."

"The excessive sweater?" Sharp asked.

"Lance is right," Morgan agreed. "Kevin was far too nervous during our interview. In addition to sweating bullets, Kevin couldn't hold eye contact or keep his hands off his face. He knew Tessa, and he's hiding something. I want to know what."

"Did the police collect DNA from any of the other kids?" Sharp asked. "The forensic reports aren't in, but the medical examiner found a number of hairs on her body and clothing. Different colors. Different lengths. None of those have been tested yet."

Morgan shook her head. "No. It seems they focused only on Nick from the very beginning. But she could have picked up hairs hugging her friends."

"But they could still be compared to the DNA of the fetus," Sharp said, "if we think the unknown father is a suspect for her rape and murder. A condom prevents the transfer of DNA via semen, but it's hard to rape a woman without leaving any biological evidence behind. I've no doubt that forensics will turn up other sources of DNA. The difficulty lies in determining what belongs to the killer and what could have been transferred through normal activities."

Lance stood and rubbed his thigh. He said his bullet wound was fine, but it clearly still bothered him. "So what's *our* theory?"

Morgan set her marker on the narrow ledge of the whiteboard. "Tessa was alone at the lake. We know she was upset with her grandparents. She texted Felicity about her breakup with Nick. Then she called Jacob's house but was denied access to him. What happened next? Someone had to come back to the lake and attack her. He brought a condom and a knife with him. He knew she was there and planned to kill her."

"But who?" Lance asked.

"I want to get a copy of last year's high school yearbook," Morgan said. "Then we can see who Tessa hung out with last year."

"The autopsy says she was approximately eight weeks pregnant, so she got pregnant in July," Lance pointed out. "Not during the school year."

Morgan nodded. "True, but I doubt very much that Tessa slept with a boy she didn't know."

Sharp jerked a thumb at his growing lists of Witnesses and Suspects. "We need to gather as much information as possible about every one of these people. Lance, how about we get your mom on that?"

Lance fumbled a pencil. "My mom?"

His mom? Morgan's curiosity piqued. Other than the revelation about his father's disappearance, Lance didn't talk much about his family or past.

Sharp nodded. "She's the pro at accessing online information, and we need the help." He gestured toward the board. "In case you hadn't noticed, this case is a total cluster. Our best alternate suspect is a seventeen-year-old with a lawyer for a father."

"My mom has never helped us with a case. She might not want to get involved," Lance protested.

"You won't know until you ask." Sharp pinned Lance with a look. "She might appreciate being useful. It could be good for her."

Lance looked doubtful.

"Do you want me to ask her?" Sharp offered.

"No. I have to check on her today anyway." But Lance didn't look happy about the idea. "No promises."

"Understood." Sharp nodded.

"We need to interview Robby Barone, Felicity Weber, and Jacob Emerson. I have no doubt Mr. Emerson will be in on Jacob's interview." Morgan abandoned her file, went to the board, and started a list of Questions.

Who was the father of Tessa's baby?

Who doesn't have an alibi for Thursday after the party?

"I'd like to visit the crime scene as well. Daylight might give us a whole different feel for the area." Morgan shivered as she remembered being in the woods in the dark, seeing Tessa's body in the harsh beam of the flashlight, the girl covered in blood.

And the word written across her forehead: SORRY.

CHAPTER NINETEEN

The afternoon sun warmed Lance's back as he and Morgan walked toward his Jeep.

"Are you sure you don't mind?" Lance asked. "I could drop this list off to my mom, and then meet you later."

He'd given Sharp a hard time, but his boss was right. His mother might be thrilled to be able to help. She had long days and nothing to fill them. But could she handle the facts of the murder case? All Lance had brought was a list of names and addresses—no photos or details of the crime. Still, his mom was fragile. Who knew what would upset her?

Lance couldn't deny that he was embarrassed for Morgan to meet her. He could sense a no-turning-back sharing moment on the horizon. But Morgan was a friend, not a date, and she was the most understanding, giving woman he'd ever known. She didn't judge people. She'd taken a former drug addict into her home and made her part of her family. She took care of her cantankerous grandfather. She understood what it meant to care for the people she loved without qualifications. Lance had learned the hard way that not everyone was willing to make sacrifices.

"That's silly. After all the things you do to help my grandfather? Of course I don't mind," Morgan said as she got into the passenger seat. "I'm happy to meet your mom."

Lance slid behind the wheel. "I'd better give you some background first. Remember when I told you about my dad disappearing?"

"Yes." Her seatbelt clicked into place.

He pulled away from the curb. It was easier to talk about his mom if his eyes were on the road. He didn't want to see the shock and pity on Morgan's face as she pictured his childhood.

Before he could change his mind, Lance dove into his story headfirst. "About a year after he was gone, my mom started showing signs of anxiety and depression. It probably began earlier, but I was just a kid. I didn't notice until it started to affect my life. At first, the symptoms were more quirky than alarming. Mild OCD, depression, that sort of thing. I figured she was just sad. Hell, I was sad too. I missed my dad, and with the way she was retreating from life, it felt as if I was losing her too."

Morgan didn't comment, but he could sense her scrutiny.

He continued, "Within the next couple of years, Mom went out less and less. By the time I was thirteen or fourteen, she was leaving the house maybe once a week. If she hadn't had to feed me, she probably would have willingly crawled in a hole and starved. She couldn't work. Those trips to the grocery store got farther and farther apart."

Memories flooded him. He'd worried about her committing suicide and leaving him alone.

"Didn't she have friends?" Morgan asked, her voice heavy with empathy, not pity.

Lance stopped at the corner, then turned left onto Main Street. "Her symptoms took years to fully develop. It was a gradual progression, starting with slowly cutting herself off from her friends. By the time she was sick enough for other people to notice, she'd already alienated everyone in her social circle. She didn't have any real family except me. The only person who persisted was Sharp."

"He seems like he really cares about you."

Lance took Main to the edge of town and turned onto a rural highway. The miles rolled by. Houses gave way to fields and forests. "He was still a detective then, and even though my dad's case had long since been set aside, he kept tabs on us. As you can see, we didn't live in town. It was a damned long bike ride to get anywhere.

"Sharp was the guy who drove me to hockey practice. He taught me how to drive. He forced my mom to see a psychiatrist. There were plenty of nights I stayed at Sharp's place because I needed a break from my mom's anxiety."

Once open wounds, Lance's memories were

now needle pricks of humiliation. Sharp checking their fridge and finding it empty. Lance's mother, dirty and wild-eyed, counting and arranging empty bottles, boxes of unworn shoes, and stacks of magazines. Sharp taking Lance out for a burger and letting him use his guest room to give him a respite from the stress of his mother's mental illness. The day he'd gotten his driver's license at the age of sixteen, Lance had become his mother's caretaker.

Lance pulled onto the shoulder in front of a roadside farm stand. "I'll be right back. Do you want anything?"

"No, thank you."

Lance grabbed a fresh apple pie, his mom's favorite treat, and returned to the Jeep. Morgan took the white box and held it on her lap.

"I had no idea," Morgan said after he pulled back out onto the road. "I often wondered why you stayed in Scarlet Falls when there weren't any openings for a detective. You could have applied to another police force years ago and gotten your promotion."

"My mother requires a lot of maintenance. I need to stay close." Lance turned at a mailbox. A narrow drive led to the small house he'd grown up in. After his dad disappeared, Mom refused to consider moving. It was as if she held onto the three-bedroom house and five acres as her last connection to her husband.

As if she still expected him to come home.

He parked in front of the house and looked over at Morgan. She didn't seem disturbed by his story.

"Is there anything I might do or say that could upset her?" Morgan asked, always thinking of others, never herself.

"Not really." Lance said. "But don't be offended if she's standoffish or nervous. She doesn't like visits from strangers. The only people she's comfortable with are me and Sharp."

"All right."

Lance got out of the Jeep. For a few seconds, he considered asking Morgan to wait outside, but that was cheating. Mom's therapist wanted him to treat her as normally as possible. Bringing a coworker to the house was perfectly ordinary.

Morgan carried the pie as they walked to the front porch.

"Did I mention she's also a hoarder?" he warned as he knocked on the door. No one answered, so he used his key and let them in.

"Mom?" he called out as they stepped into the living room.

He assessed a stack of shipping boxes by the door. Not too bad. Seven pairs of shoes. He'd last visited yesterday morning. These must have been delivered in the afternoon. Other than the new boxes, the living room was tidy.

A former computer science professor, his mom

had turned to online teaching years before. She also did freelance website design, security, and maintenance. With her mortgage paid off, her expenses were minimal, and her salary enabled her to indulge in far too much online shopping. Lance kept close tabs on her credit cards, but it was still impossible to keep her completely in check. If he cancelled one credit card, she applied for ten more.

He pictured the clutter that had once filled the house. They'd barely been able to walk from room to room. Antidepressants, weekly group therapy, and Lance's determination were the three keys to keeping Jennifer Kruger's living conditions sanitary, safe, and relatively sane.

Morgan wandered into the living room and inspected the hanging glass cases full of thimbles and spoons. Several chests of drawers held more of the same. "Spoons and thimbles?"

"They're small and nonflammable," Lance said. His mother had needed to keep some of her *treasures.*

"Lance, is that you? I'm in the office." His mom's voice drifted from the bedroom wing of the house.

A doorway opened into the kitchen, while a short hallway led to the three bedrooms.

Morgan detoured to the kitchen with the pie while Lance headed for the hall and the extra bedroom that had been converted into an office

211

when his mother had started working from home.

His mom sat behind the desk, hunched over a keyboard. On one side of her L-shaped desk, a computer was equipped with three monitors. A laptop was open on the second leg. A cat lounged beside the laptop. Another bathed itself in a patch of sun that streamed into the room and puddled on the floor behind the desk.

His mom smiled as he entered the room, leaned over her desk, and kissed her on the cheek.

On the outside, his mother looked ordinary. Her painfully slender frame, white hair she didn't bother to color, and deep lines in her face aged her beyond her sixty years. The one highlight of her OCD was that she was routine dependent, and her therapist had designed daily hygiene rituals with her illness in mind. She was now incapable of sleeping past her seven a.m. alarm, skipping a shower, or not washing her clothes at exactly nine o'clock every morning. The end result was a seemingly put-together older woman who functioned with a precision that even drill sergeants would envy.

But the ever-present bright sheen of apprehension that clouded her pale blue eyes gave her away. No amount of medication or therapy would ever bring her back to the woman she'd once been.

In the blink of an eye, his mother's expression shifted from resignation to fear. "Who is that in the hallway?"

Looking lawyerly—and gorgeous—in her navy-blue suit, white blouse, and heels, Morgan stepped into the doorway. She must have left the pie and her giant purse in the kitchen.

Lance gestured for her to come into the room. "Mom, this is Morgan Dane."

"It's nice to meet you, Mrs. Kruger."

He braced himself for a panic attack as his mother studied Morgan for a full minute without speaking. In his mind, Lance was already fetching antianxiety meds from the kitchen when the most extraordinary thing happened.

His mother smiled.

Rising, she came out from behind the desk and extended a hand to Morgan. "Please, you must call me Jennifer."

What the hell?

When was the last time Mom had willingly touched a stranger?

"Let me make you some coffee?" His mom led Morgan toward the kitchen. The pair of cats weaved precariously around their ankles.

Feeling like he was having an out-of-body experience, Lance followed. His mom gestured toward the round oak table that had graced the gray sheet vinyl since the house had been built. He couldn't remember the last time someone other than he, his mom, or Sharp had sat at it. Even the social worker who visited once a month usually set off an anxiety attack.

But his mom was at the counter making coffee as if she entertained on a daily basis. She pointed to a high cabinet. "Lance, get some plates down."

"OK." He did as she asked, his emotions bouncing between suspicion and guarded relief.

"Can I help?" Morgan asked.

His mother waved away Morgan's offer. "No. No. You're our guest."

Lance spent the next twenty minutes in an utter state of confusion as they ate pie and drank coffee like normal people. His mother finished an entire slice, the most he'd seen her eat in one sitting in years, and she wore the first genuine smile he'd seen in a very long time.

Who was this woman, and what had she done with his mother?

"Mom, we need to ask you for a favor." Lance collected their dirty plates and put them into the dishwasher. His mother would run the appliance at seven o'clock this evening, whether it was empty or full.

"What is it?" his mom asked.

"Morgan is a defense attorney. Sharp and I are assisting with her investigation. We're short-handed, and we could use some help running background checks."

"You want me to help you?" She perked up even more.

"Yes," he said.

"Of course I will." She rose, a flustered hand

going to her throat as she scurried back to her office.

Lance rushed after her. Was she going to freak out? What had he done? "I don't want to give you any stress."

But his mom slid behind her desk. Did she really just crack her knuckles over her keyboard? "Did you bring me a list?"

"Yes." Lance froze.

Luckily, Morgan kept her wits. From behind him, she said, "I'll get it."

When his mom looked up at him, her eyes were wet. Lance had a moment of fear before he realized it was gratitude shining from his mom's face.

Sharp had been right.

His mother was thrilled to be helping.

"So you're OK with this?" Lance asked.

She nodded. "I'm so glad you asked." Her gaze went around the office. "The fall term just began. There isn't that much I can use to fill my work hours." She focused on him. "There's nothing I'd rather do than help you and Sharp. I know I've been a terrible burden to you both."

"Never a burden." Lance rounded the desk. Resting his hands on her shoulders, he bent and kissed her on the cheek.

She turned, smiled up at him, and whispered, "She's lovely."

The waggle of her eyebrows shocked the hell

out of him, and he couldn't stifle the laugh that burst out of his chest.

Another first, his mother showing a sense of humor.

"We work together."

The gleam in her eye showed she didn't believe him. "Sure."

Morgan brought a file into the office and handed it over. His mother opened it, flipping through the pages.

"Are you going to be all right, then?" Lance asked.

"Yes. Yes. I'm going to work on these all afternoon." His mom's attention was riveted on the file.

"How long do you think it will take?" Morgan asked.

"Depends on what I find." His mom flipped through a couple of pages. "I doubt I'll be finished, but I'll have something for you by Monday."

"Then we'll leave you to it." Lance straightened. "I'll call later. If you find anything spectacular before then, would you call me?"

"I will." His mom lifted her gaze. "Will you bring Morgan back?"

"Maybe," Lance answered. "She's very busy with the case."

Mom's smile faltered.

"I'd be happy to come back," Morgan said from the doorway.

His mother beamed. She tugged on Lance's sleeve. "Bring more pie."

"All right. I'll see you tomorrow."

On Sundays, Mom had group therapy. He'd need to do her grocery shopping and mow the lawn too.

Morgan waited patiently while he stopped in the kitchen to check Mom's pill organizer and make sure she'd taken all her medication. In the living room, he picked up the boxes of shoes. The stack blocked his vision.

"Let me help." Morgan grabbed the top box.

They went outside.

"That was a surprise." He closed and locked the door behind them. "Normally she isn't good with strangers."

"Your mother is sweet."

"She certainly likes you." Lance suspected his mother had the wrong idea about his relationship with Morgan.

"I'm glad."

Lance piled the shoes in the back of his Jeep. "This is the ritual. She does OK in the daytime, but at night she gets online and orders all sorts of other things. I take everything back the day after it arrives. I return what I can and donate the rest. She tries, but she just can't help herself."

"When you said she was a hoarder, I pictured a cluttered house."

"It used to be a firetrap, but there was a breaking point when I graduated from college and came home. During the term, I'd come home every weekend, but those last weeks, I got tied up with finals and papers. I hadn't been here for a month. I couldn't even get into the house. She'd blocked all the exits except the back door. My absence had exacerbated her symptoms. She worries all the time. I can't miss a day of visiting. When I was in the hospital, even though Sharp came every day to give her an update on my condition, I had to Skype with her each morning to prove I wasn't dead."

"What happened when you came home from college?" Morgan asked.

"Sharp and I got her into an inpatient facility." Lance still remembered his shock at his mother's appearance—unshowered, in dirty clothes, fingernails chewed ragged, cuticles picked bloody. He hadn't known how she'd been able to fake it during their daily phone calls. "They got her back on the meds and balanced her moods. While she was gone, Sharp and I emptied the house." Which had required renting a Dumpster. "Now I have to enforce strict rules. If she wants to keep a new purchase, she has to get rid of something of equal size. Two cats are the maximum, but she can have all the spoons and thimbles she likes. I know it sounds weird, but the system has been working for years."

Lance closed the cargo door. They climbed back into the vehicle, and he started the engine. When he grabbed the shifter, Morgan put her hand on his.

"I like your mom." She smiled. "No one's perfect."

"Some are less perfect than others, but thank you."

"She's kind, she's alive, and she obviously loves you very much." Morgan squeezed his hand. "In the end, that's what really matters."

"I know." Lance focused on the word *alive*. Morgan had lost two parents and a husband.

"After my father was killed, my mother ran away from the memories. She moved out of the city and dragged us all with her. We didn't want to leave our friends, our lives, but there was no reasoning with her. Ian went to college in the city, so he stayed. My sisters and I had no choice." Morgan paused for a breath. "My mom never recovered from his death. A few years later, she had a massive heart attack. I always thought she died of a broken heart. Thank God for Grandpa."

"I'm sorry." Lance turned his hand over and interlaced their fingers. Their teenage relationship had been short and superficial. Morgan's mom had been alive then, though Lance had only met her once or twice. After they'd broken up, he and Morgan hadn't kept in touch.

When she turned away to stare out the window, her eyes shone with unshed tears. "Your mom is sick. Don't hold that against her. Grief can break even the strongest person."

CHAPTER TWENTY

Jail, day 3

Nick hunched over his breakfast tray. Although his stomach pinched with hunger, he waited for the older inmates to grab their trays. Like high school, much was inferred through your choice of where to sit for a meal.

At first, he'd been afraid that every inmate was forced to choose a gang, but it seemed that only a rough third of the population of D-pod were actually gang members. The Man's information wasn't exactly correct. If tattoos were accurate, the Aryan Brotherhood, the Bloods, and the Mexican Mafia were all represented, but they gave each other space, as if some sort of wary truce had been achieved.

Since surveillance cameras and guards watched 24/7, maybe they'd all agreed that attacking each other here was pointless.

The other forty-odd inmates had their own smaller social groups. A small gathering read the Bible and prayed before breakfast. There was a study group. Nick hadn't expected that. And one popular, geeky guy gave out free legal advice, which seemed to have earned him respect and maybe even gratitude, among the other inmates.

For now, Nick was still keeping to himself and observing as much behavior as possible before he would inevitably be forced to interact with the others. So far, there'd been mostly silent assessment.

He'd already learned that first-timers were called fish.

He grabbed a tray. He took the empty end of the prayer group's table. He kept his head down and ate, barely tasting the oatmeal, hard-boiled egg, and milk on his tray. The portions were small, and his stomach was not nearly full when his food was gone. Other inmates traded food, and there must have been a place to buy food because an older guy was cooking ramen in a microwave—another surprise.

Nick hadn't expected this much . . . freedom.

An odd word for the inside of a county jail, but although the men were all locked up, they moved about the room at will. No one was locked in a tiny cell. It seemed that as long as you obeyed the rules, both the official and unofficial sets— and no one was out to get you—this was how it would be.

But the way the other inmates studied Nick told him he wasn't going to be so lucky.

He ate quickly, feeling vulnerable out in the open. Depositing his tray back on the cart, he retreated to his mattress on the floor. He felt better with his back to the cinderblocks.

A few stragglers sat at empty tables. One guy cleaned tables. Another mopped the floor. Two guys played a game of chess, and a small group banded around them to watch. Nick almost wanted to go over and see if he could get in line to play, but he watched from a distance. He still attracted too much attention. There was a tension he couldn't describe building in the room. And it seemed to swell whenever one of the other inmates made eye contact with him.

The walls were depressing. The food was depressing. On top of fear, sheer hopelessness weighed on him like a steel blanket. Halfway through the morning, a short, stocky white guy with a full sleeve of multicolored tattoos approached. He sat on the closest steel bench and faced Nick. Had he been assigned to interview him?

"So, you're the beast?"

"Beast?" Nick asked, confused.

"You raped a girl, right?" the man asked, his eyes creasing with disapproval.

"No." For the first time, Nick made purposeful and prolonged eye contact. Anger kept his voice and gaze steady. "I didn't."

The man considered Nick's answer. "What's your story?"

Nick sensed a test. "My girlfriend was raped and killed. The police and the DA pinned it on me. I just want to get out of here, find the one who did it, and do her justice."

"Half the men in here claim they're innocent. Why should I believe you?"

Nick shrugged, exhaustion sliding over his body in a wave. He'd been afraid to close his eyes. Hell, he was afraid if he blinked, someone would kill him. But lack of food and sleep was wearing on him. He didn't know how much longer he could keep up the hypervigilance. "If you don't want to, there isn't anything I can do about that."

"This is true." The inmate nodded. "I'm Shorty."

OK.

"I'm Nick." *What the hell?* Not knowing what else to do, he reached out a hand.

Shorty shook it with only the briefest of hesitations.

What did an introduction mean? Had that been a test?

This was so confusing. He felt like he'd been dumped into a reality TV show with no description of the game he was supposed to play.

During the next few hours, three other inmates introduced themselves to Nick and asked for his story. Were they comparing notes? Nick kept his statements simple and honest and hoped that came through.

Not much else he could do. Everything depended on Ms. Dane.

Nick got up to use the toilet. He passed by a cell. A hand grabbed his uniform collar and yanked him off his feet into the dark space. He landed on his side, his shoulder smashing into the concrete. A body jumped on top of him. A fist slammed into his face. Pain exploded through his nose and mouth. Nick tasted blood. He wrapped his arms around his head to block the blows while he got his bearings. Adrenaline shot through his bloodstream, shocking his heart into a panicked frenzy.

Questions fired through his mind. Would the guards see? Were there cameras in the cells? Nick had never ventured inside one.

Were they going to kill him?

Trying to block the raining fists, Nick squinted around his forearms. One man was delivering the beating, but others watched from the doorway. They seemed to be standing guard.

A punch connected with his ribs. He couldn't protect his head and his torso at once. Primal instinct sent a blast of energy through him. He was going to die if he didn't fight back. As shitty as his life was, he couldn't just let it go.

Nick rolled a shoulder to cover his face. He lashed out a hand. His fist connected with his attacker's body.

The guy got to his feet and delivered a kick to

Nick's ribs. The pain just about split him in two. He coughed and wrapped his hands around his middle. When the foot came in for a second kick, Nick grabbed the ankle and pulled. Surprised, his attacker went down on his back. Nick scrambled to his feet, his chest heaving, his lungs crying for air.

Blood dripped down his face and onto his uniform. He almost went after his attacker, and then stopped when he recognized Shorty—and saw the three larger inmates in the doorway. They helped Shorty to his feet. Then the four of them stared at Nick.

What. The. Fuck?

He couldn't take them all on.

His chest heaved. He wiped a hand across his face and waited. A few long minutes passed until one of the men tossed Nick a towel. "Get yourself cleaned up before the guards come in."

Nick nodded and wiped his face. The four men stepped aside and let him out.

Two guards burst through the door. One eyed Nick's face. "What happened?"

Snitches get stitches.

Had that been some sort of test?

"I tripped," Nick said.

"No one attacked you?" they asked, scanning the room.

"No," Nick lied. "These guys were just helping me up."

The guard frowned. Clearly they didn't have cameras inside the cells, just in the main room, and the inmates all knew it.

Who's fucking stupid idea was that?

"You're sure?" the guard asked.

"Yep." Nick wiped his nose.

The guard frowned, not convinced. "You need to go to the infirmary?"

Nick shook his head. Dizziness swam in his head. "I'm good."

The guards shot a warning look around the room. Shorty wasn't in sight. Nick wondered if his knuckles were bleeding. He limped to the toilet and relieved himself. Returning to his mat, Nick put his back to the wall. He huddled on the mattress, pain and cold blotting out every other sense.

And waited.

He might have to spend a year or more in this place. The thought of living out the rest of his life in a concrete box made him want to throw up.

Or kill himself.

Today he'd received a beating. He had no idea why.

Or what was next.

CHAPTER TWENTY-ONE

He lifted his binoculars and watched the three girls standing at the edge of Scarlet Lake. He guessed the girls were about sixteen. The sun reflected off the water like a mirror. One girl handed something to her friend. A joint?

He adjusted the focus of his binoculars to zoom in on the girl's face.

Yep. They were passing a joint around.

He shifted his aim lower. Tight yoga pants cupped tighter asses. He licked his lips. A hand slid down to his crotch. He rubbed himself through the fabric of his pants before giving in to the urge and lowering his zipper.

But it wasn't enough.

Frustrated, he zipped up.

There was no doubt about it. He needed to replace Tessa.

He'd thought coming back to the place where she'd died would help with his self-control by reminding him that all actions had consequences. And that he absolutely had to stay out of trouble until this whole mess blew over. But he hadn't counted on those girls and their skintight pants.

He'd wanted to be alone at the lake. To reflect. To get a fucking grip.

He'd been prepared to share the beach with dogs and families. But pretty girls brought back memories of Tessa. Not just of her death, but of all the things he'd done with her.

To her.

The girls finished their joint and turned away from the water. He followed them with his binoculars as they walked toward a car in the parking lot. The one on the left had long blonde hair. Tall, blue-eyed, and stacked, she was as different from Tessa as possible.

The blonde slid into the driver's seat. They drove away, and he lowered the binoculars after memorizing the license plate of the car. How hard would it be to find out her name?

He knew he needed to wait. It was too soon. But in reality, how long would he be able to keep his shit together?

He'd come to the lake to get a grip on his need, but he'd ended up stoking it higher.

CHAPTER TWENTY-TWO

In the passenger seat of the Jeep, Morgan blinked the tears from her eyes. Her grief was ramping up this week.

Lance was still holding her hand. The gesture was simultaneously comforting and terrifying, and she fought both the desire to snatch her hand away and crawl into his lap.

She shouldn't be surprised that she wanted some comfort. She'd thrown away her job. Her neighbors hated her. After two years in a holding pattern, she'd turned her entire professional life into a train wreck in the course of a single week.

And Lance seemed to want to be there for her. In high school, he'd kept his emotional distance, and she hadn't pressed him for a deeper relationship. They'd been young, and she'd had her own family issues. But the adult Lance was harder to resist. The more time she spent with him, the more he opened up to her.

The more she liked him.

He put his mother's welfare ahead of his own desires. He made real sacrifices to care for her, and he did it freely and without resentment. He was willing to help Morgan solve Nick's case, and she knew that if Bud couldn't pay, Lance would still be in.

He was a man you could count on. A man *she* could count on.

But this wasn't the time. Regret pinged in her heart as she pulled her hand out from under his. All her focus needed to stay on Nick and his defense. When it was over, she would reassess her personal life. A few months ago, she hadn't thought she'd ever be attracted to another man. But she had to admit it—she definitely was.

She turned to study Lance's profile, her gaze sliding from his face over his muscular chest and arms. She definitely liked what she saw, and there was no mistaking the fact that her girl parts were perking up.

He gave her a quizzical look. "What?"

"Nothing." She turned away, her face hot.

"Any return call from Jacob's father?" Lance asked.

"Let me check. He's an attorney, so it wouldn't surprise me if he makes us wait a bit just to show he can." Morgan pulled out her phone. "That's what I would do. There's always some game-play involved with lawyers. But he knows we'll just get a subpoena, so in the end, he'll cooperate."

"That's annoying."

"That's the legal system." Morgan opened her email account. "I'm surprised. Jacob's father returned my email already. He wants to meet."

"Where?"

"Let me call him." Morgan made the call and got an immediate response. A minute later, she ended her call and lowered the phone. "He says we can drop by the house now."

"Maybe he isn't a game player."

Morgan shook her head. "He's a lawyer. He's playing an angle. I just don't know what it is, which makes me uncomfortable."

"It's sad that our legal system is a game," Lance said.

"Isn't it?" Morgan said. "I've spent most of my career trying to figure out the other side's ulterior motive."

"Doesn't that get old?"

"Faster than you can imagine," Morgan agreed.

"Then why do you do it?"

"Today, I'm doing what I do for Nick," Morgan said. "I just know in my heart that he's innocent. That's never happened before in my career. I've always been convinced that the people I've prosecuted were guilty. But this time is different in every way."

"Then we won't stop until we solve the case. Where to next?" Lance stopped at an intersection, and Morgan gave him the address of the Emerson residence.

"That's in your neighborhood. Do you know the Emersons?"

"No. My grandfather knows both the Emersons

and the Palmers in passing but not well. Grandpa isn't a social butterfly." And since she'd moved back to Scarlet Falls, Morgan had avoided people as much as possible.

"Does he have an opinion on Jacob Emerson?" Lanced asked.

"Grandpa has an opinion on everything," Morgan said. "But he's probably had more contact with the parents than their teenage son. The only reason Grandpa knows Tessa and Nick is because they both were in our house regularly."

As Lance turned down the Emersons' street, a BMW parked in the driveway. A young blond man climbed out of the car and disappeared into the house.

"That looked like Jacob," Morgan said.

"I wonder where he was." Lance parked the Jeep at the curb in front of the Emersons' house. "What's our approach?"

She gathered her tote and thoughts. "I'll ask questions and take notes. I want you to watch them both. Facial expressions. Body language. Just like it was with Kevin Murdoch, their words will only be part of the story."

They walked up the driveway and rang the bell. A maid in a gray uniform admitted them. Built of cedar and glass, the house sat on high ground with a stunning view of the river. Morgan had thought her grandfather's view was prime, but it didn't compare to this one. The maid led them to the back deck, where Mr. Emerson and his son sat at a round table.

Seventeen-year-old Jacob was blond and athletic. Sitting next to his father, he had none of the arrogance he'd displayed in the fight video. He wore a blue polo shirt, dark jeans with no holes, and boat shoes. Forty-eight-year-old Phillip Emerson, in gray slacks and a white shirt, looked as if he'd just walked off the golf course. His blond-and-silver hair was cut short. They both stood as Lance and Morgan stepped outside. The maid moved aside as introductions and handshakes commenced.

"Would you like an iced tea?" Mr. Emerson asked.

"Yes. Thank you." Morgan accepted, hoping the polite and social feel of the meeting would spill over into cooperation.

The maid disappeared. Morgan and Lance took seats at the table. The maid returned in a minute and set a glass in front of each of them.

"First of all, I'd like to thank you for your cooperation," Morgan said.

Mr. Emerson flashed a cold smile. "We both know you can subpoena my son. While we can be civilized about the situation, let's not pretend it's anything other than a legal requirement. My son has already told the police what he knows. You've no doubt already read his statement.

He'll answer all your questions as required by law, but nothing more."

"We appreciate your candor," Morgan returned. She opened her tote and pulled out a notebook, where she'd jotted down a list of questions. She'd let the interview guide itself, but there were specific points where she wanted to compare today's answers to Jacob's original statement.

Mr. Emerson leaned his tanned forearms on the edge of the table. "I'm also well aware that this is a fishing expedition. You'll grab hold of anything that might cast doubt on your client's innocence. I won't let my son be Nick's Hail Mary pass. So please keep your questions on point."

Morgan nodded. So much for cooperation. What had she expected? If she proved Nick innocent, someone else had to be guilty. Mr. Emerson was well aware that his son, as Tessa's ex-boyfriend, would be high up on the list of alternative suspects.

"Jacob," she began. "You attended the lake party last Thursday night?"

"Yes, ma'am." Jacob folded his hands in his lap.

"What time did you arrive?" she asked.

"I don't know exactly. I wasn't checking the time." His words were careful.

"Can you give me your best estimate?" she asked.

"Shortly before nine o'clock," Jacob said.

"Were you the first one at the party?"

He shook his head. "No."

"Who was already there?"

"I don't remember." He didn't break eye contact, but there was a slight twist to his mouth and a gleam in his eye that felt . . . mocking.

As if he was lying.

And he was good at it.

She moved on. "When did Nick and Tessa arrive?"

"I wasn't watching the clock so I can't give you the time."

Morgan tried to pin him down. "Before or after you got there?"

"After," he said.

Morgan made a note. She set down her pen and gave him her full attention. "Can you tell me what happened between you and Nick?"

"Nick and Tessa arrived at the lake. I said hello to her. She said hi back. Nick jumped between us and told me to stay away from her. He shoved me. I shoved back. We exchanged a few punches. It was over quickly. Nick and Tessa left. I stayed for another hour or so, and then went home." Jacob recited this part without inflection, as if he'd memorized it.

"Were either of you injured in the fight?" she asked.

Jacob gave his head a slight shake. "I wasn't."

"What about Nick?"

"It was dark. I couldn't see," Jacob said.

Morgan changed her tactic, trying to elicit an emotional response. "Why do you think Nick got angry when you greeted Tessa?"

Mr. Emerson broke in. "There's no way for my son to know what the other boy was thinking."

"You're right. I'm sorry. I'm just trying to understand what happened." Morgan nodded. "Jacob, did you consume alcohol at the party?"

Jacob's gaze dropped to the table. Real shame or fake? "I had a couple of beers."

"Do you think your judgment was impaired?" Morgan asked.

Mr. Emerson leaned forward. "Please be specific, Ms. Dane. Exactly what do you mean by impaired?"

"Did you fight with Nick because you were drunk?" Morgan asked.

"I fought with Nick because he attacked me." Jacob's enunciation sharpened with irritation. Finally, a reaction.

"And all you said to Tessa was *hello?*" Morgan pressed.

But Mr. Emerson butted in. "Already stated."

Jacob's expression shuttered, his father's interruption giving him time to smooth the annoyance from his face.

Morgan returned to her list. "What did Tessa and Nick do next?"

"They left." Jacob's voice had returned to its monotone.

"Did they drive or walk?" she asked.

He answered without moving. "They drove."

"His car or hers?"

"His." For a guy who said he wasn't interested in Tessa, Jacob had been watching her every move.

"Tell me how the rest of the night played out." Morgan set down her pen and watched him.

"I stayed at the party for a while, then I went home." Jacob was going to make her drag every answer from him.

"Did you see Nick and Tessa again that night?"

"Yes. They came back to the party later," Jacob answered. "They argued."

"Did Nick leave before Tessa?"

"I don't know. I wasn't paying attention." Jacob returned to his fallback position.

Morgan pretended to check her notes. "Tell me about your relationship with Tessa."

Jacob shrugged. "We didn't have a relationship. We dated a couple of times last spring, but we weren't into each other. I've known her for years. My relationship with Tessa was more brother-sister."

Mr. Emerson's smile was sad. "My wife and Tessa's grandmother thought they would make a handsome couple."

238

"So you hadn't spent much time with Tessa in the past few months?" Morgan clarified.

Jacob shrugged. "Not really."

Morgan closed her notebook. "That's all the questions I have for you right now, Jacob, unless there's anything else you want to tell me?"

He shook his head.

"Then thank you both for making time to see us this afternoon." Morgan rose and offered them both her hand. Lance, Mr. Emerson, and Jacob stood when she did.

The maid showed them out. Morgan waited until they were in the car. "Well?"

Lance started the Jeep and pulled away from the curb. "I don't trust that kid. I didn't feel sincerity coming from him. How did his answers match up to his police interview?"

"This is from Jacob's police statement." She cleared her throat and read. "Nick and Tessa arrived at the lake. I said hello to her. She said hi back. Nick jumped between us and told me to stay away from her. He shoved me. I shoved back. We exchanged a few punches. It was over quickly. Nick and Tessa left. I stayed for another hour or so, and then went home."

"That sounds like what he said today."

"It is exactly the same statement. Word for word."

"So? His dad is a lawyer. Of course he coached him."

"You're right. I should have expected it." Morgan stuffed the notebook into her bag. "Do you still have the video of the fight on your phone?"

"Yes." He handed it to her and gave her his passcode.

"When I interviewed Nick, he said that he punched Jacob because Jacob knocked Tessa down when she tried to break up the fight." Morgan pulled up the video and played it. She watched the scene play out exactly the way Nick described. "Jacob conveniently left that out of his version."

"He has a very selective memory."

"You picked up on that too?"

"Yes." Lance drummed his fingertips on the steering wheel. "He remembered everything that made Nick look guilty."

"Omitting something from his statement isn't the same as lying. Mr. Emerson provided Jacob with an alibi, and his phone records back that up, which is why I didn't bother asking him about it. There goes our opportunity. We have no motive."

"Jealousy?" Lance suggested.

"We have no evidence that Jacob wanted Tessa for himself."

"So where to next?" Lance asked.

She checked her messages. "I still haven't heard from Felicity." Since she already had a connection with Felicity, Morgan had called the girl directly. She consulted her notes. "That puts Robby Barone on the top of our to-question list."

Lance frowned. "The Barone place gave me the willies. Maybe I should go there alone or take Sharp."

"Or perhaps *I* should go there alone. Mrs. Barone might be more willing to talk to another woman."

"No."

Morgan shifted her attention from her notes to Lance's profile. "Excuse me?"

Lance pulled over to the shoulder. "I'm sorry. I didn't mean for that to come out so authoritatively."

"I should hope not," Morgan said dryly. "You know I have plenty of experience with criminal investigations? I take care, but I also do my job."

Lance turned his shoulders to face her. "I already stopped there to talk to Robby Barone once and got a very bad feeling about the place."

"What kind of bad feeling?"

"Like both Robby and Mrs. Barone were afraid that the mister would come home while I was there."

"Maybe they're scared of him," she said.

"And afraid of him discovering them talking to me."

Morgan considered the options. "If she was nervous because her husband is the jealous type, then a visit with another female is less likely to cause friction." Morgan mentally reviewed the police interview reports. Robby had been briefly questioned at the bowling alley. Horner had never brought him down to the station for a more formal interview. Clearly, the police didn't think Robby had anything exciting to add to the statements they'd already taken.

"We'll go together." Lance pulled back onto the road. "Can you text Sharp and let him know where we're going? If we never come back, at least he'll know where to look for our bodies."

CHAPTER TWENTY-THREE

Lance drove toward the Barone place. He still didn't like taking Morgan there, but he was going to have to put a leash on his inner guard dog. She'd been a prosecutor for six years. She knew her business, and the Barones wouldn't be the first hostile witnesses she'd interviewed.

"What do we have in background information on the Barones?" he asked.

Morgan took a file from her giant bag, flipped through some pages, and began to read. "I'll summarize. No one at the Barone house has a criminal record. Robby, or Robert William Barone, is the second of six kids. He turned sixteen four months ago. His license was issued on his birthday. He has one older sister and four younger ones. The oldest is eighteen. The youngest is eight."

"Six kids in ten years?"

"My kids are two years apart," Morgan said.

"But you don't have six of them," Lance pointed out.

"We talked about having another."

"Did you?" Why was he surprised? She was only thirty-three, and she clearly enjoyed her kids. So did he, come to think of it, which was a far scarier revelation.

Morgan turned a page. "Ivy Melissa Barone, age thirty-six, has no record of employment. This is interesting. Ivy doesn't have a New York State driver's license."

"Medical condition?" Lance hadn't noticed any obvious impairment when he'd spoken to her.

"She had six kids so she can't be too frail. Pregnancy and childbirth aren't for the weak." Morgan's finger skimmed the paper. "She doesn't appear in many places. Birth certificate, Social Security registration, marriage certificate, the birth certificates of her six children. And that's all the information on her. She owns no vehicles or real estate."

"She doesn't have a job, she doesn't drive, and she lives a good distance from town. Mrs. Barone doesn't get out much."

"The oldest daughter is eighteen. She doesn't have a driver's license either."

"Robby does," Lance said, "though he's only sixteen."

"Yes. And while Robby attends Scarlet Falls High, all five girls are homeschooled." Morgan frowned and a deep-in-thought line creased above the bridge of her nose.

"Homeschooling is getting more and more common."

"It is, but in this situation, it feels more like

Dwayne doesn't like the women to have outside contact."

Lance agreed, and he didn't like the impression he was forming of the family.

Morgan continued. "Dwayne David Barone is fifty. He's worked for Marker Construction for twenty-five years. His position is listed as supervisor. The house is in his name only, as are the cable and utility bills. There's no mortgage. The property operates as a farm and produces a small income. All taxes are current."

"So no red flags about Dwayne Barone?"

"No." Morgan glanced at him. "Except for the lack of information about him. Also, there are no credit cards issued to any of the Barones."

"That's unusual," Lance said. "Mrs. Barone was awfully anxious for me to leave before her husband came home."

"Possible domestic violence?" Morgan suggested.

Lance nodded. "My impression of her was that she was scared."

"There's no record of domestic disturbances or arrests or restraining orders," Morgan said. "But just because no one ever reported a crime doesn't mean one never occurred. Plenty of domestic abuse victims are too intimidated to call the police."

Lance turned into the driveway. Robby's Toyota sat next to the house. A Ford Bronco in remarkable condition for its age was parked in the shade cast by the barn. The hood was up, and a man leaned over the engine. The German shepherds went ballistic, and the man straightened and stepped away from the vehicle.

That can't be Robby's father.

Lance estimated him at six-six and two hundred forty pounds. Dwayne's middle name should have been "The Rock" instead of David. He took a few steps away from his vehicle, his posture relaxed but ready, his stance almost military-like.

"There's no record of Dwayne serving in the military?" Lance navigated around a rut in the gravel lane.

Morgan checked. "No."

Lance stopped the Jeep next to the Bronco and got out of the vehicle.

"Hello," he said.

"Can I help you with something?" Dwayne held a torque wrench in one hand. Grease stained his gray coveralls, and his shaved head gleamed. He set his wrench in the toolbox at his feet, took a bandana from the back pocket of his coveralls, and wiped his hands. Despite the sweat, Mr. Barone was a cool customer.

"Yes." Lance took a business card from his pocket while Morgan made the introductions.

"I'm representing Nick Zabrowski," she said.

Dwayne shook their hands. "What can I do for you?"

"I'd like to ask your son, Robby, a few questions," Morgan said.

Dwayne's eyes narrowed in suspicion. "Why?"

"I'm interviewing all of the kids that attended the lake party on Thursday night." Morgan smiled.

"He already spoke to the police." Dwayne shifted his weight onto his heels and crossed thick arms over his chest.

"Yes." She nodded. "We know. But I need to question everyone involved in the case in order to prove Nick is innocent."

"The police seem to think he's guilty," Dwayne said.

Did Lance hear a slight echo of distrust when Dwayne uttered the word *police?*

Morgan nodded. "They've made a mistake."

Lance played his card. "It doesn't seem to concern them that they might have the wrong man."

Dwayne didn't bite on the comment, but a flicker of irritation accompanied his almost imperceptible nod.

"Is Robby here?" Morgan's gaze drifted to the house.

"He is. I suppose if I don't let you talk to him, you'll get a subpoena?" Another interesting fact about Dwayne Barone: he knew a thing or two about the law.

"Yes. I wouldn't have a choice. It's my job to give Nick the best possible defense." What

Morgan didn't say is that she'd probably depose Robby if he had anything relevant to say today.

"I'll get him. Wait here." Dwayne's request was clearly an order. He stalked away and went into the house.

"I guess we're not getting an invite inside," Lance said. He'd really wanted a look at the family dynamics, a chance to poke around their home.

"No. That's clear," Morgan agreed.

Two minutes later, Dwayne returned with Robby in tow. Their relationship could be summed up by the bow of Robby's head and the hunch of his shoulders. Dwayne stood at the boy's side, one enormous hand dwarfing the boy's shoulder. The contact could have been intended as comfort, but Robby seemed cowed.

"Hi, Robby." Morgan introduced herself and Lance. "I'm representing Nick."

"I know who you are," Robby mumbled.

"Mind your manners." Dwayne's fingers tightened, and a brief wince crossed Robby's face before he smoothed it over.

"I need to ask you a few questions," Morgan said.

Robby lifted his eyes. There was no sign of cockiness in them, only defeat and humiliation. "Yes, ma'am."

"When did you arrive at the party?" She began with routine facts to get the interview warmed up. Robby's answer agreed with everyone else's.

"Tell me what happened between Jacob and Nick." Morgan's head tilted. If Dwayne hadn't been there, intimidating the hell out of his son, her gentle voice and demeanor would have encouraged Robby to talk.

But Dwayne *was* there, with his anvil-size hand as a constant reminder of whatever order he'd given his son.

"I don't know." Robby's eyes drifted to his left sneaker.

He knows plenty.

"You saw the video, right?" Morgan prompted. Smart of her not to inform Dwayne that Robby had been the one to show the video to Lance.

"Yeah," Robby admitted. "Jacob and Nick got into it." His voice sharpened when he said *Jacob*.

"But you don't know what started the altercation?" Morgan asked.

"No." Robby shook his head, purposefully avoiding eye contact. "I wasn't close enough to hear."

Liar.

Robby's pants should have burst into flames.

"Did you see Nick and Tessa after the fight?" Morgan asked.

Dwayne's fingers moved, ever so slightly, but Lance didn't miss the boy's very small flinch.

"No." Robby's jaw tightened. Tears moistened his eyes.

Morgan tried a few more questions, but Robby refused to admit knowing anything else, like who had left the party at what time, or who had been the last person to see Tessa alive.

"I can't tell you anything else." The boy's gaze lifted. For a few seconds, his stare burned with anger.

"Thank you, Robby. I really appreciate that you tried." Morgan gave the boy an understanding smile.

Robby's head bobbed once in acknowledgment.

The slap of wood on wood sounded as loud as a gunshot. Everyone turned toward the house. Two slim redheaded girls carried baskets of laundry toward a clothesline. They wore the same type of below-the-knee, shapeless cotton dress that their mother had worn when Lance had first come to the house.

"Get back inside," Dwayne barked at them.

They paused for a split second, their eyes opening wide, and then turned and bolted for the house. A few items of wet clothing fell from the smaller girl's basket.

Morgan shot Dwayne a frown, then quickly lifted the corners of her mouth into a forced and tight smile. "Thank you very much for your cooperation, Mr. Barone."

Dwayne nodded, his eyes hard.

Lance felt Dwayne's eyes on his back all the way back to the Jeep.

He slid behind the wheel, closed the vehicle door, and started the engine. "How old were those girls?"

"About twelve and fourteen." Morgan fastened her seatbelt. "And they're terrified of Dwayne."

"I think everyone that lives in that house is terrified of him." Lance steered the Jeep onto the main road and drove away from the farm, his fingers tight on the wheel. Robby wasn't a Boy Scout, but he didn't deserve his father's treatment.

"Why was it such a big deal for the girls to be outside while we were there?" Morgan asked.

"I don't know, but I think we should find out."

"There's no love lost between father and son." Morgan turned her head to glance at the farm-house through the rear window. "The kids we've seen take after their mother, very small and slim . . ." Her voice trailed off.

"While Dwayne looks like a retired WWE star." Lance finished her thought. "Dwayne has to be disappointed in his son. His only boy is a ninety-eight-pound weakling."

"Dwayne's a bully," Morgan said.

"How old is he again?" Lance asked.

"Fifty."

"And Ivy is thirty-six?"

"Yes."

"How old was she when they married?"

"Oh. She must have been young." Morgan

scrolled on her phone. "She was seventeen when they married, and Dwayne was thirty-one." Morgan looked up.

"What did you think of thirty-one-year-old men when you were seventeen?" Lance asked.

"At seventeen, anyone over the age of twenty-five was gross," Morgan said.

Lance made a right at a stop sign. "Not only did Ivy marry very young, she had her first baby within a year."

"I don't know what to think about that." Morgan tapped a finger on her lower lip. "Or how it might be relevant to Tessa's death. I'd like to know if Tessa knew Dwayne."

"When I spoke with Mrs. Barone, she said that Tessa had been the same age as her oldest daughter."

"I wonder if Tessa ever paid a visit to the farm."

Lance said, "I can't see Dwayne approving playdates, and I definitely think Dwayne has to approve everything that happens on that farm."

"Yes." Morgan frowned. "Those two girls were clearly scared. I don't like it, but I still can't figure out how that might connect to Tessa's murder."

"Me either. I'll get my mom to do some deeper digging into the Barone family. What did you think of the way Robby practically spat out Jacob's name?"

"He doesn't love Jacob, that's for sure," Morgan said.

Lance scrubbed a frustrated hand down his face. "You know this whole investigation would be easier if everyone wasn't lying."

CHAPTER TWENTY-FOUR

As Lance drove away from the Barone farm, Morgan set down her phone. It was four p.m. Where had the day gone? They'd made so little progress. She needed to regroup, to go back to the beginning and look at the crime anew.

"Let's visit the crime scene before it gets dark," she said. "Do you have a camera?"

"In the console." Lance lifted his arm.

Morgan retrieved the camera. Though the police had already photographed the scene, they were viewing the case from an entirely different angle. When she'd worked on homicide cases for the Albany County DA, she'd always visited the crime scenes to make sure she had an in-person perspective. Photos and diagrams weren't enough to visualize how the crime played out. She'd caught more than one criminal in a lie because he'd gotten slight details wrong.

Lance pulled onto the road and made the next left.

Morgan reviewed her notes on the crime scene during the drive out to the lake. Lance turned down the same dirt lane they'd used the night they'd found Tessa's body. He parked short of the clearing.

As she climbed out of the car, Morgan's stomach curled. Every sense—the crunch of dead leaves underfoot, the scents of pine and lake water, the sound of the breeze ruffling the branches overhead—brought back the memory of finding Tessa's body.

In person, she'd seen the girl at night, with the darkness concealing many of the details. But the police and autopsy photos had highlighted every bloodstain, every smudge of dirt, every deep wound and small scratch on Tessa's body. Now, Morgan's mind superimposed those new details onto her memory.

A hard shiver rattled her bones, and Morgan could feel eyes on the center of her back. Was it her imagination? She scanned the surrounding forest. The trees were dense, and even in the broad daylight of late afternoon, the woods provided plenty of shadows.

"Are you all right?" Lance stepped up to her side.

"Yes." Morgan shook off her fear. "Hold on." She opened her tote and took out her pair of emergency flats. After changing her shoes, she left her heels in the Jeep.

"Is there *anything* you don't keep in that bag?" Lance pressed the button on the fob. With a beep, the vehicle's doors locked.

"I like to be prepared." Morgan fell into step beside him.

The overwhelming sense of being watched closed over her again. The hairs lifted on the back of her neck, her instincts practically screaming for her attention. She stopped to survey the woods.

"Are you sure you're all right?" Lance asked.

She lowered her voice. "I feel like we're not alone."

"This place is giving me the creeps too." His gaze followed hers.

"It's probably just knowing what happened here that's making us nervous." She forged ahead. "I could be paranoid. When I was ten, we took a family camping trip to the Catskills. I spotted a couple of deer and wandered away from camp. Before I knew it, I was lost. They didn't find me until morning."

"You spent the night out in the woods alone?"

"Yes." Morgan set off toward the clearing. "I've never had much love for the woods or the dark since."

"And I'm sure finding Tessa's body didn't improve your opinion of either."

They walked up the dirt tract and paused at the edge of the clearing. In the daylight, the spot should have been pretty. But instead of seeing the play of sunlight on coppery foliage, Morgan's eyes focused only on the shadows.

Except for the charred wood in the bonfire pit, the clearing was bare. The forensic team had collected the litter as evidence.

Lance moved closer, and the tension in his body told her he felt it too. As much as she hated to admit it, his presence was the only reason she could stand to be in the clearing.

"I'll start at the clearing, and we'll work our way to the place where we found the body." Lance began to shoot photos.

Morgan took a notepad out of her bag and started drawing a sketch. She studied the clearing and surrounding forest. "Her car was parked over there."

The Accord now sat in the police impound garage. Tessa's purse had been found on the passenger seat.

She added details to her sketch. "Nick said when he left, Tessa was sitting in her car."

Morgan went to the spot where the Honda had been parked. A sense of dread slithered through her belly, leaving it cold and empty, as she envisioned Tessa's last moments. "She's sitting in her car, crying. She sends the text to Felicity, telling her BFF about her breakup with Nick. Then she calls the Emerson house to talk with Jacob."

"But Mr. Emerson answered the call." Lance lowered the camera.

"That's what he says. What if he didn't? What if Jacob answered?"

"What if Tessa told Jacob she was pregnant?" Lance said. "And he drove out to the clearing."

"The police didn't ask for a DNA sample from Jacob. They were focused on Nick from the very beginning. When the police interviewed Jacob, they didn't know Nick wasn't the father of Tessa's baby. They assumed it was Nick. They didn't know they were looking for two different men. Plus, Jacob's father is an attorney. He would never have allowed it. He would have known the implications and demanded a warrant."

"What are the chances of forcing Jacob to submit to DNA testing?" Lance asked.

"Without new evidence? Slim. Mr. Emerson would fight it for sure. Plus, Jacob and Tessa dated five months ago. She was only eight weeks pregnant. There's no basis."

"I watched that fight between Jacob and Nick," Lance said. "Jacob was angry to see Tessa with Nick. Who's to say they didn't have a brief reconciliation over the summer?"

Morgan hated to think of Tessa going out with Nick and cheating on him with Jacob, but Lance's theory was possible. She couldn't let her personal relationship with Tessa or Nick get in the way of her investigation. Tessa *had* cheated on Nick. But with whom?

"We won't get a court order based on a hunch. We'd have to get some evidence that Jacob and

Tessa had had contact . . ." Morgan counted backward. "Mid to end of July."

"Or evidence she was seeing someone else back in July," Lance added.

She made a note in her phone. "I'll need to pick through Tessa's cell phone records from the whole summer."

The police had focused on the last few weeks of Tessa's life. Even after learning of her pregnancy, Horner hadn't done much to look for the father of Tessa's baby.

Lance frowned at the lake. "So everyone else leaves. Tessa is alone in her car. Why would she get out of her car?"

"I can think of a couple of reasons." Turning in a circle, Morgan scanned the forest. "She was mad at her grandparents. She didn't want to go home. She took a walk to clear her head."

"Or someone arrived."

"Someone she knew. Jacob, if we're thinking he was the father of her baby and that Mr. Emerson lied about handling the call, and that she actually talked to Jacob." Morgan wouldn't have gotten out of the car alone in the dark, but she wasn't a frightened, pregnant teenager.

"Would he really have to kill her if he'd knocked her up? His family has plenty of money. This isn't 1950."

"In some ways, social pressure hasn't changed as much as you might think. I'm sure Tessa was feeling pretty desperate. She hadn't even graduated high school. Her grandparents are old-fashioned. The stigma of being a teen mom would alienate her from everyone." Morgan thought of the girls who had gotten pregnant back in her high school days. They'd all dropped out of school, unable to handle being ostracized.

"It was early enough for her to get an abortion, or she could have given the child up for adoption," Lance said.

"True. But I'm sure she was still panicked about the pregnancy." Morgan's heart ached when she thought about Tessa going through her personal crisis alone. Her grandmother was too out of touch to be a confidant.

"Could she have threatened the father?" Lance said.

"If a paternity test proved Jacob was the father, how would that have affected his plans for law school?"

"Doesn't seem like enough motivation to kill her," Lance said. "Legally, the most Jacob could have been forced to provide is financial support. No one could force him to raise the child. His family could afford to pay Tessa."

"That's how you and I would approach a critical decision, but we're talking about two teenagers. Tessa clearly engaged in risky behavior."

"Like unprotected sex," Lance said. "She was sleeping with Nick and at least one other boy."

"Exactly. Plus, they all admitted to drinking beer. Jacob said he drank a couple of beers. Maybe it was much more," Morgan added.

"That all said, we don't know for sure that Tessa was killed because she was pregnant. We have no evidence that she told anyone." Lance took a few shots of the opposite side of the clearing. "The police have held that piece of information back from the press. No one has mentioned it, not even the Emersons."

"If she told the father and he killed her because of it, it's not knowledge he would admit to having." Morgan walked across the clearing to the entrance of the game trail. "She got out of her car. They argued. She ran, and he chased her."

What had it been like for Tessa that night? Alone in the dark.

Lance snapped a few pictures of the area where the Honda had been parked. Then he followed Morgan down the game trail to the edge of the lake. Trampled cattails and torn pieces of crime scene tape marked the location where Tessa's body had been found.

Other than the limp, dirty yellow tape, the only other sign that a young woman had been killed there was a small memorial of teddy bears, notes, and flowers at the water's edge.

A chill swept over Morgan as she stared at the patch of thick reeds that Tessa had lain in. Standing in the safety of daylight and Lance's company, she could barely restrain the urge to run. "The mud here is too wet for footprints. Any imprints would have filled in."

"The police didn't find any on the bank either. Too much sand in the soil, and there were so many tire tracks and footprints at the clearing."

"The police had no way of knowing who came before or after the party."

"Why did she run in this direction?" Mud sucked at Morgan's shoes as she picked her way toward the water and the broken path of reeds that had led to Tessa's body. "On the other side, there's a path that leads to the public parking lot, the gazebo, and picnic tables."

Lance followed her. "There wouldn't have been anyone there at that time of night to help her. She was running blind, terrified out of her mind."

But Tessa had barely made it out of the clearing. Morgan stared at the lake, aware in every fiber of her body that a young girl had been brutally murdered on that very spot of marsh. Tessa's blood had leaked from her body and soaked into the mud. Had she been awake? Had she known she was dying?

Alone in the dark.

They were quiet for a few minutes. A breeze rushed through the reeds, their heavy heads swaying.

The snap of a twig made them both jump. Lance spun toward the sound. He wrapped one thick arm around Morgan, sweeping her behind him.

"What is it?" The hairs on the back of Morgan's neck lifted as she peered around his body and whispered, "A deer?"

"I don't think so." Lance's gaze swept the trees as he and Morgan backed toward the game trail. "Someone is out here."

CHAPTER TWENTY-FIVE

Lance's hand automatically went to the Glock at his hip.

The sound had come from deeper in the woods.

"Let's go back to the Jeep." He steered Morgan down the path toward the clearing, keeping his body between her and the origin of the noise.

He should have listened to his instincts when they'd first gotten out of the car. But he'd thought they were both spooked by the scene itself.

Oh hell, they still could be.

Morgan pointed toward the impromptu shrine. "Looks like plenty of other people have been here. It's probably just someone who wants to pay his respects. Or satisfy his curiosity."

"I'm sure you're right," Lance said. Was their visitor Jamie Lewis? She'd been at the party, and no one seemed to know how she'd gotten there. Could she be hiding out here in the woods?

"Should we call the police?" Morgan asked as they stepped back into the clearing. Out of the underbrush, they turned and headed for the grass and dirt tract where they'd left the Jeep.

"And say what? We heard a twig snap while we were out in the woods?" Lance put Morgan in front of him and glanced over his shoulder. He couldn't see anyone, but damn, he could feel eyes on him.

"Good point," Morgan said. "But we need to know who's been hanging around the crime scene."

"You're right." He led the way back to the Jeep. "Let's allow whoever was here to think we left. Maybe they'll come out of hiding."

They returned to the Jeep. Lance turned the vehicle around and drove back toward the main road. When the tires rolled onto the pavement, Lance headed for the public recreation area on the shores of the lake. He parked in the gravel lot. A small beach and the lake lay in front of them. To one side, the gazebo and narrow dock stretched out onto the water. On the other side of the beach, picnic tables clustered under the trees. He removed his binoculars from the console.

"Should we try to sneak up on whoever is out there?" she asked.

"Yes." He handed the binoculars to Morgan. "First, let's watch the woods and see if our exit flushed anyone out of their hiding spot."

They watched and waited. Lance scanned the trees with his camera. Morgan used the binoculars. After fifteen minutes, nothing had moved that was larger than a squirrel. Lance set down the camera. "I don't see anyone. Maybe there wasn't anyone there. Can we be that paranoid?"

"I know I can." Still carrying the binoculars, Morgan opened her car door. "Let's get a look at the clearing from this approach."

They got out of the vehicle and walked to the beach. They passed the picnic tables and gazebo. The beach was a man-made sandy spot a hundred feet wide. At the end of it, the shoreline reverted to dirt, weeds, and cattails, then gradually eased back into forest.

"There's the trail," Morgan said in a low voice, pointing.

A rough footpath led through the trees. Lance kept a sharp eye out, but saw no one as they walked through the woods to the clearing.

"That was much closer than I remembered." Morgan paused at the edge.

"Teenagers never use the public area. It's safer to use the dirt lane and park in the woods. The police have to go out of their way to see them."

"Some things never change," Morgan said as they turned back. At the beach, she raised the binoculars to her face again, sweeping the shore-line. She pointed to the woods on the opposite side. "Do you see something black and shiny?"

Lance followed her gesture and spotted another opening in the trees. "Yes."

"How do we get over there?"

"I'm sure there are game trails all around the lake."

Morgan started forward. "The police focused on the clearing and the wooded area immediately around it. I saw no statements or pictures from the other side of the lake."

"No reason to. The body was located. The scene secured."

"A suspect identified almost immediately," Morgan added.

They found a path that meandered along the bank. Twenty minutes later, they stood on the opposite bank, staring at a makeshift camp. A black two-man tent had been pitched in a stand of pines. Ashes filled a stone-rimmed circle. A tiny plume of smoke drifted from the center, as if the pit had recently housed a fire. Lance glanced inside the tent. A sleeping bag, cooler, and battery-operated lamp made a cozy space. Next to the sleeping bag, a small shovel, a backpack, and a box occupied the corner.

"Someone's been camping," Morgan said. "Can you see what's in the pack?"

Lance gently lifted the flap. Inside the bag, he saw a pair of jeans, several sweatshirts, and a winter coat. "Clothes."

"Female or male?"

"Hard to say." Lance shifted the pack to see more of the items. The clothes looked large, but Jamie Lewis was tall and most photographs he'd seen of her showed her dressing grungy. "There're also matches, nylon rope."

"Let me see. Maybe I can recognize the brands." Morgan leaned over the bag.

A shot rang out through the woods. Lance dove on top of Morgan, pulling her to the ground and covering her with his body. His heart went into a full sprint, his pulse echoing in his ears, blocking out sound like the bass line at a rock concert.

"Did someone shoot at us?" she asked from under him, her voice filled with disbelief. "Or was that a firecracker?"

"Gunshot." Lance would never confuse the sound of a gunshot with anything else. Pulling his handgun, he scanned the little camp but saw no one to shoot back at. A tent didn't provide much cover. He spotted a fallen tree. "Can you belly crawl?"

"Yes."

Lance nudged her toward the moss-covered log. "Get behind that."

The half-rotted log provided inadequate cover but hiding behind it was better than being completely exposed. Morgan wiggled her skirt higher up her thighs and snaked forward in an impressive army crawl.

The telltale clack of a bolt-action rifle made the hair on Lance's neck stand straight up. Another shot pinged into a tree ten feet to his left. Morgan moved faster. More concerned about her than himself, Lance kept his bigger body between her and the origin of the shots as he followed her. In two minutes, he had her wedged between the log and his body. He dug his cell phone out of his pocket, called 911, and reported shots fired.

He ended the call and whispered in Morgan's ear, "Police won't be here for at least ten minutes. Then they have to find us in the middle of the woods."

"And who knows how the shooter will respond to their arrival." She lifted her head an inch off the ground. "We should move."

If the shooter decided to circle around and come at them from the rear, they were sitting ducks. Footsteps crunched in leaves. The sound grew louder, as if the shooter was approaching.

"Move." Lance pushed her forward.

Morgan crawled. When they'd reached the safety of a large oak tree, they got to their feet behind the massive trunk. Lance glanced around the trunk. Another shot zipped into a neighboring tree. Bark chips flew through the air.

"He's following our movements," Morgan said, her back pressed to the trunk. "Why isn't he hitting us?"

"Either he isn't a great marksman or he doesn't want to hit us." Lance bet on the latter. Each shot seemed to be the same distance away.

"Why are you shooting at us?" Lance yelled.

"Get away from my camp!" a male voice shouted.

"We just want to talk to you," Lance answered,

trying to pinpoint the location of the shooter.

Clack clack. Another bullet hit the neighboring tree almost exactly in the same place as the previous shot. The shooter was putting his bullets in precise locations.

Was he trying to drive them away or pin them down?

"You're thieves!" the man yelled. "You're here for my valuables."

Valuables?

"Let me try," Morgan mouthed. She cleared her throat then called out, "If you stop shooting at us, we'll leave. We stumbled on your camp by accident. We mean you no harm."

"Leave me alone," the voice shifted from angry to sad.

Morgan frowned. "We understand, and we're sorry we disturbed you."

A few seconds of eerie silence followed, then the heart-wrenching sound of sobbing.

"We're unarmed, and we don't want to take your things," Morgan said, her voice sympathetic and calm.

But the shooter's cries were anything but stable. "She's dead. She's dead. Dead, dead, dead."

Lance and Morgan shared an *uh-oh* glance. Whatever slim grasp their gun-toting camper had on reality, he was losing it.

"Keep talking," Lance whispered. "I'll try to get behind him while you distract him."

Morgan nodded, raising her voice to ask, "Who's dead?"

"The girl. So pretty. So young. No one can help her now." The voice rose with anger.

"Did you see who killed her?" Morgan asked.

"So much blood." The sobbing ceased, the voice shifting to a disturbing singsong. "Everywhere."

Carefully placing each foot on solid, debris-free dirt, Lance kept his footsteps silent. He slipped behind another tree, then another. With painstaking steps, he worked his way through the trees.

"I'd like to talk to you," Morgan said. "Would that be all right?"

"No. No talking." The shooter howled. "Just leave me alone. I want to be alone. I can't hurt anyone if I'm alone."

Lance eased around the trunk of a tree and got his first glimpse of the shooter. A man dressed in desert camos sat with his back to a tree. A bolt-action hunting rifle rested across his thighs. He'd streaked his face with dirt as camouflage. His eyes looked wild and white against the dirt. The circles under his eyes were so dark and deep, he could have been a cadaver. Underneath the dirt, his cheekbones stood in sharp relief to his skeletal face.

He wiped a hand across his face, his expression a heartbreaking combination of confusion and devastation. Tears left clean rivulets from his eyes to his jaw.

"I'm sorry," Morgan called. "If you promise not to shoot, we'll leave now, and we won't bother you again."

"Go!" he screamed, and then he began to beat his head against the tree trunk at his back.

The thin sound of a siren floated through the air. Damn it! Why hadn't they come in quietly? Morgan might have talked the man down. There was no chance of that happening now.

The siren shut off, but it was too late. Fear lit the shooter's eyes. He jumped to his feet, fumbled in his panic, and dropped his rifle. He scrambled toward it. Lance took the split-second opportunity to holster his gun and dive for the man's midsection. They went down in a tangle of limbs and rolled across the ground. Lance kicked the rifle away.

Expecting a feral response, he was shocked when the shooter shifted into hand-to-hand mode. The shooter performed an instinctual, textbook sweep, tossing Lance off his body. Lance landed on his back. A forearm to his throat pinned him to the ground.

Lance wheezed. Stars peppered his vision. Bucking to upset the shooter's balance, Lance grabbed the forearm with both hands. Trapping the man's foot, he bridged over his shoulder and reversed their positions.

The shooter was malnourished and shaky. Once his initial burst of adrenaline waned, his efforts weakened, and he was reduced to kicking and bucking under Lance's body. His eyes took on a desperate light. Panic and bewilderment shone in his dilated pupils. The man obviously suffered from some mental illness.

But crazy was dangerous. Despite his pity, Lance needed the man immobilized to ensure Morgan's safety.

"Freeze!" Morgan shouted. "Or I'll shoot."

Lance did. So did the shooter.

Less than ten feet away, Morgan held the rifle in a comfortable grip. She pointed it at the shooter. "Don't even think about moving. I'm an excellent shot."

Lance flipped the shooter onto his belly, brought both of his arms to the small of his back, and pinned him with a knee. "Do you see something to restrain him?"

"Do you have him?"

"I do."

"Here." Morgan stooped, fished in the shooter's backpack, and came out with a piece of nylon rope.

Lance fastened the shooter's wrists together, and then rolled him over and hauled him into a sitting position. Agitated, he immediately began to rock back and forth. He refused to make eye contact, staring at his boots instead.

Sirens blared louder. Car doors opened and shut.

"In here," Lance shouted. "We have the situation contained."

Bodies crashed through the brush. Carl Ripton and another uniform burst from the trees, weapons drawn. Lance didn't recognize the second officer. New hire?

"Lower the rifle, ma'am. Both of you put your hands on your head. Interlace your fingers," Cop Two ordered, pointing his handgun at Morgan.

She complied, and Carl took the weapon.

"On your knees!" Cop Two yelled at Lance.

"I know them," Carl said. "You can stand down." He turned to Lance. "What happened?"

Lance explained as he maintained his grip on the now-limp man on the ground. "He's been saying odd things about a dead girl and blood. That little camp over there is his."

"Let's put him in the back of the car." Carl pointed at his companion.

"He needs a bath." Cop Two grimaced as he handcuffed the shooter and hauled him to his feet.

He held the man still while Carl patted him down. He emptied Camo Man's pockets, tossing a folding knife, some loose change, and a wallet to the ground. Carl opened the wallet and skimmed through it. "His name is Dean Voss." Carl turned to the man. "Dean? Want to tell me why you were shooting at these people?"

"The girl is dead, and it's all my fault." Dean stared at his boots. "They're coming to get me."

"Who is coming to get you?" Carl asked in a gentle voice.

Dean lifted his gaze. The eyes that swept over them were opened wide with terror. "You can't lock me up. They'll find me. They'll kill me. I have to run. I have to hide."

"It's all right. We won't let anyone get you," Carl said.

But Dean wasn't convinced. He turned and tried to pull away from the uniform. Carl took his opposite arm. Dean went ballistic, but his bound arms and weakened condition didn't allow for much opposition. Carl and Cop Two held him steady until he stopped struggling and stood still, shaky, limp, and pathetic.

"Let's get him out of here." Carl accompanied the second cop and Dean back to the road. He returned in a few minutes. "He's on his way to the holding cell, but I expect he'll be transferred to a psychiatric facility. Doesn't take an expert to see that he's unstable."

"Who's the new guy?" Lance asked.

"Rookie." Carl nodded. "This is his third day. He's very enthusiastic. Sorry about him blasting his siren."

"I remember those days," Lance said. "We were all that enthusiastic at the start."

Lance and Morgan gave Carl their statements, making sure to highlight Dean's outbursts about the dead girl and blood.

Morgan brushed dirt and dead leaves from her skirt. Dirt and sweat stained her blouse. Her face was pale and her voice shaky. Scratches crisscrossed her calves.

Carl nodded. "I'll call for a forensics team to go through his camp. Brody is on his way. He wants to talk to both of you."

"Thank you," she said.

Morgan and Lance stepped aside while Carl secured the scene. Morgan took her own pictures. Not that she didn't trust the police, but . . . they were so sure they'd already caught the killer, she wanted to be sure no new evidence got "lost."

Brody arrived before the forensics van. He gave the camp a thorough once-over before joining Morgan and Lance. Lance recapped what had happened.

Brody snapped shut his notebook. "I'll let you know if I have any further questions."

"Dean Voss is clearly connected to the Palmer murder," Morgan said.

Brody offered a brief, noncommittal nod. "I'm going to attempt to interview Dean now, but from what you and Carl have said, he's likely too unstable to give a rational statement. In that case, we'll have to wait for a psychiatric evaluation, and we'll see what the forensic team turns up."

"Can we go?" Lance asked.

"Yes," Brody said.

"You'll call us if you find anything relevant to the Palmer case?" Lance asked.

"I'll pass your request on to Chief Horner." With a frown, Brody turned and left.

What the hell did that mean?

Carl was marking off the camp with crime scene tape. He directed Lance and Morgan to the outside of the perimeter.

This is what happens when you change sides. Lance was no longer one of them. And now that he'd joined Morgan, he was likely shut out of the loop forever.

But if he'd denied her request, she would have come to the scene alone. She could have been killed.

Morgan and Lance made their way back to the beach. The dropping sun hovered over the tops of the trees and cast golden light on the lake. Lance checked the time on his phone. Six-thirty. "Half hour until sundown. Maybe we should call it a day. You can clean up at the office before you head home." He eyed the scrapes on her legs.

"Good idea." She brushed at a streak of dirt on her calf.

"Are you all right?" he asked Morgan.

"Yes. I'm afraid I'm not feeling much in the way of trust in the SFPD right now."

"Chief Horner is a pain, but Brody is a good cop. You can count on him."

"I hope so." She plucked a pine needle from her skirt.

"I'm going to call my mom and add Dean to her list of background checks. I'm sure she can dig up plenty of personal information."

Morgan said, "From Dean's ramblings, I'm convinced either he killed Tessa or he saw who did."

CHAPTER TWENTY-SIX

Morgan got out of the Jeep as soon as Lance parked behind her minivan in front of Sharp Investigations. Her scraped leg ached as she detoured to her van and removed a gym bag from the cargo area. The sun had set, and dusk settled over the quiet street. They went up the walk and climbed the steps of the dark duplex.

Lance unlocked the front door. "I didn't know you went to a gym."

"Two months ago, I bought a two-week trial membership. I went twice. The gym bag has been sitting in there since." Morgan followed him into the office.

"Sharp must be out." Lance closed and locked the door behind them.

"You obviously work out regularly." She scanned his muscles on top of muscles.

He shrugged. "My physical therapy regimen is intensive."

"It's helped you recover?"

"Yes. It's also good for releasing endorphins and purging stress."

"That was my intention with the trial membership." She had plenty of excuses about the kids

279

taking up all her time, but in reality, she just hadn't been motivated to exercise.

Or to do much else.

Lance steered her back to the kitchen. He took a first aid kit from the cabinet. "Sit down."

"I can clean my cuts myself," she protested.

"Fine." He set the kit on the table and went to the fridge. Taking out a bottle of water, he put one in front of her, then retreated to the other side of the small room, leaned back against the cabinets, and watched.

Morgan sat down and bent over her knees. Blood and dirt caked the scratches on her legs. She squirted antiseptic onto a gauze pad and began to blot. There was more dirt than blood. A few superficial scrapes on her shins were already scabbing over, but a deeper abrasion on her ankle was bright red and still bleeding. She dabbed at it, wincing at the sting. The gauze caught on something. Several large splinters were stuck in her skin. She must have picked them up from the log Lance had jammed her behind, not that she was complaining. He'd put his body between her and an active shooter.

She'd held her act together during the moment, but now that she was safe, her hands trembled as she replayed the incident in her head. She flexed her fingers to steady them. Shaking the memory away, she focused on her ankle. Once she was home and alone, she could fall apart. She tried to get a better look, but she couldn't get her ankle closer without hiking her skirt up to her hips.

And thinking about doing that . . .

Her gaze flickered to Lance, leaning on the counter, his thick arms crossed over his thicker chest. He was not the sort of man who could blend into the background. His body—and personality—took up too much space. So much that her eyes were drawn to him whenever he was in the same room.

He was so different from John. Her husband had been tall, thin, and dark, with an easygoing personality. Lance was blond, heavily muscled, and intense.

Very intense.

She blinked and looked away.

What was wrong with her? It must be the aftereffect of being shot at. Her emotions were all over the place.

"Is there a pair of tweezers in that box?" she asked.

She wanted to be blood- and dirt-free before she went home so she didn't frighten her girls. They didn't need to know she'd been in danger.

"Let me look." Lance set his water bottle down and crossed the kitchen.

But instead of searching the kit, he sat in the chair next to her and lifted her legs onto his lap, turning her sideways in her seat.

"Oh," she said, surprised. His legs were twice

281

as thick as hers and ten times more solid.

"It's probably easier for me to get these for you." Taking tweezers from the kit, he bent over her legs.

"It's OK. I can get it." A shiver in her voice belied her confident words.

He lifted his head, his gaze catching hers and holding on for a long second. Emotions darkened the blue of his eyes. Anger. Concern.

Heat.

She shivered.

"Just let me help you, all right?" His fingers wrapped around the sensitive skin of her calf. "I'm a little freaked out about us getting shot at today."

"All right." Morgan sat back. She took a drink of cold water and swallowed. "Thank you for what you did."

The tweezers hovered over her ankle. "You're welcome." He plucked a splinter free.

"I'm serious. When I think of what happened." And what *could* have happened. Her eyes burned with unshed tears. "I'm all my girls have left."

His grip on her foot tightened. "I know. That's all I could think about."

So the man who already lost a career and ten months of his life to a bullet wound had been worried about her and her girls. Warmth rose into Morgan's chest.

"I don't know what I would have done if I'd been alone." Her throat clogged.

"You wouldn't have been alone. You would have hired another investigator."

"A stranger wouldn't have been willing to be my human shield. You were. Thank you."

"You're welcome." He cleared his throat, grabbed hold of another splinter, and gently lifted it free. "You handled yourself pretty well out there."

He picked another splinter free while she tried to ignore the heat of his big hands on the sensitive skin of her ankles . . . and the heat building in her belly.

"One more," he said. "It's a big one. Hold tight."

Morgan braced herself as he worked the splinter out. "Ow."

Holding a gauze pad under her foot to catch drips, he poured antiseptic onto her ankle.

Morgan flinched at the bright sting. "That smarts."

Bending his head, Lance blew on the cut for what seemed like a long time.

A really long time.

Finally, he straightened. "Let me put a bandage on that."

He squirted antibiotic cream on the cut and covered it with two large Band-Aids. He turned to her and leaned closer, until their faces were inches apart. God, he smelled good, a little sweat and dirt layered over plain old soap. On her, the combination felt gross, but on him, it ramped up his masculinity until her ovaries practically swooned. Not that they needed any encouragement. He'd already achieved hero status with her hormones.

The pads of his fingers stroked her ankle. When was the last time a man had touched her bare skin? Years ago. So long that the sensation felt brand new.

She was almost sitting in his lap. But he didn't seem like he was in a rush to move, and frankly, a big part of her wanted to crawl all the way into his arms.

"I should get up now," she said.

"Oh. Right." Lance released her ankles.

She lifted her legs from his lap and stood. "Thank you again."

The adrenaline rush from the afternoon had long since faded, leaving exhaustion in its place. She was tired and lonely, and tired of being lonely. And being this close to Lance in such a state could be dangerous. If she didn't leave soon, she was going to embarrass herself, because all she could think about was kissing him.

Actually, kissing wasn't *all* that was on her mind.

He tossed used gauze pads into the trash. "You might want to consider wearing pants when you're not in a courtroom. Or at least when you're traipsing around the woods. Not that I don't like looking at your legs . . ."

"Really?" Was she flirting? She remembered how? Must be like riding a bike, because with him, it felt totally natural.

He lifted an eyebrow. "Really."

Oooooh.

But she was too chicken to follow through on that kiss.

For now.

"I'll just go change my clothes." She slipped out of the kitchen, went into the bathroom, and changed into a pair of yoga pants, a T-shirt, and white sneakers.

He smiled when she came out.

"What?"

"Nothing. You look cute."

"Cute?" Morgan was five nine. "I haven't been called *cute* since I outgrew all the boys in my grade in grammar school."

His grin widened as he closed the distance between them. "You're small compared to me."

He was nearly a head taller and twice as broad.

"This is true. You look like you've been bench-pressing houses."

"Maybe I have." He flexed his bicep.

Her ovaries responded with *yum.*

Annnnnd it was time to go.

"Thank you again for what you did today." She

retreated to her office and gathered some files. She still hadn't made it through all the information from the DA's office. She was determined to read every word on every page by Monday.

He followed her and stood in the doorway. "You're welcome again. What's your plan for tomorrow?"

"I'll be spending the day with my girls. I'll work before they get up and after they go to bed." She had to draw the line between work and family somewhere. One positive of self-employment: she could work from home whenever it suited her. On the downside, she wasn't getting paid.

He nodded. "I have to take my mom to her group session anyway. I'll be busy all morning."

"Monday then." She agreed. "You'll let me know if your mom finds anything juicy?"

He grinned. "I'll call you."

She tucked her files into her bag and lifted the strap over her head and across her shoulders. As she walked out of the office, her hip brushed his in the narrow hallway. He caught her by the arm. His gaze dropped to her lips.

Was he going to kiss her?

Though she had contemplated doing that very thing to him a short while before, the idea sent a shiver of warning through her already damaged heart. Beyond the undeniable physical attraction between them, she really liked this man. Everything from his courage and his kindness to his sense of humor appealed to her.

But tonight, with the combined weight of Tessa's death and Nick's future resting on her shoulders, her feelings for Lance—and the vulnerability they created—were more than she could handle.

When his head dipped lower, she stopped him with a hand in the center of his chest. "It's just too much right now." She wished she could explain more eloquently, but she couldn't summon the words. "We'll talk Monday?"

With that question, the tension between them shifted from sexy to awkward.

With a quick nod, he stepped back. For a second, he looked as if he wanted to say something, but he just followed her out to her van and didn't step away until her door was locked.

Morgan used the drive home to decompress. When she walked into the house, the girls were in the tub.

In his recliner, Grandpa lowered his newspaper and frowned. "What happened to you? You have a leaf in your hair."

She perched on the edge of the couch and relayed the day's events. There was no point in trying to minimize the danger. Grandpa would verify her story with Stella anyway.

"Thank goodness Lance was there."

"Yes," she agreed.

"I still don't like it," Grandpa said.

"Me either. Being a lawyer isn't usually dangerous. This was definitely a strange day." Morgan didn't want the day's distressing events to intrude on her family time. For now, she'd put it aside. She heard the sound of splashing and a little-girl squeal high enough only to be heard by dogs. "I'll go give Gianna a hand with bath time."

"She's great with them, you know."

"I know. I think we're the ones who got lucky when she moved in." Morgan dropped her dirt-streaked suit in the dry-cleaning basket. When she entered the bathroom, Ava and Mia both stood on the mat wrapped in towels. Gianna was helping Sophie climb out of the tub. Morgan hugged the bigger girls and braced herself for Sophie's greeting.

As expected, the child leaped into her arms, naked and wet. She pressed her face into Morgan's shoulder, soaking the T-shirt. "Mommy! I missed you."

Morgan wrapped her in a towel and set her down. "I missed you too. Tell me about your day."

"Grandpa bought me a glitter pen," Sophie began.

Mia vied for attention. "I dressed Snoozer up as a princess."

Ava hung back, unusually quiet as the younger

girls chattered. Morgan pressed her palm to Ava's forehead. Her nose was red, and her skin felt overly warm. She'd definitely caught Sophie's cold.

Gianna sat on the edge of the tub and tossed plastic toys into a mesh basket suction-cupped to the tile backsplash.

"Thanks for helping, Gianna. I can do cleanup," Morgan said.

"I've got it," Gianna said. "Why don't you do story time? They missed you today."

A fresh pang of guilt hit Morgan between the ribs as she picked up Sophie's pajamas from the vanity. "Let's get our pjs on. Want to watch a movie in my bed?"

That night, they broke all the rules, eating cookies in bed and staying up way past bedtime, but it was exactly what Morgan and her three girls needed. After ninety minutes of cuddling with cookies and Disney's *Frozen*, Ava was the only child still awake. Morgan transferred Sophie and Mia to their own beds. Sensing something was up with her oldest, she didn't rush her.

Morgan sat on the edge of her bed and brushed her daughter's hair away from her sad face. "What's wrong, baby?"

Ava twisted the hem of her Little Mermaid nightgown. "What is a rapist?"

Oh no.

She, Grandpa, and Gianna were careful to keep the news off when the girls were around, but it was impossible to isolate her children from the world.

"Where did you hear that word?" Morgan asked.

"Mandy Pinkerton said her mommy said that Nick is a rapist and that he killed Tessa and you're trying to get him out of jail." Ava's words came out rapid-fire fast in one breath.

"A rapist is someone who hurts other people," Morgan simplified. "But I don't believe Nick would hurt anyone."

"Then why is he in jail?" Ava's big brown eyes swam with questions and fear.

"I think the police made a mistake."

"What if they didn't?" Ava echoed Morgan's own fear.

Was it possible that Nick was guilty? That he'd killed Tessa in a fit of rage?

Ava crumpled another handful of her nightie. "What if Nick *is* a bad person, and they let him go? He lives right across the street. He comes in our house all the time. He could hurt us."

Morgan debated assuring Ava that Nick was innocent. At this point, she had more questions than answers about the case. In the end, she opted for the truth.

"I'm going to find out what happened, OK? I would never want a dangerous person to be let out of jail." She kissed her daughter's head. "And I promise to keep you safe."

Nodding, Ava sniffed. "I miss Tessa. Did she really die?"

"Yes." Morgan's heart ached.

"So we'll never see her again," Ava said.

"That's right. I'm sorry." Morgan put her arms around the child. Neither Mia nor Sophie had mentioned Tessa, although Morgan had told them she'd died. But Ava was clearly struggling. Her memories of John were clearer, and so was her grasp of the concept of death.

"Can I sleep with you tonight?"

"Yes." Morgan brushed her teeth and climbed into bed.

Ava took the photo of John from the nightstand and stared at it. "I miss Daddy. If he was here, he'd protect us, and I wouldn't be so scared."

"I miss him too, but you're safe here with Grandpa and me." Morgan leaned back on the pillow.

"Sometimes I forget what he looked like." Ava carefully returned the framed picture to the nightstand.

"We have lots of pictures." Morgan pulled her daughter close. She took a deep whiff of detangling spray and bubblegum-scented soap as Ava snuggled close. Who was comforting whom?

Ava drifted off quickly, but sleep eluded Morgan. It hadn't occurred to her that six-year-olds would be discussing a case of rape and murder. But she should have expected it. Kids had the most acute hearing when adults were discussing forbidden topics.

But it saddened her to think of young children learning about brutal crimes. Her girls should go to bed feeling safe and secure. They shouldn't have to worry about criminals living across the street.

Morgan stared at the ceiling, Ava's words echoing in her mind.

Was it possible that Nick *was* guilty? How would that affect the girls? Eventually they'd find out that a man their mother had welcomed into their house was a killer.

And even scarier, if Nick was innocent. Then someone else had killed Tessa. Which meant that someone in Scarlet Falls was a murderer. And that killer still roamed free.

CHAPTER TWENTY-SEVEN

"How was your Sunday?" Lance asked Morgan as he walked into the war room. By mutual agreement, Lance, Sharp, and Morgan had all used the previous day to catch up on personal commitments, read files, and let Lance's mother get a jump on the research.

Lance had taken his mom to therapy. He'd mowed her lawn, done her shopping, gone through her bills, and filled her medication organizer for the week.

"Quiet. I took the girls to the park and finished reading through the police interviews." Standing behind the table, she set down her bag and a stainless-steel travel mug and draped her jacket across the back of her chair. Easing into the chair, she crossed her legs, the cuff of her navy slacks rising enough to show her shiny black heels. Dark smudges under her eyes told him she'd spent the daylight hours with her children and worked well into the night. "What did you do yesterday?"

"The same." After he'd finished with his mom, Lance had read through files until his eyeballs burned.

Morgan seemed distracted.

"Are you all right?" Lance asked.

"Ava had some issues at school with another little girl telling her that her mommy wanted to free a rapist." Morgan propped an elbow on the table and rested her chin in her palm.

Lance pushed off the doorway. "Seriously? Some parent was talking about rapists with their six-year-old?"

"The child could have simply overheard her parents talking."

"People should be careful what they say around children."

She sighed. "Six seems too young to me to talk about rape and murder. When I took this case, I knew there would be gossip, but I thought some of the community would be on Nick's side. That doesn't seem to be the case."

"The media hasn't helped. The coverage has been distinctly one-sided."

"Neither Mia nor Sophie understand the finality of death, but Ava is starting to get it." Morgan straightened, as if shaking off her mood. "Either way, she really needed my attention yesterday."

"I'm sorry," Lance hesitated. He wanted to be her confidant, but Saturday he'd pushed too hard and she'd backpedaled. He didn't want her to retreat any further. "The girls don't need this on top of their dad's death."

Morgan shrugged. "Only Ava asks about him.

Sophie barely knew him. She was just an infant when she saw him last. John was deployed six months before he died. Mia was only two and a half. Even Ava's memories are limited. He was gone so much that his absence wasn't anything new in the kids' day-to-day lives."

Guilt stabbed him in the gut. Whatever happened between him and Morgan, she had to make the first move. How else could he be sure he wasn't taking advantage of her vulnerability? "Look, Morgan. About Saturday." He lowered his voice. "I'm sorry if I came on too strong. I don't want to do anything to add to your stress. I know you have a lot on your plate with the case and your girls. If I was out of line—"

She got up and walked closer, stopping him with a hand on his forearm. "You weren't. I'm the one who should apologize to you. I know I'm sending you mixed signals. The fact is I am attracted to you, but I don't know when or if I'll be ready to do anything about it. I don't know what I want. I'm sorry. Until this case is over . . ."

"It's probably best if we stick to friendship. I like you. I don't want to ruin what we have." But even as he said it, his brain latched onto *I am attracted to you.*

She smiled. "I like you too."

Well, shit. That didn't help.

"Grief isn't something you can rush or make

happen on cue," he said. "But maybe you should consider therapy."

Morgan frowned. "I've tried. It didn't feel right."

"Mom had to work her way through a few therapists before she found the right one. Personality and style have to be a good fit. I can give you a number."

"I'll think about it." She squeezed his arm. "Thanks for understanding."

He was the one who didn't know what the hell he wanted. Yes, he did. He wanted her. He just couldn't have her.

For instance, right now he was loving her hand on his arm. He wanted to return the touch. He wanted to drag her against him and kiss her senseless. The more they worked together, the closer he felt to her. When the case was over, he'd have to back off until he straightened out his head.

"Did you run across anything interesting yesterday?" he asked.

"Yes. I found a fascinating piece of information buried in one of the police reports." Morgan returned to her chair and removed a stack of files from her tote. "The Palmers told everyone that Tessa's parents died when Tessa was twelve. That isn't entirely true. Tessa's mother died in the car accident, but her father survived. He was responsible. He's currently serving a twenty-three-year sentence in state prison for aggravated vehicular homicide."

"Twenty-three years?" Lance whistled.

"Steep sentence, right?" Morgan tapped a finger on the table. "After Tessa's death Chief Horner interviewed the Palmers personally, and he didn't press them for details. It was mentioned quietly in the background information and never highlighted. Tessa's father has been incarcerated for six years. It was a multi-vehicle crash, his blood alcohol well beyond the legal limit, and he'd previously lost his license for driving while intoxicated. Three people died, and he was found guilty on multiple counts. There were definitely aggravating factors, but he isn't a cold-blooded killer. And he's behind bars, so maybe Horner was right to let it go."

"So why did the Palmers lie?" Lance asked.

"I suppose they didn't want people to know their son was in prison," Morgan said. "Tessa was old enough to understand the details when it happened. I wonder how she felt about pretending her father was dead." She shook her head. "Though I honestly don't see how it could be related to Tessa's case. The Palmers might have told their neighbors a lie, but they were truthful to the police, and it was so long ago."

The front door banged open, and Sharp shouted down the hall, "Anybody home?"

"We're back here," Lance called.

Sharp unzipped his gray hoodie on his way into the room. He carried a cardboard tray containing three cups. "Green tea for everybody."

Lance took a cup. Sharp offered one to Morgan.

She smiled, lifting her cup. "Thanks anyway, but I brought my own."

"That stuff will kill you." Sharp frowned.

"But I'll be awake when I go," she said.

Sharp winked. "I'll convert you yet."

Morgan wrapped both hands around her mug. "I have three kids under the age of seven. You'll pry the coffee from my cold, dead hands."

He laughed. "What did everyone accomplish yesterday?"

Morgan repeated the information about Tessa's father.

"From the beginning, I wasn't happy with the way the case was being handled." Sharp turned to the murder board. "I spent some time last night at The Pub. The boys were there and gossiping like a bunch of old ladies."

In Lance's experience, Sharp's retired and almost-retired cop buddies gossiped more than any women. Many of them were divorced and lonely. It was hard for a marriage to survive twenty-five years on the force. Some cops were closer to their partners than their spouses.

"I agree. I expect more from Brody." Lance pulled out a chair and sat across from Morgan.

Sharp took the seat next to him. "Now I

know why Brody is out of touch with the case."

"Why?" Lance asked.

"Because Horner is hoarding this case like a possessive dog. He won't let Brody do anything." Sharp's eyes brightened. "He and the DA have tied Brody's hands."

"That explains why Brody was so abrupt on Saturday," Lance said. "Sounds like he's as frustrated as we are."

"No doubt," Sharp agreed. "What's on our plate for today?"

Morgan drained her coffee. "I'm talking to Felicity as soon as she gets home from school."

"Lance?" Sharp asked.

"Waiting for a call from my mom about background data on Dean Voss and the deeper digs on the Barones and Kevin Murdoch." His phone buzzed. "And that's her now." He answered the call. "Hi, Mom. Can I put you on speaker? Morgan and Sharp are here."

"Yes," she said.

Lance turned on the speaker and set his phone on the table. "OK. We're all listening."

"I'll email you the full report, but I wanted to give you the highlights," Mom began. "Let's start with Dean Voss. Mr. Voss is a veteran. He served in the army for eight years after college, including three tours in Iraq. He's married, no kids. He was wounded twice. Four years ago, at age 30, he received an honorable discharge.

He got his teaching certificate and took a job teaching history at Scarlet Falls High School. Last year, he resigned in the middle of the year."

"Let me guess," Sharp said. "Inappropriate relations with a student."

"How did you know?" Mom asked.

"Because it just figures," Sharp said in a wry voice.

Lance's mom continued. "There were no charges filed. I had to work to get the details. The girl, Ally Somers, denied it, and apparently there wasn't any physical evidence, just a statement from another student, Kimmie Blake, who claimed to see them kissing. But Voss resigned anyway."

"Is there any connection between Kimmie Blake, Ally Somers, Jamie, and Tessa?" Morgan asked.

"That I don't know," Lance's mom said.

"Even if the accusations were a complete fabrication, there's no coming back from that in teaching." Morgan shook her head. "Do we know if Voss ever had Tessa in one of his classes?"

"I can't legally access student records," his mom answered. "But I did find out that Voss taught American History and World Cultures to sophomores and juniors, so it's very possible."

"Putting that on my list of questions for the Palmers." Morgan made a notation. "I hope they'll talk to me without me having to subpoena them to give a deposition. I don't want to look like a monster. I'll ask Felicity first. She might know who Tessa's teachers were last year."

"She might have more info on Voss as well." Lance nodded. "Kids know everything."

Lance's mom gave them Dean Voss's last known address. "He's only been living there since last May, and his wife filed for divorce two weeks ago."

Could that have sent him over the edge?

"We'll drop by Voss's place and talk to the neighbors today," Lance said. "What else do you have for us, Mom?"

"You asked for more information on the Barone family." She cleared her throat. "This took some digging, but I believe Dwayne Barone is involved with a group called the WSA."

"Well, shit." Sharp got up and began to pace the room.

"What's the WSA?" Morgan looked up from her file.

"The White Survival Alliance," Lance said. Now he *really* didn't want Morgan anywhere near the Barone place. "A local white supremacist group, a quasi-militia. They're preparing for the apocalypse."

Sharp rubbed his bald head. "A few months ago, the SFPD raided a barn behind a member's house. It was full of raw materials for making explosives. It was also booby-trapped.

Thankfully, no one was killed when it blew up."

"Mrs. Kruger?" Morgan leaned over the speaker. "Do you know Dwayne Barone's position in the organization?"

"Please call me Jennifer, and no," Mom said. "I moved from the Deep Web to the Dark. There's very little information about the WSA. They stay off the radar."

Which explained the lack of data on the family. The Deep Web included Internet pages that couldn't be found through search engines. Most of these existed for ordinary reasons: databases, web forums that required registration, or pages behind paywalls. Online bank accounts that required logins and passwords were an example. But the Dark Web went further. Sites on the Dark Web hid their identities and spoofed their locations using an encryption tool. Some sites hid their IP addresses behind multiple layers of encryption.

Lance got up and walked to the window. Talking about the homegrown militia group made him edgy. "The thing about the WSA is that they are very secretive about their roster. They keep their resources spread out. So if any one member is compromised, the rest of the group remain anonymous."

"WSA aside." Morgan tapped her pen on her notebook. "Do we really have reason to believe Robby killed Tessa? Why?"

"Unrequited love?" Sharp suggested. "What if it wasn't Robby? What if Dwayne killed Tessa? The WSA isn't just a white supremacist organization. They have a patriarchal, barefoot-and-pregnant philosophy toward women."

"That explains the way Dwayne treats his wife and daughters, but we still have no link between Dwayne and Tessa. We need to find out if Tessa spent any time at the Barone house."

"Can you keep digging, Mom?" Lance asked.

"Of course." She sounded pleased.

"Without putting yourself in danger." Lance worried about the WSA tracking her online inquiries.

"I know how to hide my tracks." She chuckled. "Don't you worry."

But he would. The WSA was nothing to mess around with.

"One more thing," Lance said to the phone. "Have you turned up anything else on Jamie Lewis's family or her mother's fiancé?"

"No," his mom said. "Nothing unusual on the Lewises or Kevin Murdoch yet. I'll send you the details as soon as I can. Later today or in the morning. I'm waiting on one more source."

"Talk to you later, Mom. Love you."

"I love you too." She ended the call.

Lance picked up his phone. "I was really hoping for some dirt on Kevin."

"Me too." Morgan made more notes in her

303

files. "I suppose there's always the chance that he's just a nervous person or he has some sort of medical condition that causes him to sweat excessively."

Lance shook his head. "Kevin's body language all but screamed pants-on-fire."

"I know. Let's wait until your mom is finished with her report. Then we'll pay Kevin a visit." She finished her paragraph. "Do you want to start with the Barones or Dean Voss today?"

"I guess we can drive by the Barones' first." Hopefully, Dwayne would be at work. The family had set off all Lance's alarms since the first time he'd set foot on the property. The last thing he wanted to do was put Morgan on the WSA's radar. "Then we can drop by Dean Voss's apartment, peek in the windows, and talk to his neighbors. He's safely tucked away in the psych ward, so it seems like a good day for it."

She stood, stretched, and reached for her blazer. "I'm ready."

"See ya, Sharp." Lance headed for the door.

"You kids be careful." Sharp waved them off. "I'm going to work on Jamie Lewis's case for the morning. I plan to talk to Jamie's best friend, Tony, and put some pressure on him. Let me know if you need me."

"Will do." Lance followed Morgan outside. Autumn had hit Scarlet Falls overnight. The air had turned cool, and leaves clogged the gutter.

They climbed into the Jeep.

Morgan set her giant purse at her feet. "I have a legal visit set up with Nick for tomorrow morning. He deserves an update, and I'd like to make sure he's all right. He might have some insight on what we've discovered so far, especially Tessa's pregnancy. I need to confirm that Nick didn't know about the baby."

They drove away from the business district. On their way, they passed Scarlet Lake. The crisp morning air sent mist rising from the water. It floated over the beach and swirled through the cattails like smoke. He and Morgan both went quiet as they drove past, but the visual was a reminder to Lance of the seriousness of the case. A young girl had been violated and murdered, and her killer still ran loose. If they didn't find Tessa's murderer, an innocent man could spend the rest of his life in prison.

And a killer would be free to strike again.

Neither he nor Morgan spoke until they reached the Barone place. Then Lance drew the Jeep to a stop on the shoulder of the road, his gaze fixed on the farm.

"Do you see what I see?" he asked.

It couldn't be.

What the hell?

CHAPTER TWENTY-EIGHT

Lance blinked hard, but it didn't change the sight. The farm looked deserted.

Morgan lowered her window. She tilted her head to the opening. "It's too quiet."

He turned past the mailbox into the driveway. There were no vehicles parked near the house. The chicken enclosure and pigpen were empty. No cows grazed in the pasture. The stock trailer and school bus that had been parked alongside the barn were gone.

They got out of the car. Lance led the way to the front door. Who knew what kind of surprises Dwayne Barone, with all of his WSA paranoia, would leave behind? Standing to the side of the doorway, he tucked Morgan behind him and knocked on the door. Nothing but eerie silence greeted them.

Lance walked to the window and peered inside. "The furniture is still here, but they took everything else."

Wire hung from holes in the wall where the TV and other electronic devices had been installed. Lance went back down the steps. Backing away from the house, he scanned the roofline. "The satellite dish is missing."

He headed for the barn, already knowing what he was going to see.

"This is creepy." Morgan followed him.

Watching their step, they checked the outbuildings. Lance took care to inspect every door before approaching and opening it. But nothing happened. Nothing at all.

The entire farm was eerie and silent and empty.

They returned to the car, turning to stare at the vacant buildings.

"Any thoughts?" Lance asked.

"No one takes their pigs on vacation," Morgan said. "Dwayne likes to live off the radar. Maybe he wasn't comfortable with our questions."

"We didn't accuse Dwayne or his son of anything."

Morgan's eyes drifted back to the house. "Maybe one of them did something really bad, and he was afraid we'd find out."

"Like commit murder. Do you like Robby or Dwayne for the crime?"

"Robby seems awfully small, not much bigger than Tessa," Morgan said.

"That boy is holding onto a lot of anger, though," Lance pointed out. "Rage can make someone stronger than he looks."

"Yes," Morgan agreed.

"And Tessa wouldn't know how to defend herself. She was just a kid." It killed Lance to think of the violence, the pain, the terror that had filled the young girl's final moments.

Morgan walked toward the back door. "But Dwayne would have no difficulty overpowering a young girl."

Lance followed her. "With one hand."

Pausing, Morgan shook her head. "We're getting ahead of ourselves. We haven't established that Tessa has ever been to the farm."

"She knew the Barones' oldest daughter from church. She didn't have to come to the house for her to have met Dwayne."

"His own family is terrified of him. Could they know he's a killer?"

"Wait a second." Lance jogged back to the Jeep and retrieved two pairs of vinyl gloves and a small black case from the glove compartment. Then he joined Morgan at the Barones' back door.

"What's that?"

"Nothing." Opening the black case, he selected two slim metal tools.

Morgan reached around him and turned the knob. The door opened. "It's not locked."

Eyeing the open door, Lance slid the lock picks back into their case. "I don't like this."

Not one bit.

Standing aside, he touched the door and let it swing inward. When nothing happened, he stepped through the opening. The large, farmhouse kitchen was bare. The Barones hadn't even left dust behind. Morgan pulled on her gloves and walked around the center island. She opened a drawer, then a cabinet. "Everything is gone."

Lance checked the fridge. "Empty."

They toured the downstairs, then went up the steps to the second floor. Morgan opened a closet. "How did they pack up and get out so quickly?"

"I wonder what Dwayne will do with the house." Lance led the way back downstairs and outside. He turned and scanned the surrounding area. There wasn't another house in sight, just fields, meadows, and woods. "It's not like we can ask the neighbors about the family. But maybe we can find out which church they attended."

"It's worth a try."

They returned to the Jeep. Morgan climbed into the passenger seat.

Lance slid behind the wheel. "What now?"

"Call the police?"

"And report what? It's not illegal to move." Lance started the engine and turned the vehicle around. "Maybe Sharp will have an idea." He called his boss and put him on speaker.

Lance told him about the Barones' vanishing act.

"I'll make some calls. Maybe your mom can think of a way to track them. Even if they want to stay off the radar, it's almost impossible these days given the amount of electronic surveillance out there. Eventually, they have to stop for gas or pay a toll. Keep me updated."

Lance ended the call with a *thanks*. He dialed his mom and explained the situation.

"Let me see what I can hack into," she said.

"Be careful. Don't do anything illegal." Or that might tip off the WSA to her inquiries.

But she made no promises, hanging up with a vague, "I'll call you."

Lance pushed the "End" button on his phone. He drove out onto the road and headed back into town. "I hope we don't totally strike out at Voss's apartment."

Dean Voss lived in an older residential section, not far from the business district. Lance pulled up to the curb in front of an old Victorian house that had been divided into apartments.

Morgan studied the doors. "I see units one through four. Dean lives in number five."

"We'll look around back."

They got out of the car and stood on the sidewalk for a minute.

"It's quiet." Morgan shielded her eyes from the late morning sun.

Lance checked his watch. Eleven o'clock. "This is a residential block. Everybody's left for school or work by now."

They walked up the driveway, which continued alongside the house to a detached single garage in the backyard. A set of wooden steps up the side of the garage led to a white door marked FIVE.

"Bingo." Lance headed for the stairs.

"Can I help you?" A woman's voice called out.

Morgan and Lance turned. A middle-aged woman in jeans and a red baseball cap stood on the back porch of the Victorian.

"Yes, you can." Morgan walked across the yard. "I'm Morgan Dane and this is Lance Kruger. We're looking for Mr. Voss."

"I'm Shannon Green." The woman nodded. "Who are you?"

"We're private investigators." Lance handed her a business card.

She studied it for a minute, holding it at arms' length and tipping her head back. "I haven't seen Mr. Voss lately. If you ask me, he's crazy pants. I hope he moves. He's scared the bejesus out of me more than once."

"How?" Lance asked.

"Skulking around the property at night like some kind of paranoid ninja wannabe. He always seemed to be watching." She pointed to the house behind her. "I live on the bottom floor. A few weeks ago, I caught him at my bedroom window in the middle of the night, trying to get a glimpse through the blinds. I went out and bought those blackout drapes just to make sure he couldn't see in."

"Did you complain?"

"I called the landlord." She rolled her eyes. "He couldn't care less about any of us. I reported the incident to the police. They came out and talked to him. He told them he was just walking by. Wasn't his fault that my blinds were open. They blew me off. I'm thinking about getting a dog. A big one. But if Voss moves, I won't have to."

"Do you remember the last time you saw Mr. Voss?" Morgan asked.

"Not exactly, maybe a week ago?" Shannon shrugged.

Lance glanced over his shoulder at Voss's apartment. "Do you know what's in the garage?"

"No." Shannon shook her head. "But Voss rents it with his unit."

"Does he ever have any company?" Lance asked.

Shannon's hands dropped to her sides. "Not that I've ever seen."

"Thank you for your help," Morgan said.

The neighbor went back inside her apartment.

After her door closed, Lance turned back to the garage and stared at it. He really wanted to see Voss's personal space. "There's a window next to the door. Maybe we can get a look inside."

Even knowing that Voss was locked up, Lance felt like he was being watched. The place gave him the creeps. He scanned the sides of the building and spotted a surveillance camera mounted under the eave above a door on the far side of the garage. Conveniently, the neighbor wouldn't see Lance pick the lock. He picked up a thin branch from the ground and hung it over the camera so that the dead leaves covered the lens.

"I did not see that," Morgan said.

"See what?" Lance checked the rest of the building for cameras but didn't find any more.

A tall hedge blocked the view from the street. Lance removed his lock picking tools from his pocket. The deadbolt took some work to pop, but he got it.

"Breaking and entering?" Morgan looked over his shoulder.

"Just looking around. We won't disturb anything." He pulled gloves from his pocket and handed her a pair. "We did it at the Barone house, and you didn't mind."

"They had clearly vacated the house, and the door was unlocked. Technically we only entered," she whispered. "And there weren't any nosy neighbors."

"You could wait in the car." He knew damned well she wouldn't. "If we find anything, we'll just slip out and call the police." Lance pushed the door open and stepped onto a concrete slab. Despite the warmth of the September morning, the garage was cold and damp. Lance hesitated at the threshold. A huge pile of shipping boxes occupied half the space.

Morgan sidestepped to the pile. "They're empty. Most are from major retail chains." She shifted a box. "Walmart, Amazon, Home Depot. Mr. Voss is quite the online shopper."

"But what did he buy?"

She peeked inside a few boxes. "No packing slips."

There were only two other items in the garage: a motorcycle and a chest freezer. Lance walked to the freezer and opened it. Dozens of packages, wrapped in thick layers of plastic wrap, filled the freezer.

"What's in those?" Morgan stood next to him and peered inside.

"I'm not sure I want to know, but I suppose we should look." Lifting one of the frozen packages, he picked at the edge of the plastic and began unrolling it. The Styrofoam meat package made him exhale in relief. "You have no idea how glad I am to see hamburger patties."

"Right?" She picked up another and opened it. "Five pounds of chicken legs."

Lance closed the lid and continued to inspect the space.

The motorcycle was equipped with the equivalent of saddlebags, two storage compartments behind the seat. Lance opened one. Empty. The second contained MREs and foul weather gear.

"Lance." Morgan stared at the ceiling.

He followed her gaze. A rectangle had been cut

into the ceiling. A slightly smaller rectangle was set inside. "Pull down steps?"

There was only one place they could lead: to Voss's apartment.

"No string," Morgan said.

Correction: the stairs led *from* the apartment above.

"I think they're designed to be exit only."

"Now what?" Morgan asked.

"I really want a look inside his apartment."

"You can't pick the lock to his front door. The neighbor will see."

Lance bent over and laced his fingers together. "See if you can grab the edge of the board. I'll give you a boost."

She stepped into his hands and he lifted her. Once he straightened, she maintained her balance by leaning into him. Lance closed his eyes to the sight of her thighs at his eye level, mentally filing his idea under *seemed like a good idea at the time.*

"I've got it." Morgan transferred some of her weight to the stairs and the platform descended, the steps unfolding.

Lance set her on the floor. He tested the steps, then climbed. His head poked through the opening into a dim space. A closet? He went all the way inside. As his eyes adjusted to the dim space, he found the door and opened it into a bedroom, or at least what was supposed to be a bedroom.

An unrolled sleeping bag occupied the space where a bed should have stood. A makeshift desk held a monitor showing the live surveillance camera feed from the back door and a second that appeared to be from inside the front entrance. Heavy blankets were nailed over the windows.

"Mr. Voss is more than a little paranoid." Lance pivoted. "Shit."

Voss had written on the walls. He'd covered every inch of white wallboard with a bizarre collage of mathematical equations, nonsensical phrases, hand-drawn maps, and lists of random objects.

Lance whistled softly. "Looks like the neighbor's diagnosis is correct. Voss is crazy pants."

"Voss was military." Morgan walked the perimeter, taking pictures of the walls in sections. "He gathered provisions. Put in a back door. Had an escape plan, complete with a well-stocked secret vehicle."

"So what the hell was he doing out in the woods?"

"Maybe his paranoia went into overdrive."

"This is more than paranoia." Lance scanned the drawings and annotations.

"Psychotic break?"

"Something like that. I don't think we can assign rational explanations to Voss's activity."

"There's a camera trained on the front door," Lance said. "Stay out of its view."

They went through the rest of the apartment, which consisted of a tiny living area and a kitchenette. A card table and four chairs were the only furnishings. The corners were crammed with stacks of books. Lance found a stack of packing slips on the table. He flipped through them. Most of Voss's purchases were for home-monitoring equipment, nonperishable food items, and camping gear.

"Found his bills," Morgan said from the kitchenette. "He's maxed out his credit cards. Hasn't paid a utility bill in ages. His rent is overdue. If he wasn't in jail, he might not have a place to live soon."

"Do you see a laptop?" Lance asked. Voss must have used a computer for his online ordering.

"No. I wonder if it was at the camp site." Morgan continued to search the kitchen. "There's a bit of dust in here, but not more than would accumulate in a week or two. The rest of the place seems relatively clean."

"So he was tidy before he went over the edge," Lance said. "You know what I don't see? Any sign the police have been in here."

"Maybe they haven't gotten around to going through his apartment yet. They need a warrant, and he's in custody, so I doubt they see any reason to rush."

Lance went to the corner and began reading the book titles. Voss had paranoid taste in reading material. Conspiracy and spy thrillers, military memoirs, and how-to books about survival, prepping for doomsday, and staying off the radar. Lance considered the credit card bills. Maybe Voss hadn't gotten around to reading the off-the-grid books yet.

Halfway down a high stack, Lance's eye stopped on an odd-shaped hardcover bound in navy-blue leather. Gold script on the binding read SCARLET FALLS HIGH SCHOOL with last year's date.

"What did you find?" Morgan peered over his shoulder. "A yearbook?"

Lance tugged it from the pile. He flipped through the pages. Voss had been considerate enough to flag his own pictures with Post-it Notes.

Morgan pointed to a photo of a large group of kids in athletic shorts. Several adults flanked the group. "Voss was an assistant track coach."

"Was Tessa on the track team?"

"No."

Lance went to the next bookmarked page. "He ran the video-gaming club. Tessa isn't there either." He turned to the next Post-it. "Bingo."

The photo was labeled YEARBOOK COM-MITTEE. Voss stood on one side of a group of twenty kids.

Morgan frowned and moisture glistened in her eyes as she pointed to a slim girl in the middle of the group. "There's Tessa."

"So Voss knew her."

"Yes."

"Do you see the girl who accused him of inappropriate behavior?" Morgan checked her notes. "Kimmie Blake. Or Ally Somers, the girl Kimmie claimed Voss kissed."

"Neither are on the yearbook committee." Lance went to the individual headshots section of the yearbook. "Here's Kimmie Blake." He turned pages. "And this is Ally Somers."

Lance snapped a photo of the important pages, then returned the book to its original location. "We'll get our own copy and look through it more thoroughly to see if we can find any connections between Kimmie, Ally, Jamie, and Tessa."

"Do you need to see anything else?" Morgan asked, her eyes sweeping the room.

"What's in the cabinets?"

"Normal kitchen stuff. I even checked the undersides of the drawers."

"No secret compartments?"

"None that I could find," she said.

Lance ducked into the only bathroom, a four-by-eight space with a pedestal sink, a narrow shower stall, and toilet. He opened the medicine chest over the sink. Clean spots on the shelves indicated missing pharmaceuticals.

"Was Voss taking any prescription meds?" Morgan asked from the doorway.

"If he wasn't, he should have been."

"Now that we've established that he knew Tessa, we can subpoena his medical records."

"That's progress." Lance turned off the light and exited the bathroom. As they walked back to the bedroom closet, he ensured the apartment was exactly the way it had been before they'd entered.

They used Voss's escape hatch. Lance folded the steps and eased the platform to the ceiling. It sprang back into place with a quick snap. Lance opened the exterior door an inch to find that the side yard was empty. They slipped out and walked around to the front of the garage. Looking up, Lance spotted a note taped to the front door.

"Hold on a second." Lance went up the steps. "It's a package delivery notification. I guess the credit card companies haven't cut him off yet."

Lance turned back to the stairs. *Boom! Crack.*

The stairway trembled. Light flashed under his feet. He grabbed for the railing. Too late! Wood splintered, and the stairs collapsed.

CHAPTER TWENTY-NINE

Morgan's heart dropped into her stomach as the stairway crumbled in front of her, and Lance plunged to the ground in a cloud of smoke and dust.

"Lance!" She rushed forward.

The structure had broken apart. Lance landed in the middle of the rubble. The small cloud of smoke dissipated in a few seconds in the breeze. Had Voss set a small explosion as a booby trap?

Morgan climbed over a pile of wood. He was on his back with several boards piled on top of him. He wasn't moving. Her heart stuttered. He had to be all right. He just had to be.

Fear turned her hands clammy and her belly cold as she crouched next to him. "Can you hear me?"

He stirred. "Yes."

Thank God.

Morgan exhaled. Her head swam with relief. She put a hand on the ground to steady herself.

"Don't move." She lifted a board off his torso. "Does anything hurt?"

"I'm all right." He tried to slide out from under two joined steps pinning him across the thighs.

"You shouldn't be moving!" She squatted and picked up the wood. She wobbled under its weight. No doubt adrenaline helped her lift it.

"Don't do that," Lance yelled as he sat up. "You're going to hurt yourself."

Staggering sideways, she dumped it into the grass.

"Morgan, I'm OK."

"You're bleeding." Wary of pointy broken boards and protruding nails, she stooped next to him and ran her hands over his arms and legs.

Lance froze.

"What's wrong? Where does it hurt?" She ran her hands up his sides. Did he break a rib? She stopped at his shoulders. His eyes were grinning at her.

She sat back. "You're not hurt, are you?"

He was working hard not to laugh. "I told you I wasn't, but maybe you should check every inch of me just to make sure."

She swatted his shoulder. "Be serious. You could have been badly hurt."

"But I'm not. See?" In one fluid movement, Lance surged to his feet and scooped her off the ground.

"Oh!" Surprised, she grabbed at his shirt. My, he was strong. She was no tiny waif, but he carried her as if she were. "It looked as if there was a small explosion before the stairs collapsed. I think Voss must have set up a trap. Which

322

would be insane because he obviously gets packages delivered."

"Keyword: insane. Let's get away from the building in case Voss has left any other surprises for visitors." Lance carried her across the grass.

"Put me down. This is backward. You're the one who's injured." Despite her protests, and against her entire modern, professional woman image, she enjoyed the way he made her feel small and feminine. All those muscles weren't just for show.

"Nothing a couple Band-Aids won't fix."

"Oh my God!" A door slammed, and Shannon raced down the porch steps. "I called 911. Are you both all right?"

"We're fine." Without putting her down, he sat on the back steps.

It took her a few seconds to think she should probably get off his lap. She scrambled to her feet and looked him over. Blood dripped from a few small cuts on his arm, and his pants were torn at the hem.

"Do you have a first aid kit in your Jeep?" she asked.

"Yes."

Before she could retrieve it, sirens approached. A minute or two later, strobe lights flashed on the side of the house. An officer in uniform jogged down the driveway toward them. Carl. He had one hand on the weapon on his hip. "Is everyone all right?"

"We're fine." Lance said. "Just a couple of scrapes."

"What happened?" Carl scanned the mess.

"I don't know," Lance said. "Morgan and I came to talk to Dean Voss's neighbors. I went to his door and knocked in case he had a roommate. I heard a boom and crack and the stairs gave out."

Not exactly the truth, but close enough.

Lance twisted his arm to inspect a cut. "I didn't see any signs of rot or neglect." He paused. "But there was smoke, and I thought maybe I saw a flash of light. I suspect some sort of rigged explosion. Maybe there was a tripwire or pressure trigger I didn't see."

"I saw flames under your feet," Morgan added.

Carl inspected some pieces of rubble. "Look at this neat hole."

Lance walked closer, his eyes narrowing. "You know what that looks like?"

Carl nodded. "A small, controlled explosion."

"Looks like the damage left after an explosive door breach." Lance surveyed the debris. "With Voss in the psych ward, we have to assume he booby-trapped the staircase and I triggered it. I wonder what he did in the military."

"I'd better call forensics," Carl said as he stepped away and spoke into the radio mic on his shoulder.

Morgan rubbed her arms. Despite the heat of the sun, a cool wind swept across the yard, stirring dead leaves and small bits of debris. Her suit jacket didn't seem warm enough. "You could have been blown up."

Voss was crazy, but he was locked up. She'd like to believe he couldn't hurt anyone ever again, but he just had.

Carl returned. "Horner is on his way. He wants you to wait here."

Lance sighed. "This day just keeps getting better and better."

The police chief arrived fifteen minutes later. Horner talked to Carl and inspected the scene. Then he approached Lance and Morgan. "What were you doing here?"

"We came to talk to Voss's neighbors." Lance repeated his story to the police chief. "The stairs collapsed."

"Voss knew Tessa Palmer," Morgan added. "He taught at the high school and ran the yearbook committee that Tessa was on."

Suspicion narrowed Horner's eyes. "How did you learn that?"

"The yearbook." Morgan didn't mention where they'd seen the yearbook. "Tessa and Voss were both in the photo for the yearbook committee. The photos were probably taken in the beginning of the year, and no one bothered to take Voss out after he quit."

"Voss hasn't been with the school since late winter," Horner said. "There's no evidence he and the Palmer girl were in contact since."

"He left because of accusations of misconduct with a student," Lance pointed out.

Horner's voice and gaze sharpened. "There was no evidence. Charges were never filed."

"That doesn't mean it didn't happen," Morgan said.

Lance gestured to the debris-strewn yard. "Clearly, Voss could be violent or unstable enough to commit murder."

Horner leaned closer. His gaze flickered to Morgan, then back to Lance. Anger gleamed in his eyes. His mouth opened and closed. Morgan could read his desire to warn them off the case, but legally, he didn't have an argument. Nick's defense team had every right to investigate. But Horner resented the fact that they'd uncovered evidence he'd missed.

Finally, he blew air from his nose like an irritated pony. "I can't stop you from sticking your noses into the case, but I'm giving you a warning. Don't break the law in doing so."

"I assure you, I know the law very well," Morgan said.

Horner snorted. "Just watch your step, counselor. Because if you don't, we will."

And now he'd crossed Morgan's line. "Are you threatening me, Chief?"

"Of course not." Horner took a step back. "But your client is guilty as sin. He killed Tessa Palmer. Voss had nothing to do with it."

"I'd like to remind you that I'm required to conduct a full investigation into the case." Morgan enunciated each word carefully. It took quite a bit of control not to say *because you didn't conduct a proper investigation before you arrested my client,* but it was implied. "I'm going to file a subpoena for Voss's DNA to be compared to that of Tessa's child."

Horner's jaw clamped tight. "You do what you have to do, counselor, and so will I. Don't forget to come down to the station to sign an official statement." He walked away.

"What did he mean by *so will I?*" Morgan asked.

"I don't know, but he's up to something. I don't trust him." Lance turned toward the Jeep. "Let's get out of here."

Morgan watched the police chief's stiff posture for a few seconds before turning to follow Lance.

She brushed some dust from her suit. She'd torn the hem of her slacks, and the leather was scraped off the heel of her shoe. Back in the Jeep, Lance took out his first aid kit and cleaned the cuts on his arm and covered them with a few Band-Aids.

"Are you OK?" he asked.

She felt his gaze on her face but kept her focus

out the window. "I'm fine. But I'm sure you'll have some bruises tomorrow."

The incident had left its mark on Morgan. She cared about him more than she wanted to, felt more than she was ready for. Her head began to throb. She propped an elbow on the passenger door and rubbed her temple.

Lance stopped at the diner at the edge of town.

"What are you doing?"

"I think we both need a break." He removed his seatbelt and turned toward her. "You look tired. I know Tessa's murder really rocked you, and you're trying your best to save Nick. But you can't neglect yourself."

"I'm fine." She reached for the door handle.

"Just remember. This case will go on for a long time. You're no good to Nick if you run yourself ragged."

"I know. I just haven't been hungry." She opened her car door. "But I could really use some coffee."

"Did you eat breakfast?"

"Yes."

"Donuts don't count."

Damn it.

"That's what I thought," he said. "You'll eat too. Some protein might help with that headache."

"You're as bossy as Sharp," she said without rancor. Despite her determination to keep her distance, smart-assing him felt good. The promise of a huge cup of coffee cheered her.

He grinned back at her. "Only when I need to be."

She shot him an exaggerated eye roll, and his grin widened. The light in his eyes took him from handsome to irresistible.

What *was* she going to do with him?

Lance followed her inside and found a booth overlooking the parking lot. Lance ordered a turkey sandwich. Ignoring the lunch menu, Morgan splurged on a giant stack of French toast and a latte.

"French toast is not protein," Lance protested.

"Sure it is. The bread is soaked in eggs."

The waitress brought their drinks.

Morgan settled back and sipped her latte. The caffeine hit her system with a pleasant buzz. "I hope the police and forensics team are careful going into Voss's apartment."

"They will be. But considering we already poked around inside, it's probably safe."

The caffeine eased her headache. Their food came and Morgan plowed through her French toast like a soldier. When she pushed her plate back, nothing remained but a few sprinkles of powdered sugar.

"Wow," Lance said. "Not going to lick the plate?"

"Hey, you wanted me to eat."

"I did."

Morgan grabbed the check.

Lance reached for her hand. "Let me get that."

She snatched it out of his reach. "It's an expense."

"You're not getting paid. You have no income to expense." He tried to tug the handwritten green slip from her hand. She held on, giving him a stubborn look, and he gave up. He was already working on the cheap for her. She wasn't going to let him incur additional expenses.

"Eventually, I'll have to think about what I'm going to do about a job." She slid out of the booth.

"I'll get the tip." Lance tossed some cash on the table. "Do you need money?"

She led the way to the register at the front of the diner. "No, but thank you for asking. Living with Grandpa, my expenses are low. We're not rolling in cash, but we have a roof over our heads, food on the table, and a little left over." She paid the bill. "But I'm already thinking about saving for college tuition for three."

"You could be a defense attorney. I know quite a few prosecutors who've switched sides. The private sector pays better than the DA's office."

"I've thought about it, but I don't think I can defend guilty people and sleep at night. I know in my heart that everyone deserves the best defense.

The legal system wouldn't work without the balance of prosecution and defense, but my dad was a cop. My grandfather was a cop. My sister and brother are both cops. I grew up believing that criminals belong behind bars. Defending anyone who walks through my office door just isn't for me. I'm not saying I could never defend another person, but I'd have to be convinced they were innocent."

"Like Nick?" Lance shoved his wallet into his pocket.

"Yes."

They walked through the tiled lobby, out onto the concrete, and right into Tessa's grandparents. The Palmers had aged twenty years since Tessa had died. Mrs. Palmer's skin was the pale, translucent color of parchment paper. She wore no makeup. Her hair was uncombed, and she clutched the lapels of her sweater together at the base of her neck as if she were freezing. Mr. Palmer's eyes were rheumy and red. They looked like they hadn't eaten or slept in weeks.

"I'm so sorry." Morgan had no other words to express her sympathy. She understood sorrow too well, but losing a child took the Palmers to a place she couldn't even contemplate without risking a panic attack.

Mr. Palmer shot Morgan a glare she felt right into the pit of her stomach. Her French toast flipped over.

Mrs. Palmer drew up, her face an angry mask. "How could you do this to Tessa?"

"You're a disgrace." Mr. Palmer took his wife's elbow and steered her toward the diner. As they passed, he spit on Morgan's shoe.

Morgan flinched as if he'd hit her. Lance moved to step in front of her, but Morgan put a hand on his forearm and held him back. "Leave them be."

"He had no right to do that."

"They're grieving, and they think I'm defending their granddaughter's killer." Morgan took a tissue out of her purse, stooped, and wiped her shoe. She couldn't hold the Palmers' reactions against them. She understood the raw, over-whelming nature of grief too well. "I don't know how I would react if I ran into the defense attorney who represented the men responsible for John's death or my father's killer."

She tossed the tissue into a garbage can.

Lance unlocked the Jeep, and they got in. She could still feel the Palmers' wrath. Looking up, she saw them through the plate glass window. Mrs. Palmer was staring right at her.

"The only thing I can do for them is find the man who really killed Tessa." Morgan blinked away from the old woman's glare. "Ready to get back to work?"

"You bet." Lance backed out of the parking spot.

Morgan opened her purse, found a roll of antacids, and chewed two. The encounter with the Palmers had left her with indigestion. "We should talk to Voss's wife."

Lance turned the Jeep around. "An excellent idea. There is no better source than a soon-to-be ex."

"Wives usually know if their husbands are straying." But would she have known if her husband was a killer?

Lance's phone rang. He stopped the Jeep and answered the call. "Thanks for letting me know."

"That was Carl," Lance set his phone on the console. "Dean Voss escaped from the hospital."

CHAPTER THIRTY

Lance shifted into drive. He locked the doors. The thought of Voss running loose made Lance want to put Morgan on a plane to Australia.

"No!" Morgan turned to stare at him. "How did Voss escape?"

"He slipped out of his restraints, knocked out an orderly, and stole his uniform and ID. The man might be insane, but he's very intelligent." Lance drove onto the road.

"Did he escape before or after his booby trap went off?" Morgan asked.

"Just after. He must have set it before he shot at us at the lake."

"Where do you think Voss will go?"

"Since he set his own place to self-destruct, I'd bet either to his wife or to hide in the woods. In case he picks his wife, we'd better catch up with Mrs. Voss before he does."

Mrs. Voss wasn't at home, nor was she at the bank branch where she worked as the assistant manager. The branch manager told them she'd just left. Lance saw no sign of Voss at either location. If everyone was lucky, he'd head for the wilderness to hole up.

"Is she afraid of her husband?" Morgan asked. "If I'd just filed for divorce from a violent and unstable man who just escaped from the psych ward, I'd go into hiding."

Lance called his mother and asked her to research Mrs. Voss's family and friends. Then he turned to Morgan. "Where to now?"

The meal had improved her color, until they'd run into the Palmers. He understood that Tessa's grandparents were grieving, but that didn't mean he liked them lashing out at Morgan.

"Would you mind stopping at my house? Ava stayed home sick today. I'd like to check on her, and Felicity doesn't get out of school for another hour."

"Of course." Ten minutes later, Lance parked in the Dane driveway. Inside the house, Ava greeted Morgan with a big hug and smile.

"She's much better," Grandpa said from his recliner.

Morgan lifted her daughter's chin. "Back to school tomorrow."

Ava nodded. "Grandpa got me a milkshake at McDonald's."

"That sounds yummy," Morgan said. "I have to run to my room for a minute. I'll be right back."

After her mother left the room, Ava's gaze landed on Lance. "What happened to your arm?"

He glanced down. He'd lost a Band-Aid. "Just a scratch."

"Does it hurt?" Ava asked.

"Just a little," Lance said.

"You need a Band-Aid."

Lance pretended not to melt when she took him by the hand and tugged him into the kitchen.

She pointed at an upper cabinet. "The box is up there."

He opened the cabinet and took down a white box with a red cross on the top. He handed it to her.

"You sit here." She steered him to a chair, set the box on the table, and opened it. Then she carefully selected a pink princess bandage and applied it to his arm. Leaning over, she kissed the bandage. "All better."

Lance felt his heart crack wide open. Some tough guy he was.

"I have to go play with Gianna." She jumped off the chair.

"Thanks, Ava," Lance called as the child skipped out of the kitchen, nearly colliding with Morgan as she walked in.

"I have to go. Love you, baby," Morgan called after her daughter.

Morgan led the way out of the house, stopping to say good-bye to her grandfather on the way out.

As she reached for the Jeep's door handle, Lance spotted a suspicious bulge just below her right kidney. "Is that your gun?"

"Yes." She'd added a belt to her slacks, no

doubt to accommodate her holster. "You can see it?"

"Just when your jacket tightened." He'd known she had a weapon but had never seen her armed.

She adjusted the holster. "I haven't carried in a very long time. I've only taken my gun out for the occasional trip to the range."

"Do you practice regularly?"

She laughed. "As if Grandpa would allow me not to." They settled into the front seats of the vehicle. "Felicity doesn't live far from here." Morgan gave him the address and Lance drove out of the neighborhood.

The Webers lived in a Cape Cod-style house. The blue-gray clapboards, white trim, and black shutters were freshly painted. A white picket fence enclosed a front yard full of lush grass. Lance parked at the curb, and they went to the door. Felicity opened the door before they knocked. Her long blonde hair fell in a long braid down the center of her back.

"Come on in." Felicity stepped back.

The front door opened directly into the living room. Felicity led them straight through to a small, tidy kitchen. Behind it, a screened porch looked onto a tiny yard of well-kept grass. They went through the French doors onto the porch. Felicity sat in an Adirondack chair and hugged her knees. Morgan and Lance took a wicker love seat facing her.

Morgan started. "Thanks for talking to us."

Tears filled Felicity's eyes. "I can't believe Tessa's dead."

"I know." Morgan reached out and touched her knee. "I'm sorry."

Felicity sniffed. "You don't think Nick did it?"

"No." Morgan said in a firm voice.

"Me either," Felicity agreed.

"Why do you say that?" Lance asked.

Morgan had been concerned with Lance intimidating Felicity, but she didn't seem the least bit nervous. Just sad.

The girl pulled her braid over her shoulder and stroked it. "First of all, Nick really liked Tessa, and he treated her real nice."

"In what way?" Morgan asked.

"He was considerate, kind, gentle even." She chewed on the end of her braid. "I can't picture him ever hurting a girl."

"He fought with Jacob," Lance reminded her.

Anger flashed in the girl's eyes. "Because Jacob was mean to Tessa. Nick was protecting her."

Lance leaned his elbows on his knees. "You don't like Jacob?"

"Jacob is an asshole." Felicity scowled. "If I had to pick someone who would rape—" She paused for a second to press a hand to her mouth and compose herself. "—a girl, it would be Jacob."

Morgan's body tipped forward, as if the girl's words pulled at her. "Why do you say that?"

"Because of other things he's done." Felicity surged to her feet and paced the gray-painted floorboards.

"Did he ever do anything to Tessa?" Morgan asked.

The girl stopped, nodding. "There was this party at the beginning of the summer. I wasn't there, but apparently Tessa passed out. The next day, she said she'd only had two beers. She was in really bad shape, though, and she didn't remember much about the party. Then Jacob sent her a picture on Snapchat."

"What's Snapchat?" Morgan asked.

"It's an app that lets people share pictures and messages that self-destruct after they're read." Lance said. "It was designed to be a way for kids to share things without having to worry about their pictures or messages haunting them on the Internet for the rest of their lives."

"So if they were drunk or someone took a photo of them smoking pot, there's no proof," Morgan said. "What kind of picture did Jacob send Tessa?"

A tear rolled down Felicity's cheek. "She was naked, and he was doing things to her."

Lance and Morgan shared a look.

"Do you know when this happened?" Morgan asked.

"Around the beginning of July." Felicity wrapped her arms around her waist. "I don't remember exactly."

Right about the same time Tessa got pregnant.

"But the pictures on Snapchat are temporary, so they were wiped from Tessa's phone." Frustration bubbled in Lance's chest. Jacob Emerson was a predator, and Lance wanted to nail him.

"Technically they disappear from your phone." Felicity took her phone from the back pocket of her shorts and began scrolling. "But I made Tessa take a screenshot. I wanted her to keep a copy because Jacob is such an asshole that it wouldn't surprise me if he pulled a stunt like this again. I didn't want Tessa to regret not keeping the pics. But she didn't want to keep them anywhere her grandparents could see them. She was so embarrassed."

So embarrassed that she didn't go to the police. Humiliation was one of the reasons that only a third of rape victims reported their assaults.

"I copied the pictures to my cloud account," Felicity said.

The police wouldn't have known they ever existed, even if they got a search warrant for Felicity's phone. Plus, if Jacob ever got a hold of her phone, he couldn't delete the pictures.

"Do you still have them?" Morgan perched on the very edge of her seat.

"Hold on a minute. I have to download them."

Felicity watched her phone, then handed it over. Then she turned away, as if unable to look.

Morgan held the phone toward Lance. Even knowing what to expect, the first photo made him suck wind. An unconscious and naked Tessa sprawled on a rug. A fully clothed Jacob knelt between her legs, both hands on her breasts.

"Hell." Disgusted, Lance looked away.

There were four pictures, each worse than the last. Lance gave them a quick glance, then got up and paced to the window. Just viewing the images made him feel dirty, as if Tessa was being violated all over again. The anger that had been building throughout the case went from a simmer to a boil. Jacob Emerson was just seventeen, but Lance wanted to beat the hell out of him for what he'd done to Tessa.

So much for Jacob's statement that he thought of Tessa as a sister.

Morgan lowered the phone and spoke to Felicity. "These pictures are evidence now. I need your phone, and you'll have to give a formal statement."

Felicity nodded. "OK."

"Why didn't you show these to the police?" Lance asked.

"They only asked me about the last two weeks." Felicity shrugged. "I didn't think something that happened a couple of months ago could be important. I guess I should have, but I've been so upset since Tessa died. I'm not thinking straight."

Damned Horner . . .

He and the DA had been so positive Nick was their perpetrator, and in such a rush to make an arrest and ensure the public that a violent offender was off the streets before the upcoming election, they'd neglected to fully investigate other suspects. They'd taken clean-cut Jacob at face value.

Morgan collected the phone, and they left Felicity's house.

"Do you think he drugged her?" Morgan asked.

"There's no way to prove it." Lance led the way back to the Jeep. Morgan pulled her phone out of her bag.

"Who are you calling?" he asked.

"The DA. We need to have a meeting." Morgan scrolled on her phone. "We need a DNA sample from Jacob Emerson to see if he's the father of Tessa's baby. There are several ways I can make that happen, but frankly, Bryce can do it faster. I have to share any information I uncover in the investigation anyway."

The discovery process was a two-way street. The prosecutor had to share all the evidence he intended to present against Nick, but the defense had the same obligation.

"Do you think he'll cooperate?" Lance asked as they paused on the sidewalk.

"If he fights it, there's a chance the judge

would deny our request based on the fact that someone has already been arrested for the crime. Jacob isn't a suspect. Plus, the fact that he got her pregnant doesn't mean he killed her, but it would prove he lied. His father knows this and will fight hard to keep us from getting a sample."

"But this is new evidence."

"Yes, and I'll get Jacob's DNA eventually, but I want it to happen sooner rather than later. I want Nick out of jail." She tapped a finger to her lower lip. "Bryce takes his case to the grand jury tomorrow. If he gets his indictment the same day this new evidence goes public, he'll look like a fool."

"But he can't put off the hearing."

"No, he can't, and he can still get his indictment, but he's not going to be happy that Jacob lied. Lying witnesses create reasonable doubt. Bryce doesn't like to take cases to court he isn't confident of winning." Morgan's focus shifted to her call as she asked for Bryce. "Tell him he's going to want to see me." She paused for less than a minute. "Thank you."

She lowered the phone. "He'll see us now." Confidence gleamed in her eyes.

"What is it?" he asked.

"For the first time, I think we've found a solid flaw in the case against Nick."

Thirty minutes later, they parked in the municipal complex and locked their handguns in the glove compartment of the Jeep. Lance followed Morgan to the DA's floor. His secretary didn't make them wait. The DA rose as they walked into his office.

Morgan and Lance slid into two chairs facing the DA's desk.

Bryce gave Lance a nod, then turned his laser focus on her. "What is this all about, Morgan?"

Morgan pulled Felicity's phone, now in a plastic bag, from her pocket. Through the clear plastic, she tapped on the pictures app and pulled up the photos of Tessa. She handed the phone to Bryce.

Lance had seen the DA in action in the courtroom. Bryce Walters could compete for an Oscar any day, but even Bryce couldn't maintain his poker face when viewing the images of Tessa. Lance was relieved when disgust flashed briefly in Bryce's eyes. Lance had been afraid that personal ambition would make the DA blind to the injustice.

Bryce set down the phone and dragged a hand across his face. "Whose phone is this?"

"Felicity Weber's," Morgan said. "Jacob sent Tessa these pictures via Snapchat. Tessa took a screenshot but didn't want to hold onto them in case her grandparents saw her phone. Felicity stored the images on her cloud account in case

Jacob pulled another similar stunt in the future, either with Tessa or someone else."

Bryce sat back. "So what do you want?"

"I want a DNA sample from Jacob," Morgan said.

"Why?" Bryce asked. "Nick's sperm was found in her body. That's verified."

"These pictures date back to early July," Morgan said. "Right about the time Tessa would have become pregnant. If Jacob raped her in July and she got pregnant, she could have confronted him that night. That's motive."

Bryce rested his elbows on the table and steepled his fingers. "But why kill her? So he got her pregnant? It's not the end of the world."

"Bryce, those pictures show Jacob molesting an unconscious girl. She couldn't have possibly given consent, while Jacob appears to be in control of all his faculties. If he got her pregnant that night, he raped her. She could have put him in jail." Morgan gestured to the phone sitting on Bryce's desk. "Even if he didn't kill Tessa, Jacob Emerson is a predator. This is a whole separate charge."

Bryce's jaw sawed back and forth, as if his molars—and brain—were grinding away at the evidence of Jacob's crimes.

"The press would have a field day with those photos," Morgan added.

Anger flared in Bryce's eyes, but he blinked it

away and leaned back. "I'll have the police bring Jacob in for questioning and obtain his DNA."

"I want the test expedited."

Bryce shook his head. "I can't promise that. Even a positive test doesn't prove he killed her."

"You already did it in this case," Morgan argued. "The presence of lubricant proves that a condom was used the night of Tessa's murder. Jacob could have raped and killed her without leaving his sperm behind."

Bryce crossed his arms over his chest. "That's a stretch."

"So you'll expedite the tests that put my client in jail, but you won't do the same for the tests that might get him out? I *will* go to the press, Bryce. It won't reflect well on you if you're willing to let Nick rot in jail to protect a privileged, wealthy young man."

"This won't affect the grand jury hearing tomorrow. My evidence is solid. Your client will be indicted." Bryce glared.

"We both know you'll get your indictment because a grand jury hearing is completely one-sided. I don't get to present evidence," Morgan acknowledged. "Furthermore, we both know those pictures don't have to prove Nick is innocent or that Jacob is guilty." She stabbed the air in the direction of the phone. "Those photos are reasonable doubt."

"I talked to Chief Horner today," the DA said.

"He said you want Dean Voss's DNA tested as well. Grasping at straws, Morgan?"

"Not at all," she answered. "Just conducting a thorough investigation."

Lance felt the *zing* of that comment bounce around the room.

He admitted that the case had appeared pretty open-and-shut at the beginning. Originally, even he had thought Nick looked guilty. He'd lost faith in the criminal justice system over the years. Too many criminals walked on hard charges. But maybe this time the system would actually work the way it was intended.

Morgan's body shifted forward an inch. "Did Chief Horner tell you about the accusations against Dean Voss last year? And that he was on the yearbook committee with Tessa?"

She never raised her voice, but her posture and tone had become commanding in a way he hadn't expected. She slid into the offensive in a perfectly ladylike fashion. It was like watching Perry Mason disguised as Donna Reed. Lance imagined she often took opposing counsel by surprise.

"I'll have the test expedited." The DA's eyes went flat. Clearly, he hadn't expected Morgan's direct attack either. "Be careful, Ms. Dane. You're stirring up more than a few hornets' nests. You're bound to get stung."

CHAPTER THIRTY-ONE

Jail, day 5

Nick retrieved an evening chow tray from the cart. As he turned, Shorty gestured to him. Nick walked over, and Shorty motioned to the empty spot on the bench next to him. "You can eat here if you want."

No one had bothered him much since his beating two days ago. Nick had added staying far away from cell doorways to his growing list of habits. He'd also spotted other blind spots and avoided them as well.

Nick sat down, hoping no one would attack him in full view of the surveillance cameras.

"I'm not that hungry. You want an extra biscuit?" Shorty asked.

Nick hesitated. Trying to analyze the subtext was giving him a headache. If he took the biscuit, did he owe Shorty something in return? If he didn't take the offer, would Shorty be offended?

If there was one thing he'd learned since he'd arrived here, it was that jail operated on a system of respect. The worst thing a man could do was show disrespect to another. Every man had a place on the hierarchy, a spot he'd earned.

Insults, even perceived ones, threatened that established pecking order.

Chaos resulted.

Plus, Nick figured if he stuck with honesty, he wouldn't have to remember what he'd said. "I appreciate the offer, but I can't help but wonder why you're making it. If I accept it, does that leave me with any obligation?"

Shorty tossed the biscuit onto Nick's tray. "You're a smart kid. We trade food all the time, but this is a one-time peace offering."

Spurning the biscuit would be offensive and signal that Nick held a grudge. Had the beatdown been a test?

"In that case, I accept," Nick said. The meatloaf tasted like cardboard, but hunger drove him to eat every bite. At home, he would have bypassed the soggy green beans, but today Nick ate every scrap of food on his plate.

The two guys on the opposite side of the table joked between themselves. They didn't give Nick a second look. He realized that he was no longer being eyeballed. Had he passed whatever test he'd been put through?

They finished eating, shoveling their food with the concentration of the perpetually hungry.

Shorty lowered his voice. "Do you have your PIN yet?"

Nick shook his head. He was still waiting to be issued his prisoner personal identification number, which he would need to do everything from make phone calls to purchase items at the commissary.

"That sucks," Shorty said. "We're making a spread tonight. I could spot you."

A spread was a meal the inmates put together with food they'd purchased from the commissary like tuna, ramen, coffee, and candy. Nick had watched them have one the first night he'd been here.

"Thanks for the offer, but I'd rather wait until I can contribute. I don't want to mooch." Nick had already seen one man smacked around for welshing on a debt.

Shorty nodded. "Next time."

Nick wandered to the chess players and watched two games. Neither of the players was very good. Nick could have wiped the board with either of them, but he thought that wouldn't be the best idea. Still unsure about his status, he remained a silent observer, limiting his involvement to a low-key congrats to the winner.

A Spanish soap opera played on the TV on the wall. He had no idea who had the remote, if anyone.

Even after Shorty's olive branch and his seeming acceptance among most of the inmates, the hair on the back of Nick's neck still bristled. He would never be able to let his guard down. The constant state of vigilance wore on his nerves. Did all the men in this place feel the same? The Man didn't appear to be nervous. Was that an act? Sure, he was the size of an armored truck, and he had a group of like-sized buddies, but the AB was outnumbered six to one. Plus, there were several other gangs that looked equally deadly. The brothers with the BLOODS tattoos weren't fucking Boy Scouts.

The truth hit Nick with shocking clarity.

They have nothing to lose.

The Man had said he was being charged with manslaughter, and he was a repeat offender. Once his trial was over, was he going to state prison for the rest of his life?

Their lack of fear wasn't due to a lower threat level, but indifference.

Nick's breaths tightened. His palms began to sweat. What would happen if he was found guilty? He'd go to state prison for a minimum of twenty-five years. Best case scenario: he'd be forty-five years old before he could get out.

Worst case: he'd get life without parole and never see the outside again. He'd spend the rest of his life in a concrete cage. He'd listened to the experienced prisoners talk about the state prison, about living in a four-by-eight with one hour of yard time a day.

His vision dimmed as this real possibility swept over him. Hopelessness was a thousand pounds sitting in the center of his chest. It pressured his lungs and cut off his air until he choked.

Stop it!

"You OK, man?" Shorty asked.

"Yeah. I'm cool." Nick beat a fist on his chest and coughed. "Just need a drink of water."

He got up and walked to the water fountain, beating back the impending panic attack. How could he even feel sorry for himself when he was alive and Tessa was dead? He pictured her face, her smile, her eyes.

Then the photo the cops had shown him of her dead body.

Slipping in when he was vulnerable, grief swamped him. He missed her so much it hurt, and knowing he'd never see her again made him feel like he'd been stabbed in the heart too.

He held onto the vision of Tessa, dead, and let his fury build. In here, anger was a much more useful and acceptable emotion. Anger made him appear strong.

She'd broken up with him, but Nick just knew she hadn't wanted to. The way she'd cried didn't make sense otherwise. If breaking up made her miserable, why did she do it? Just days before they'd been really happy together.

The more he thought about it, the less it made sense, and the more his chest ached.

If he ever found the man who'd killed her . . .

He leaned over the water fountain and drank.

Cool liquid slid down his throat but did nothing to chill the hot swirl of emotions in his belly.

In the far corner of the space, a dozen inmates were working out. With no exercise equipment, they were creative about it. A pair took turns sitting on a bunk while the other bench-pressed him. Another guy sat on his partner's shoulders while he did push-ups. But Nick didn't trust anyone enough to buddy-up, and he prayed he wasn't here long enough to develop any tight bonds. Some of these men had been here a long time.

He turned back toward the chessboard. Two new players had started a fresh game. Watching seemed the safest option. Nick headed back across the room. He stepped aside as an inmate exited a row between tables. The man passed close. Too close, Nick realized, but it was too late to get out of the way.

The man's shoulder bumped Nick's, and the rest played out in slow motion. A quick twist of the orange-clad body. The sharp sting of a blade sliding into Nick's belly. A second and third hot slice of agony as the man punched the weapon into Nick's gut again and again. The instinctive response to cover the wounds, to keep his insides from gushing out. The hot rush of blood between his fingers.

No one came to help. Orange bodies slunk backward, unsure of the situation.

Unwilling to get involved.

An alarm blared. It sounded far away, muted by the throb of Nick's pulse in his ears. Cold swept over him, in him. He dropped to his knees.

The door burst open. Feet pounded on concrete. Men shouted. Nick fell sideways, his shoulder hitting the concrete.

Hands rolled him to his back and moved his hands from the wounds.

Pressure.

He blinked at the ceiling. Fluorescent lights blurred and dimmed as shadows leaned over him. He knew they were guards by their shape and voices.

More shoes beat on cement.

Someone grabbed Nick's chin. "Stay with me."

But he couldn't. He drifted. Sounds and light faded. His heartbeat slowed. Pain consumed him, and the darkness that followed was a relief.

CHAPTER THIRTY-TWO

Morgan sailed out of the municipal building, her step brisk, her mind whirling. "I can't wait to tell Nick tomorrow. We finally have a break in his case. I'll stop by Bud's house and give him the good news tonight. He needs some encouragement."

Nick's dad needed hope, and she couldn't wait to give it to him.

"I wouldn't build his hopes up too much." Lance fell into step beside her on the sidewalk. Since they'd gotten word of Voss's escape, Lance hadn't stopped scanning their surroundings. "This won't mean much until the DNA test comes back."

At six thirty in the evening, the visitors' lot was mostly empty.

"It'll mean one of the prosecution's key witnesses lied, and the video with Nick fighting Jacob just took on a whole new meaning. Nick's account looks a lot more truthful than Jacob's now. Bryce might not want to admit it, but between those photos and Voss's camp near the murder site, I can poke a hundred holes in his case against Nick." At the end of the walk,

Morgan stepped off the curb. "Bryce relied on an abundance of physical evidence without the due diligence of making sure there wasn't an alternate explanation for it."

Her phone rang as they reached the Jeep. Bud's name was displayed on the screen. Morgan answered the call. "Hi Bud. I was just going to call—"

"Morgan." Bud's voice was hoarse. "I just got a call from the jail. Nick's been stabbed."

Morgan froze. "What?"

"Stabbed," Bud said. "By another prisoner. That's all I know. I'm on my way to the hospital."

"I'll meet you there." Numb, she lowered the phone and explained. "We need to go to the hospital."

Lance opened the passenger door for her. "Let's go."

The ride passed in a blur of landscape. "This isn't right. It's not fair. Nick was locked up with hardened criminals because he didn't have enough money for bail *and* a defense. He had to choose."

Morgan closed her eyes and rested her forehead against the cool glass. She could feel the case breaking apart, the knots in the DA's case unraveling as she picked at the evidence. But she hadn't been quick enough for Nick. All her efforts hadn't been enough.

"If only I'd questioned Felicity earlier—"

"Stop that!" Lance cut her off. "You've done everything possible. You've investigated a case when the police and the DA failed to do their due diligence. You've come up with two alternative suspects and destroyed the credibility of one of the prosecution's witnesses. You have nothing to regret. This is not your fault. The blame here rests on the DA and Chief Horner. They were so sure they had an open-and-shut case."

She nodded, but she didn't really agree. In hindsight, she could have done better. She could have realized the police were interested in Nick as a suspect before they'd actually arrested him. She should have checked on him after they'd found Tessa's body. She'd known he'd be one of the primary suspects as the boyfriend of the victim.

Lance reached across the console and grabbed her hand. "You are amazing. You've stuck by Nick when no one else would."

At the hospital, they parked in the ER lot and went in through the sliding doors. They found Nick's father in the hallway of the ER, both hands pressed to his forehead. Ten feet down the hall, a sheriff's deputy leaned against the wall. The fact that he was outside the room told Morgan that Nick was in bad condition. So bad that there was no chance he could escape or be aggressive.

"Bud!" Morgan rushed forward.

357

Bud lowered his hands, his eyes shell-shocked. "He's in emergency surgery. Another prisoner stabbed him in the belly three times with some sort of homemade knife. A shiv, they called it."

Blinking back a tear, Morgan put her hand on Bud's arm. "I'm so sorry."

He covered her hand with his. "You have nothing to be sorry about."

Morgan didn't say anything about the case. It wasn't the time. "Did they say anything about his condition?"

Bud swallowed. It looked as if it took some effort. "He's lost a lot of blood. They don't know if he's going to make it."

Lance steered Morgan and Bud toward a waiting room. The guard stayed in the hall. "I checked with the nurse. The surgeon will come and talk to us when he gets out of the OR."

"Can I call someone for you, Bud?" Morgan asked.

He pressed a hand to his lower back. "No. My sister is coming from Manhattan. She should be here in a couple of hours."

Morgan called home and told her grandfather not to expect her. Lance brought coffee, but the first sip turned sour in Morgan's belly. Bud paced. Lance called Sharp and updated him. Morgan dropped into a chair to wait. Lance sat next to her. Hours passed in a tense, silent fog. Morgan lost track of the time, but pins and needles in her legs forced her to get up and walk the hallways multiple times. Bud's sister arrived and paced with him.

A shadow fell across the doorway. Morgan startled to attention as a green-scrubbed surgeon walked into the room, his surgical mask still tied around his neck.

He swept the skullcap off his head. "Mr. Zabrowski?"

Bud nodded, frozen in place in the middle of the room as if he was afraid to get closer to the doctor.

As if he was afraid to hear if Nick was alive or dead.

"I'm not going to lie to you. His injuries are severe. He suffered three stab wounds to the abdomen. The worse of which was the laceration to the liver. We've repaired the damage but he lost a lot of blood. He's received several units to replace his blood volume." The surgeon paused, his mouth grim. "The next twenty-four hours are critical. He's young and strong, and he made it through the surgery without any major complications. He's in recovery now." The surgeon's gaze swept the room. "Once he gets settled in the surgical intensive care unit, you'll be able to see him." He glanced around the room. "Immediate family only. Do you have any questions?"

Bud shook his head.

"I know it's a lot to take in. Follow the signs to the SICU waiting room. A nurse will come out and get you after Nick is settled." The surgeon walked out.

Bud exhaled a long breath and then turned to Morgan. "I'll call you. Thank you for everything. You're the only one who believes in him."

Morgan took Bud's hands and gave them a squeeze. Then Bud and his sister left the room.

"Come on. I'll take you home." Lance put an arm around Morgan's shoulder.

But her hands began to shake. She rolled her fingers into fists and clenched them to stop the tremors, the stress and fear of the day finally breaking through her control. "No. I don't want to go home like this." She glanced at the time on her phone. "It's midnight." If she went home now, she'd wake Grandpa.

She felt lost, her limbs loose and uncoordinated, ready to fly apart. The weight of Lance's arm around her shoulder was all that held her together.

"Can I go home with you tonight?" she asked.

His fingers dug into her arm for a brief second. Then he relaxed. "Sure. Let's go."

She let him steer her through the hallways to the exit. The cool night washed across her face. She inhaled, the crisp air a bracing shot of energy in her lungs.

Lance drove back into town and parked in the driveway of a one-story house. He'd been to her house so many times, it felt odd that she'd never been to his. He pushed a button on his visor and opened the garage door.

They got out of the Jeep, and Morgan stared at the neat ranch-style home. "You live close to the office. You could walk."

"I do if I'm going to be in the office all day, but that's rare. Usually I'm running around all day. There's a lot of legwork to the job."

She followed him into the garage. "Do you like it?"

"I wasn't expecting to, but yes," Lance said.

Hockey equipment filled half of the two-car garage.

"You still play?"

"I coach a team of unruly kids. I haven't actually been on the ice since I was shot."

Morgan followed him inside. The door opened into a living/dining room combination. The kitchen was straight back, and the hallway that opened off the living room probably led to the bedrooms. The house was neat, almost stark, with minimal furnishings and no decoration. In the living room, a small couch and a recliner faced a TV. But the big surprise was the baby grand piano that took up the entire dining room.

As Morgan followed him back to the kitchen, a creeping and cold numbness slid over her. Her hands started trembling again.

"Can I get you anything? Are you hungry?"

Lance turned to stare at her, his gaze searching, assessing. "Tea or coffee?"

"No." Morgan pictured Bud's face as the surgeon gave him the news. "I wonder how Nick is." Emotions too conflicted to identify surged in Morgan's chest. Anger, frustration, helplessness, all boiled together into a toxic stew. "Do you have anything to drink?"

"I'm not sure. Let me look." Lance opened and closed three cabinets. In back of the lazy Susan, he found a bottle of whiskey, still in its box. Obviously a gift, the bottle had a red bow tied around its neck. "Since I started working for Sharp, I gave up most alcohol as part of his get-Lance-healthy campaign. He's not opposed to organic wine or beer. The guys on the SFPD gave me this as a good-bye gift."

He splashed a tiny amount into a glass and handed it to her. She took a small sip. The whiskey burned a path from her tongue to her belly. Finally, some warmth.

"Do you mind if I take a shower?" he asked.

"Not at all." She took another swallow of whiskey. "I'll be here."

He disappeared down the hall.

She reached for the bottle, poured a more generous shot, and tossed it down. Slowly, the numbness receded, like floodwater after a storm. Her phone rang. She fumbled in her pocket to draw it out.

"Yes?" She held her breath.

"This is Bud's sister. He asked me to call you with an update. He's with Nick now. His blood pressure has come up a bit. So that's good news. I have to go now. Bud needs me."

"Thank you for calling," Morgan said.

Bud's sister ended the call. Morgan wandered to the piano. She sat and placed her glass of whiskey on a conveniently placed coaster. She'd taken lessons as a little girl, but now the only song she could plunk out was "Chopsticks."

Lance returned. He was wearing a pair of athletic shorts and a snug T-shirt. A towel hung around his neck. He rubbed it over his head, making his short blond hair stand straight up.

"Nick is holding on."

"Good."

She played a few notes. "I hope you don't mind."

"Of course not." He joined her on the bench.

"Play something."

He nudged her over a few inches. She'd been around him enough to know that he favored classic rock so the opening chords of "Hallelujah" shocked her. When he opened his mouth and sang, she was even more surprised. His voice was deep and smooth, inflective and filled with emotion.

She joined him on the chorus but lost her

voice as they reached the cold and broken verse. Something cracked deep inside her. She let him finish solo. By time the final notes faded to silence, tears streamed down her face.

She turned and faced him. "This isn't right. Teenagers shouldn't die. Tessa should be alive, and Nick should be thinking about which movie to take her to this weekend. How did this happen?"

She picked up her whiskey, wishing it would hurry up and numb her.

"This isn't the way to handle it." Lance reached for her glass. "How about some food? An omelet?"

"I'm not hungry." She pulled her drink out of his reach. "Maybe I don't want to handle it. Maybe I'm tired of handling everything. Maybe I just want to stop thinking for one night."

She got up, went into the kitchen, and poured another shot. Lance followed her.

Her mind turned endlessly, like a merry-go-round that never stopped. Images of Tessa, bloody and shredded and covered in dirt; pictures of wounds; autopsy reports; crime scene photos. The slideshow ran 24/7, as if it had been burned into her retinas.

She tipped the glass back. The next shot slid down her throat and into her belly. She welcomed the heat. A few seconds later, it soothed and smoothed her raw edges. It was merely a Band-

Aid over a gaping wound, but if a Band-Aid was all you had, you used it.

Right?

"Morgan . . ." Lance pressed closer. His body nearly touching hers. He took her arm and turned her to face him. His hand settled on her bicep.

If she'd thought the whiskey made her hot, the proximity to him sent her temperature off the charts. Lance had the power to make her forget everything. To shut off her brain and simply *feel*. She put the glass down and splashed more whiskey into it. "I'm going to prove Nick is innocent, even if he . . ." She didn't want to verbalize her worst fear. In the beginning, she'd been terrified that she was going to fail Nick, and he would go to prison for murder. His life would be over. Prison was dangerous, but she'd never expected someone to try to kill him in his first five days in the county jail. But did she want to solve the case for Nick or for herself?

If Nick died, she'd risked everything for nothing.

The community hated her. She'd lost her job before she'd even started.

This was hardly the first case where she'd bucked popular opinion. Her whole family was devoted to serving justice. Her entire life she'd been raised to respect the law. Those who didn't obey it deserved to suffer the consequences. She'd spent years doing her best to put criminals behind bars. This case was no different. The police had arrested the wrong man. A killer was still out there, and Nick was in intensive care, maybe dying, because of their mistake.

She thought of Nick playing chess with her grandfather or blowing bubbles for the girls on the front lawn and couldn't reconcile those images with a boy on the brink of death.

Not fair. Not fair. *Notfairnotfairnotfair.*

Tears burned in the corners of her eyes. She tipped the glass and took another mouthful of whiskey. The taste mellowed on her tongue, and her thoughts grew fuzzy.

"I know you're hurting tonight, but whiskey isn't the answer," Lance said. "I should know. I tried that route last winter. Made everything worse."

Morgan sipped. Alcohol might not be the answer, but frankly, she was out of ideas. "Then what *is* the answer?"

Would Nick still be alive in the morning?

He hadn't done anything to deserve what had happened to him. Morgan couldn't believe he could intentionally hurt anyone. "Do you believe Nick is innocent?"

"I'm not convinced he's guilty," Lance said. "But I don't think we've found the truth yet."

"Is my judgment skewed? Do I just want him to be innocent so badly, I'll do anything to prove it?"

Warmth bloomed on her skin. Setting her glass on the counter, she pulled away from Lance's touch and took off her suit jacket.

"I don't know." Lance took her arms firmly in both hands. "But whatever happens, none of it was your fault. You've already given me serious doubts about the DA's case. We'll solve this case. We will find Tessa's killer."

"Even if Nick . . ." She couldn't finish the sentence.

But Lance understood her. "Yeah. Even then."

Her palms landed on his shoulders. Though he wasn't 100 percent convinced Nick was innocent, she should be glad to have him on the investigation. She needed someone close by who was objective. Someone to keep her in check.

Tomorrow. She'd think about the case tomorrow.

Right now, the last thing she wanted was to be in control. She wanted to blot out all her thoughts and simply *feel.* The whiskey helped. She leaned closer and inhaled the cedar scent of his skin. Rising onto her toes, she settled her mouth on his.

With all of the things that felt wrong in her life, this wasn't one of them. His mouth tasted of mint. She delved deeper, her tongue sweeping into his mouth. She needed more. Skin. *His* skin. Up against hers.

She tugged at the hem of his shirt.

Her hands slipped under the fabric and up the hard muscles of his back. He was solid and so utterly, deliciously male. The more she touched, the more she tasted, the more she wanted. She opened her eyes. His had gone deep blue, the want in them stealing her breath as he returned her kiss with equal heat.

His fingers grasped her hips and pulled her against him. A groan slid from deep in his chest, and a hard length pressed against her belly.

A tiny voice in the back of her mind warned that she wanted this particular man far too much and that the heat building between them was spiraling out of control.

She silenced it by sliding her hands between their bodies to caress the hard ridges of his abdomen. He hissed, his entire body stiffening.

Lance eased back, his hands taking hers and pulling them out from under his shirt. "Let me make you some tea and maybe something to eat."

"I don't want a cup of tea." She curled her fingers into his T-shirt. "I want you."

Pure need flashed in his eyes. He wanted her back. He squeezed his eyes closed for a few seconds. When he opened them, the desire had cooled. "You don't know what you want right now."

"Don't tell me what I want." Frustration flared in Morgan's belly, thick and hot, two years of grief and pain finally edging into anger. Why was the world so damned unfair? She'd had a man she'd loved with all her heart ripped away from the family who needed him. How did she let go of that?

There was another man in her life she could love, and he was standing right in front of her. And damn it, she *did* want him.

She closed her eyes, leaned forward, and pressed her forehead to Lance's chest.

He wrapped his arms around her and rested his cheek on the top of her head. "I can't explain your feelings, but I know mine. We both know what would happen tonight. This would become a way for you to exorcise your demons. We're friends, and I care about you. You're a beautiful, amazing woman. Making love to you would be a religious experience. Any man in his right mind would jump at the chance to share your bed. But I won't have our friendship tainted by this. I won't be something you get out of your system. I won't be someone you regret."

Sure, she'd felt some attraction from him, but never the depth of emotion she'd seen in his eyes tonight.

Tonight, everything had felt different, more intense. Was it just because of the stress of the day or were their feelings real? Lance was right. They shouldn't make such an important decision under this much stress.

He was working hard to make the right decision, and she was being selfish.

"I'm sorry. You've done so much for me, and I just keep asking for more." She leaned back, shame washing through her, wiping out the effects of the whiskey. "I'm just so tired of not letting myself feel anything." She pulled out of his embrace.

"I know." He pulled her close again. "And I'm sorry."

Reluctantly, she stepped back. "I didn't mean to hurt you."

"You didn't." Only because he'd stopped her.

She rubbed her arms, missing the heat of his body. "Do you mind if I use your shower?"

"Not at all. Do you want some clothes to put on?"

"That would be great."

Lance led her into a guest bedroom. "There's a shower in the hallway bathroom. Towels are under the sink. The sheets on the bed are clean. Call me if you need anything."

I need you.

But the words died on her lips.

He brought her a pair of shorts and a T-shirt. "These have a drawstring."

She took the clothes and showered. No matter how hot she turned the tap, she barely felt the water on her skin. She felt numb from the inside out.

Whiskey was not her friend.

The shirt hung to mid-thigh and the drawstring barely kept the shorts on her hips. Dressed, she slipped into the guest bed, setting her gun on the nightstand. But sleep wouldn't come. She stared at the ceiling until the first gray streaks of dawn brightened the sky. Then she slipped out of bed. She stuffed her gun into her purse, stepped into her shoes, and left the house.

The sky turned pink as the sun peered over the horizon. She encountered no other humans on the six-block walk to Sharp Investigations where her van was parked. She grabbed the change of clothes she'd started keeping in the back since the incident at the crime scene. Taking the key for the building Sharp had given her out of her purse, she approached the front door. She'd change before going home to see her girls. It would be hard to explain why she was wearing Lance's clothes.

A scraping sound lifted the hairs on the back of her neck. She spun, but the street was empty. Twenty feet away, a tall hedge separated Sharp's lot from the property next door. Morgan backed toward the office, senses on alert. The hedge rustled. Backlit by the rising sun, a figure stepped out of the hedges. His shadow fell over the grass.

CHAPTER THIRTY-THREE

Lance woke to a dark house. He'd worried about Nick in the ICU, crazy Dean Voss on the loose, and Morgan falling apart in his arms.

Especially that last part.

His hand brushed the empty, cold pillow next to him. It was a freaking miracle he'd resisted taking her to bed. Beyond the physical desire, she was everything he'd ever wanted in a woman, a beauty that went soul deep and an irresistible combination of strength and fragility.

He didn't know how she handled the amount of stress and responsibility on her shoulders. Looking after just his mother overwhelmed him at times.

His joints felt like rusty hinges after a night of very little sleep. All he wanted was a cup of strong coffee and a hot shower. There was no way in hell that Sharp's green tea would cut through Lance's brain fog.

But as he got out of bed, he sensed the place was empty. He pulled on a pair of shorts and went to the guest bedroom. The door was ajar. He peered inside.

Morgan was gone.

Damn it.

There was only one place she could have gone. Her van was at the office. Lance tugged a T-shirt over his head, stepped into shoes, and went outside. Voss was still loose and dangerous.

The sun was peering over the horizon as he hurried to his Jeep. In front of the office, Lance parked at the curb and jumped out of his vehicle. As he walked toward the building, his heart skipped at the sight of her purse and a small duffel bag on the walkway halfway to the front door.

Drawing his gun, he went inside. "Morgan?"

"Back here." The feminine voice from the kitchen made him nearly light-headed with relief. He picked up her purse and duffel and carried them inside.

Morgan sat at the kitchen table. She still wore his clothes. Blood wept from an abrasion on her knee. The stray dog leaned against her legs. Sharp, dressed in shorts and a T-shirt, was making a pot of tea.

As Lance stepped into the kitchen, the dog bristled and growled, getting between him and Morgan.

He stopped. "What happened?"

"Someone was outside." Morgan's hand settled on the dog's head. "I tripped and skinned my knee. She chased him away."

"Did you see who it was?" He set her things on the empty chair next to her.

Morgan shook her head. "He was in the hedges next door. The sun was in my eyes as he stepped out. When the dog came running from around the back of the house, he ran back through the hedge."

"Did you call the police?" Lance asked.

Sharp shook his head. "He didn't do anything illegal."

Lance swore. "Did you check the surveillance footage?"

Sharp reached behind him for an iPad. He swiped through a couple of screens and handed the iPad to Lance. "The sun was behind him. Average size guy, dressed in jeans and a black hooded jacket. It looked like his face was covered with something."

"That's not very helpful." Lance watched the video. The figure was a barely detailed shadow, an outline of a man. He stepped out of the hedges. Before he'd taken two steps, a white blur charged him. The man turned and bolted. "That dog is a rocket."

"I'm going to send the image to a friend and see if he can get any more details out of it," Sharp said.

Morgan stroked the dog's head. "If we assume the man was Tessa's killer, that would rule out Robby Barone and his father. Robby is too small and his father is too large."

"What if the man had nothing to do with the

case?" Sharp asked. "He could have been a prospective burglar casing the building next door."

"Or it was Jacob Emerson," Lance suggested. "I'm sure the DA has already called his father. Maybe he doesn't appreciate the prospect of being swabbed for DNA."

"Dean Voss is another possibility," Sharp said. "Trying to kidnap a woman on a public street is pretty crazy. The SFPD, the sheriff's department, and the state police are looking for him, but he's slippery."

"Don't forget Kevin Murdoch," Lance added. "I know we haven't turned up any dirt on Jamie's soon-to-be stepfather, but I haven't counted him out yet."

"There's one person who is completely ruled out." Morgan applied a Band-Aid to her knee. "Nick. And on that front, Bud messaged me that Nick is stable and improving faster than the doctors expected. They think he's out of the woods."

"That's a relief," Lance said.

Sharp set a cup of tea on the table in front of her.

"Thank you," she said.

Lance tried to catch her eye, but she was entirely too focused on stirring a spoonful of honey into her tea.

Suddenly, she stood without drinking any tea.

"I'd better change and get home if I want to see my girls before they go to school."

Sharp handed her a Band-Aid, and she left the room with her duffel. The dog followed her. They heard the bathroom door open and close. A few minutes later, Morgan returned dressed in a pair of jeans and a light sweater. The dog remained plastered to her shins. "Thank you for rushing to my rescue, Sharp."

"Between the Glock in your hand and the dog, you didn't need much rescuing," Sharp said.

"I still appreciate it." Morgan shifted the duffel bag in her hand and grabbed her purse from the kitchen chair. "I'll be back in a couple of hours. Then we can look for Voss's wife."

"Sounds like a plan." Lance walked her to the front door.

She stooped to pet the dog's head. "Thank you. You have to stay here, at least for now."

Lance followed her outside, making sure the dog didn't get out the front door.

On the sidewalk next to her van, she turned to him. "I'm sorry about last night."

"Nothing to be sorry about," Lance said. "You were upset about Nick."

Their gazes locked for a few seconds.

Her eyes were sad and resigned. "It wasn't all right, and I *am* sorry." She turned away and slid into the driver's seat, tossing her purse and duffel bag across the console. "It won't happen again. I promise."

And didn't that just unleash a flood of regret?

If only things were different. If she wasn't hung up on her dead husband. If there weren't three innocent little kids that would be affected by any fallout. If his mother's mental illness didn't consume so much of his life.

Too many *ifs*.

But he'd been completely honest the night before. He wouldn't be a regret. Not with her.

"Text me when you're home?" he asked.

She nodded and closed the door.

Lance watched her drive away. The empty hole in the pit of his stomach worried that by taking the high road last night, he'd passed up his only opportunity to make love to her.

He shook off his mood and went back inside. Sharp was in the kitchen when Lance returned.

"I want to know why that man was outside my house this morning," Sharp said.

"But did he follow her here or lie in wait?" Lance asked.

"Good question. I also wonder if he knew I live upstairs."

"He definitely didn't know about the dog." Lance walked back to the kitchen. The dog was in the corner, eyeing them suspiciously. "Rocket Dog gave him quite a surprise."

"Don't look at her. It makes her nervous."

Sharp ignored the dog. She cowered under the table as he filled bowls with food and water and set them in the corner as if he did it every day. "So why was Morgan dressed in your clothes this morning?" Sharp asked with his typical bluntness.

"It's not what you're thinking." Lance went to the fridge and poured a glass of filtered water.

Sharp raised his hands. "I didn't make any assumptions."

"It was late when we left the hospital last night. Morgan stayed in my guest room. Nothing happened." Lance didn't know why it felt important that Sharp know that.

Sharp said, "Of course nothing happened. You'd never take advantage of her."

"I wanted to," he admitted. "Does that make me a jerk?"

That kiss had nearly done him in.

"No. It makes you human." Sharp slapped him on the back.

A knock sounded at the door. Lance walked to the foyer and looked through the window. "It's Tony Allessi, Jamie Lewis's best friend."

He opened the door.

Tony's Mohawk had changed color to bright green. "I know it's early. I wanted to stop on my way to school. I need to talk to you. It's about Jamie."

Lance stepped aside. Sharp was in the hallway

behind him. He gestured to his office. "Let's go in here."

Tony paced a nervous square in front of Sharp's desk. Lance crossed his arms and leaned on the wall. Sharp sat down behind his desk. "What can we do for you, Tony?"

Tony stopped. "It's Jamie."

"Have you seen her?" Sharp asked.

"No. That's just it." Tony resumed his tour of the room's perimeter. "Since she left home, we've met twice a week at the lake. I brought her food and other stuff she might need. She didn't tell me where she was staying, but I knew she was OK."

"And now?" Lance pushed off the wall.

"She missed our last couple of meetings. I don't know where she went. I looked everywhere I could think of. Nobody's seen her."

Sharp frowned. "Since when?"

"Since the night Tessa Palmer died." Tony stopped behind a chair and put both hands on the back. His fingers clenched. "I'm really worried."

Sharp nodded. "Smart of you to come to us."

"Make a list of everywhere she might have gone." Lance went to the war room and returned with a blank sheet of computer paper. He handed Tony a pen from Sharp's desk.

"OK." Tony eased into the chair and leaned on the desk as he wrote. "But I already checked out all these places."

"Make another list of anyone else Jamie might have gone to for help," Sharp added.

Tony finished writing and pushed the list across the desk. "I wrote my cell phone number on the bottom, in case you want to ask me anything else."

"Thanks, Tony." Lance escorted him out the door, and then returned to Sharp's office.

"Damn it. We need to find this kid, and we need to make sure she's safe." Sharp waved Tony's list. "I'm going to start on this list. If this kid is still around, someone has seen her."

Lance headed for his office while Sharp left via the front door. As Lance settled in his chair, he heard crunching from the kitchen, then the sound of the dog lapping water.

There were too many people hiding in this town. They had to find Jamie for her own sake, and the police needed to locate Dean Voss for everyone else's.

CHAPTER THIRTY-FOUR

Morgan walked through her front door. Sophie was already up. She stood on a stool in the kitchen "helping" Gianna make pancakes.

"Morning." Gianna caught Morgan's eye. "Any new updates?"

"Nick is doing better." Morgan nodded. She'd talked to Bud in the car. She'd also left a message for the county sheriff. He needed to provide her with the details on Nick's attack.

"Mommy!" Sophie leaped from her chair and raced to Morgan.

Morgan caught her in midair and kissed her on the forehead. With her daughter's thin limbs wrapped around her waist, she walked toward the hallway. "I'll wake Ava and Mia." A chatty breakfast with her girls was exactly what Morgan needed to regroup.

She helped them dress, brushed and braided their hair, and walked them to the bus stop. Sophie refused to let Morgan touch her hair, saying she would wait for Gianna to make her kitten ears.

As the bus approached, she took Sophie's hand, kissed Mia and Ava, and watched her two oldest girls climb the big steps into the school bus. She and Sophie turned toward the house.

Sophie skipped. "Me and Gianna are baking cookies today."

"You are?"

"Uh-huh." Sophie nodded. "Kitten ones."

"Kitten cookies sound yummy."

"We have chocolate chips for their eyes and licorice for whiskers."

Morgan opened the door and they went inside.

Gianna had cleaned up the kitchen from breakfast. She closed the dishwasher door. "If you bring me the basket of hair things, I'll make your kitten ears."

"Meow." Sophie skipped from the room.

"I can't thank you enough. She seems really happy."

"I already told you. I love being with the girls." Gianna smiled. "I feel like I have little sisters."

"Tomorrow you have dialysis. I know you offered to be their nanny, but you must promise that you'll tell me if they're too much for you," Morgan said. "This situation will only work if we communicate."

"OK." Gianna wiped her hands on a dishcloth. "But my dialysis treatments line up with Sophie's preschool schedule. As long as I can catch a nap afterward, we should be fine."

"We still have to discuss a salary for you."

Gianna gave her head a stubborn shake. "No."

"I'll let it go for now, but we will have this discussion again." Morgan turned toward the doorway.

"My answer won't change," Gianna called after her.

Morgan showered and dressed in black slacks and a cotton blouse, tucking her Glock into her inside-the-waistband holster behind her right hip. After slipping into a blazer and flats, she kissed Sophie good-bye and headed for the office.

Tessa's murder needed to be solved. Nick was going to live, but he was still in danger of going to prison.

She went through the front door of the office and walked down the hall toward the war room. Lance was coming out of the kitchen and nearly collided with her. His hair was still damp. She'd shoved the previous night in the back of her mind, but the cedar scent of his shower gel brought it back with a rush. The feel of his muscles under her hands. The smell of his skin. The taste of his mouth.

Heat rushed to her face.

Last night she'd been upset, and whiskey had lowered her inhibitions, but this morning she was 100 percent sober. There was no denying that she still wanted him.

But was she ready to do something about it?

And after her behavior last night, was he still interested in her? She'd been an idiot.

She ducked into the war room. Lance followed.

Sharp stood in front of the whiteboard. "Do we have an update on Nick's condition?"

"Yes," Morgan said. "Bud called while I was in the car. The doctors are very pleased with his improvement. He's been upgraded from critical to stable and should be moved out of intensive care this morning."

Lance exhaled. "That's great."

"I'm waiting to hear from the sheriff. I want to know who stabbed Nick and why," Morgan said. "The inmate who attacked him took a huge risk. He needed a reason to attack Nick. It could have been simple jail violence, but there's a greater chance that it wasn't."

Lance crossed his arms over his chest. "It's not that hard to arrange a hit on the inside, but why?"

"Maybe the real killer assumed if Nick died, we wouldn't have a client, and we'd stop investigating." Morgan walked the length of the room and back. "Which means we've made someone uncomfortable. We're on the right track."

Lance pointed to photos of Robby Barone and his father. "I talked to my mom. She's found nothing on the Barones. They seem to have disappeared into thin air. She has found several small corporations linked to other suspected members. She's digging through layers of shell companies to see if they own real estate."

Sharp said, "I called a couple of my pals. There's been no sign of Dean Voss. The local, county, and state cops are all looking for him. They do know that Voss was in special forces. He's not going to be easy to find."

"They're looking for Rambo." Lance sighed.

"Exactly," Sharp agreed.

Morgan said, "We're going to try to talk to Mrs. Voss today in hopes that she has some idea where her husband is hiding."

"Good luck with that." Sharp rubbed a hand over his head. "She's cooperating with the police. They're watching her. They think Voss might try and contact her."

Damn.

Morgan stared at the board. "Who's left on our suspect list?"

"Jacob Emerson," Lance said. "Could that have been him following you this morning?"

Morgan took the image captured on the surveillance video and fastened it to the board with a magnet. "This could be either Dean Voss or Jacob Emerson. They're about the same size and build."

Lance shook his head. "For argument's sake, let's assume the same man stalked Morgan this morning and arranged the attack on Nick. If that's true, then I can't see Jacob Emerson having the contacts to orchestrate a jail hit."

"Could his father have arranged that? What

385

kind of law does Mr. Emerson practice?" Sharp asked.

Morgan opened her file and flipped to Mr. Emerson's pages. "He specializes in medical malpractice, but he's also defended some DUIs, which means he's spent time in the courtroom and jail."

Morgan's phone vibrated. "This is the sheriff."

She answered the call. "Morgan Dane."

"Ms. Dane," the sheriff said. "What can I do for you?"

"Thank you for returning my call. Who stabbed my client, sheriff?"

The sheriff began, "The man's name is Zachary Menendez. He's awaiting trial on three counts of first-degree murder."

"Do you have any idea why he did it?"

"So far, Mr. Menendez has exercised his right to remain silent." The sheriff's voice reflected his contempt. "But I know the charges already filed against him are pretty tight. He's expected to go to jail for the next hundred years. He's a very violent man. I'm not sure he needs a reason to hurt people."

Morgan didn't believe that for a second. Menendez could have stabbed anyone in that pod. Why did he choose Nick? "What else do you know about him?"

"He has mental health issues," the sheriff said. "He's a heroin addict, and he's been homeless since he was discharged from the military five years ago."

"Do you have any of his military records?" she asked. *Could he know Dean Voss?*

"No. He was in some kind of special forces. The military isn't fond of sharing that sort of information," the sheriff replied. "You don't need to worry about your client when he returns to jail. We've transferred Menendez to isolation. He'll be charged with attempted murder, on top of the other charges he was already facing."

"Thank you for the information." Morgan didn't discuss any possible lawsuit on Nick's behalf. She was determined that Nick would never return to jail. "I'd like to see the surveillance footage of the incident."

"Of course." But the sheriff didn't apologize for the stabbing. The man was smart enough to know that an apology could be interpreted as an admission of fault and that Morgan would likely file a civil suit on Nick's behalf.

"Thank you," Morgan offered.

"You're welcome. Let me know if you need any more information." The sheriff ended the call.

Morgan summarized the call for Sharp and Lance. "The man who stabbed Nick was in special forces. How do we find out if he served with Dean Voss?"

"We need to talk to Voss's wife," Lance said.

"She might either know Menendez or someone else who served with her husband."

"Good luck." Sharp turned back to the board. "I have a meeting scheduled this morning with Jamie Lewis's parents. Then I'm going to see what else I can learn about Menendez."

"Any luck finding Jamie?" Morgan asked.

"No," Sharp said. "The last time anyone saw her was the night Tessa disappeared."

"I don't like the sound of that." Morgan stood, slinging the strap of her tote over her shoulder. "I hope nothing's happened to her."

Morgan and Lance went out to the Jeep. They drove the first few blocks in silence.

She stared out the passenger window as they drove through Scarlet Falls. Close to the town center, homes were large and well-kept, with wide porches, trimmed shrubs, and neat patches of green grass. But who knew what was happening behind those freshly painted closed doors? She lowered her window a few inches. The crisp morning air smelled of dead leaves and wood smoke. The tension between her and Lance crackled like a bonfire. Had she damaged their relationship?

She glanced sideways at him. "I hope I didn't ruin our friendship."

"You didn't." But his body language contradicted his words. The muscles of his jaw clenched, and his fingers tightened on the wheel for just a second. If she hadn't been watching for it, she wouldn't have noticed.

She turned away to stare out the windshield, exhaustion sliding over, weighting her limbs like a thick comforter. She shook it off. Repairing their relationship would have to wait. Nick's case needed all her energy.

CHAPTER THIRTY-FIVE

Mrs. Voss lived in a development of small homes on postage-stamp lots. Upkeep was a mixed bag. Some lawns were mowed and raked, others overgrown. Lance parked at the curb of a small bungalow. No peeling paint or dangling shutters, but the grass needed mowing. He surveyed the surrounding houses but saw no sign of Dean Voss.

Across the street, a police car sat at the curb. Lance recognized the young cop in the driver's seat. Really? Horner had put the rookie on duty to watch for an ex-special forces soldier?

Lance scanned the property. "I guess Mrs. Voss hasn't had time to mow the lawn."

Morgan gathered her tote. "If one of my neighbors had grass that high, Grandpa would be at their door asking if everything was all right. Then he'd have seen to the grass."

"Either this isn't that kind of neighborhood or Mrs. Voss isn't that kind of neighbor."

Two doors down from the Vosses', a garage door opened and a man emerged to fetch his garbage can from the curb.

"Let's find out." Morgan got out of the car.

She and Lance walked toward the neighbor.

The sky was overcast, and the lack of sunlight made the morning feel cool.

"Hello," she called.

The neighbor was middle aged. He wore khaki pants and a blue polo shirt with the logo for an electronics store on the chest.

Morgan made the introductions. "Do you know the Vosses?"

"I'm Ned Burke," the neighbor said. "I know them just enough not to want to get closer. They aren't very friendly, and the husband is a hothead. I just moved in last March. Couldn't open my windows. The whole neighborhood could hear them fighting. It's been quieter since he moved out. I heard he completely lost his shit. Doesn't surprise me."

"Have you seen Dean since?" Morgan asked.

"Yes." The neighbor nodded. "He came a couple of weeks ago to bang on her door. I went outside to ask him to keep it down, and he told me if I didn't mind my own fucking business, he'd make me."

Lance didn't like the image of Voss he was forming in his head, a man with a violent temper who'd been trained to hurt people. "What happened?"

"I called the police." The neighbor huffed. "They didn't respond for fifteen minutes. He continued to harass his wife until he heard the sirens. Then he took off."

"Have you talked to Mrs. Voss recently?" Morgan asked.

"No. I'm staying out of it." The neighbor pulled a set of keys from his pocket. "I have to get to work."

"Thanks for the help." Lance handed the neighbor a business card. "If you see Dean around, would you give us a call?"

The man tucked it into his pocket. "Sure. Right after I call the cops. But if I were you, I wouldn't be looking for Dean Voss. That man is nuts."

The uniform was standing outside his car when they walked back toward Voss's house.

"Can I see some ID?" the rookie asked.

Lance pulled his license from his wallet. "Don't you remember us?"

"I still need your license number." The rookie took Morgan's ID as well. "Wait here." He took their IDs back to his car. He returned a few minutes later and handed their documents back to them. "Thank you."

Morgan and Lance went to the door. Lance pressed the doorbell. The window curtains to the left shifted. A few seconds later, the door opened as far as the chain would allow. A woman's thin face appeared in the gap.

"Mrs. Voss?" Morgan asked.

The woman's nod was uncertain and full of suspicion. "Who are you?"

Morgan introduced them. "Can we ask you a

few questions about your husband? We had an encounter with him a few days ago."

"You're the people he shot at?" Mrs. Voss asked.

"Yes," Morgan said.

The door closed, the chain scraped, and Mrs. Voss opened the door wide. "I suppose I owe you a few minutes."

"Thank you." Morgan stepped over the threshold.

The living room was dark, the curtains and blinds closed.

Mrs. Voss led them into a tiny but tidy kitchen. The vinyl floor was spotless and the countertops gleamed in the overhead light. A spray bottle of cabinet cleaner and a pile of rags sat on the floor. She sat at a round oak table and folded her hands in front of her, their skin red and irritated.

"I don't know what to do, so I clean." She rubbed at her knuckles. "I've been afraid to leave the house, even though the police are following me everywhere. Yesterday, I went to the store. I was so scared, I barely managed to get milk and bread before I had to leave."

"There's a police officer right out front." Morgan slid into the seat next to her.

Mrs. Voss blew out a quick breath. "They don't know Dean. If he wants to get me, one uniformed officer won't be able to stop him."

"You don't have to convince us that he's

dangerous," Morgan said. "He tried to kill us."

Mrs. Voss shook her head. "If Dean wanted to kill you, you'd be dead."

"How good of a marksman is Dean?" Lance leaned on the counter. He'd suspected Voss had intentionally missed them.

"Dean hits what he aims at. Every time." Mrs. Voss rubbed her hands together.

"Has your husband always been violent?" Morgan asked.

Mrs. Voss plucked a tissue from the box and blotted her eyes. Her voice grew harsh. "No. This all started last winter, when that little bitch accused him of kissing another student."

Morgan leaned her forearms on the table. "You don't think Dean was guilty?"

"Dean has his issues, but he would never be inappropriate with a student." Mrs. Voss met Morgan's gaze, then Lance's. She might be frightened of her husband, but she was equally sure he hadn't made advances toward his student. "Under all his delusions, Dean is a good man. A moral man."

"But you're afraid of him now?"

"You don't understand. The Dean that's running around town in a state of paranoia isn't really him." Mrs. Voss leaned back, crumpled her tissue in her hand, and hugged her waist. "Dean came back from Iraq a changed man. Whatever happened over there destroyed him. But he went

394

to therapy. He talked to other vets. He worked damned hard to pull himself together for the whole first year. When he felt steady enough, he applied for his teaching certificate. He'd gotten his master's degree in history while he was in the service."

More tears formed, and she dabbed at her eyes and nose. "He loved teaching. It gave him purpose. He loved the kids, and the kids seemed to love him back. I thought he'd made it. The nightmares had stopped. He was actually sleeping through the night. The longer he worked at the school, the more like his old self he became."

She paused again. A small shudder shook her body, then a sigh. "Then that girl went to the principal and said she'd seen him kissing another girl. Dean denied the accusation, and so did Ally Somers, the girl he was accused of kissing. There was no proof. None. Except that one statement from Kimmie Blake. But his reputation was tarnished, and his career over. He quit. After that, depression hit him hard. He became volatile. He refused to go back into therapy. It was too much. He'd already remade himself once. He couldn't do it again. He sank from depression into paranoia."

Mrs. Voss went silent.

"Does your husband ever mention Tessa Palmer or Jamie Lewis?" Morgan asked.

"I don't think so," Mrs. Voss said. "Of course, I know Tessa's name from the news."

"Has your husband ever mentioned a man named Zachary Menendez?" Lance asked.

Mrs. Voss shook her head. "No. Why?"

"We thought they might have served together in the military," Lance explained, disappointed. An established connection between Voss and Menendez would have simplified matters, but Mrs. Voss's denial didn't totally rule it out.

"The name isn't familiar," Mrs. Voss said.

"What happened in May?" Morgan asked gently. "Why did he move out?"

"He hit me." Mrs. Voss pressed the tissue to her face. A small sob sounded behind it before she sniffed and lowered her hands. "I don't know which one of us was more horrified, but I knew something had to change. I couldn't live with him unless he was willing to get help. Frankly, I was afraid of him. So I gave him an ultimatum. If he wanted to stay in our marriage, he had to get treatment."

Tears poured down her cheeks, and this time, she didn't bother to wipe them away. "I meant well. I thought he loved me enough that he'd work to keep our marriage together, but Dean was too far gone by then. He left. Got his own apartment. He refused to answer my calls. I didn't know what to do. In my heart, I still love him. But how do you live with a man who scares the hell out of you? Even after Dean moved out, I'm still afraid to close my eyes at night. He's become unpredictable and irrational. He's come over a couple of times to apologize and beg for me to take him back. But when I say no, he flips out. I finally filed for divorce. I can't help a man who won't let me."

A dog barked outside, and Mrs. Voss jumped from her chair. She went to the window over the sink. With one forefinger, she separated the mini blinds and peeked between the slats.

Lance crossed the kitchen and peered over her shoulder. "Do you think he'd come here in the middle of the day?"

"Dean wouldn't let a little thing like daylight stop him." Mrs. Voss eased back from the blind. When the house remained quiet, she paced. "Getting the divorce papers seemed to be the last straw. He came here the day he received them. He begged me to take him back. He said he loved me. But he couldn't go through therapy again. It was too much. I asked him to leave. He started shouting. I locked the door, but he didn't leave until the police came." She stopped in the corner and turned. Her hands gripped the counter on either side of her. "He's at some kind of breaking point. I could feel it."

A floorboard overhead creaked. Mrs. Voss's gaze shot to the doorway. A few seconds later, a man stepped into the opening. He pointed a rifle into the kitchen.

How the hell did he get inside?

Lance's pulse jump-started, and he automatically shifted sideways to try and put himself between the armed man and the women in the room.

"Stop." Dean Voss's tone was soft but commanding. He was dressed in desert camouflage BDUs that would have blended with the dead leaves of autumn. His face was smeared with dirt, and he carried a rifle like a man who was comfortable with his weapon.

Lance considered his options. He didn't have many. He had no time to draw his gun. So how would he keep Voss from hurting his wife or Morgan?

"Don't move," Voss said.

"Don't worry." Lance raised his hands. The rifle was aimed in the dead center of his chest.

CHAPTER THIRTY-SIX

Morgan's heart stuttered as she recognized Dean Voss. His face was thin, his eyes feral. She kept both of her hands on the table in front of her.

Voss jerked the gun at Lance. "Put your hands on your head. Interlace your fingers." He shifted his gaze to Morgan for a second. "You too."

"Dean, they were just talking to me," his wife said.

"No." Voss shook his head. "They want to take you away. They want to hurt you. The only way you'll be safe is if you come with me."

"I won't go," she said. "You need me. You need help."

"The only kind of help I need is the kind that'll make me disappear. They want me to pay for what I did." Voss's voice softened. "I have to pay." He lifted his chin. There was too much white around his eyes. They blazed with a crazy light.

"Dean. No one wants to hurt you. They want to help."

"No," he shouted. His grip on the rifle tightened until his knuckles were as white as his eyes. "That's just what they told you to make you cooperate."

Dean Voss was clearly paranoid and likely delusional. Morgan could not draw her gun before Voss shot Lance. Talking Voss down from his paranoid ledge was their only option. Plus, she'd never shot another human being and didn't want to start now if it could be avoided. Though she would do it to protect Lance.

A fist banged on the front door. "Hey, Mrs. Voss. Is everything OK in there?"

The rookie.

That was not going to help.

Voss's eyes widened. He grabbed Morgan by the hair and dragged her from her chair. Pain burst in her scalp. She cried out. Both of her hands went to the top of her head, an instinctive attempt to alleviate the pulling.

Lance lunged forward, but the rifle in his face stopped him.

"I'm OK, Lance." Morgan got her feet under her body. Standing eased the pressure.

Lance put his hand up in front of his chest and inched back a half step. "You don't want to hurt a woman, do you, Dean?"

Dean laughed. "What does it matter? The world is backward. I get accused of a crime I didn't commit but never caught for the one bad thing I did do."

"What did you do, Dean?" Lance asked.

"Can't tell. Promised. But I gotta pay." Dean's head bobbed in rhythm with his words. "She's dead. It's my fault."

"Who is dead?" Morgan asked. Was he confessing to Tessa's murder?

The rookie banged again. "Mrs. Voss?"

"Tell him you're fine." Dean pulled Morgan closer. The rifle remained pointed at Lance. Voss's unwashed body smelled ripe with fear. Morgan breathed through the pounding of her heart and trembling of her hands. She needed him to put down the rifle. If Voss fired at Lance at a distance of five feet, the bullet would rip right through him.

"Dean," his wife begged. "Don't hurt them. I'll go with you. We can be together forever."

"We'll never get away." Voss shook Morgan by the hair. Her scalp screamed.

"I'll tie them up, and we'll go," his wife pleaded. "Just you and me. I know you'll be able to make us disappear. You were right all along. We're not safe here."

Voss nodded. "If you mean it, get rid of the cop at the door."

"Mrs. Voss?" the rookie shouted through the door. "If you don't open this door, I'm going to break it down."

"Coming!" his wife called out toward the door as she wiped her palms on her jeans. She lowered her voice. "I'll get some rope."

She ran out of the room. Morgan didn't know whether to expect her to return or not. Mrs. Voss could run right out of the house if she wanted to escape. But she didn't. She hurried back into the kitchen, a coil of nylon rope in her hand. "Put your hands behind your back," she said to Lance.

He complied, and she tied his wrists. Morgan's racing pulse echoed in her ears. She couldn't allow her own wrists to be tied. They'd all be at Voss's mercy.

"Zip ties would have worked better," Voss said. "And take her weapon."

Damn. He'd spotted her gun under her jacket.

"I couldn't find zip ties." His wife tied a knot. She moved a chair behind Lance, and he sat while she bound his ankles to the chair legs. "This will hold them long enough." She took Lance's gun from his holster, then moved on to Morgan's. "What should I do with the guns?"

"Give them to me," Voss said.

Once Lance was tied, Voss set the rifle down on the counter and tucked Morgan's gun into his waistband. He brought Morgan to a second chair. She had to act now. She wasn't going to get another chance. But it had been years since she'd practiced physical self-defense. Would she do it correctly? If she didn't . . .

Before he could force her into the chair, she slapped her hands on the top of her head, crushing the fingers entwined in her hair. Pinning his hand to her scalp, she dropped to her knees and bowed her head toward his knees, bending his hand backward. Bone crunched as his wrist broke. His useless fingers released her. He reached for her with his other hand.

No! She wouldn't allow him to get a fresh hold on her.

She scrambled a few feet away, fear tightening around her throat like fingers. Breathing hard, Morgan rolled onto her back and kicked out. Voss jumped out of the way and tried to get around her feet, but she kept her legs drawn up and prepared to fire another kick.

Lance sprang to his feet. Mrs. Voss's knots must have been all show. Lance dove across the room, tackling Voss around the waist. They landed hard on the floor and rolled in a tangle of limbs, coming to a stop with Lance on top. With a grunt, Voss heaved Lance off him.

"Mrs. Voss. I'm coming in." The rookie kicked at the door. It didn't open. He kicked again.

Morgan hoped he'd called for backup. She climbed to her feet and raced for the door. She opened it, and the rookie stumbled inside. He recovered his balance and lifted his drawn handgun. Pointing it at the men on the floor, he shouted, "Freeze."

Voss jumped to his feet and ran. Lance lunged after him, grabbing his shirt. Voss spun around, his right hand cradled against his body.

Boom!

The gunshot reverberated in the small room. Voss stopped midstride. Lance froze. Morgan's heart skipped a beat. A red stain bloomed across Voss's chest. He fell to his knees and swayed for a few long seconds before crashing facedown to the floor.

The rookie didn't move. His gun was still pointed at Voss. Lance was on his knees beside Voss. "Get me a towel."

Crying, Mrs. Voss ran to the kitchen and brought a dish towel. Lance put it over the wound on Voss's chest and applied pressure. "Call for an ambulance."

The rookie jumped to action. Holstering his weapon, he used his radio to call for assistance.

Morgan's knees felt like water as she stumbled to Lance's side. Despite Voss's attack, she didn't want him to die. He couldn't help what he'd done. He wasn't sane. "How is he?"

"Bleeding way too much." Lance said. "I need another towel."

Mrs. Voss brought him a stack. Then she dropped to her knees beside her husband. She grabbed his hand. "Dean? Dean, don't you give up."

Lance caught Morgan's gaze. He shook his head. The bullet had hit Voss in the center of his chest, right over his heart.

Morgan put two fingers to Voss's neck but felt nothing. "No pulse."

Lance started CPR and performed chest compressions until the paramedics arrived. Then he stepped back. The paramedics worked on Voss for ten minutes before shaking their heads. "He's gone."

Mrs. Voss began to weep. Morgan went to her, putting an arm around the woman's shoulders.

The next few hours passed in a blur of *I can't believe that just happened.* More police arrived. Morgan's and Lance's guns were recovered from the scene and kept as evidence until they were cleared by ballistics. Though everyone agreed the rookie had shot Voss, a thorough investigation dotted every *I* and crossed every *T.* The police determined that Voss had scaled a tree and broken in through an upstairs window at the back of the house.

Morgan, Lance, and Mrs. Voss went to the police station to give statements. They were separated and put in individual rooms. Numb, Morgan recounted the incident like a robot. She wasn't even aware that she was shivering until an officer brought her a jacket and a cup of coffee. As the adrenaline faded, her scalp throbbed from her encounter with Voss, but other than a few bruises, she was uninjured.

It was after lunch by the time Morgan emerged

from the tiny, windowless room. Lance was waiting for her.

Lance led Morgan out of the station. The sun had emerged while they were inside, and as much as Morgan craved heat, the warmth of its rays felt wrong.

"He shouldn't have died." Morgan shivered in the sunlight. She'd given the officer's jacket back before leaving the station. "He was mentally ill."

"Do you think he killed Tessa?" Lance opened the Jeep door for her.

Morgan replayed Voss's words. "I don't know. He wasn't any more specific than the first time we encountered him. I've no doubt that Voss's words will help Nick's case, but I wish we had more."

"We know Voss had a campsite not far from where Tessa's body was found. He was suffering from delusions and paranoia." Lance closed the door, rounded the vehicle, and slid behind the wheel. "Hopefully forensics will be able to tie Voss to the crime scene."

"Why would he have killed Tessa?" Morgan asked.

"He was delusional. Maybe he thought she was someone else. If he really was falsely accused, he could have mistaken her for Kimmie Blake, the girl who made the accusation."

"Or, if he really was interested in his female students, maybe he was attracted to Tessa."

Morgan's phone vibrated. She glanced at the display. "It's the DA."

She answered the call.

"Can you come to my office?" he asked.

"Yes." She looked at Lance. His clothes were stained with Dean Voss's blood. "Thirty minutes?"

Bryce agreed, and Morgan ended the call.

"What was that about?" Lance drove out of the parking lot.

"Bryce wants to see me." She checked the time. "Which is interesting because he's supposed to be in a grand jury hearing in two hours."

"Do you think he'll drop the charges?" Lance asked.

"Maybe." Morgan rubbed her head. Her scalp still stung from Dean Voss's grip in her hair. "If you drop me back at the office, I'll get my minivan."

"Or I could take you to the courthouse."

"I think I'll be safe enough there," she said. "Besides, you need a shower and fresh clothes."

"Where are you going after the courthouse?" he asked as he drove toward the office.

"To see Nick." She crossed her fingers that she'd have the best news for him.

When they reached Sharp Investigations, Lance dropped her next to her minivan. "I'll meet you at the hospital."

She drove to the courthouse. With her stomach

growling and her energy flagging, Morgan detoured to the vending machines for a pack of Peanut M&M's. She ate them on the way to Bryce's office. His secretary waved her through immediately. Morgan went in, not sure what to expect.

He stood as she entered and gestured to a guest chair facing his desk. Had she not decided to defend Nick, she would have started her job with the DA's office the day before. Had it only been a week and a half since she'd had dinner with Bryce? It felt like much longer.

Bryce leaned back in his chair and stared at her for a few seconds, then he shifted forward. "I'm dropping the charges against Nick Zabrowski. *Not* because I'm convinced he's innocent but because Dean Voss's cryptic confession creates too much doubt. The police will continue to investigate, and there's no guarantee we won't seek an indictment against your client at some future date."

But for now, Nick wouldn't have to go back to jail. Equal amounts of relief and anger rushed through Morgan, but she held her tongue. Lashing out at Bryce for putting Nick in jail—where he was stabbed—wouldn't help. In fact, the less she spoke to Bryce the better. Every word that came out of her mouth would give the DA information.

"If a man isn't proven guilty, then he is innocent in the eyes of the law," she said.

Bryce didn't comment on Nick's innocence. "I'll call off the guard and have Nick's handcuffs removed."

Morgan nodded. "I'm headed to the hospital to speak with Nick now."

But they both knew that public sentiment wouldn't necessarily be as easy to sway, not until *someone* was convicted of Tessa's murder.

"You are a diligent investigator, Ms. Dane," Bryce said as they both stood. "I might be willing to extend another offer to you."

Morgan shook his hand. When she tried to pull her hand from his grip, he held on. The gesture felt slimy. Everything about Bryce Walters felt slippery, and the fact that he was playing nice made her doubly suspicious. "Thank you, but I'll pass."

"Suit yourself." Releasing her hand, he straightened. His flat smile couldn't cover the irritation in his eyes. He was up to something. But what?

"How did the Emersons take the request for Jacob's DNA?" she asked.

"About as well as you would expect. Phillip Emerson is filing a harassment lawsuit against the township."

"It won't stand up."

"I'm not worried about it. The photos from last July of his son with Tessa Palmer are damning. If Tessa was still alive and willing to testify, we'd likely be filing sexual assault charges against Jacob." Bryce came out from behind his desk.

"You're not?" Disappointment filled Morgan. Tessa deserved better. Morgan rose from her chair.

"It's hard enough to get a conviction in a sexual assault case with the victim's testimony and DNA evidence. Without either of those things . . ." Bryce lifted a shoulder. "You know the odds."

"This is why so few rapists ever spend a day in prison," Morgan said.

She left without a single regret for losing the job with the DA's office. When she'd worked for the prosecutor's office in Albany, the DA had power, but he hadn't run his office like a fiefdom the way Bryce did.

She couldn't wait to tell Nick he was free, at least for now. She wished she had a real confession from Dean Voss. As much as she wanted to tell Nick she'd found Tessa's real killer, Voss's vague statement wasn't enough to convince Morgan. Reasonable doubt would keep Nick out of prison, but it wouldn't restore his reputation.

More importantly, if Voss wasn't Tessa's killer, then a murderer was still loose in Scarlet Falls.

CHAPTER THIRTY-SEVEN

Lance showered and dressed in clean clothes before heading to the office to give Sharp all the details on Voss's self-destruction. Today's incident was another unwelcome reminder of his own shooting last fall.

Sharp was at his desk typing on his laptop when Lance walked in.

Lance dropped into a chair, his foot tapping as he gave his boss a complete rundown of the incident at Voss's house.

Sharp closed his laptop. "Was the shooting justified?"

Lance replayed those few pivotal seconds in his mind. "Voss had put down his rifle in the kitchen. He had Morgan's weapon on him, but his hands were empty. He was running away. I was chasing him. He turned at the last second and the rookie shot him."

Sharp's jaw tightened. "The officer could have shot you."

"But he didn't. His aim was true, and I won't be the one to judge him." Lance tried to stop his leg from bouncing, but the adrenaline rush at the Voss house had left him twitchy. "I don't know what the rookie saw from his angle before he fired. We both know how fast these situations go down. He had one second to make up his mind. When Voss turned, he was cradling his right hand under his left arm. It's possible it looked as if he was drawing Morgan's weapon from his waistband."

"The rookie had no way of knowing he had a broken wrist," Sharp added.

"But everyone is going to judge him as if he did."

"They will." Sharp sighed. "Morgan really broke his wrist?"

"She did." Unable to sit still, Lance got up and paced the floor in front of Sharp's desk. "I don't know why everything she does always comes as a surprise. Her father and grandfather were both cops. Her sister is a detective. Her brother is NYPD SWAT."

"The pearls and heels throw you off."

"That'll teach me to judge people by their appearances." Lance paused, one hand on the back of his neck.

"What's wrong?"

"I don't know. Maybe I'm still revved from the shooting."

"I have some information for you." Sharp picked up a pair of reading glasses and focused on the paper in front of him. "The man who stabbed Nick—Menendez—has a wife and a six-year-old son. The child has a heart defect. Their medical bills have already driven them into bankruptcy," Sharp said. "Yet Mrs. Menendez made a hefty deposit into her bank account recently. Considering the prior balance was eleven dollars, I think the deposit is significant."

"Someone paid Menendez to stab Nick."

"Yes." Sharp's eyes gleamed.

"Do you know who?" Lance asked.

Sharp nodded. "The sheriff might not be keen on sharing, but I have my own contact at the jail. My man says the sheriff knows who ordered the hit."

Suddenly that piece of the puzzle clicked into place for Lance. "Tessa Palmer's father."

"Bingo," said Sharp. "He did it from inside prison. Apparently, her father has some clout in prison."

"And access to money," Lance added.

"The sheriff's office is following the money trail. They'll find out who financed the hit."

"So revenge motivated the attempt on Nick's life."

"Yes. The poor kid was jailed *and* stabbed for something he didn't do."

Lance's phone buzzed. "It's Morgan." He answered the call, and she summed up her meeting with the DA and Nick's certain freedom. Relief flooded Lance. "Great. I'll see you at the hospital."

He ended the call and relayed the conversation to Sharp. "Morgan says the DA dropped the charges against Nick."

"Hallelujah," Sharp said.

"Don't get too excited. Nick is still considered a suspect."

Sharp swore. "Voss's confession was too wishy-washy, but it will force Horner and the DA to take a fresh look at the case. Plus, forensics will have Voss's DNA to compare to evidence found at the scene."

Lance resumed his pacing. "*I'm* not convinced that Dean Voss killed Tessa Palmer."

"Voss was seriously impaired. He might not have been aware of what he was doing."

Lance stopped. "I could see him stabbing her thinking she was someone else, but rape? That's a whole different crime. One that doesn't fit with Dean Voss's personality at all. His wife doesn't think he did it either, and she was afraid of him for other reasons."

Sharp got up and walked down the hall to the war room. He stood in front of the whiteboard. "If it wasn't Voss, then who killed Tessa?"

"The only other suspects are Jacob Emerson and Kevin Murdoch."

"I respect your instincts. You and Morgan both have enough experience to know when you're being lied to, but we have no *evidence* to support a case against Kevin except the timing of Jamie's vanishing act."

"You're right." Lance stepped up next to him and pointed to Jacob's photo. "We know *he* sexually assaulted Tessa back in July. It doesn't seem like a big stretch that he'd do it again. When she resisted, he got angry."

"His father says he was home, and the GPS on his cell phone confirms that."

"Either Phillip Emerson is lying or Jacob slipped out of the house without his father knowing. Kids do it all the time."

Sharp scanned the board from one end to the other. "I think you're right. Rape shapes the whole dynamic of the crime. Rape happens when a man sees something he wants and takes it."

"Voss's violence came from his fear, his paranoia, his delusions."

"He hit his wife," Sharp said.

"Yes. But even she said he was moral, that he would never have hurt one of his students. Rape is about power. It's aggressive. Voss acted defensively, like a cornered animal."

"A rapist has no regard for women. Jacob is an entitled little prick who already demonstrated his lack of respect for Tessa when he assaulted her unconscious body." Sharp took Jacob's photo and moved it to the center of the board. "We have no hard evidence that he killed Tessa. Yet we both believe that he's the most likely suspect."

"He was laughing in those pictures. He enjoyed humiliating her."

"Your assessment of his expression is not evidence," Sharp said. "Let's backtrack. Jacob saw Tessa at the party. She was with Nick. This angered him. What if she refused to sleep with him when they dated? The only way he was able to have sex with her was to drug her. Yet she was obviously having sex with Nick, giving him what she'd denied Jacob."

Lance picked up the thread of the theory. "He snuck out of his house. He brought a condom. He planned to rape her, to take what she wouldn't give him but he was entitled to."

"How did he know she would still be at the lake?" Sharp asked.

"That I don't know. When he left the party, she was sitting in her car, crying. Maybe he just hoped she'd still be there."

"She called his house that night," Sharp reminded him. "Either it was Jacob who took the call or he overheard her conversation with his father. We don't know what was said. We only have Phillip Emerson's statement, which he could totally have changed to protect his son. What about the knife? Do you think he brought it with him to kill her?"

"I don't know. Maybe he brought it to facilitate the rape, then she made him angry. Jacob doesn't have the best self-control."

Sharp and Lance exchanged a glance.

"We can't prove any of this," Sharp said.

"Nope."

"There's one person who was at that party and not interviewed by the police." Sharp hurried from the room. He returned with Jamie Lewis's picture. He fixed it to the board with a magnet. "No one has seen Jamie Lewis since that night, not even her best friend. I spent all morning checking places on Tony's list. I called all her friends, and I'm halfway through the locations Tony thought Jamie frequented. So far, I've found no sign of her. What if Jamie saw the murder and it scared her so much she left town?"

"It's a possibility." Lance rubbed the ache at the base of his skull. "I'm going to cruise by the Emerson house before I join Morgan at the hospital. I would love an opportunity to talk to the maid without the family around."

"Watch yourself. Phillip Emerson is already screaming harassment."

Lance shrugged. "He's filed suit against the township. We're private."

"You know what I mean."

"I do." Lance went to his office to retrieve his keys. "What are you doing next?"

"I'm still working on the list of Jamie's hiding places. I'm packing bribe money and considering asking a few of my retired friends for help. They know this town inside and out. If Jamie Lewis is anywhere in this area, I'm going to find her."

"I'll check in when I know something." Lance headed for the door.

The Emerson house was quiet when Lance parked at the curb. Originally, he'd only planned to watch the house for a few minutes, but since the Emersons utilized their garage, it was impossible to see who was home from the outside. Lance used the telephoto lens on his camera to look through the windows. The only activity he saw was the maid dusting.

He watched for another ten minutes. No sign of Jacob or Phillip Emerson. *Enough tiptoeing around these people.*

Lance slipped out of the car, walked up to the front door, and rang the bell.

The maid answered. She was in her mid-fifties. She wore a plain gray uniform with a white apron. Her gray-and-brown hair was bound in a tight bun.

"Yes?" she asked.

"I'm here to see Mr. Emerson." Lance smiled.

"You were here before." She frowned.

"Yes. Is Mr. Emerson in?"

"Which Mr. Emerson?" she asked.

Lance was not going to be accused of harassing a minor. "Mr. Phillip Emerson."

The maid shook her head. "No. I'm sorry. Mr. Phillip isn't home. Would you like to leave a message?"

"Yes." Lance offered her a business card. "Please tell him I'd like to speak with him."

The maid took the card. "In the future, please call for an appointment."

"Who's at the door, Myra?" a voice called from the hall behind the maid.

Jacob Emerson stepped into view. His face tightened as he recognized Lance. "What are you doing here?"

"I just wanted to ask your father a few questions." Lance smiled.

"You have balls. I'll give you that." Jacob pushed the maid aside. "I'll handle this, Myra. Go back to work."

With a nod, the woman backed away.

"There's no use sniffing around here. You won't find any evidence because I didn't kill Tessa." Jacob crossed his arms over his chest.

"The same way you didn't molest her unconscious body?" Lance asked.

Jacob's lip curled. "When my father gets home, he's going to be pissed."

He's a minor. You can't punch him.

But Lance wanted to smack the sneer off this kid's face. "Is he out cleaning up more messes for you? That must be a full-time job for him."

"You know nothing about us." Jacob's face flushed red. "My father is a great man. Right now he's visiting a sick friend at the hospital. Take your accusations and get off our property before I call the police."

But Lance was already headed toward his Jeep. Emerson was going to the hospital.

Where Morgan was visiting Nick.

Coincidence?

With everything else that had happened on this case, Lance was not willing to bet Nick's or Morgan's safety on a coincidence.

Could they have been wrong? Had the man who'd stalked Morgan at the office been Phillip Emerson, not Jacob? He must have known that it was Morgan who'd petitioned for Jacob's DNA. And he must have been angry. Parents will do anything to protect their children. How far would Phillip go?

CHAPTER THIRTY-EIGHT

Rage pulsed inside him. It grew and fed on itself until it had a will of its own.

Morgan Dane was going to ruin everything. Someone else had been arrested. The evidence he'd planted had been solid—until Ms. Dane stuck her nose into his business.

There was no question that she had to be stopped. But how? Her sidekick, the former cop, was always at her side, and he acted like her personal bodyguard.

He'd spent all night devising a plan to stop her investigation. Step number one: finish what the county jail had left undone. She couldn't defend a dead client.

He entered the hospital through the main doors. This wasn't the city. The medium-size community hospital had little need for security. There were only two people behind the reception desk in the lobby. An elderly woman sat at a computer, looking up patient room numbers and handing out visitor passes with a polite smile. Seated behind her, a security guard in his mid-fifties drank coffee and talked over the counter with a man in a suit wearing a hospital ID. Hospital administration?

He set his shopping bag at his feet, used the hand sanitizer, and collected a pass from the old lady. He headed for the elevator bank at an unhurried pace. No one asked what was in the bag. No one cared.

The security cameras tracked him as he stepped inside. But he had nothing to hide.

Yet.

On the third floor, he took care of his legitimate business. Then he needed to improvise. Nick Zabrowski had been transferred from the ICU to the fourth floor that morning.

He ducked behind a set of double doors that separated the more public hallways from the less-traveled ones. He passed signs for Radiation and the Cardiac Cath Lab and found the nearest restroom.

The day before, he'd bought green scrubs at a uniform supply store. He changed into them, folding his regular clothes and stuffing them into the shopping bag. His costume was authentic right down to his rubber shoes. The salt-and-pepper toupee covered his hair, and black-framed glasses concealed his eyes. He inserted rolls of cotton gauze in his mouth to disguise the shape of his face. When he was satisfied that no one would recognize him, he went back out into the hallway.

He walked down the hall, scrolling on his phone to discourage attention. He paused as an orderly rolled a patient on a gurney out of a doorway labeled Magnetic Resonance Imaging. There was an outer room that appeared to exist for prepping patients before their test. This outer room was empty. A desk was pushed against the wall, a white lab coat tossed carelessly over the chair. With a glance in each direction down the hall, he ducked inside long enough to grab the lab coat. The ID badge clipped to the pocket showed the photo of a young man. Not a problem. He merely turned the ID over to hide the picture. Then he transferred his knife from his bag to the pocket of the lab coat.

Continuing on, he took the elevator to the fourth floor.

In a patient room on the right side of the hall, he spotted an elderly man sleeping heavily. The room was marked with a yellow card that called for Contact Precautions. A cart loaded with gloves, masks, and gowns sat next to the doorway. He stuffed his shopping bag into the bin labeled Medical Waste and helped himself to a face mask. He tied it around his face and tugged it down past his mouth, as if he'd just come from the operating room.

The nurses bustled at the station down the hall. No guard stood at the doorway. Perhaps there was a sheriff's deputy inside the room.

He glanced through the doorway. No guard.

Convenient.

Also lazy.

Who was he to judge? The lack of a guard made his job easier.

But he'd better hurry. Someone could come into the room at any moment. He entered the room, picking up the chart at the foot of the bed in case he was interrupted.

Nick Zabrowski slept peacefully. His eyes didn't even flutter. His chest rose and fell in a deep and even rhythm that suggested sedation or exhaustion. Maybe both.

An IV line ran into one arm. No handcuffs. Interesting. Not that it mattered. Nick wasn't in any condition to get out of bed.

Or fight back.

He wasn't hooked up to any heart monitors, so no alarms would ring when his own heart ceased to beat. He wouldn't even need the knife he'd brought. No. He could make Nick's death quiet and neat.

This was going to be easier than he'd expected. And when he was finished here, Morgan Dane was next. That bitch had ruined everything, and she was going to pay.

He grabbed the pillow from the empty bed.

CHAPTER THIRTY-NINE

Consciousness tugged at Nick.

He resisted. The last thing he wanted to do was wake up. He'd done that earlier, and pain had slammed into him with the force of a bus.

On one hand, the pain had assured him that he was alive when he'd been certain he wasn't. On the other, the agony had been so intense, he'd considered the advantages of being dead.

As he floated from the heavy depths of drugged slumber, the fire in his belly encouraged him to stay asleep. He was flat on his back, tethered to the bed by wire and tubes. Why be awake when he couldn't move anyway?

Sure, the nurse had told him earlier that movement would aid his recovery, but really, what was his motivation to get better? The sooner he healed, the faster they put him back in jail.

What was the point?

Even if Morgan managed to convince a jury that the prosecution hadn't proven his guilt, the whole town had already tried and convicted him. He would never be innocent in their eyes unless

Tessa's real killer was caught. Even then, he suspected some people would be forever convinced he'd committed the crime.

An image of Tessa formed in his mind, and physical pain took a backseat. The knife he'd taken in the belly couldn't compare to the invisible one twisting in his heart.

Tessa.

Dead.

Really, why bother waking up? Why had they saved him? They should have let him bleed to death.

He let his mind sink, welcoming the utter blackness and wishing it smothered him.

A rubber sole squeaked on the floor. He'd been in the hospital a few years before, for an emergency appendectomy. The nurses had been in and out of his room constantly. But this time, they entered his room only when absolutely necessary, and usually their entrance meant something painful was going to happen. He sensed resentment from the hospital staff, but then who would want to take care of a man arrested for a brutal rape and murder?

Thinking of how Tessa had died amplified his grief. How dare he feel sorry for himself when she'd suffered far worse.

He stirred, stretching a leg out. The small movement tensed his severed abdominal muscles and red-hot agony sang through him in a fresh burst of pain. His next breath hurt so much, he tried not to repeat it.

But his stupid body had other ideas. He couldn't simply stop breathing. He opened his mouth, and his lungs sucked in air. The deeper-than-usual breath causing enough pain that he nearly blacked out.

Unfortunately, he didn't.

Shit that hurt.

He concentrated on slow and shallow breathing, his focus completely absorbed by minimizing movement and the resulting pain. A few breaths later, he gave up on being unconscious and opened his eyes. Daylight from the window blinded him. He squinted at a blurred figure clad in green scrubs moving around his room.

Nothing unique about that.

He blinked dry eyes a few times, his vision gradually clearing, the figure taking a man's shape. Gray hair. An older doctor.

The figure picked up a pillow and walked closer. At first Nick thought he was going to make him sit up.

He opened his mouth to say, "I can't." But his voice sounded like rusted metal. He swallowed and tried again.

But his words were cut off when the pillow came down on his face. Nick reached for the man, but his arm was tethered by the IV. His free hand grabbed at the man's shirt and pulled, but he had the strength of a newborn baby.

His lungs burned. The pain in his belly went ballistic.

But soon it would all be over. He gave up, stopped fighting, let go.

And waited for the end.

CHAPTER FORTY

Morgan stepped out of the elevator. She couldn't wait to tell Nick the DA had dropped the charges against him. She followed the signs to his room and walked inside.

A doctor was on top of Nick. At first, she thought maybe he was administering CPR, but then she saw the pillow over Nick's face.

Oh my God.

He was trying to kill Nick.

She shook off her shock.

"Hey," she yelled, grabbing the man by the back of his collar and pulling him off Nick. The man had been focused on smothering Nick, and she took him by surprise. He tumbled backward off the bed and onto the floor. His glasses flew across the room and his dark hair fell off, revealing a blond-and-silver head.

But Morgan had no time to stare at the wig on the floor.

Nick!

She lunged to his bedside.

"Help!" she screamed, hoping her voice would carry to the hallway. "Somebody help me in here." Without turning her back to the man on the floor, Morgan snatched the pillow from Nick's face.

Is he breathing?

She jabbed the call button with her forefinger. *Come on.* The attacker was scrambling to get his feet under his body. Morgan faced him, keeping her own body between him and Nick.

Shock rippled through her as she recognized Nick's attacker.

Phillip Emerson.

Dressed in scrubs and a lab coat, he stood. His jawline was oddly puffy. He reached into his mouth and pulled out two wads of cotton.

"You bitch." Emerson pulled a knife from the pocket of his lab coat.

The knife shone in the fluorescent light. Fresh fear washed over Morgan. She glanced around for a weapon or something to use as a shield. She couldn't run. Nick would be defenseless. But there was nothing between her and Emerson.

Not. A. Damned. Thing.

Morgan couldn't even reach the curtain that went around the bed. Sweat dripped down her back as her heart kicked into high gear. She had no weapon. No way of protecting herself or Nick.

"What's wrong?" A nurse hurried through the doorway. Her momentum carried her to the foot of the bed before she realized what was happening and stopped. Her eyes opened wide in shock as she glanced between Emerson and Morgan.

"Get help!" Morgan yelled.

The nurse raced from the room.

Emerson lunged at Morgan. The knife beelined for her midsection. She barely blocked it with the back of her forearm.

But he came at her again. "You destroyed my life."

Morgan wanted to respond, but her heart was pumping hard enough to make her breathless.

She had nowhere to go that didn't leave Nick vulnerable. Never had she wished she had her weapon more than right at that moment. Fear turned her belly to ice. But as frightened as she was, she couldn't run away.

She couldn't let Emerson kill Nick.

A security guard appeared in the doorway, his weapon drawn and aimed at Emerson. "Stop right there. Put down the knife."

But the guard's hands were shaking so badly Morgan almost wished he'd put the gun away. He could just as easily shoot her or Nick as hit Emerson.

Emerson grabbed Morgan by the bicep and pulled her in front of him. Her back slammed into his chest. He put the knife to her throat, forcing her to be his human shield.

"Move out of the way or she's dead," he said, tightening his grip on her arm.

Emerson's breath was hot in her ear, and the acrid scent of panic rose from his skin. He moved sideways, yanking her with him.

The guard kept his gun trained on Morgan and Emerson as they shuffled toward the door. If the guard pulled the trigger, even by accident, he'd hit Morgan.

Emerson pulled her along the floor toward the door. The guard backed up as they neared. What would happen when they reached the corridor? Surely, there were more guards. What would Emerson do when he realized he'd backed himself into a corner and there was no escape?

His forearm was across her windpipe, the blade of the knife kissing the side of her neck. Morgan couldn't remember whether her jugular vein or carotid artery was on that side, but it didn't matter. He could kill her by slicing either one.

CHAPTER FORTY-ONE

Lance raced down the hallway.

An orderly shouted at him. "You can't go down there. The floor is closed off. There's a hostage situation."

Lance ignored him. He skidded around the turn and pulled up short.

Emerson was backing down the corridor. Dressed as a doctor, he dragged Morgan along the hallway, hiding behind her body and holding a knife to her throat. Lance wasn't a violent man, but at that moment, he *wanted* to kill Phillip Emerson.

Lance reached for the weapon on his hip, then realized the SFPD hadn't returned it yet.

Fuck.

Thankfully, he still had his backup piece. Nobody had asked for it and he hadn't volunteered.

His heart knocked against his ribs. He couldn't let anything happen to Morgan, but he could see the desire to hurt her in Emerson's eyes.

A security guard had his weapon drawn and pointed at Emerson and Morgan. The guard was obviously out of his element because his hands were shaking hard. Terror filled Lance as he imagined the security guard shooting Morgan by mistake.

Lance stopped at the end of the hall. "Let her go, Emerson!"

If Morgan moved just a few feet . . . one clear shot. That's all Lance needed.

"One step closer and I will cut her lovely throat," Emerson said, his voice oddly cold.

He wanted to do it. Lance could read the desire to end it on Emerson's face. He knew he was trapped. He knew there were only two ways out of the situation: prison or a body bag. He looked as if he wanted to take Morgan with him.

Morgan's gaze met Lance's. One of her hands grasped Emerson's forearm, as if to pull it away from her neck. She wheezed, "I can't breathe."

"Shut up!" Emerson shifted his grip, lifting his arm from her windpipe and grabbing a handful of her hair with his free hand instead. Her head tilted back, exposing her throat. But now there were a few inches between Morgan's neck and the blade.

"We know Jacob killed Tessa. You can't cover up for him anymore," Lance said.

"Jacob didn't kill Tessa," Emerson shouted. "How stupid are you? *I* killed her."

"I don't believe you," Lance shot back. "Jacob drugged and raped her back in July. Then he got mad that she was giving Nick what she'd refused to give him. He decided to teach her a lesson and got carried away."

Emerson kept shaking his head. The knife quivered next to Morgan's throat.

Lance needed a distraction. "Did you know Tessa was pregnant?"

Emerson's eyes went wild. "That's impossible."

"The police didn't make that public," Lance continued.

"You're lying." Emerson scanned the hallway and edged toward Lance. "Move back."

Lance kept pushing. "No one blames you for covering for your son. That's what parents do, right? But the DNA test will come back, and it'll show that Jacob was the father of her child."

"He was not!" Emerson jerked his head toward the corridor that led to the elevator. "Now move out of the way or I'll kill her."

If Emerson thought he was doomed, he might kill her anyway. Hatred gleamed darkly in his eyes.

Morgan's free hand was on her thigh. She was shaking her fist, as if trying to get Lance's attention.

He watched as she extended three fingers, then two, then one.

What is she going to do?

Her hand shot upward between her neck and the blade while her body dropped to the floor.

Blood streaked the back of her arm as the knife sliced it open.

As soon as she hit the floor, Lance had a clear shot at Emerson. He squeezed the trigger twice.

The bullets struck Emerson in the shoulder and chest. He jerked backward. The knife sailed from his grip and clattered to the floor.

Morgan rolled away, and Lance rushed forward. He had a boot on Emerson's arm, pinning him down. Emerson's fingers clawed for the knife.

"You're going to pay for what you did." Lance loomed over him, anger coursing hot through his veins. "You and your son."

"My son had nothing to do with it," Emerson wheezed. "*I* killed Tessa Palmer."

Lance leaned closer. "Did she threaten to tell everyone how Jacob raped her?"

"No." Emerson shook his head. "I didn't even know about those pictures until the police called me." He wet his lips with his tongue. "I loved her."

Lance couldn't believe what he'd heard. "What?"

"I loved her from the first time I met her." Beads of sweat broke out across his brow. Blood welled from the wounds and stained the green scrubs and stolen lab coat red. "She was the most beautiful thing I'd ever seen. She was going to betray me. She made me do it. It was all her fault."

A doctor rushed forward and began treating Emerson, but he grabbed Lance by the shirt.

"You have to hear this. In case I die. Jacob didn't do it." Emerson licked his lips again and kept talking. "Jacob came home from the party. He told me about the fight with Nick over Tessa. He was in his room when she called. She told me to meet her at the gazebo. If I didn't show up, she'd tell everyone. I knew she was going to break it off with me so she could be with Nick. Jacob had said they'd gone off together, but I had to have her one more time." He took two wheezing breaths. "Afterward, she was crying. She said it would never happen again. She was going to tell her grandparents. I lost it. How could she turn on me? I loved her. I barely remember attacking her, chasing her, killing her. It's all a blur. I couldn't stop myself. When it was over, I realized what I'd done . . . I knew she'd been with Nick that night, so I drove to his house and buried the knife in his yard."

His hand dropped from Lance's shirt, too weak to maintain his grip. "It was me. Not Jacob." His eyes rolled back in his head, and he passed out.

Lance holstered his weapon and went to Morgan. A nurse was holding a pressure bandage on her arm. Emerson's blade had sliced the outside of her arm open from wrist to elbow. But the wound wasn't critical, and relief poured through Lance like cold water.

He could have lost her.

"Did you hear any of that?" He took her uninjured hand.

"Yes." Her face was grim, either from the pain or from the truth they'd finally discovered. "Tessa moved here when she was twelve. I wonder how long it was going on?"

"Long enough to be sick." Lance watched two orderlies hoist Emerson onto a gurney and wheel him away. He almost wished his aim had been a little truer. Lance had no pity for Emerson, not after what he'd done.

"And long enough to be a felony," Morgan said.

Long enough for exposure of his crime to be a motive for murder.

"I'll bet she was going to tell him she was pregnant, but he never gave her the chance." Lance turned from the sight of Emerson disappearing down the hallway. "I can't believe that either Emerson or his son could be the father. Two monsters, one family."

Morgan's face was pale, her features pinched with pain. Enough of the Emersons. He wasn't going anywhere. There would be plenty of time to worry about him later. He rubbed her hand, and she smiled at him through the pain.

A doctor approached Morgan. "Let's have a

look." He lifted the bandage and checked the wound. "That's a nasty cut. You're going to need some serious stitches."

She nodded. "But better my arm than my neck."

The thought almost made Lance sick.

"I was impressed at how you slipped out of his grip," Lance said.

Although he should have expected her to act heroically, considering how she'd broken Dean Voss's wrist earlier. But even after seeing her in action, he had trouble reconciling her feminine appearance with her abilities.

She was a girly girl who could kick serious butt. He'd have to get used to that fact.

"I've told you before that my dad and granddad trained me in self-defense, but remind me that I need to practice now and then. I'm lucky I remembered." Morgan gritted her teeth as Lance and the young doctor helped her to her feet. "I knew if I could get out of the way, you'd take care of the rest."

Lance squeezed her fingers.

"Let's get you down to the ER." The nurse guided Morgan toward a wheelchair.

Lance held onto Morgan's hand. He didn't care where they were going.

He wasn't letting go.

CHAPTER FORTY-TWO

Morgan held her bandaged arm against her body as she slid into Lance's Jeep. "What time is it?"

"Almost midnight." Lance closed the car door, rounded the vehicle, and got into the driver's seat. "Are you in pain?"

"Nope. Not yet." The painkillers the hospital had given her made everything fuzzy. Her mouth tasted like she'd eaten cotton balls.

"I'll have you home in fifteen minutes."

Morgan didn't remember the drive. She must have dozed off. The next thing she knew she was home and Lance was helping her into the house.

Her grandfather held the door open. Gianna was waiting in the hall.

"She's fine," Lance said. "Just a little spacey."

"If you can get her to her room, I can take over from there." Gianna followed them down the hall.

"I only hurt my arm. My legs are fine. I can walk." But Morgan wobbled more than walked.

Lance half carried her to her bed. "Looks like she doesn't tolerate painkillers any better than alcohol."

She stretched out. "I can hear you." But she couldn't sit up. Her head felt like a water balloon.

"Thanks for saving my girl," her grandfather said from the doorway.

Lance's answer surprised her. "Wasn't me. She saved herself."

"Not exactly," she mumbled. She knew she wouldn't be here without him.

He straightened and shifted away from the bed.

She grabbed for his hand. Her eyes welled with tears. Gratitude and something more filled her with contentment. "Thank you."

"Anytime." He leaned down and kissed her hand before setting it on the bed. "Get some rest."

Morgan must have fallen asleep. When she opened her eyes again, morning blasted through the blinds. She threw an arm over her eyes. Pain sliced through her arm. "Ow."

She sat up. She was still wearing her slacks from the night before. But someone had removed her bloody blouse and replaced it with a soft flannel button-up. Her feet were bare, a blanket drawn over her. She eased her shoulders higher on the pillow. Her mouth was desert dry.

"Hey, how do you feel?" Gianna stood in the doorway.

"Like I ate chalk."

"Want some water?"

"Yes." Morgan shook her head. "And coffee."

"Lance left a few pain pills for you if you need them."

"I'll stick with over-the-counter if possible. Clearly, I have no tolerance for anything stronger." Morgan swung her legs over the side of the bed.

"Take it slowly, OK?" Gianna suggested.

"I will." Morgan eased to her feet. The room remained stationary. She walked to the bathroom. But when she came out, she decided being upright was overrated and went back to bed. Her head ached.

Gianna brought her water and coffee.

"It's like I have the worst hangover ever."

"The coffee should help." Gianna handed it over. "I guess there's no worry about you becoming an addict. You wouldn't be awake enough."

Morgan drank. The coffee went down her throat like liquid gold. "Where are the girls?"

"School." Gianna said. "The bus came a half hour ago."

"Where's Sophie?"

"Your grandfather has her outside with Snoozer. He didn't want her to wake you."

The caffeine cleared the cobwebs in Morgan's head. "Wait. It's Wednesday. You have to get to dialysis."

"Will you be all right by yourself? If not, I'll

call a cab and your grandfather can stay with you."

Morgan drained her mug. "I'm fine now that I'm caffeinated. Seriously, I have a cut on my arm. That's it."

"You were pretty out of it last night." Gianna hesitated at the door.

"The drugs are out of my system now. I'm fine." To prove it, Morgan got out of bed. Her head felt like someone had just bowled a strike in it, but she faked a smile as Gianna left her bedroom. The second they all left the house, she was getting right back in bed.

"Mommy!" Sophie ran at her.

"Sophie!" Grandpa called. "Remember Mommy's arm."

Sophie slid to a stop, her sneakers squeaking on the wood floor of the hall.

"It's OK. You can hug me." Morgan crouched down, holding her injured arm up high.

Sophie gave her a gentle hug and a kiss on the cheek before spinning around and rushing back to the door. "Grandpa is taking me to school." She hefted her Hello Kitty backpack onto her shoulders. Taking Grandpa's hand, she tugged. "Come on. I'll be late."

"Are you sure you're all right?" Grandpa's eyes were worried.

"i'm perfectly fine," Morgan said. "I'm going to get another cup of coffee."

"I'll be back in an hour," Grandpa said.

Gianna took Sophie's hand and the three of them went out the front door. Morgan heard the deadbolt sliding home.

As soon as the house was empty, she went back to her bedroom. But now that the coffee was buzzing through her system, she couldn't sleep. Giving up, she went to the kitchen, refilled her mug, and took it back to her bed.

The previous night, when Phillip Emerson had put a knife to her throat, she'd realized that life was short.

Despite all the people she'd lost, it had taken a threat to her own life to bring her to her senses.

For the last two years, she'd been squandering her life. Her children were the only things that gave her any joy, and that wasn't right.

She opened the nightstand and took out the letter that she'd been avoiding for two years. Tears burned the corners of her eyes as she read her husband's handwriting on the outside of the envelope. *Morgan.*

"I'm sorry," she said to John's photo as she slid a finger under then flap. "I couldn't read this before."

Tears blurred the page as she read the words her husband had written to her before he'd left for Iraq. The letter he'd left with his commander in case he didn't make it home. The fact that she'd never been able to read it before now suddenly felt selfish. The note was short. John had never wasted words. He hadn't been a poet, just a good man. He'd always gotten to the point and said what was on his mind. His final letter was no different.

Morgan,
If you're reading this letter, then I didn't come home. I'm sorry for that. It was a lot to ask of you to be my wife. Just know this: I loved you and our girls with all my heart. Even from six thousand miles away, I have no doubt the four of you will be the very last images in my mind. However short our time was together, your love is the precious thing that I will take with me.

I didn't give my life for a lofty idea of patriotism. I gave it so people like you, Ava, Mia, and Sophie would be safe and free. I did my duty. Now I want you to do yours. Honor my life by living yours. Don't waste a second on the idea that you being happy would somehow be disloyal to me. Live. Laugh. Love. Don't hold back. Make me proud.
Love you always, John.

She wiped the tears from her face, folded the letter, and put it back in her drawer. She'd transfer it to the safe deposit box so the girls would always have it. But she would never read it again.

She lifted his photo from her nightstand. "You're right. I've been walking around half living. It isn't fair to the girls, and it isn't fair to me. Thank you for making me see that."

Carrying his picture, she walked to the girls' bedroom and placed it on their dresser. She would never forget him or the love they had, but it was time to let him go.

It was time to live.

CHAPTER FORTY-THREE

Lance walked into the ice arena. The kids were already warming up. Coach Zack leaned on the half wall and watched as they circled the rink.

Zack turned. "Hey, Lance. Are those your skates?"

"They are." Lance sat on the bench and exchanged his athletic shoes for the black hockey skates.

"Does your therapist know about this?"

"I've been approved for some light skating." Lance tightened the laces. "So don't expect anything exciting."

But it felt damned good to step out onto the ice.

The kids raced over. He had a brief moment of panic that he'd get body slammed, but they gave him room, zooming around him and shouting encouragement.

"Coach Lance!"

"Awesome."

Lance grinned. A year and a half ago, these same kids distrusted cops so much they'd barely speak to him. Their trust had come slowly. But when he'd been shot, every single one of them had visited him in the hospital.

He followed instructions and kept his ice time short, hanging up his skates to help Zack coach from the sidelines.

It was dark when he parked in his driveway and opened his garage door. He should have been in a good mood, but he wasn't. He hadn't heard from Morgan since he'd driven her home from the hospital the night before. But then, the case was over. They wouldn't be spending much time together. Would their friendship go back to where it was before Tessa's murder? Did he even want that?

Shit.

Lance was in the garage when Sharp's Dodge Charger cruised to the curb. Sharp hurried up the driveway, a file tucked under one arm. "Wait until you see what I have."

"You look excited." Lance led the way into the house.

Sharp waved the folder. "Your instincts and Morgan's were dead on about Vanessa Lewis's fiancé."

"I thought Kevin Murdoch was clean." Lance turned on the lights and they walked into the kitchen.

Sharp opened the file on the counter. "Kevin Murdoch *is* clean."

Lance peered over his shoulder at a photo of a fat bald guy. "Who is that?"

"Kevin Murdoch." Sharp's smile was all teeth.

"Then who is dating Vanessa Lewis?"

Sharp flipped to the next page. "Byron Dixon. Registered sex offender who moved from Florida three years ago and stole Kevin Murdoch's identity. Dixon raped a thirteen-year-old girl and served eleven years in prison. A month after his parole, he moved here and used the new identity to evade the sex offender registry. Then he befriended and began to date Vanessa. He actually is an accountant and has been working out of his apartment doing income taxes and small business accounting."

"Poor Jamie." Lance was angry but not surprised. At last count, there were nearly seven hundred fifty thousand registered sex offenders in the U.S. It was too easy for them to slip over state lines and through the reporting cracks.

"Yeah. He must have done something, and when she heard her mother was marrying him, she couldn't take it." Sharp closed the file. "I called the Feds. They picked him up fifteen minutes ago. Jamie doesn't have to worry about him anymore."

"So if we can find her, she'll be safe."

"We'll keep trying, but that kid is a ghost."

"I'll call her friend, Tony," Lance said. "Maybe he can get word to her that she's safe."

"Just thought you'd want to know." Sharp picked up the file. "Have you talked to Morgan?"

"No."

"Then that explains your miserable mug."
Sharp shook his head. "Just call the woman. You
know you like her. You just can't get out of your
own way."

"Sharp, we've been over this. Relationships
and my mom don't mix."

"Don't give me that bullshit." Sharp got in his
face. "You're afraid. Morgan's different. I see
the way you look at her. She's the one that might
count."

Lance turned away from Sharp—and the truth.

"Goodnight, Sharp."

Sharp huffed as he headed toward the door.
"Don't be a dumbass."

After the door had closed behind him, Lance
settled at his piano and indulged himself with
broody music. He'd moved on to Coldplay when
his doorbell rang. No one except Sharp ever
stopped by. Lance went to the door.

Through the peephole he saw a tall figure with
a Mohawk. Lance opened the door. Tony Allessi
stood on the doorstep, and next to him was a tall,
lanky girl.

Jamie Lewis.

"Come in." Lance stepped aside.

Jamie stumbled. Tony grabbed her arm and
tugged it over his shoulders. As he helped Jamie
into the brightly lit kitchen, Lance could see that
something was very wrong with the girl. Her skin
was simultaneously deathly pale and flushed.

"Sit down." Lance pulled out a kitchen chair. Jamie fell into it.

"She's sick." Tony's hand went to his Mohawk. "I didn't know where else to bring her."

Lance crouched in front of Jamie. She obviously hadn't showered in some time. Her hair was greasy, and her eyes dull. He put a hand on her head. "She's burning up."

"I can't go home," she mumbled.

"Yes, you can. Kevin is history."

She blinked.

"Kevin isn't Kevin," Lance said. "He's a sex offender from Florida, and you don't have to worry about him anymore."

"He said no one would believe a crazy girl." She started to cry.

"I know." Lance grabbed his keys. "Let's get you to the ER and call your mom. Everything is going to be OK."

The girl's knees gave out as she stood. Lance scooped her into his arms and carried her out to the Jeep. He called her mother on the way to the emergency room. A nurse escorted Jamie into the triage bay while Lance and Tony headed for the waiting room.

Vanessa Lewis hurried through the sliding door. Her face was streaked with tears and fear. "Where is she? Is she all right?"

Lance stood. "The nurse took her back. I'm sure they'll let you in."

451

Vanessa gave her name at the counter.

"I can't believe I let a monster near my child." She dug in her pocket for a tissue. "He was so nice."

"He's an experienced predator," Lance said. "This was not his first time. He knew what he was doing."

The electronic door opened and a scrub-clad nurse called, "Mrs. Lewis?"

So did Lance. But it wasn't going to happen overnight. Both Jamie and her mom would need time and professional help if they were going to get through this together.

CHAPTER FORTY-FOUR

Two days later

Lance went into the office late Friday morning after stopping to check on his mom. Sharp was on the phone. The dog was curled up in a bed in the corner. Lance waved as he passed the doorway. Then he settled at the card table in his office and stared at the single file in front of him: his father's case.

He still hadn't opened it. Yes, he wanted to know what had happened to his dad, but if Sharp hadn't found any clues in twenty-three years, what were the chances any existed?

What were the chances that Lance would get sucked into a past that he'd thought he'd made peace with? He also considered the effect any digging into the past would have on his mom.

The front door opened and closed. Morgan walked past his doorway. Surprise pulled Lance to his feet. He hadn't seen her since he'd dropped her at her house Tuesday night.

The dog bolted from Sharp's office to greet her, and Lance wanted to do the same. He listened to her talk to the dog in a ridiculous high-pitched voice.

"What a pretty girl you are. Did Sharp give you a bath?"

The patter of dog toenails on hardwood followed Morgan's footsteps down the hall.

Lance went to the war room. She was clearing the board and filing the evidence from Nick's case. Instead of a suit, she wore jeans, a black sweater, and a pair of brown boots on her feet. A silk scarf in gray and turquoise was artfully knotted around her throat. The bandage on her arm peeked out from the hem of her sleeve. Her face was still pale, but her eyes were clear and blue and beautiful as always.

She was still talking to the dog. "Look at your new collar and tags."

The dog sat at her feet and listened with a cocked head. The collar around her neck was purple, and a hot-pink dog tag stamped with the name "ROCKET" hung from its metal loop.

What would Morgan do now? With the charges against Nick dropped, she didn't need to play defense attorney anymore. He was going to miss seeing her every day, but it was probably for the best. If they worked closely together, she would be too hard to resist.

He leaned on the doorjamb. "How's the arm?"

She turned. "Itchy but otherwise fine." She pulled the photos of suspects out from under their magnets and put them in the box.

"Can I help?" He started at the opposite end of

454

the board. "What are you going to do with all this stuff?"

"Keep it for now, I guess." Morgan paused, a picture of the crime scene dangled from her hand. "I'll decide when I hear from Bryce."

"No word from the DA yet?"

"No." Morgan scratched at the edge of her bandage. "I was hoping he would make an official announcement before Nick gets discharged from the hospital. I don't want any more incidents with the neighbors."

"Do you expect any?"

"Who knows? I have no idea why it is taking so long to file charges against Emerson. Without a formal arrest and press release, people will still think Nick is guilty."

Her phone rang, and she read the display. "It's Bryce."

She took the call. A confused line formed over the bridge of her nose as she listened. Lance could hear Bryce's voice but couldn't make out the words.

"All right. Thanks for calling, Bryce." She set the phone down, her face pale. "The DNA results came in."

"And?" Sharp said from the doorway.

"They're inconclusive." She crossed her arms. "Normally, we expect the probability of paternity to be either 99%, which means you've accurately identified the biological father of a child, or 0%, which would mean Jacob is definitely not a paternal match, but Tessa's baby was 26% match with Jacob Emerson."

Lance leaned on the wall as the truth hit him. "Because Jacob and the baby were half-siblings. Phillip was the father."

"It's disturbing on so many levels," Morgan said, reaching down to stroke the dog's head. The dog leaned on her shins.

"Like father, like son," Sharp said. "Considering what his father did, it's no shock that Jacob has no respect for women."

"Yes." Morgan shivered. "These families knew each other . . . were friends. They spent time together. Tessa even spent the night a few times when her grandfather had a heart attack several years ago. She was about twelve when Phillip started to molest her."

Sharp rapped a knuckle on the wall. "I'd like to shoot him myself."

Morgan continued. "The police conducted a thorough search of the Emerson house. In the back of Phillip's office closet, they found a box that contained photos of Tessa and what the police believe to be a lock of her hair. Bryce said the photos went back six years, to when Tessa's parents died and she came to live with her grandparents. Phillip has been charged with Tessa's rape and murder. Bryce says they'll make a public statement later today. So Nick is in the clear."

456

"The fallout should prove to be interesting for the mayor's reelection campaign," Sharp added. "But then, you reap what you sow."

"The DA's office and the police chief are scrambling for a spin on this," Morgan said. "My guess is that the mayor will distance himself from both of them. But I doubt he has enough time before the election to make up for this disaster."

"I thought he might fire Horner and let him take all the blame," Sharp said.

Lance shrugged. "That still might happen. We'll just have to wait and see. What is the DA going to do with Jacob?"

"Unfortunately, I don't think he can do anything to Jacob. Without a victim to testify, the case is dead in the water. But I have more news," Morgan said. "I spoke to the sheriff this morning. They were able to track the deposit that hit Menendez's wife's bank account. You'll never guess who arranged for the money transfer."

"Tessa's grandfather?" Lance guessed.

Morgan shook her head. "Her grandmother. When confronted, she also admitted to nailing that cow heart to my door. The sheriff's department arrested her this morning."

"Did anyone ever find out what Dean Voss confessed to doing?" Lance asked.

"Yes," Morgan said. "A member of Dean's old unit called Mrs. Voss to offer his condolences. He said Dean had accidentally shot and killed a young Iraqi girl. He couldn't give her any more details than that. The incident was part of a classified mission and they aren't allowed to talk about it."

"Poor Voss." Sharp shook his head.

"My guess is that he saw Tessa's murder and it severed any remaining thread of sanity he was holding onto. Maybe he felt guilty for not being able to stop Emerson." Morgan put the last photo in the box and closed the lid. She looked around the office. "I suppose we can box all this up and put it in storage now."

"I hope Nick can move on from this," Sharp said.

"Physically he's going to be fine, thank goodness, but his emotional recovery will be more difficult." Morgan shifted the box to the floor. "I talked to Bud this morning. He's putting the house up for sale. He and Nick are going to move in with Bud's sister in Manhattan for a while. He thinks the city might be a totally fresh start for them."

"That might be the best thing for Nick," Lance said. "I have some news too. Vanessa Lewis called me earlier this morning. Jamie is out of the hospital and recovering at home from pneumonia. They have an appointment scheduled with a new psychiatrist, but the specialist they saw at the hospital thinks Jamie's bipolar diagnosis was bullshit. Fake Kevin was already getting handsy with her and telling her that no one would believe her because she was crazy. So Jamie was freaking out. She stayed out of his way the best she could, but when her mom announced they were getting married, Jamie knew that when Fake Kevin moved in, the abuse would get serious. So she left."

"Fake Kevin has to deal with federal charges, plus state charges in Florida and New York," Sharp said. "He's going away for a long time."

"Good," Lance continued. "It seems Kevin targeted Vanessa from an online support group for parents of teens with learning disabilities."

"Ugh. I hope he rots in prison." Sharp turned for the hallway. "Morgan, let me know if you need help clearing out your office or ordering furniture."

Lance turned his head toward the empty doorway. "Did I hear him right?"

"You did," Sharp called from the hall.

Morgan blushed. "Sharp made me an offer. He thinks adding a lawyer to the team will be a benefit."

"Plus, she's damned good at this," Sharp shouted from the kitchen. "And she classes up the place. Makes us look legitimate."

Morgan got up and closed the door. "Working together isn't a problem, is it?" She walked closer.

"No, of course not." Lance didn't move as she stopped right in front of him.

How did he feel about it, really?

Poleaxed.

"Are you sure you want to do this?" he asked.

"It's a good fit for now. When the girls were born, John was away. I worked a lot. I didn't realize how insane our life was. But after being home with them for the last two years, I don't want to give up all my time with them. Except for the occasional crazy case, I can set my own hours. I hear your boss is pretty flexible."

"He is," Sharp shouted through the door.

She reached up and placed a hand on Lance's chest. "Is it OK with you? I don't know where *we* stand."

Lance's heart did a touchdown dance. "It's fine with me. More than fine." Geez. He sounded like a blubbering idiot.

"Good. I was wondering if you wanted to go out on a date or something."

Yes. Yes. Yes!

For crying out loud, be cool.

He cleared his throat. "I'd like that." But he shouldn't be so selfish. She'd only met his mom once, on a good day. Morgan had no idea what she was getting herself into. Being involved with him could be complicated.

"Good. I hope the boss is OK with fraternization in business." A smile curled her mouth.

He wanted to taste it.

"He encourages it." Sharp's voice came through the door.

"Go away, Sharp." Lance put a hand on her waist and tugged her closer. "So where do we start?"

"Beats me." She leaned into him. "I haven't dated in more than a decade."

"How about lunch?"

"Lunch would be nice."

"Just kiss her already," Sharp yelled.

Lance bent his head and pressed his mouth to hers. The kiss was unhurried, her mouth soft and warm. She sighed, a sound of utter contentment, and leaned into him. The softness of her body nestled into the hardness of his. Though the kiss remained sweet, he tasted the promise of much more on her lips.

He lifted his head. "We make a pretty good team."

"We do." She smiled. Looping her arm around his neck, she pulled him down for another, not-so-tame kiss that left them both breathless.

Who knew what would happen tomorrow? He and Morgan had enough combined baggage to sink an ocean liner, and she had no idea of the chaos his mother brought to his life.

But she fit against him in a way that made him think well beyond lunch. Today he was going to live in the moment. He'd waited too long for this simple kiss.

But it had been worth every second.

ACKNOWLEDGMENTS

As always, credit goes to my agent Jill Marsal, and to the entire team at Montlake Romance, especially my managing editor Anh Schluep, developmental editor Charlotte Herscher, and author herder/tech goddess Jessica Poore.

Special thanks to Leanne Sparks for her patience and help with some of the procedural elements of this story. She saved me weeks of research.